Angel's Big Day

WRITTEN BY
Rob Anderson

ART BY
Jay Fosgitt

Wings Over Yakyakistan

WRITTEN BY
Christina Rice

ART BY
Agnes Garbowska

Apinkalypse Now

WRITTEN BY
Thom Zahler

ART BY
Tony Fleecs

The Vines That Bind

WRITTEN BY
Thom Zahler

ART BY
Agnes Garbowska

COLORS BY
Heather Breckel

LETTERS BY
Neil Uyetake

SERIES EDITS BY
Bobby Curnow

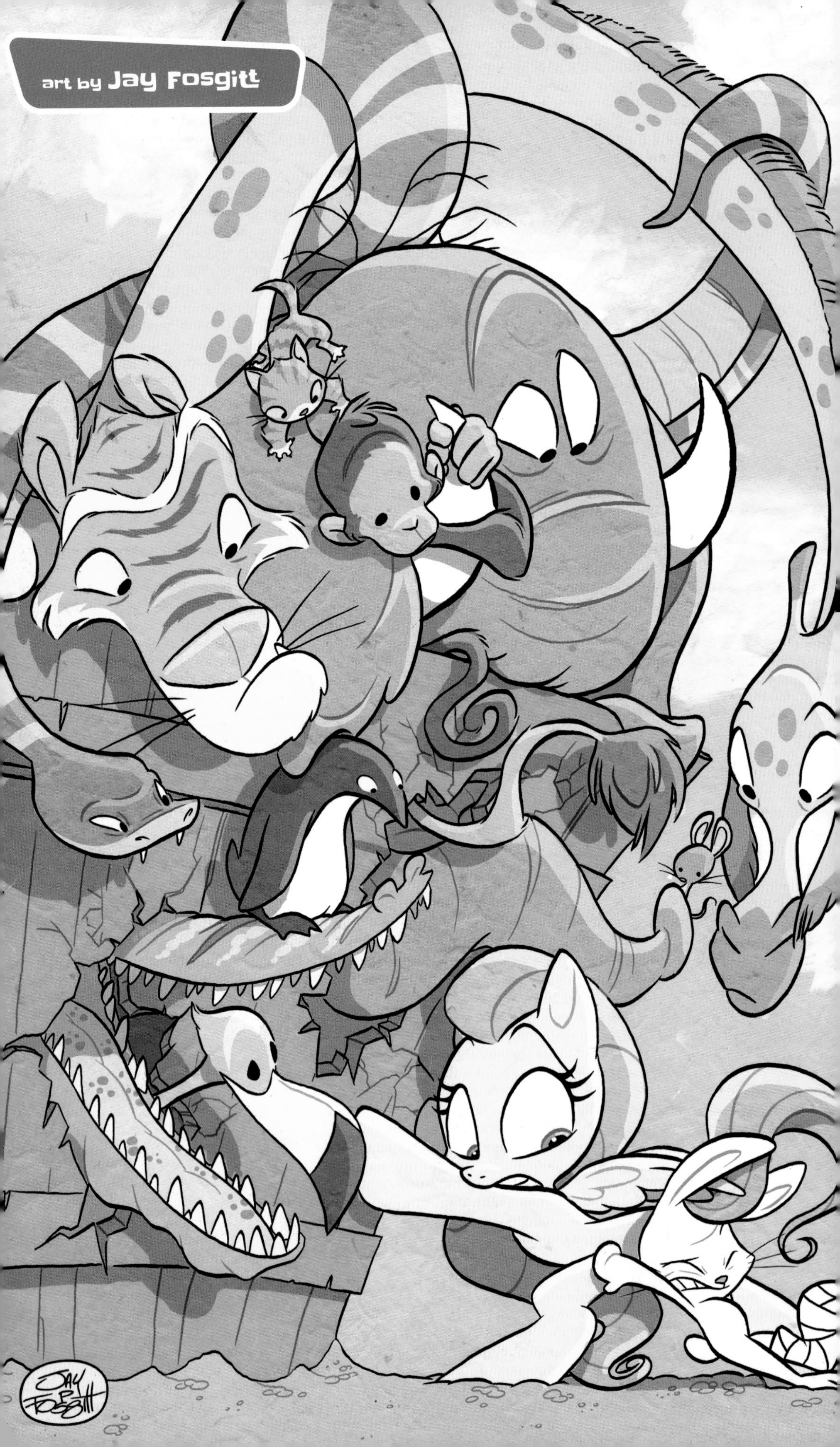
art by Jay Fosgitt

my LITTLE PONY
Friendship is Magic

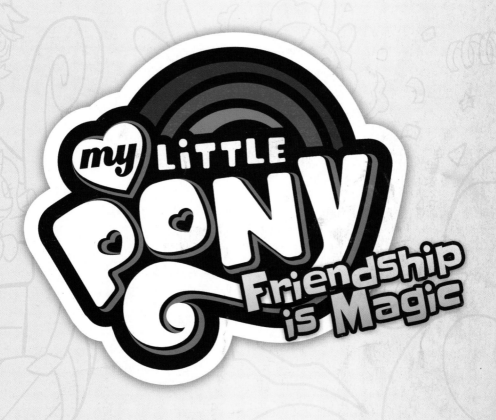

COVER BY
Tony Fleecs

COLLECTION EDITS BY
Justin Eisinger and Alonzo Simon

COLLECTION DESIGN BY
Neil Uyetake

PUBLISHER
Ted Adams

Special thanks to Meghan McCarthy, Eliza Hart, Ed Lane, Beth Artale, and Michael Kelly.

For international rights, contact licensing@idwpublishing

ISBN: 978-1-68405-029-1

20 19 18 17   1 2 3

Licensed By: Hasbro

www.IDWPUBLISHING.com

Ted Adams, CEO & Publisher • Greg Goldstein, President & COO • Robbie Robbins, EVP/Sr. Graphic Artist • Chris Ryall, Chief Cre Officer • David Hedgecock, Editor-in-Chief • Laurie Windrow, Senior Vice President of Sales & Marketing • Matthew Ruzicka, CPA, Financial Officer • Lorelei Bunjes, VP of Digital Services • Jerry Bennington, VP of New Product Development

Facebook: facebook.com/idwpublishing • Twitter: @idwpublishing • YouTube: youtube.com/idwpublishing
Tumblr: tumblr.idwpublishing.com • Instagram: instagram.com/idwpublishing

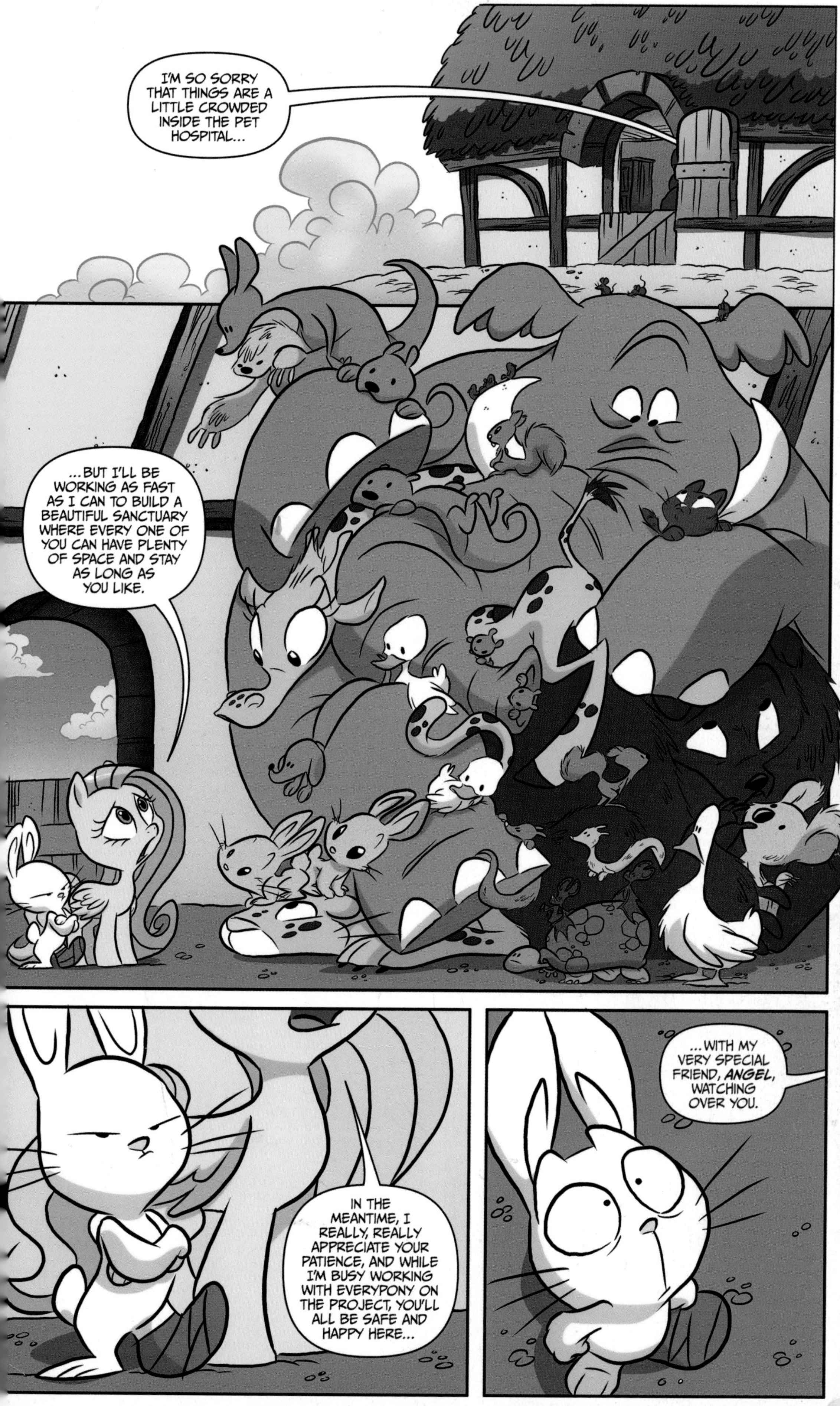
I'M SO SORRY THAT THINGS ARE A LITTLE CROWDED INSIDE THE PET HOSPITAL...
...BUT I'LL BE WORKING AS FAST AS I CAN TO BUILD A BEAUTIFUL SANCTUARY WHERE EVERY ONE OF YOU CAN HAVE PLENTY OF SPACE AND STAY AS LONG AS YOU LIKE.
IN THE MEANTIME, I REALLY, REALLY APPRECIATE YOUR PATIENCE, AND WHILE I'M BUSY WORKING WITH EVERYPONY ON THE PROJECT, YOU'LL ALL BE SAFE AND HAPPY HERE...
...WITH MY VERY SPECIAL FRIEND, ANGEL, WATCHING OVER YOU.

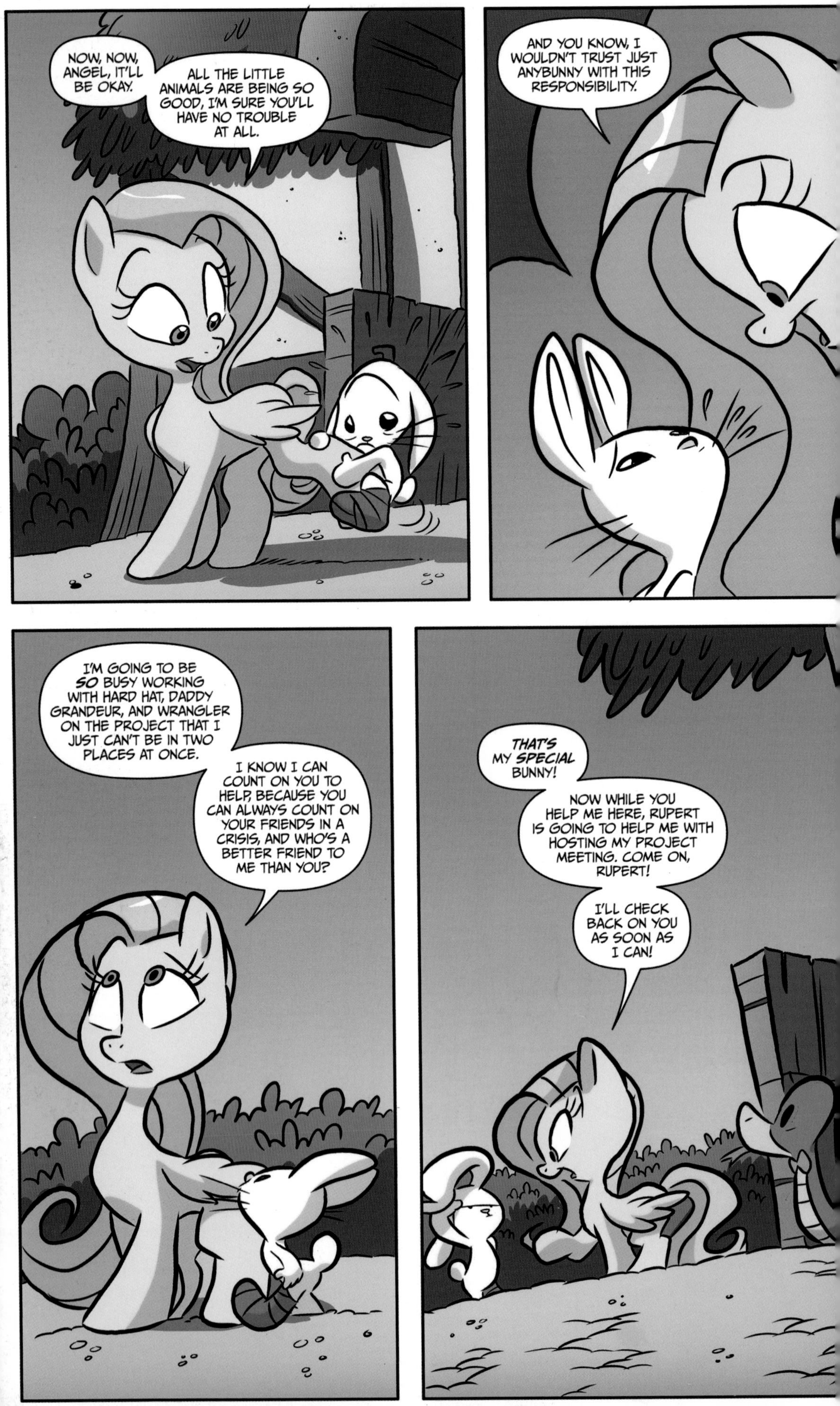
NOW, NOW, ANGEL, IT'LL BE OKAY.
ALL THE LITTLE ANIMALS ARE BEING SO GOOD, I'M SURE YOU'LL HAVE NO TROUBLE AT ALL.
AND YOU KNOW, I WOULDN'T TRUST JUST ANYBUNNY WITH THIS RESPONSIBILITY.
I'M GOING TO BE *SO* BUSY WORKING WITH HARD HAT, DADDY GRANDEUR, AND WRANGLER ON THE PROJECT THAT I JUST CAN'T BE IN TWO PLACES AT ONCE.
I KNOW I CAN COUNT ON YOU TO HELP, BECAUSE YOU CAN ALWAYS COUNT ON YOUR FRIENDS IN A CRISIS, AND WHO'S A BETTER FRIEND TO ME THAN YOU?
THAT'S MY *SPECIAL* BUNNY!
NOW WHILE YOU HELP ME HERE, RUPERT IS GOING TO HELP ME WITH HOSTING MY PROJECT MEETING. COME ON, RUPERT!
I'LL CHECK BACK ON YOU AS SOON AS I CAN!

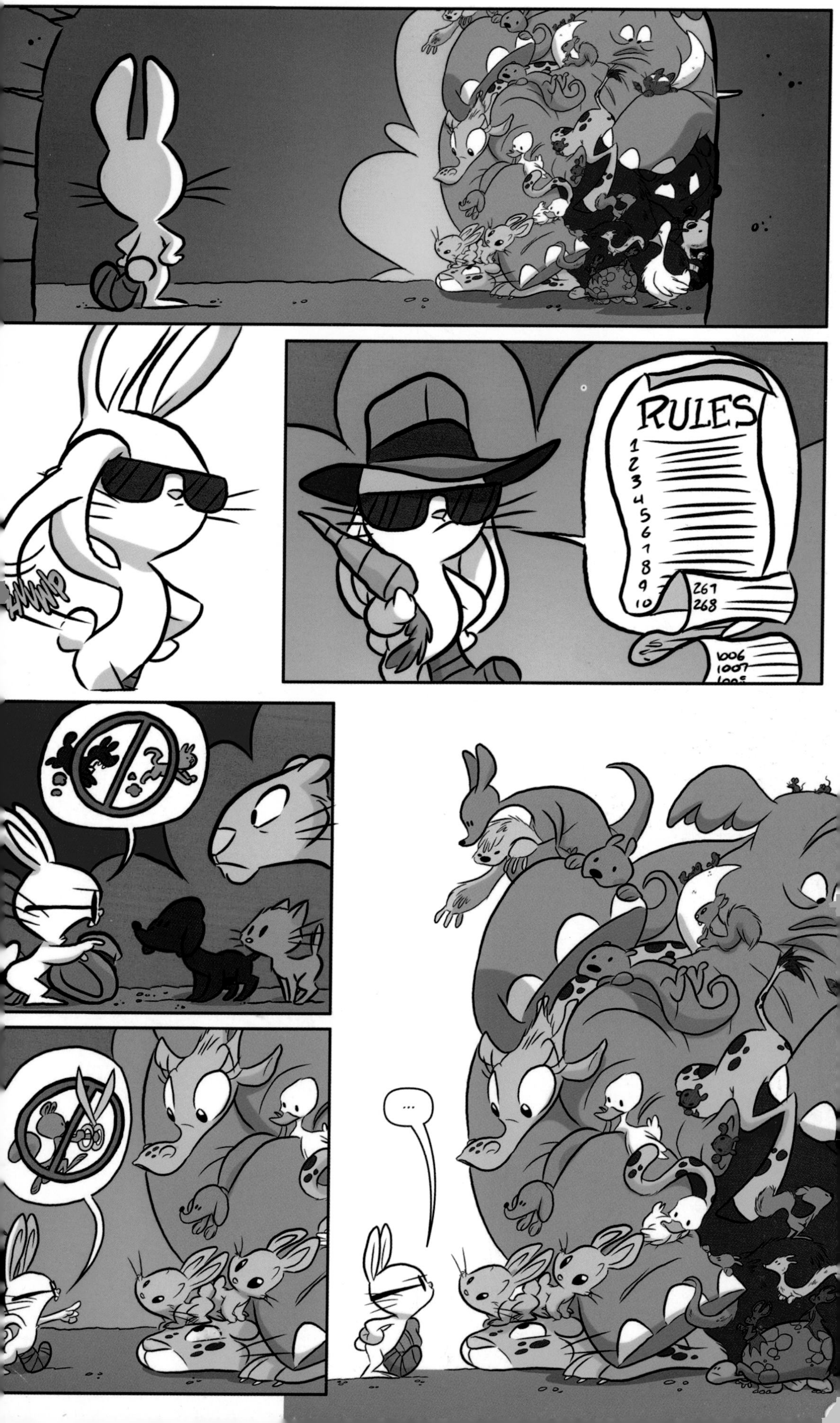

WHUMP
RULES
1
2
3
4
5
6
7
8
9
10
267
268
1006
1007
...

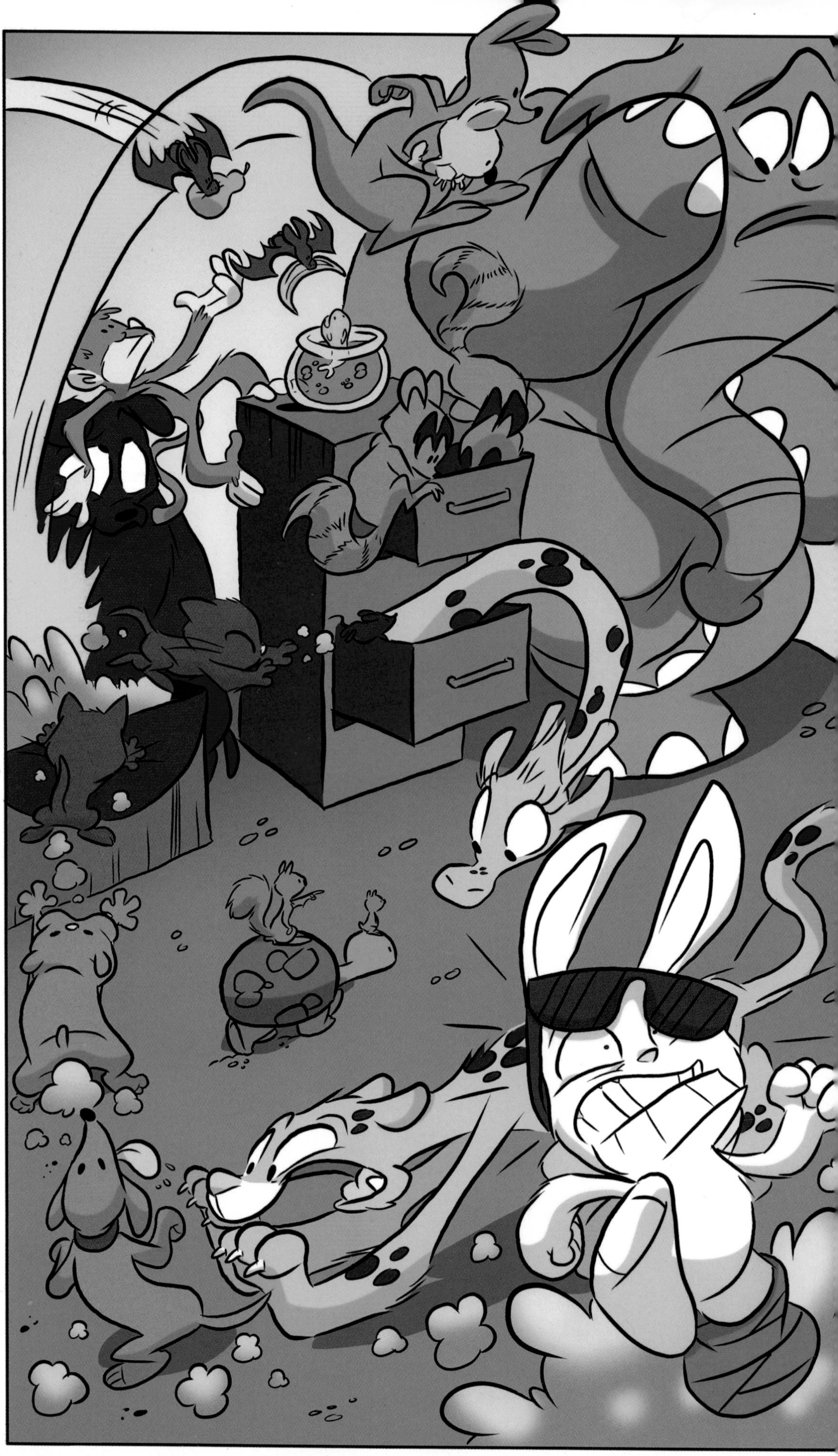

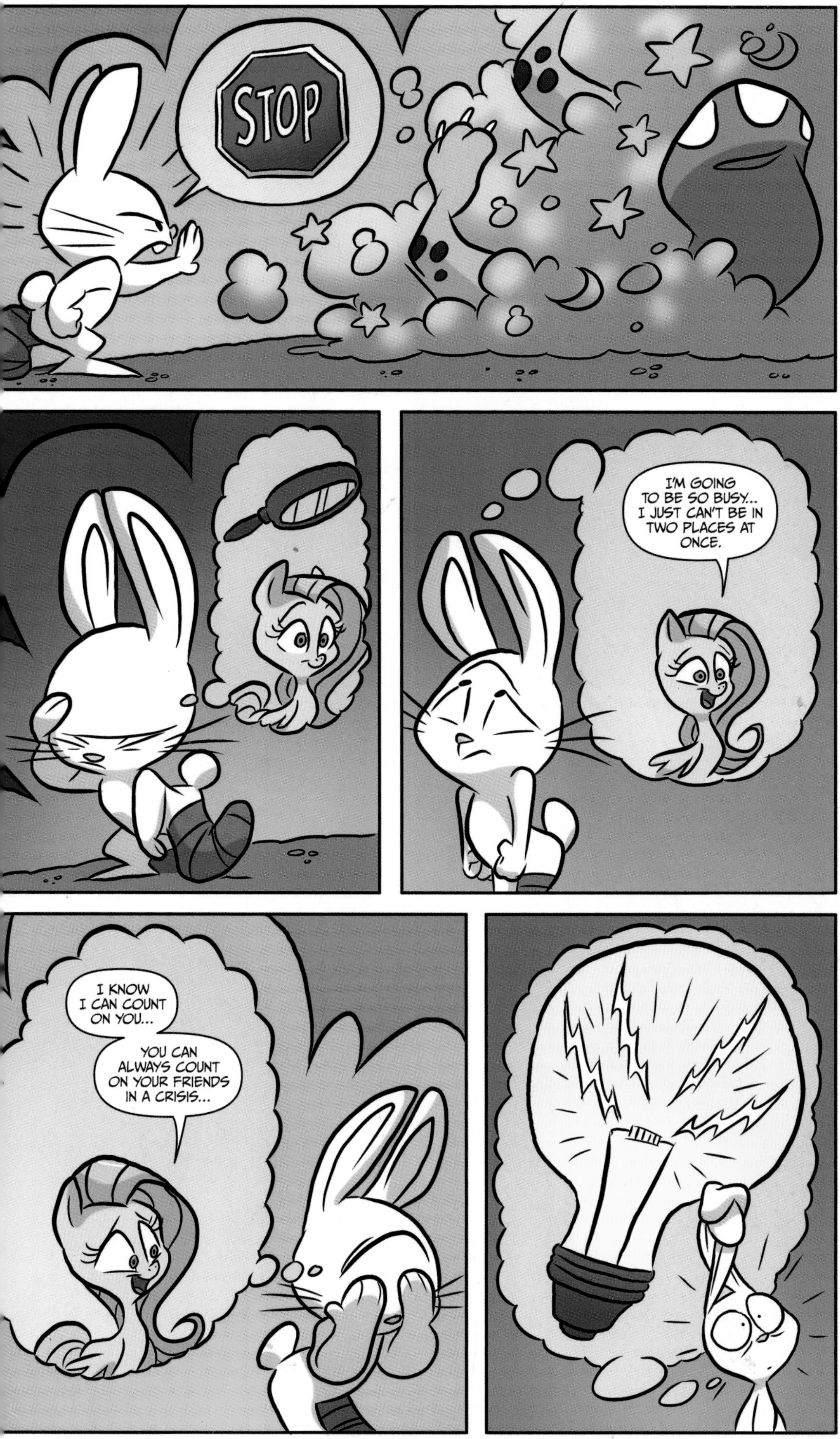
STOP
I'M GOING TO BE SO BUSY... I JUST CAN'T BE IN TWO PLACES AT ONCE.
I KNOW I CAN COUNT ON YOU...
YOU CAN ALWAYS COUNT ON YOUR FRIENDS IN A CRISIS...

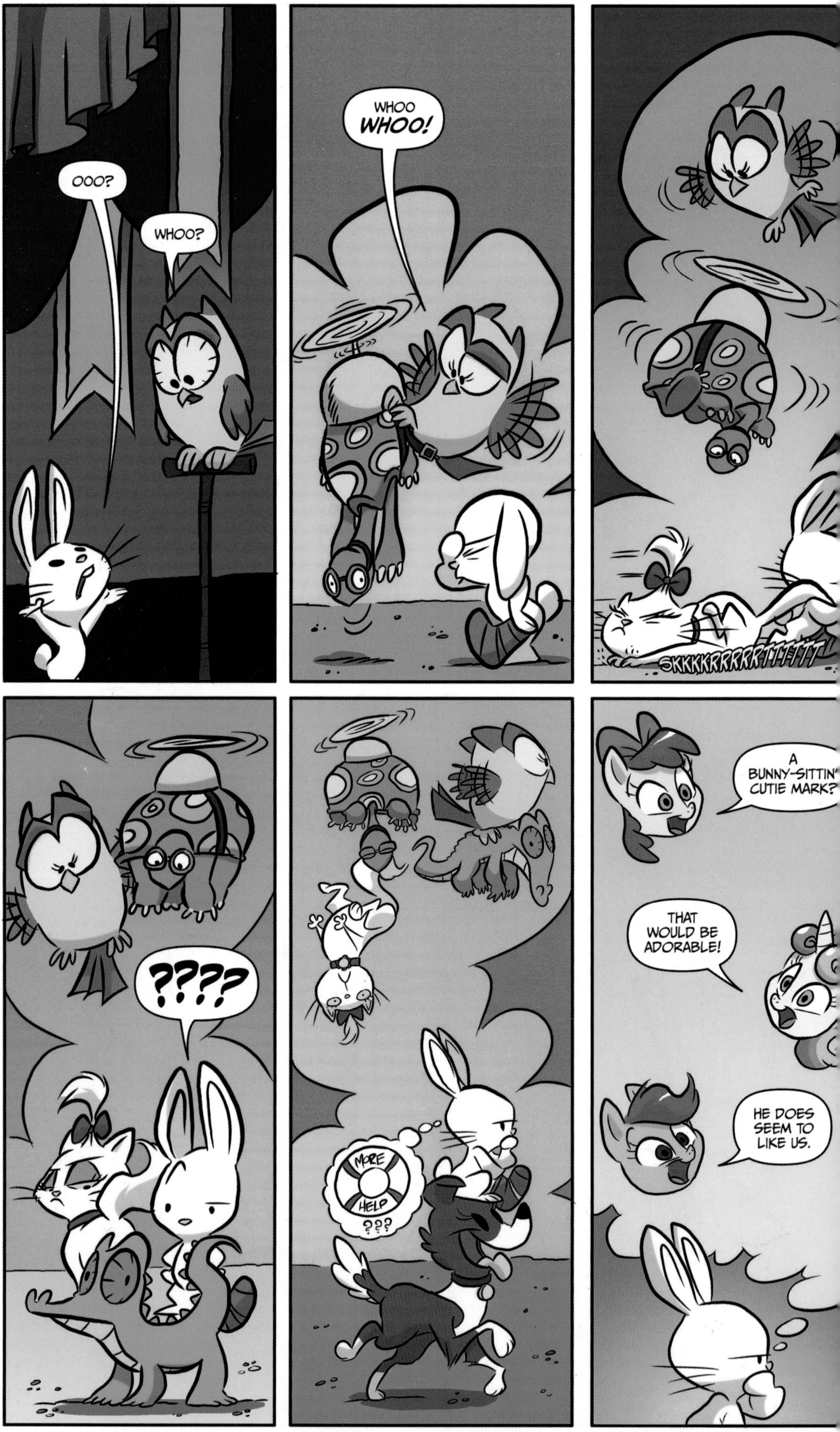
OOO?
WHOO?
WHOO WHOO!
SKKKKRRRRRTTTTTT
????
MORE HELP ???
A BUNNY-SITTIN' CUTIE MARK?
THAT WOULD BE ADORABLE!
HE DOES SEEM TO LIKE US.

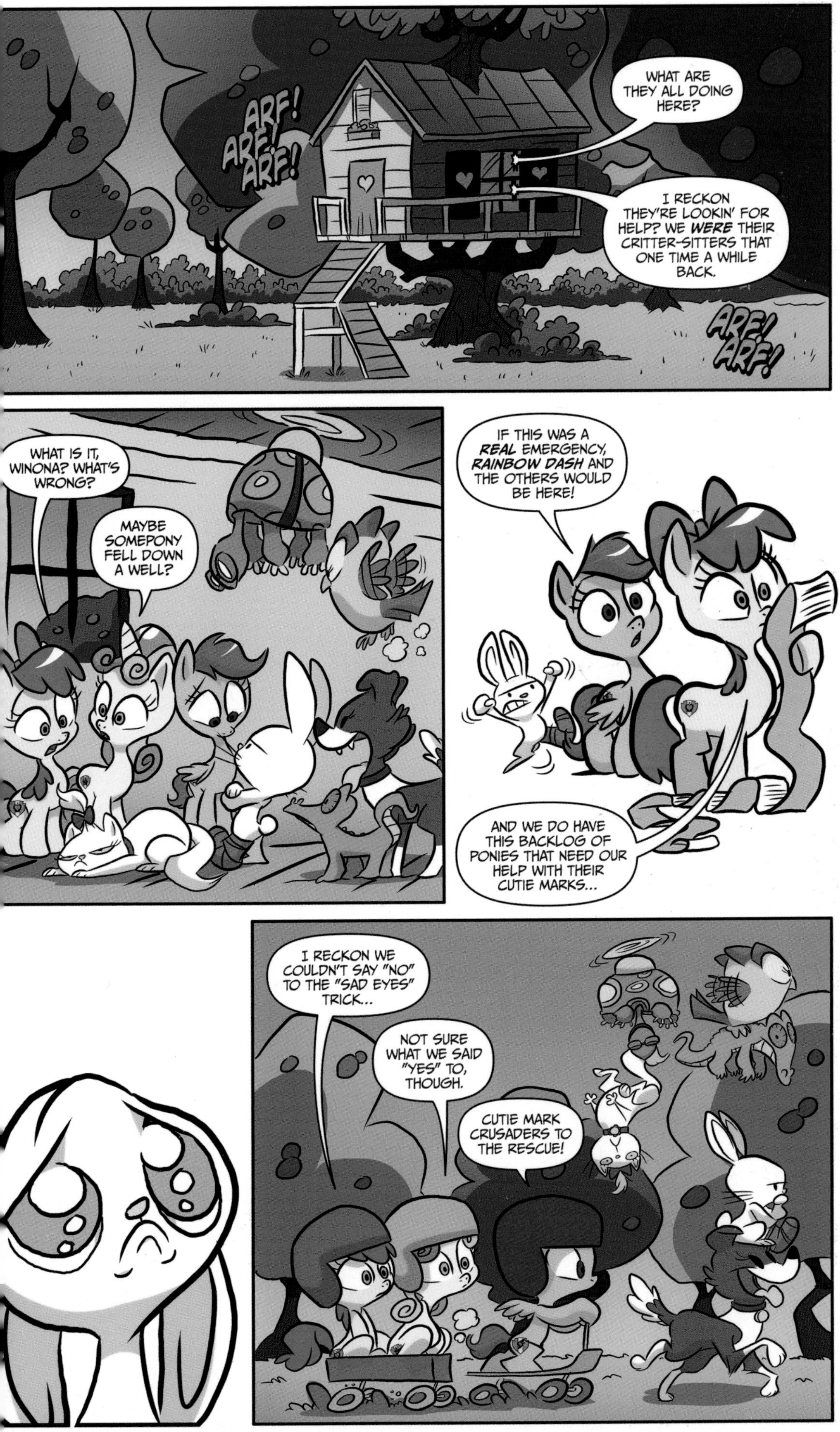
ARF! ARF! ARF!
WHAT ARE THEY ALL DOING HERE?
I RECKON THEY'RE LOOKIN' FOR HELP? WE **WERE** THEIR CRITTER-SITTERS THAT ONE TIME A WHILE BACK.
ARF! ARF!
WHAT IS IT, WINONA? WHAT'S WRONG?
MAYBE SOMEPONY FELL DOWN A WELL?
IF THIS WAS A **REAL** EMERGENCY, **RAINBOW DASH** AND THE OTHERS WOULD BE HERE!
AND WE DO HAVE THIS BACKLOG OF PONIES THAT NEED OUR HELP WITH THEIR CUTIE MARKS...
I RECKON WE COULDN'T SAY "NO" TO THE "SAD EYES" TRICK...
NOT SURE WHAT WE SAID "YES" TO, THOUGH.
CUTIE MARK CRUSADERS TO THE RESCUE!

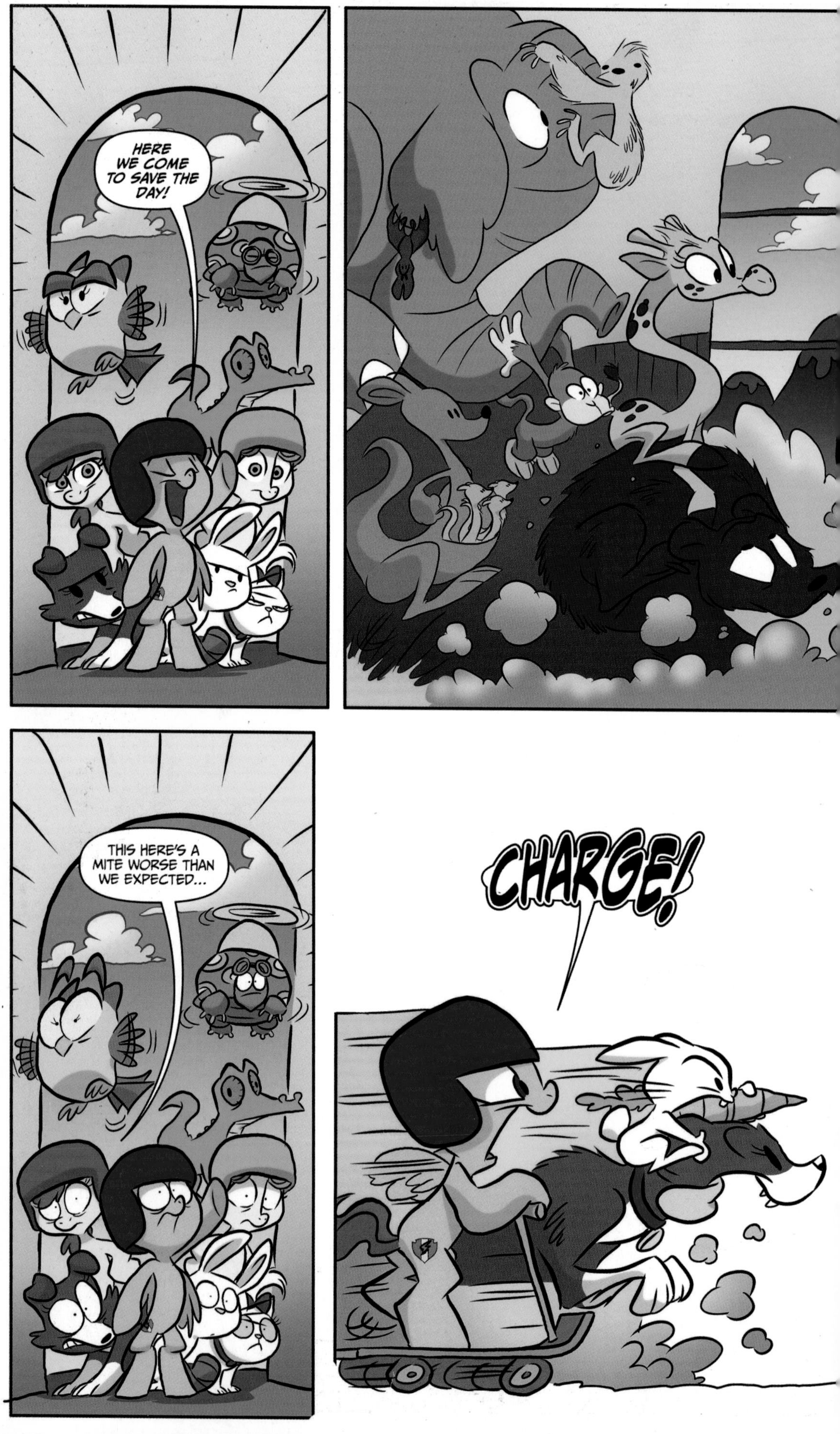
HERE WE COME TO SAVE THE DAY!
THIS HERE'S A MITE WORSE THAN WE EXPECTED...
CHARGE!

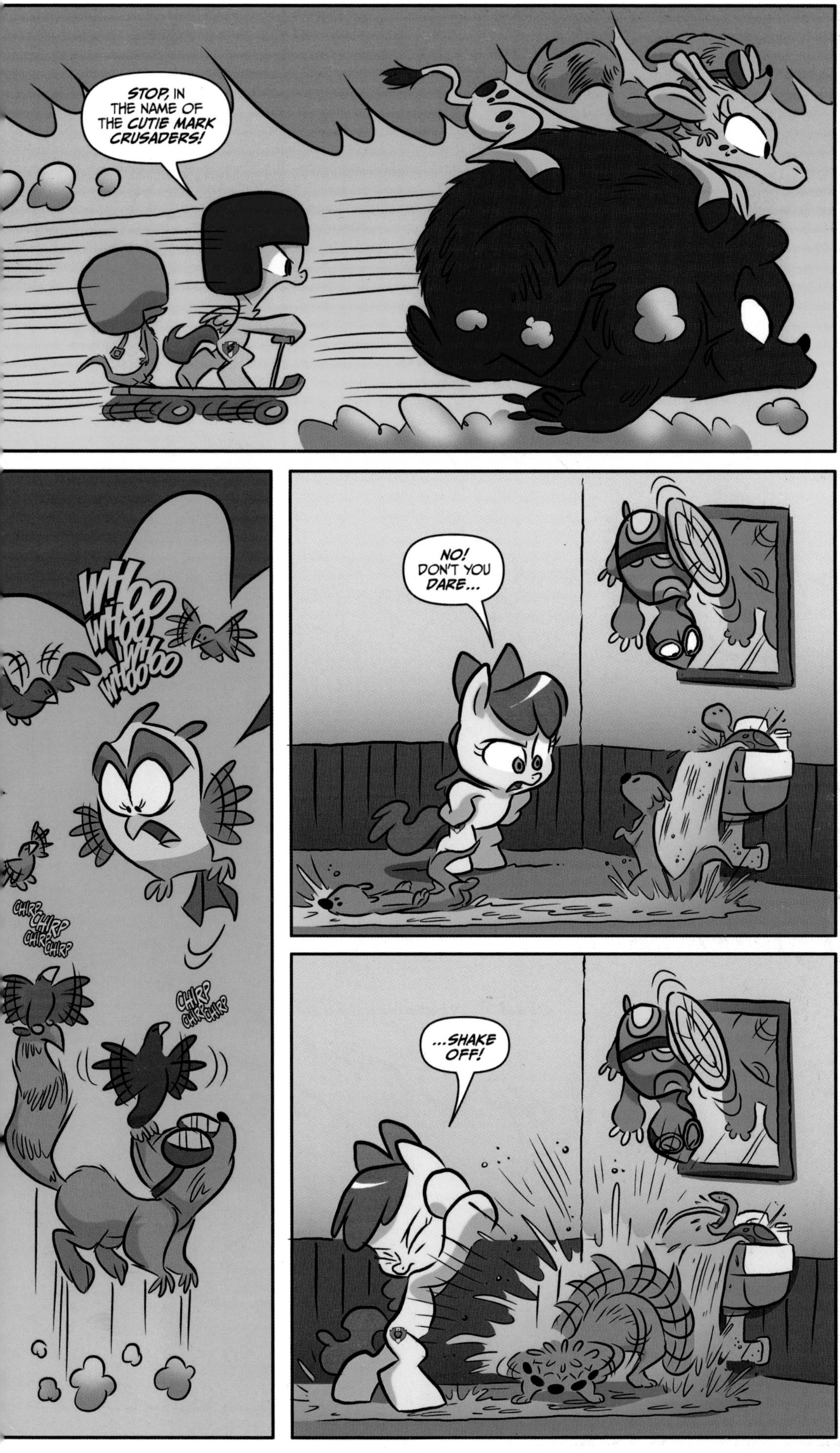
STOP, IN THE NAME OF THE CUTIE MARK CRUSADERS!
WHOO WHOO WHOO WHOO
CHIRP CHIRP CHIRP CHIRP
CHIRP CHIRP CHIRP
NO! DON'T YOU DARE...
...SHAKE OFF!

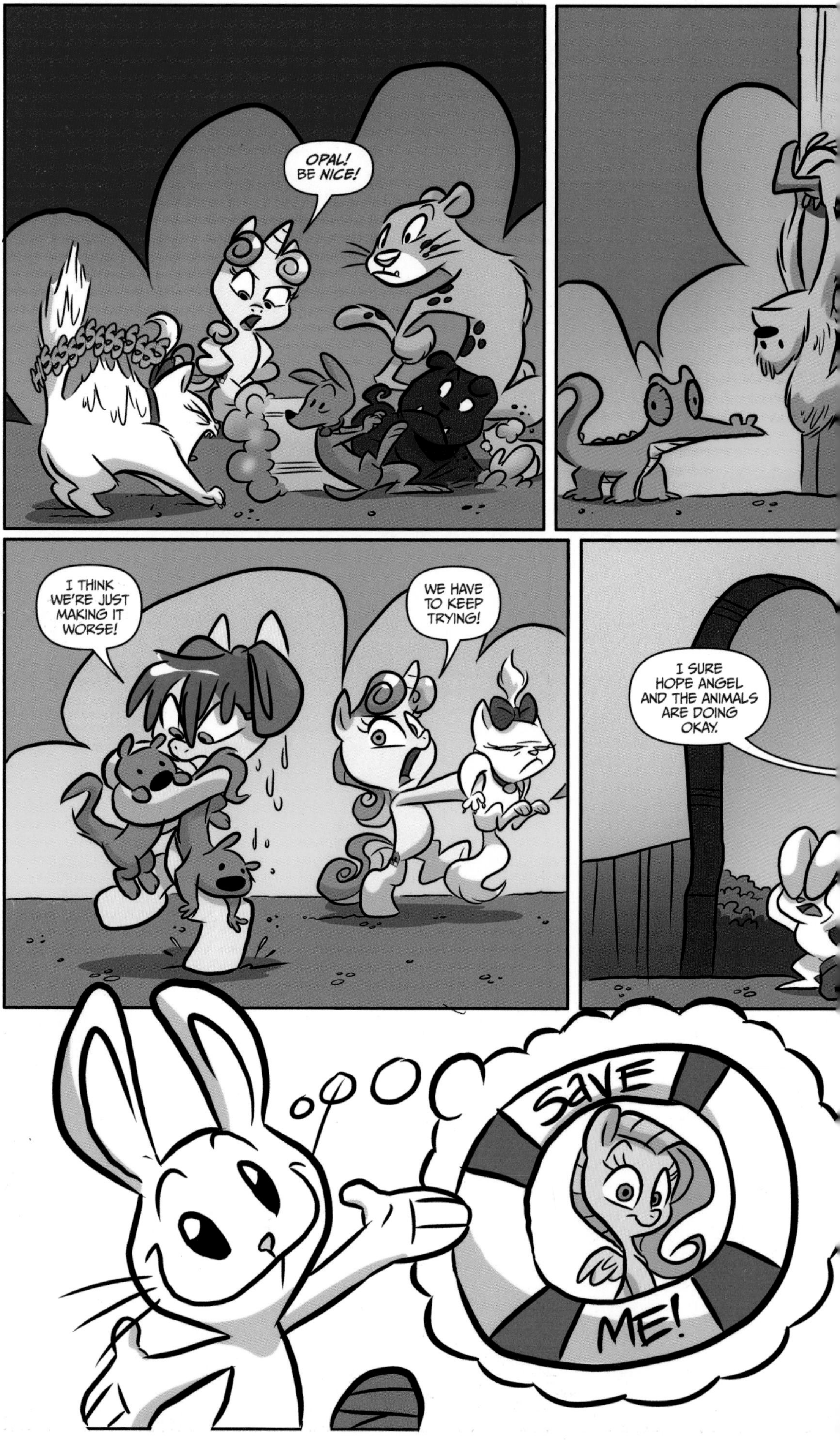

OPAL! BE NICE!
HISSSSSSSSSSSS
I THINK WE'RE JUST MAKING IT WORSE!
WE HAVE TO KEEP TRYING!
I SURE HOPE ANGEL AND THE ANIMALS ARE DOING OKAY.
SAVE ME!

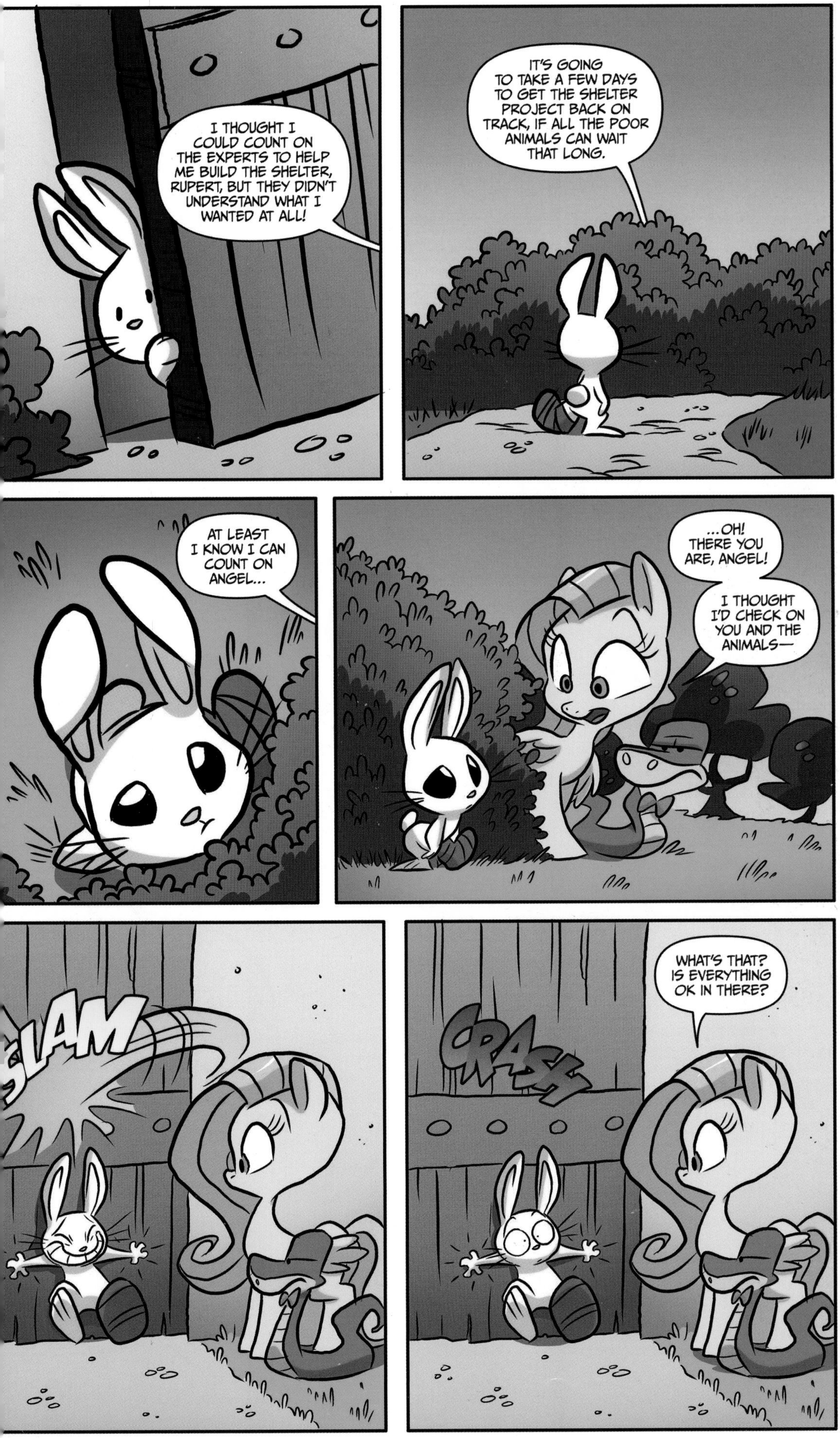
I THOUGHT I COULD COUNT ON THE EXPERTS TO HELP ME BUILD THE SHELTER, RUPERT, BUT THEY DIDN'T UNDERSTAND WHAT I WANTED AT ALL!
IT'S GOING TO TAKE A FEW DAYS TO GET THE SHELTER PROJECT BACK ON TRACK, IF ALL THE POOR ANIMALS CAN WAIT THAT LONG.
AT LEAST I KNOW I CAN COUNT ON ANGEL...
...OH! THERE YOU ARE, ANGEL!
I THOUGHT I'D CHECK ON YOU AND THE ANIMALS—
SLAM
CRASH
WHAT'S THAT? IS EVERYTHING OK IN THERE?

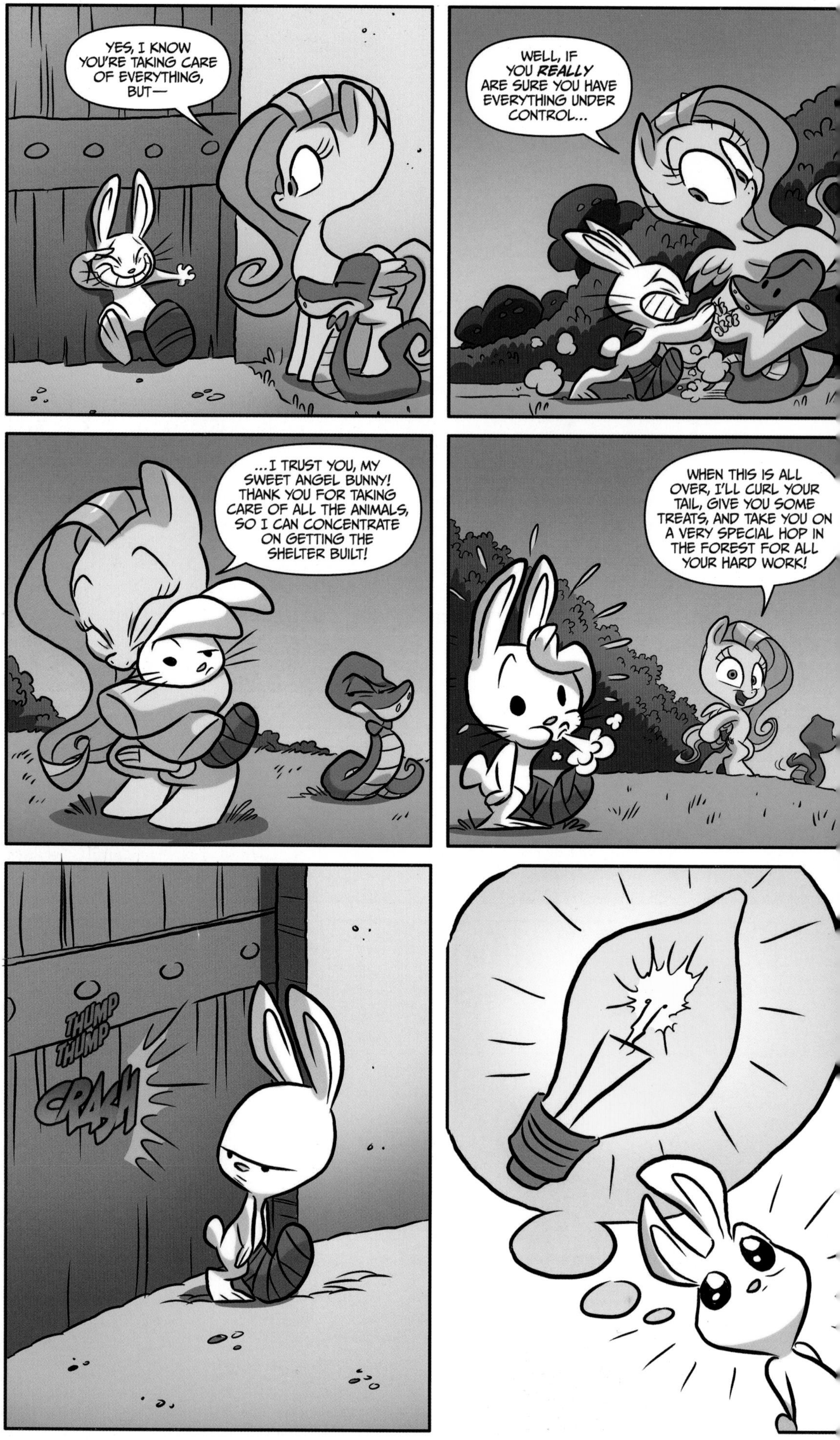
YES, I KNOW YOU'RE TAKING CARE OF EVERYTHING, BUT—
WELL, IF YOU *REALLY* ARE SURE YOU HAVE EVERYTHING UNDER CONTROL...
...I TRUST YOU, MY SWEET ANGEL BUNNY! THANK YOU FOR TAKING CARE OF ALL THE ANIMALS, SO I CAN CONCENTRATE ON GETTING THE SHELTER BUILT!
WHEN THIS IS ALL OVER, I'LL CURL YOUR TAIL, GIVE YOU SOME TREATS, AND TAKE YOU ON A VERY SPECIAL HOP IN THE FOREST FOR ALL YOUR HARD WORK!
THUMP
THUMP
CRASH

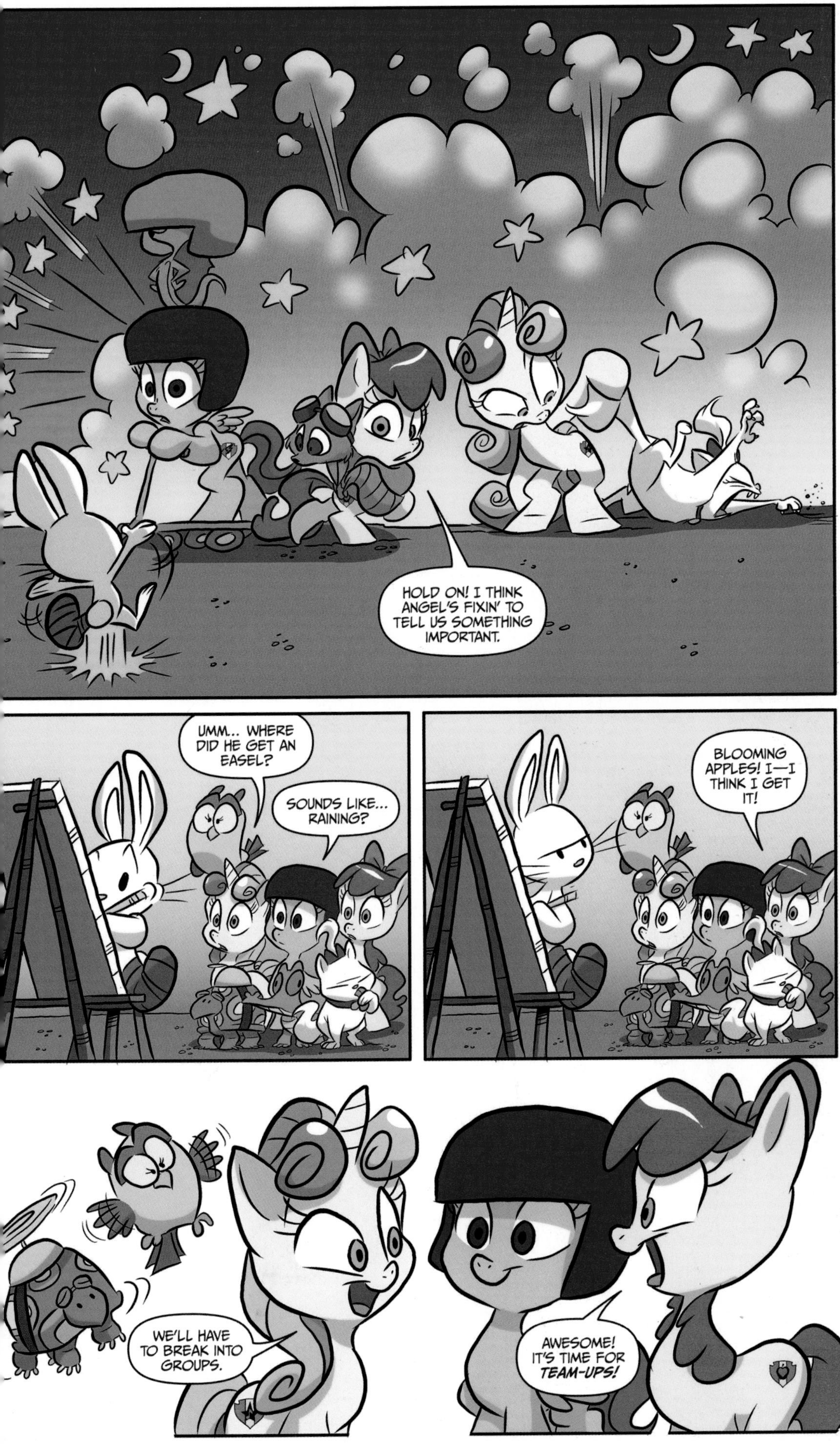
HOLD ON! I THINK ANGEL'S FIXIN' TO TELL US SOMETHING IMPORTANT.
UMM... WHERE DID HE GET AN EASEL?
SOUNDS LIKE... RAINING?
BLOOMING APPLES! I—I THINK I GET IT!
WE'LL HAVE TO BREAK INTO GROUPS.
AWESOME! IT'S TIME FOR *TEAM-UPS!*

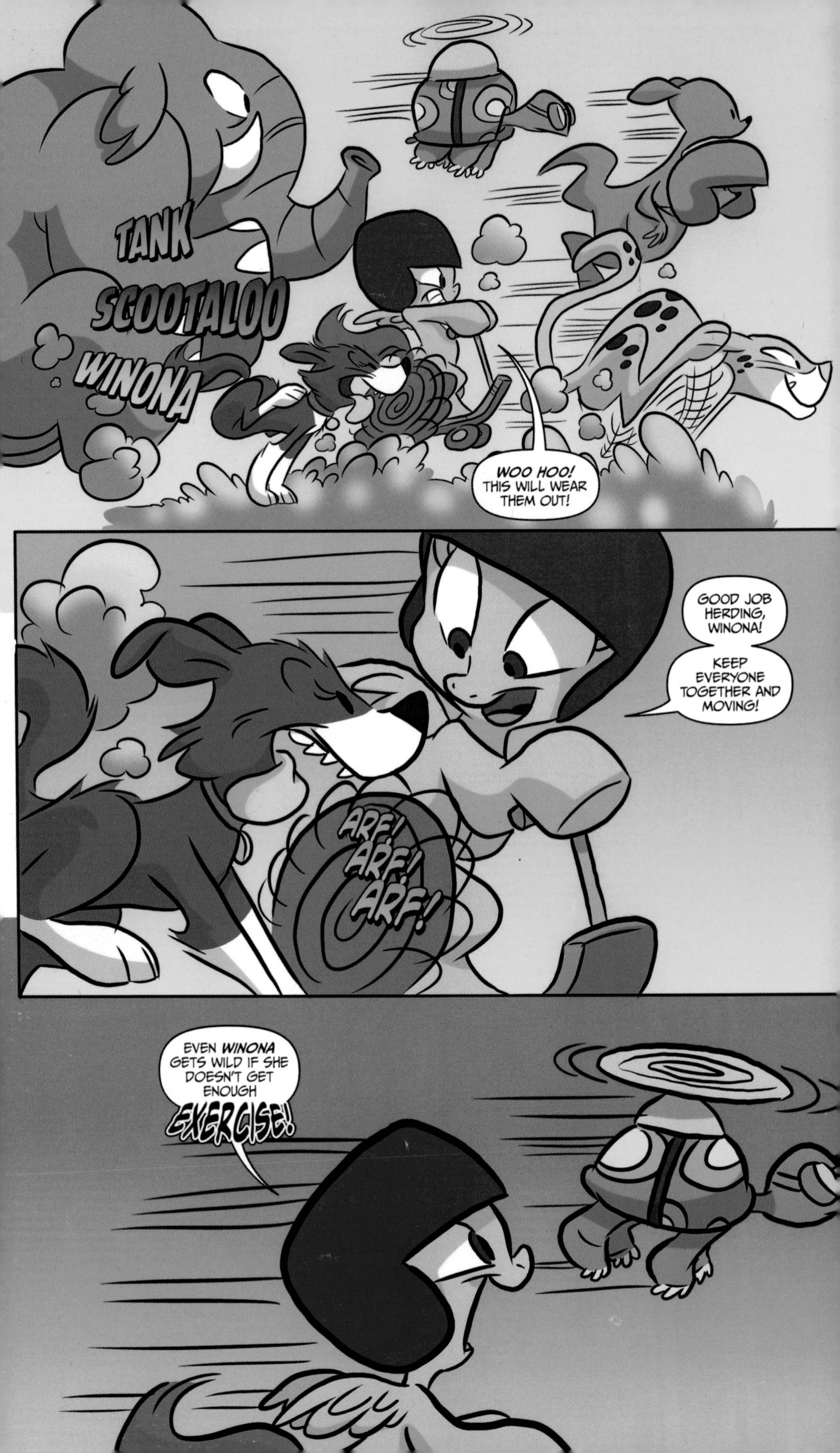
TANK
SCOOTALOO
WINONA
WOO HOO! THIS WILL WEAR THEM OUT!
GOOD JOB HERDING, WINONA!
KEEP EVERYONE TOGETHER AND MOVING!
ARF! ARF! ARF!
EVEN WINONA GETS WILD IF SHE DOESN'T GET ENOUGH EXERCISE!

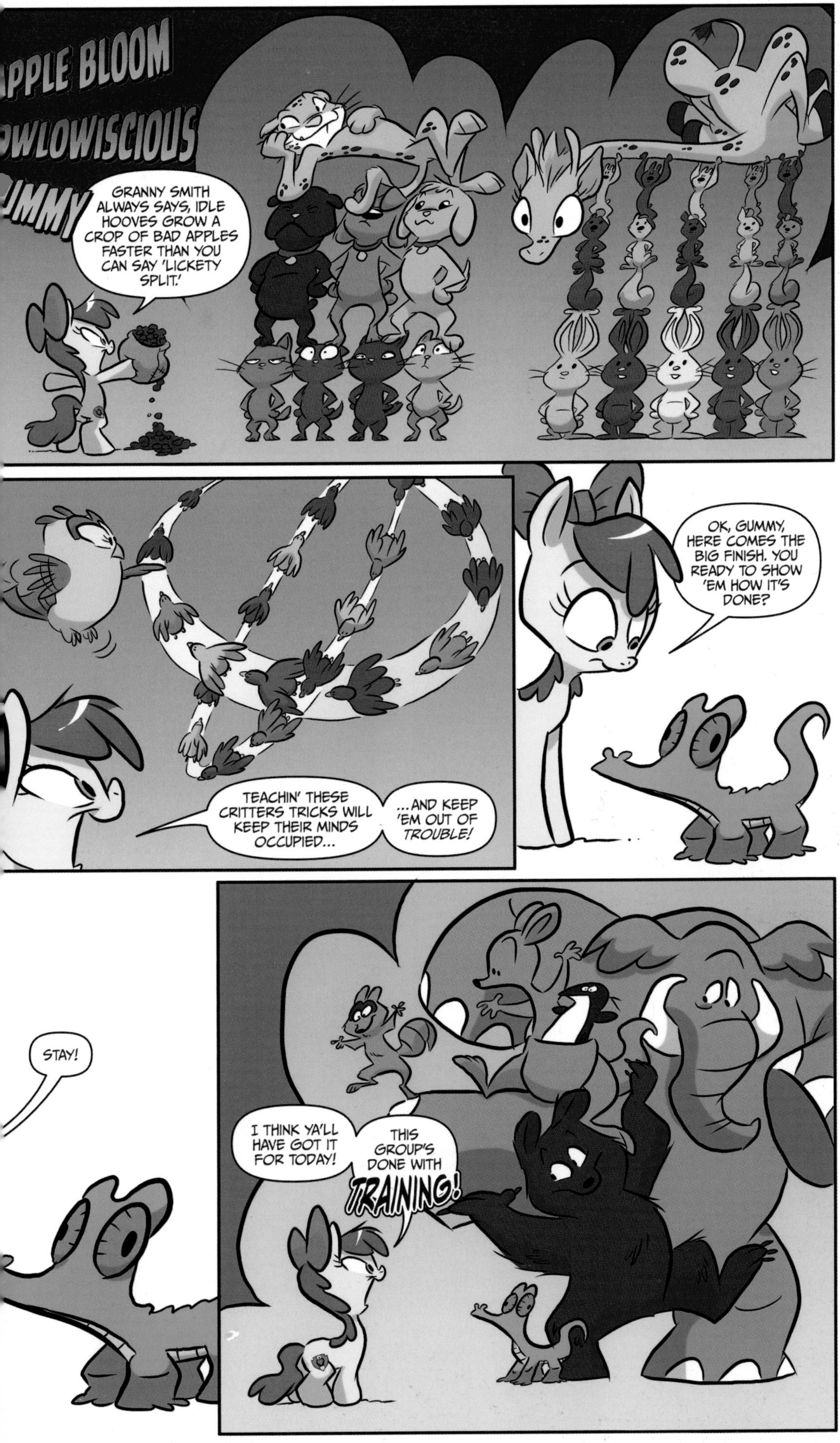

APPLE BLOOM
HOWLOWISCIOUS
GUMMY
GRANNY SMITH ALWAYS SAYS, IDLE HOOVES GROW A CROP OF BAD APPLES FASTER THAN YOU CAN SAY 'LICKETY SPLIT.'
OK, GUMMY, HERE COMES THE BIG FINISH. YOU READY TO SHOW 'EM HOW IT'S DONE?
TEACHIN' THESE CRITTERS TRICKS WILL KEEP THEIR MINDS OCCUPIED...
...AND KEEP 'EM OUT OF TROUBLE!
STAY!
I THINK YA'LL HAVE GOT IT FOR TODAY!
THIS GROUP'S DONE WITH
TRAINING!

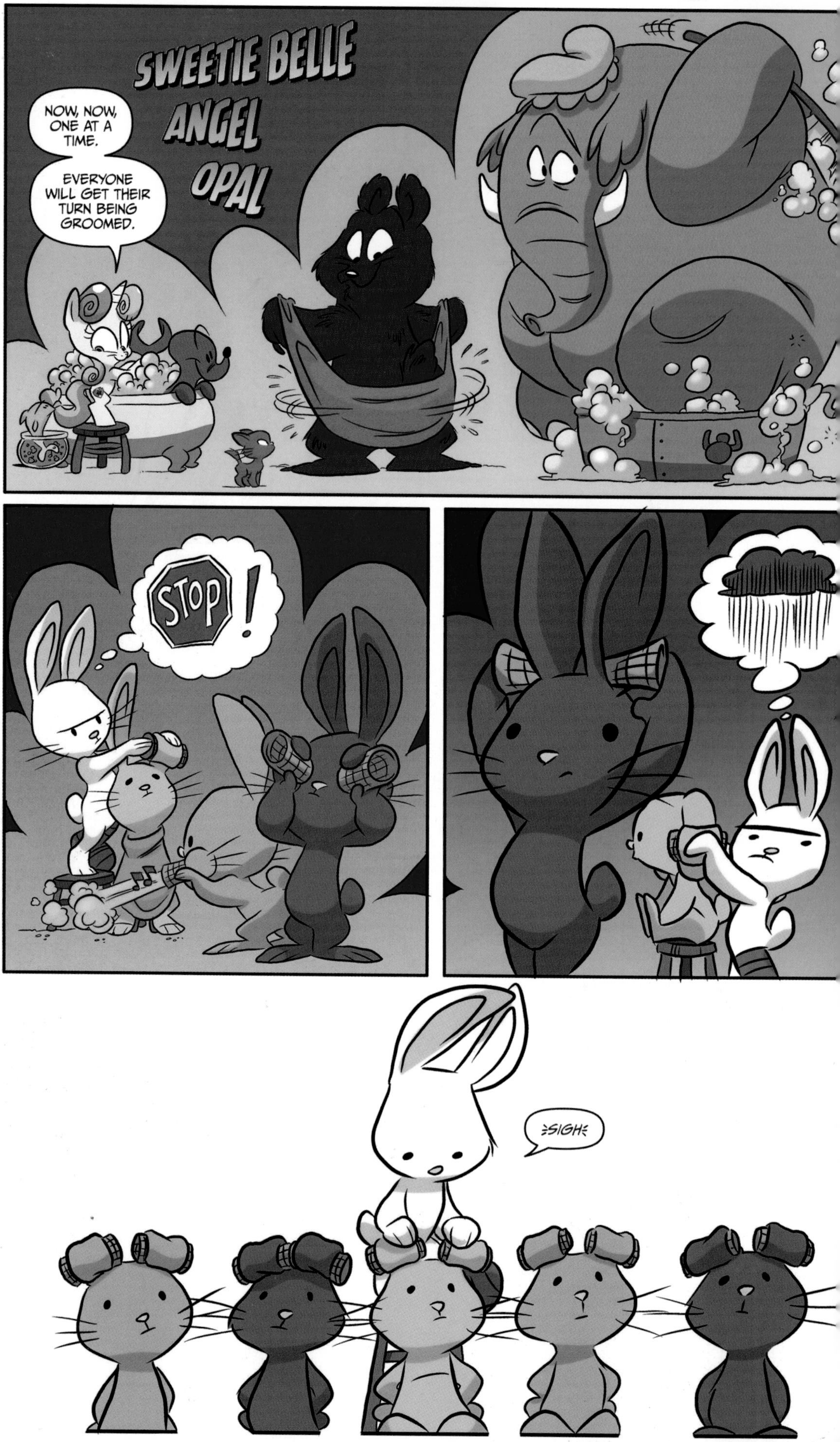
SWEETIE BELLE
ANGEL
OPAL
NOW, NOW, ONE AT A TIME.
EVERYONE WILL GET THEIR TURN BEING GROOMED.
STOP
!
SIGH

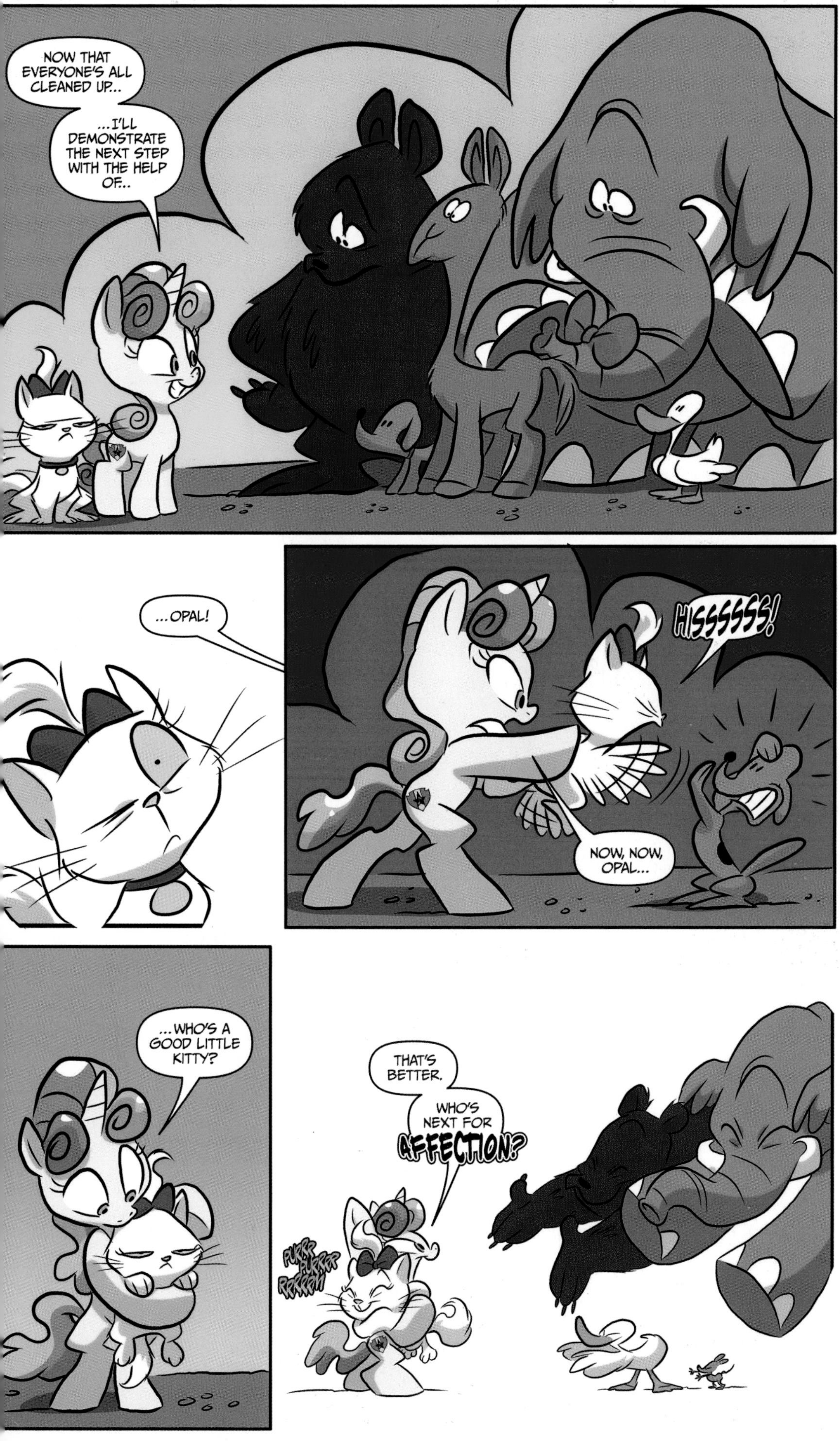
NOW THAT EVERYONE'S ALL CLEANED UP...
...I'LL DEMONSTRATE THE NEXT STEP WITH THE HELP OF...
...OPAL!
HISSSSSS!
NOW, NOW, OPAL...
...WHO'S A GOOD LITTLE KITTY?
THAT'S BETTER.
WHO'S NEXT FOR AFFECTION?
PURRR PURRRR RRRRRH

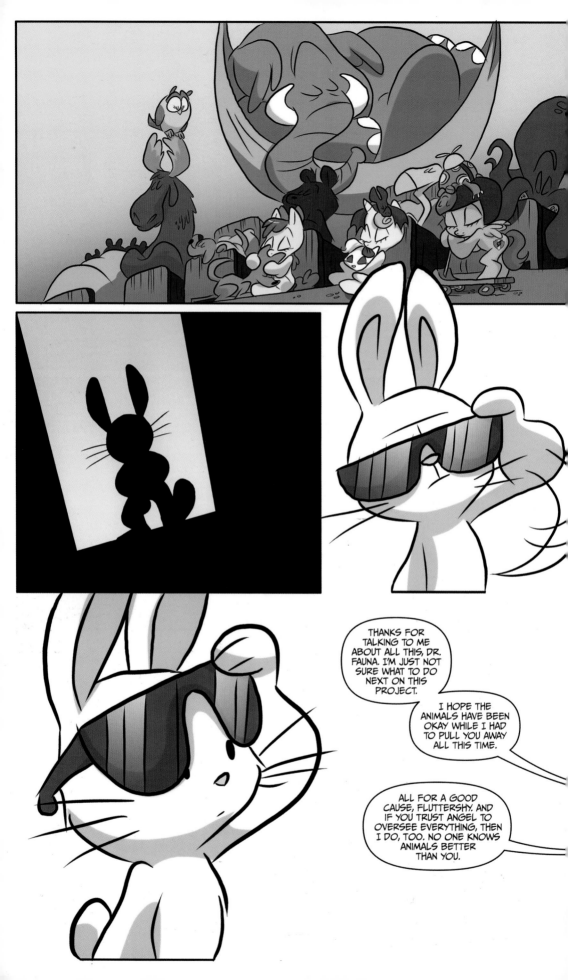

THANKS FOR TALKING TO ME ABOUT ALL THIS, DR. FAUNA. I'M JUST NOT SURE WHAT TO DO NEXT ON THIS PROJECT.

I HOPE THE ANIMALS HAVE BEEN OKAY WHILE I HAD TO PULL YOU AWAY ALL THIS TIME.

ALL FOR A GOOD CAUSE, FLUTTERSHY. AND IF YOU TRUST ANGEL TO OVERSEE EVERYTHING, THEN I DO, TOO. NO ONE KNOWS ANIMALS BETTER THAN YOU.

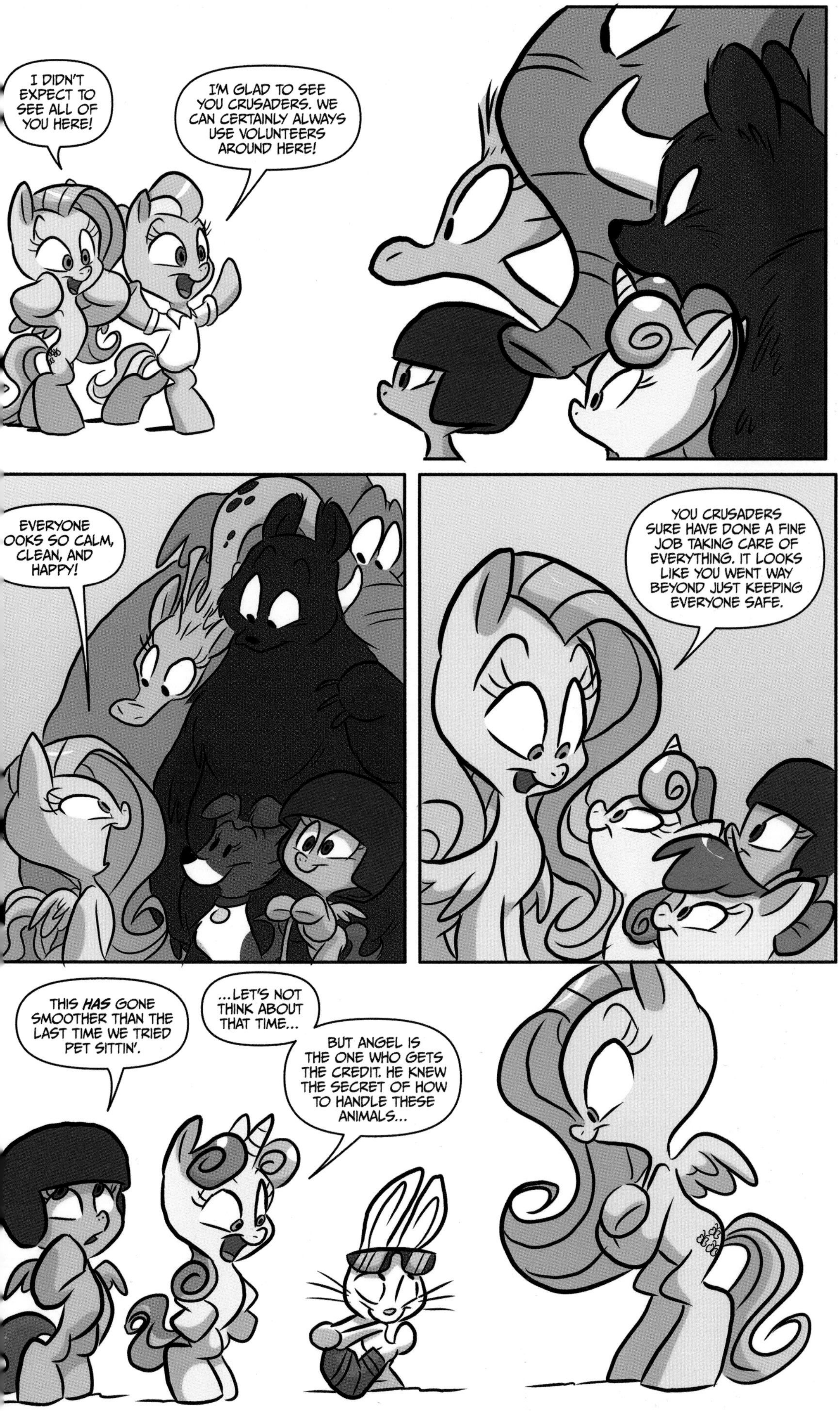
I DIDN'T EXPECT TO SEE ALL OF YOU HERE!
I'M GLAD TO SEE YOU CRUSADERS. WE CAN CERTAINLY ALWAYS USE VOLUNTEERS AROUND HERE!
EVERYONE OOKS SO CALM, CLEAN, AND HAPPY!
YOU CRUSADERS SURE HAVE DONE A FINE JOB TAKING CARE OF EVERYTHING. IT LOOKS LIKE YOU WENT WAY BEYOND JUST KEEPING EVERYONE SAFE.
THIS *HAS* GONE SMOOTHER THAN THE LAST TIME WE TRIED PET SITTIN'.
...LET'S NOT THINK ABOUT THAT TIME...
BUT ANGEL IS THE ONE WHO GETS THE CREDIT. HE KNEW THE SECRET OF HOW TO HANDLE THESE ANIMALS...

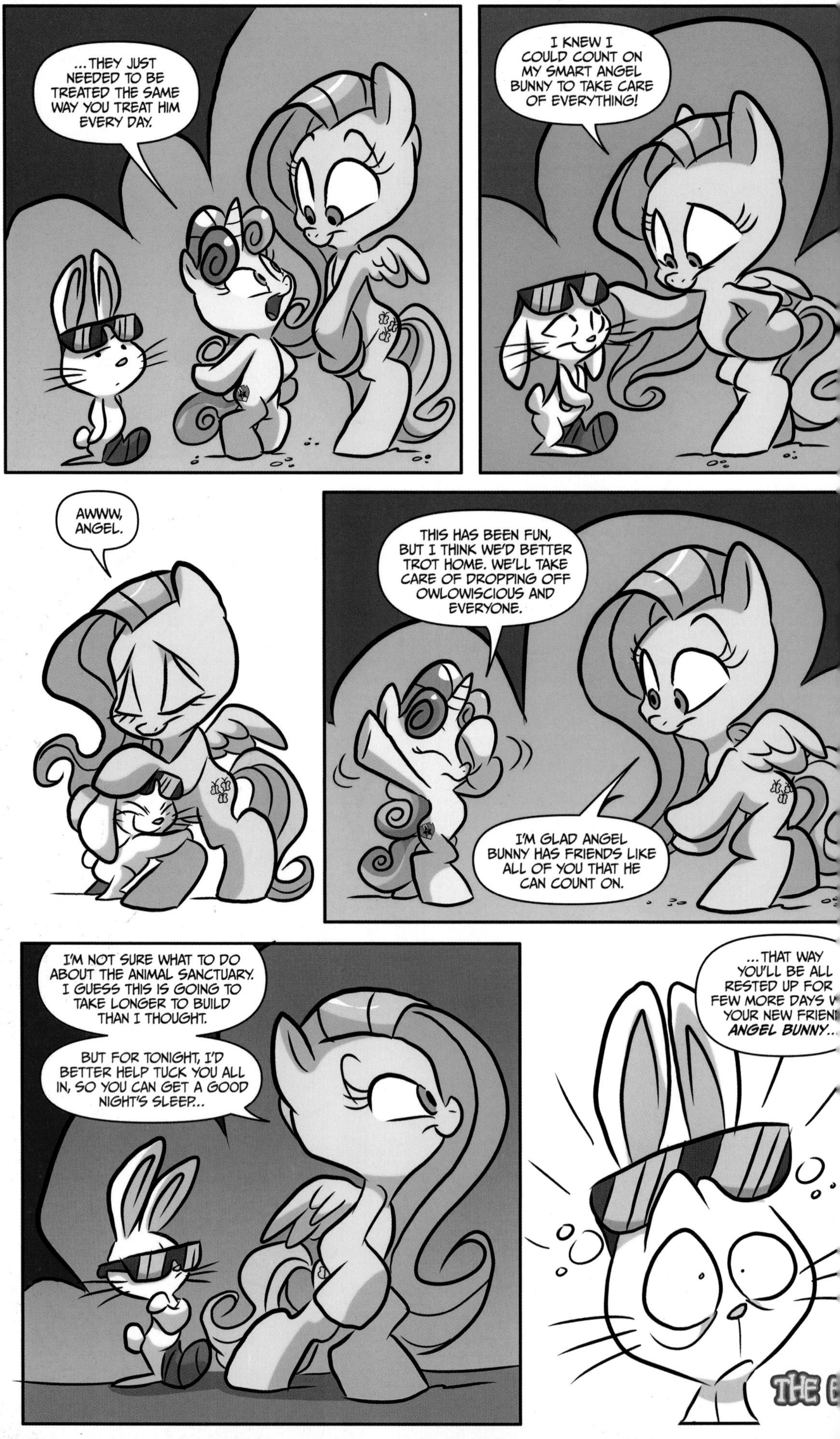
...THEY JUST NEEDED TO BE TREATED THE SAME WAY YOU TREAT HIM EVERY DAY.
I KNEW I COULD COUNT ON MY SMART ANGEL BUNNY TO TAKE CARE OF EVERYTHING!
AWWW, ANGEL.
THIS HAS BEEN FUN, BUT I THINK WE'D BETTER TROT HOME. WE'LL TAKE CARE OF DROPPING OFF OWLOWISCIOUS AND EVERYONE.
I'M GLAD ANGEL BUNNY HAS FRIENDS LIKE ALL OF YOU THAT HE CAN COUNT ON.
I'M NOT SURE WHAT TO DO ABOUT THE ANIMAL SANCTUARY. I GUESS THIS IS GOING TO TAKE LONGER TO BUILD THAN I THOUGHT.
BUT FOR TONIGHT, I'D BETTER HELP TUCK YOU ALL IN, SO YOU CAN GET A GOOD NIGHT'S SLEEP...
...THAT WAY YOU'LL BE ALL RESTED UP FOR FEW MORE DAYS YOUR NEW FRIEN ANGEL BUNNY...

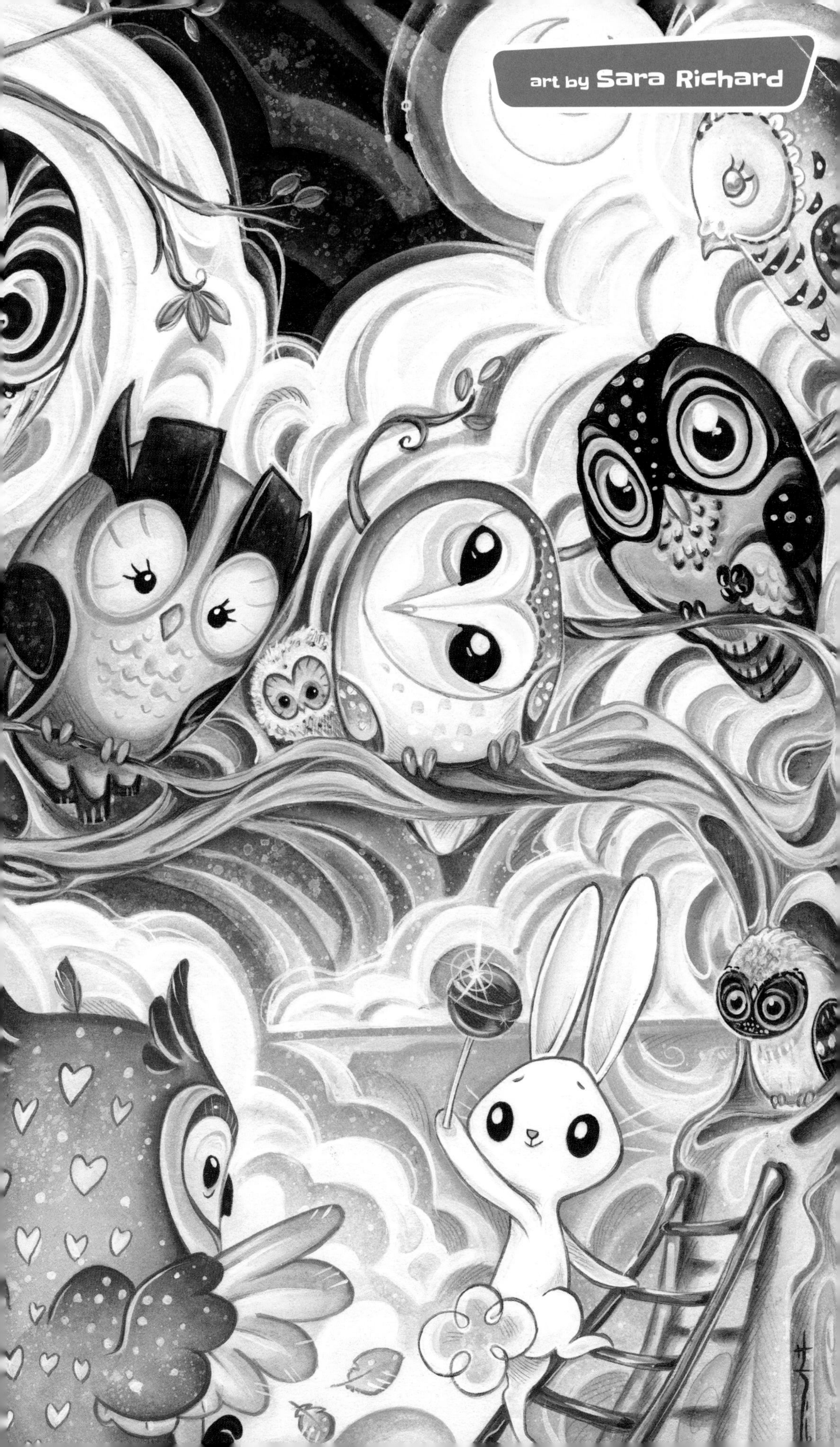

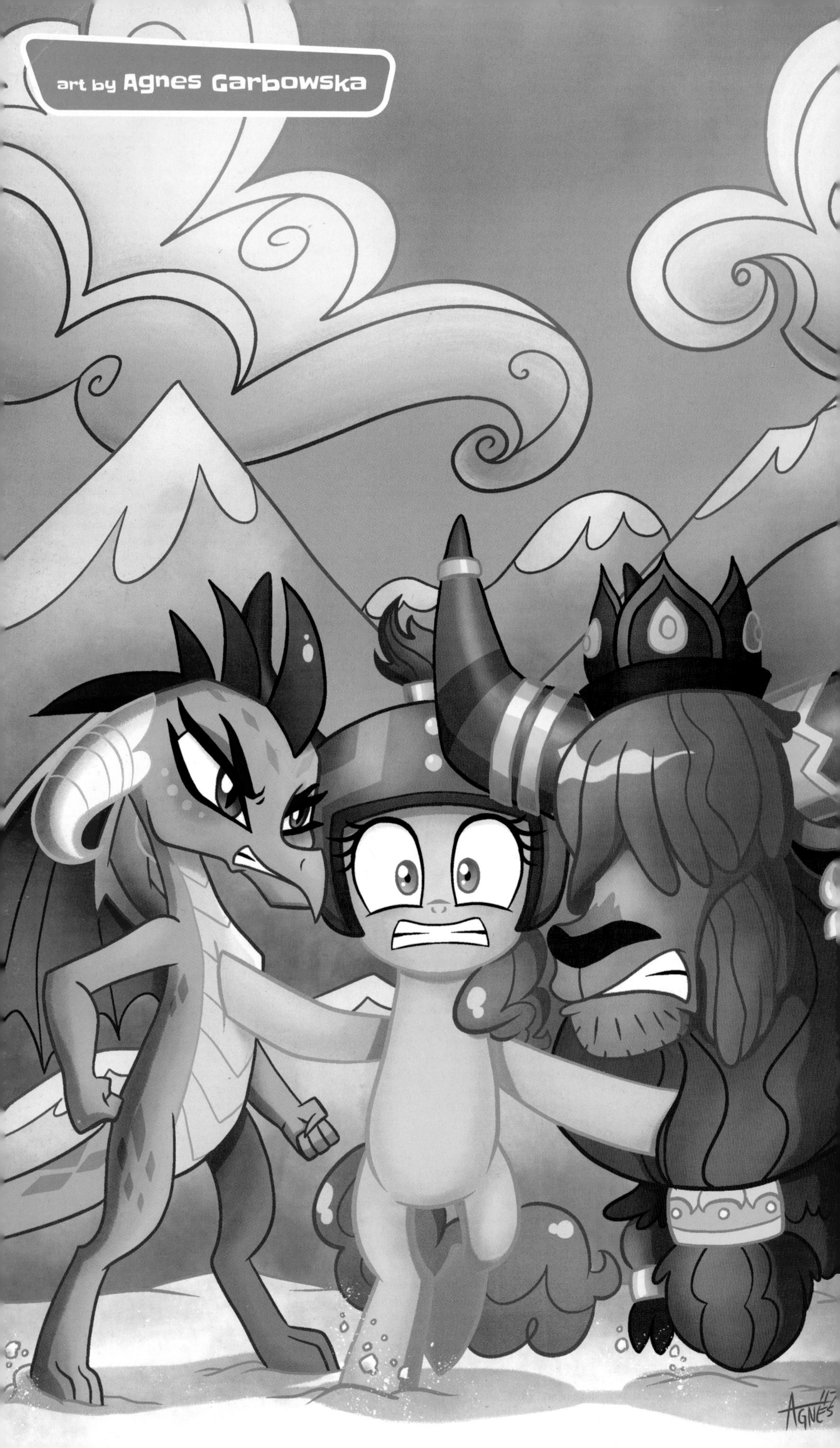
art by Agnes Garbowska

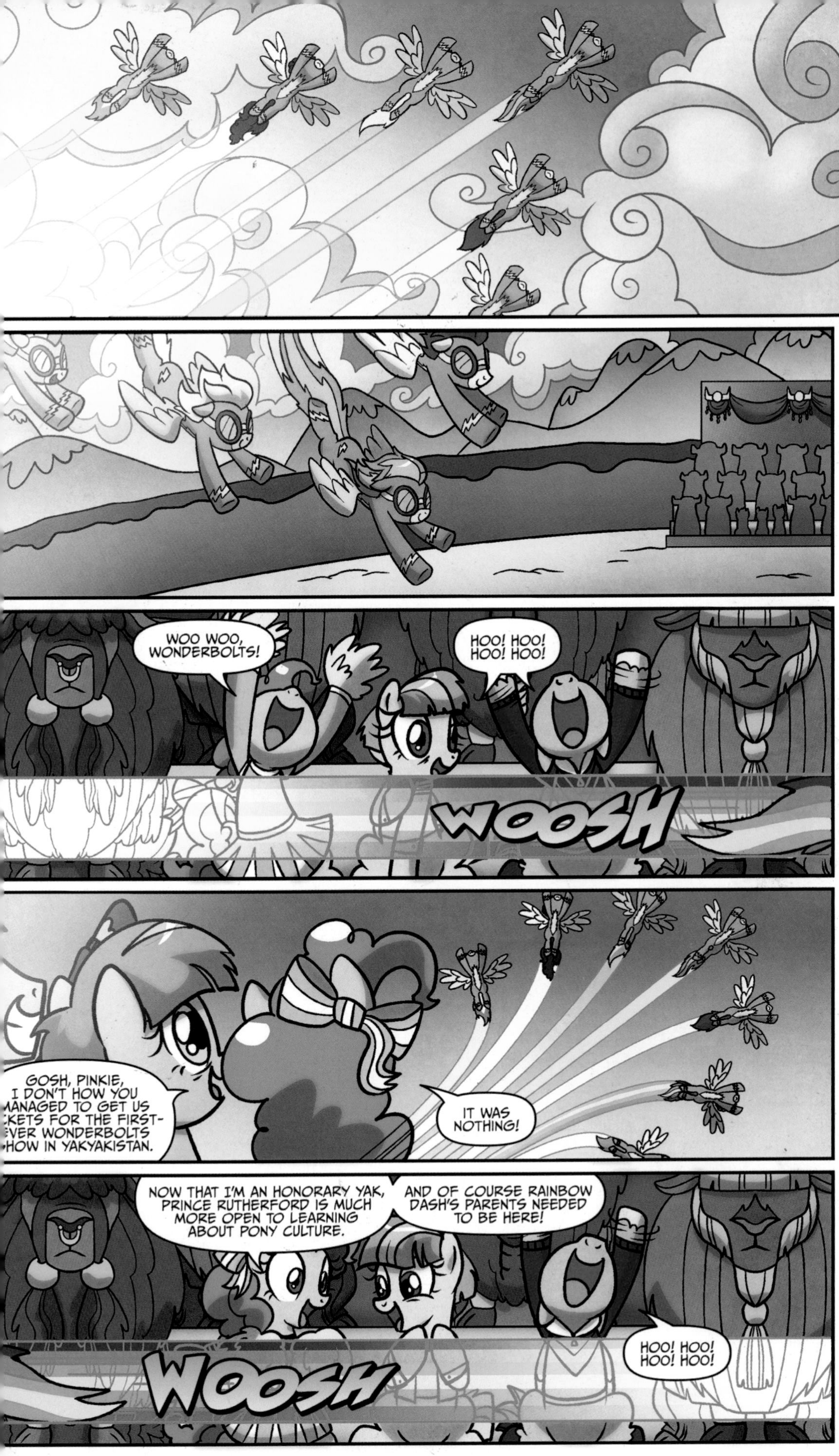
WOO WOO, WONDERBOLTS!
HOO! HOO! HOO! HOO!
WOOSH
GOSH, PINKIE, I DON'T HOW YOU MANAGED TO GET US ...CKETS FOR THE FIRST-...EVER WONDERBOLTS ...HOW IN YAKYAKISTAN.
IT WAS NOTHING!
NOW THAT I'M AN HONORARY YAK, PRINCE RUTHERFORD IS MUCH MORE OPEN TO LEARNING ABOUT PONY CULTURE.
AND OF COURSE RAINBOW DASH'S PARENTS NEEDED TO BE HERE!
HOO! HOO! HOO! HOO!
WOOSH

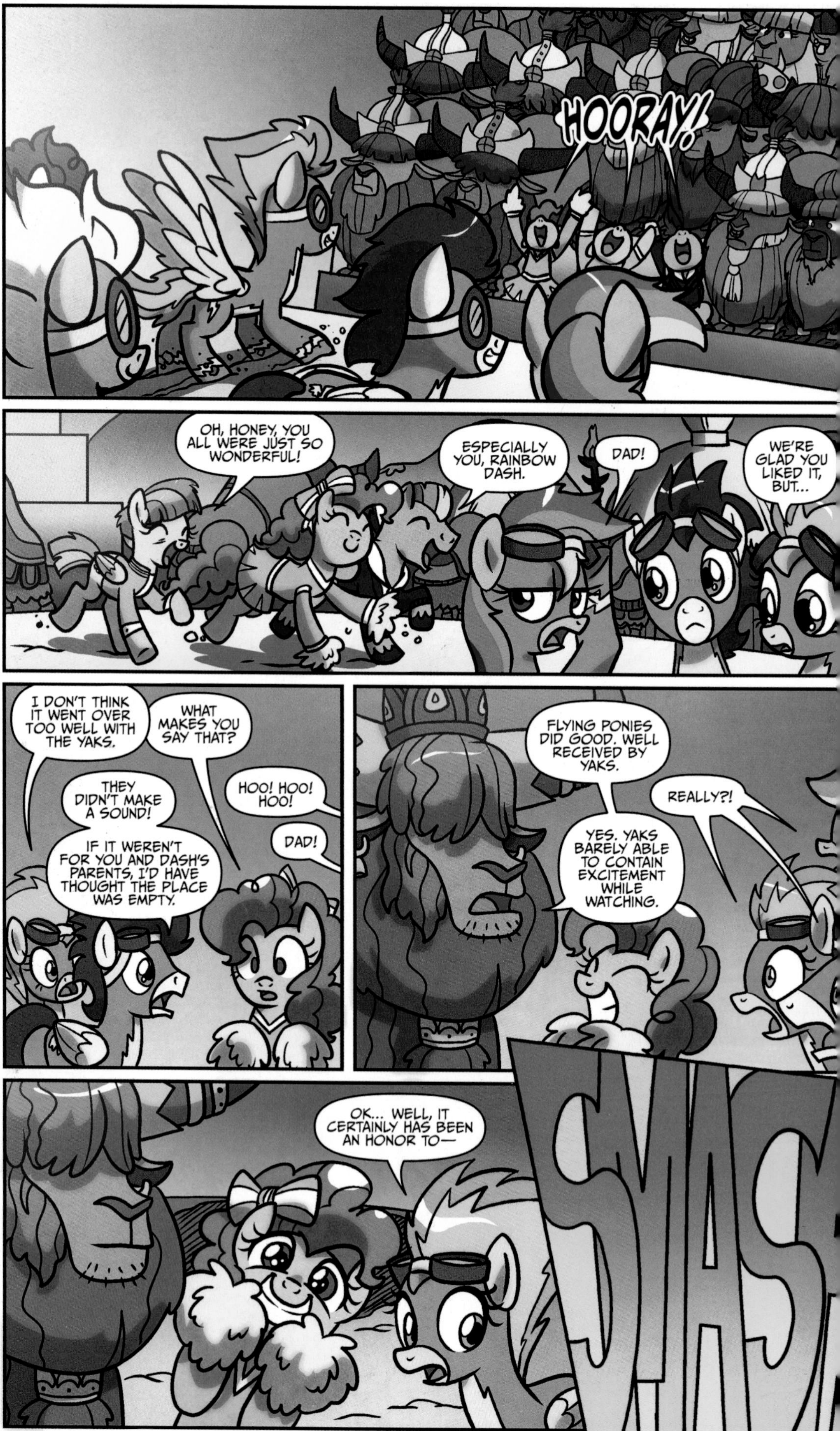
HOORAY!
OH, HONEY, YOU ALL WERE JUST SO WONDERFUL!
ESPECIALLY YOU, RAINBOW DASH.
DAD!
WE'RE GLAD YOU LIKED IT, BUT...
I DON'T THINK IT WENT OVER TOO WELL WITH THE YAKS.
WHAT MAKES YOU SAY THAT?
THEY DIDN'T MAKE A SOUND!
IF IT WEREN'T FOR YOU AND DASH'S PARENTS, I'D HAVE THOUGHT THE PLACE WAS EMPTY.
HOO! HOO! HOO!
DAD!
FLYING PONIES DID GOOD. WELL RECEIVED BY YAKS.
REALLY?!
YES. YAKS BARELY ABLE TO CONTAIN EXCITEMENT WHILE WATCHING.
OK... WELL, IT CERTAINLY HAS BEEN AN HONOR TO—
SMAS

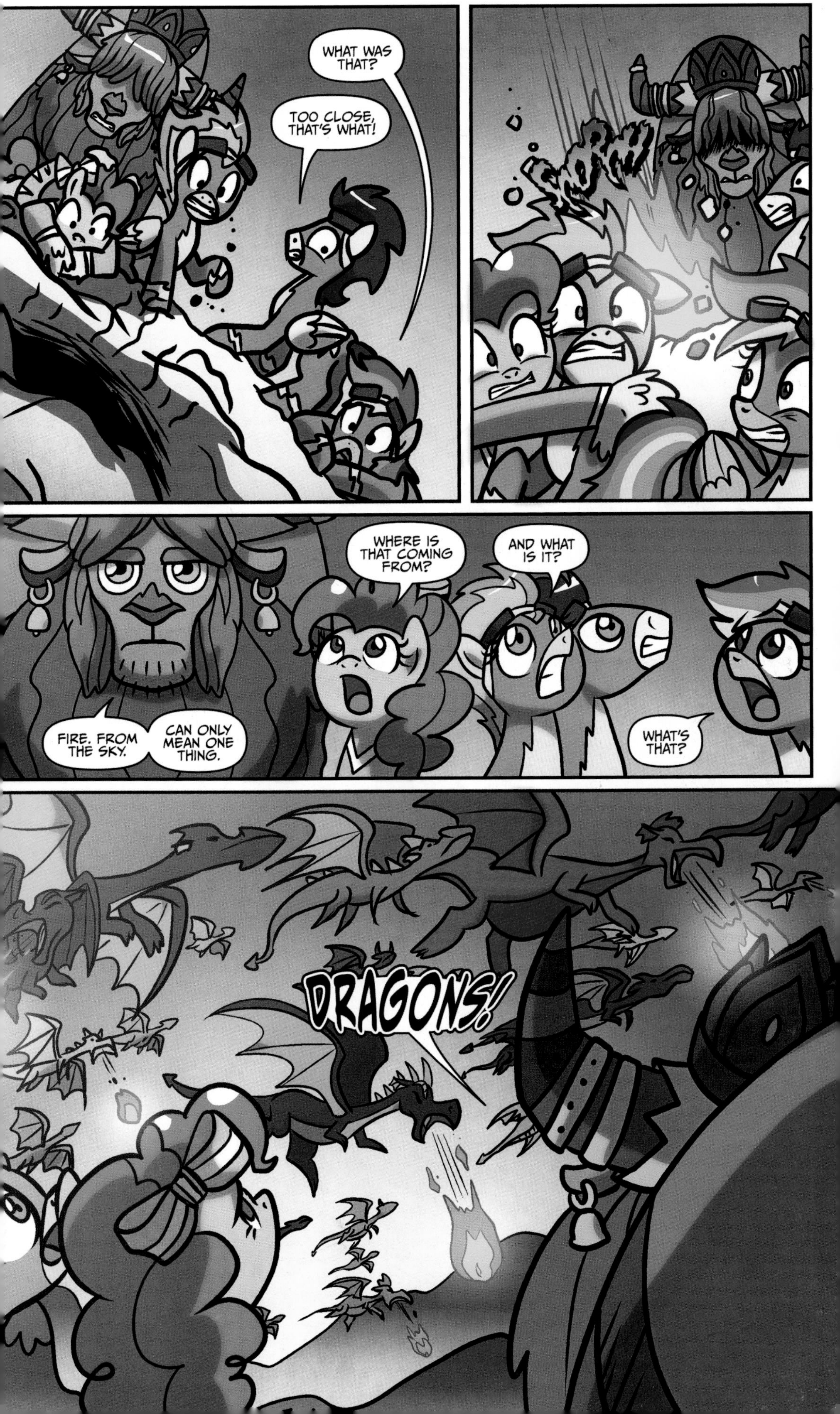
WHAT WAS THAT?
TOO CLOSE, THAT'S WHAT!
WHERE IS THAT COMING FROM?
AND WHAT IS IT?
FIRE. FROM THE SKY.
CAN ONLY MEAN ONE THING.
WHAT'S THAT?
DRAGONS!

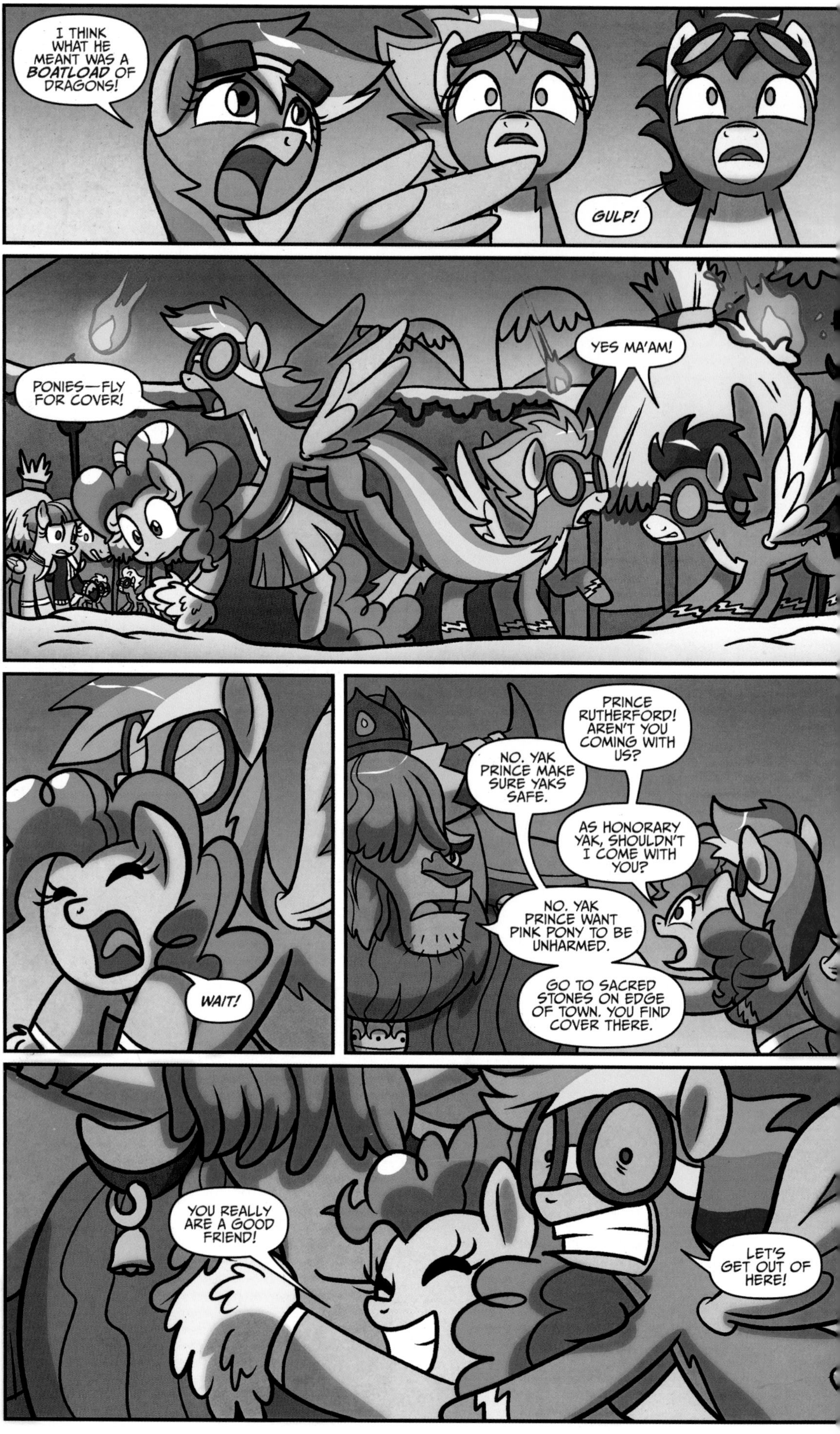
I THINK WHAT HE MEANT WAS A *BOATLOAD* OF DRAGONS!
GULP!
PONIES—FLY FOR COVER!
YES MA'AM!
WAIT!
PRINCE RUTHERFORD! AREN'T YOU COMING WITH US?
NO. YAK PRINCE MAKE SURE YAKS SAFE.
AS HONORARY YAK, SHOULDN'T I COME WITH YOU?
NO. YAK PRINCE WANT PINK PONY TO BE UNHARMED.
GO TO SACRED STONES ON EDGE OF TOWN. YOU FIND COVER THERE.
YOU REALLY ARE A GOOD FRIEND!
LET'S GET OUT OF HERE!

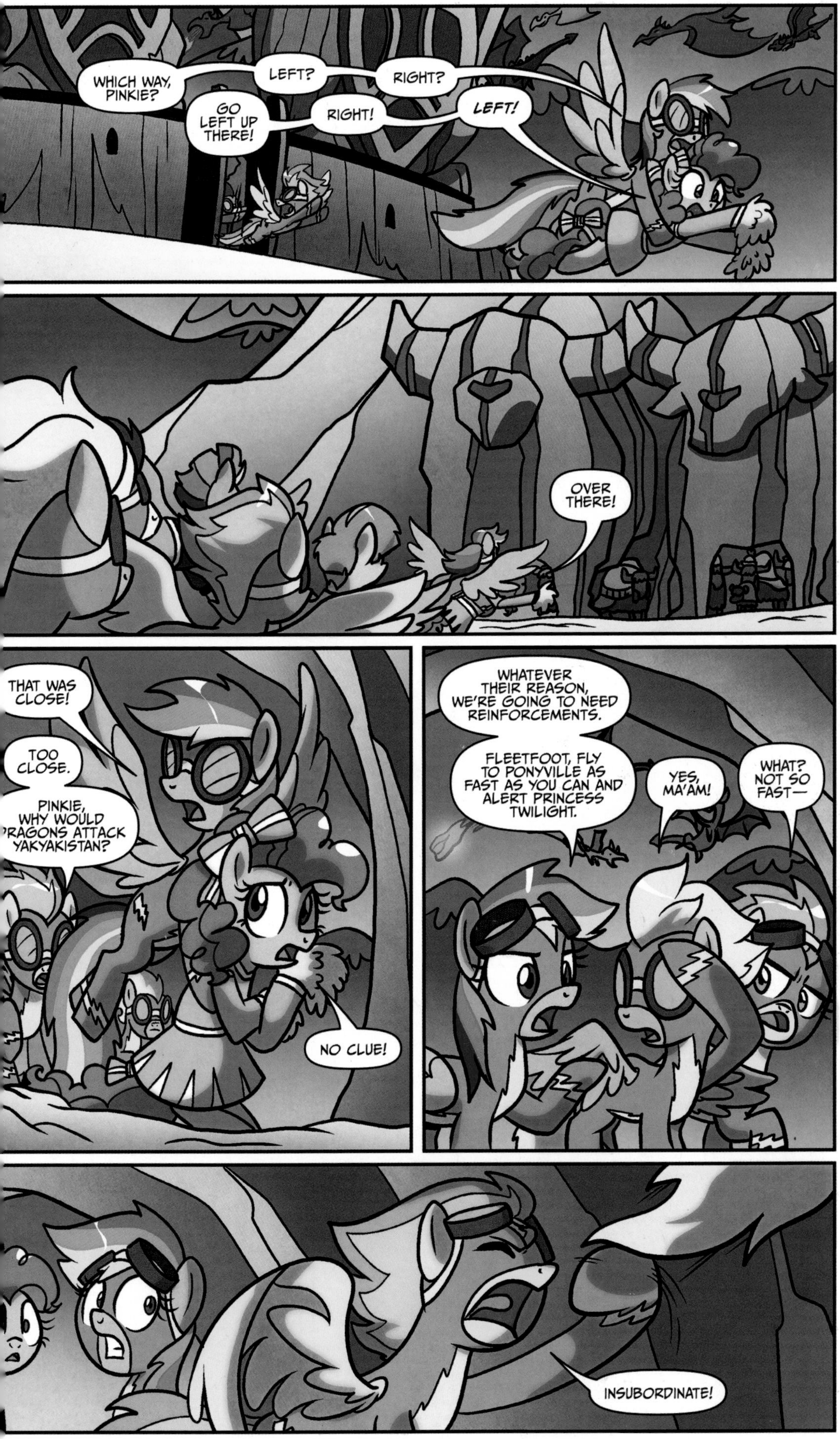
WHICH WAY, PINKIE?
LEFT?
RIGHT?
GO LEFT UP THERE!
RIGHT!
LEFT!
OVER THERE!
THAT WAS CLOSE!
TOO CLOSE.
PINKIE, WHY WOULD DRAGONS ATTACK YAKYAKISTAN?
NO CLUE!
WHATEVER THEIR REASON, WE'RE GOING TO NEED REINFORCEMENTS.
FLEETFOOT, FLY TO PONYVILLE AS FAST AS YOU CAN AND ALERT PRINCESS TWILIGHT.
YES, MA'AM!
WHAT? NOT SO FAST—
INSUBORDINATE!

WHO'S IN CHARGE HERE?

LAST TIME I CHECKED, THERE WEREN'T ANY CAPTAIN'S STRIPES ON YOUR JACKET... RAINBOW *CRASH!*

WHAT? THIS ISN'T FORMATION FLYING, IT'S A DRAGON ATTACK!

WE DON'T HAVE TIME FOR THIS!

WE NEED TO FIGURE OUT OUR PLAN OF ATTACK.

PINKIE, DO YOU HAVE YOUR PARTY CANNON?

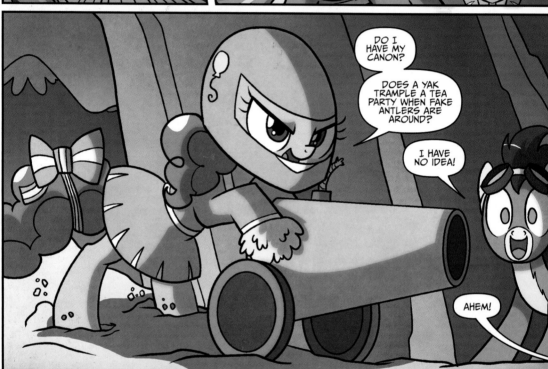

DO I HAVE MY CANON?

DOES A YAK TRAMPLE A TEA PARTY WHEN FAKE ANTLERS ARE AROUND?

I HAVE NO IDEA!

AHEM!

THERE IS NO PLAN, BECAUSE WE'RE *NOT* ATTACKING!

SO WE'RE JUST GOING TO SIT BY AND WATCH YAKYAKISTAN GET SCORCHED?

LISTEN, DASH, I KNOW YOU'RE USED TO RUNNING INTO FIRES WITH TWILIGHT AND THE REST OF YOUR FRIENDS.

AND THAT SAVING EQUESTRIA FROM SOME CATASTROPHIC DISASTER IS NO BIG DEAL FOR YOU...

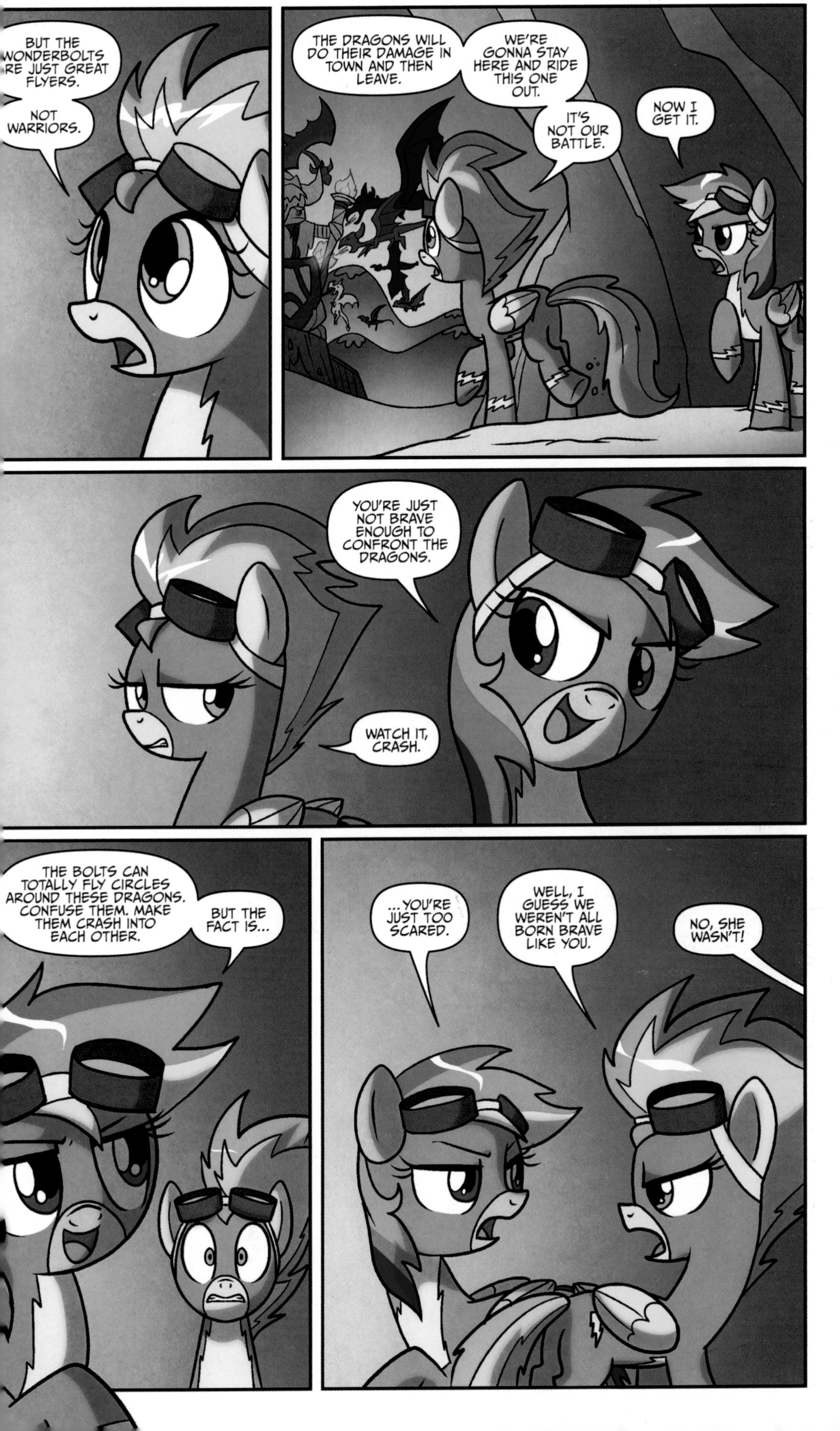
BUT THE WONDERBOLTS RE JUST GREAT FLYERS.
NOT WARRIORS.
THE DRAGONS WILL DO THEIR DAMAGE IN TOWN AND THEN LEAVE.
WE'RE GONNA STAY HERE AND RIDE THIS ONE OUT.
IT'S NOT OUR BATTLE.
NOW I GET IT.
YOU'RE JUST NOT BRAVE ENOUGH TO CONFRONT THE DRAGONS.
WATCH IT, CRASH.
THE BOLTS CAN TOTALLY FLY CIRCLES AROUND THESE DRAGONS. CONFUSE THEM. MAKE THEM CRASH INTO EACH OTHER.
BUT THE FACT IS...
...YOU'RE JUST TOO SCARED.
WELL, I GUESS WE WEREN'T ALL BORN BRAVE LIKE YOU.
NO, SHE WASN'T!

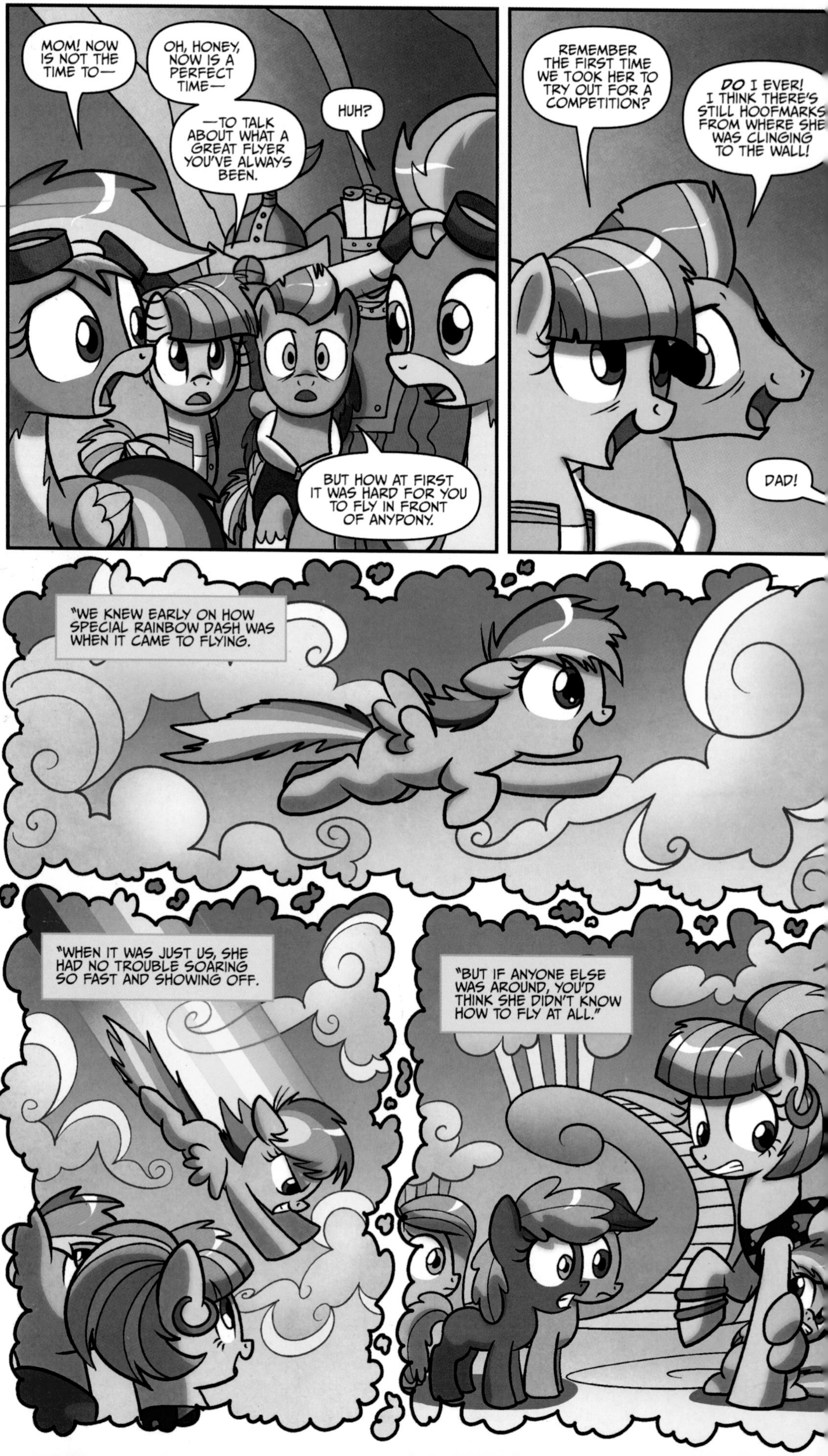
MOM! NOW IS NOT THE TIME TO—
OH, HONEY, NOW IS A PERFECT TIME—
—TO TALK ABOUT WHAT A GREAT FLYER YOU'VE ALWAYS BEEN.
HUH?
BUT HOW AT FIRST IT WAS HARD FOR YOU TO FLY IN FRONT OF ANYPONY.
REMEMBER THE FIRST TIME WE TOOK HER TO TRY OUT FOR A COMPETITION?
DO I EVER! I THINK THERE'S STILL HOOFMARKS FROM WHERE SHE WAS CLINGING TO THE WALL!
DAD!
"WE KNEW EARLY ON HOW SPECIAL RAINBOW DASH WAS WHEN IT CAME TO FLYING.
"WHEN IT WAS JUST US, SHE HAD NO TROUBLE SOARING SO FAST AND SHOWING OFF.
"BUT IF ANYONE ELSE WAS AROUND, YOU'D THINK SHE DIDN'T KNOW HOW TO FLY AT ALL."

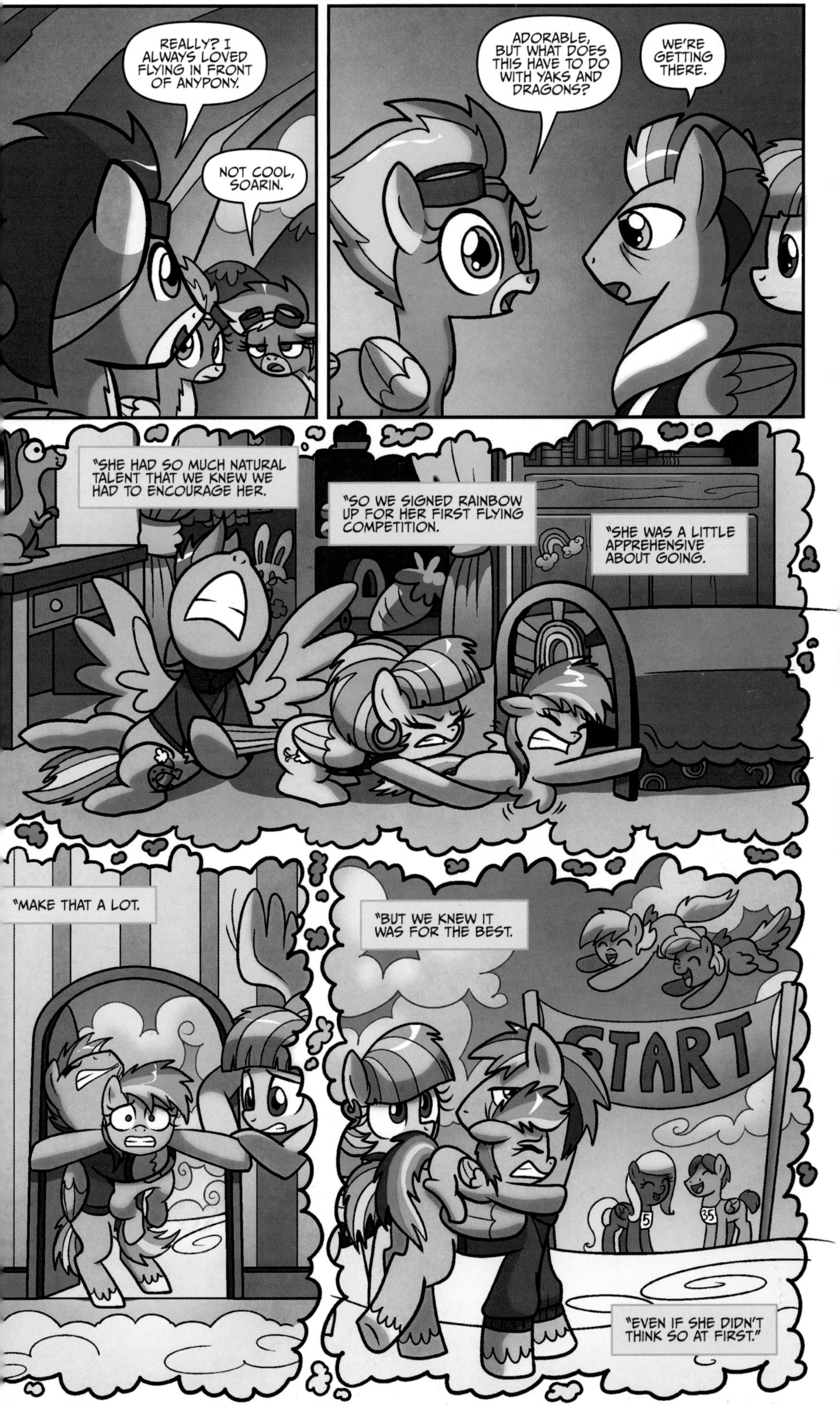

REALLY? I ALWAYS LOVED FLYING IN FRONT OF ANYPONY.
NOT COOL, SOARIN.
ADORABLE, BUT WHAT DOES THIS HAVE TO DO WITH YAKS AND DRAGONS?
WE'RE GETTING THERE.
"SHE HAD SO MUCH NATURAL TALENT THAT WE KNEW WE HAD TO ENCOURAGE HER.
"SO WE SIGNED RAINBOW UP FOR HER FIRST FLYING COMPETITION.
"SHE WAS A LITTLE APPREHENSIVE ABOUT GOING.
"MAKE THAT A LOT.
"BUT WE KNEW IT WAS FOR THE BEST.
START
5
35
"EVEN IF SHE DIDN'T THINK SO AT FIRST."

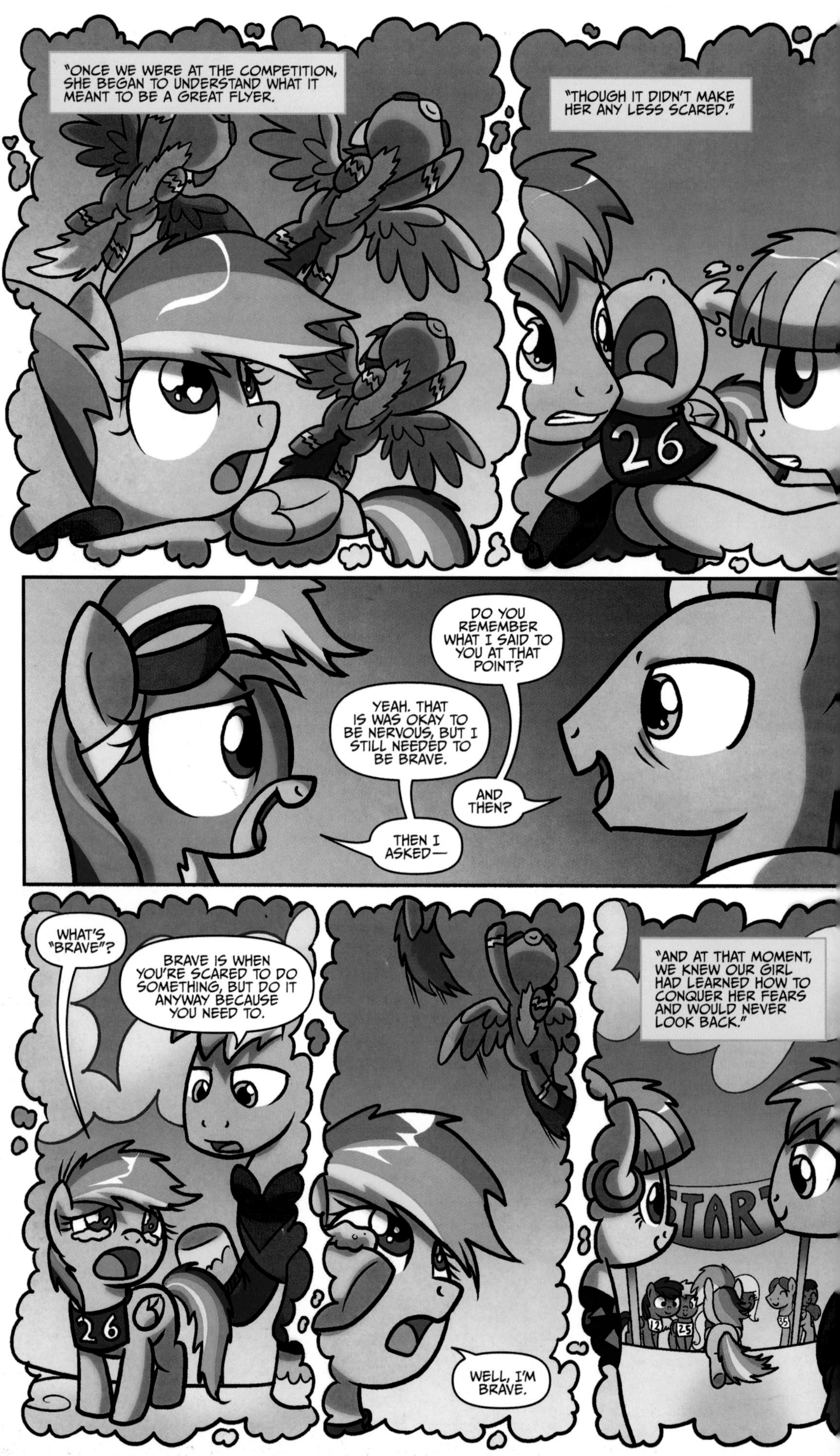
"ONCE WE WERE AT THE COMPETITION, SHE BEGAN TO UNDERSTAND WHAT IT MEANT TO BE A GREAT FLYER.
"THOUGH IT DIDN'T MAKE HER ANY LESS SCARED."
26
DO YOU REMEMBER WHAT I SAID TO YOU AT THAT POINT?
YEAH. THAT IS WAS OKAY TO BE NERVOUS, BUT I STILL NEEDED TO BE BRAVE.
AND THEN?
THEN I ASKED—
WHAT'S "BRAVE"?
BRAVE IS WHEN YOU'RE SCARED TO DO SOMETHING, BUT DO IT ANYWAY BECAUSE YOU NEED TO.
26
WELL, I'M BRAVE.
"AND AT THAT MOMENT, WE KNEW OUR GIRL HAD LEARNED HOW TO CONQUER HER FEARS AND WOULD NEVER LOOK BACK."
START
12
25
35

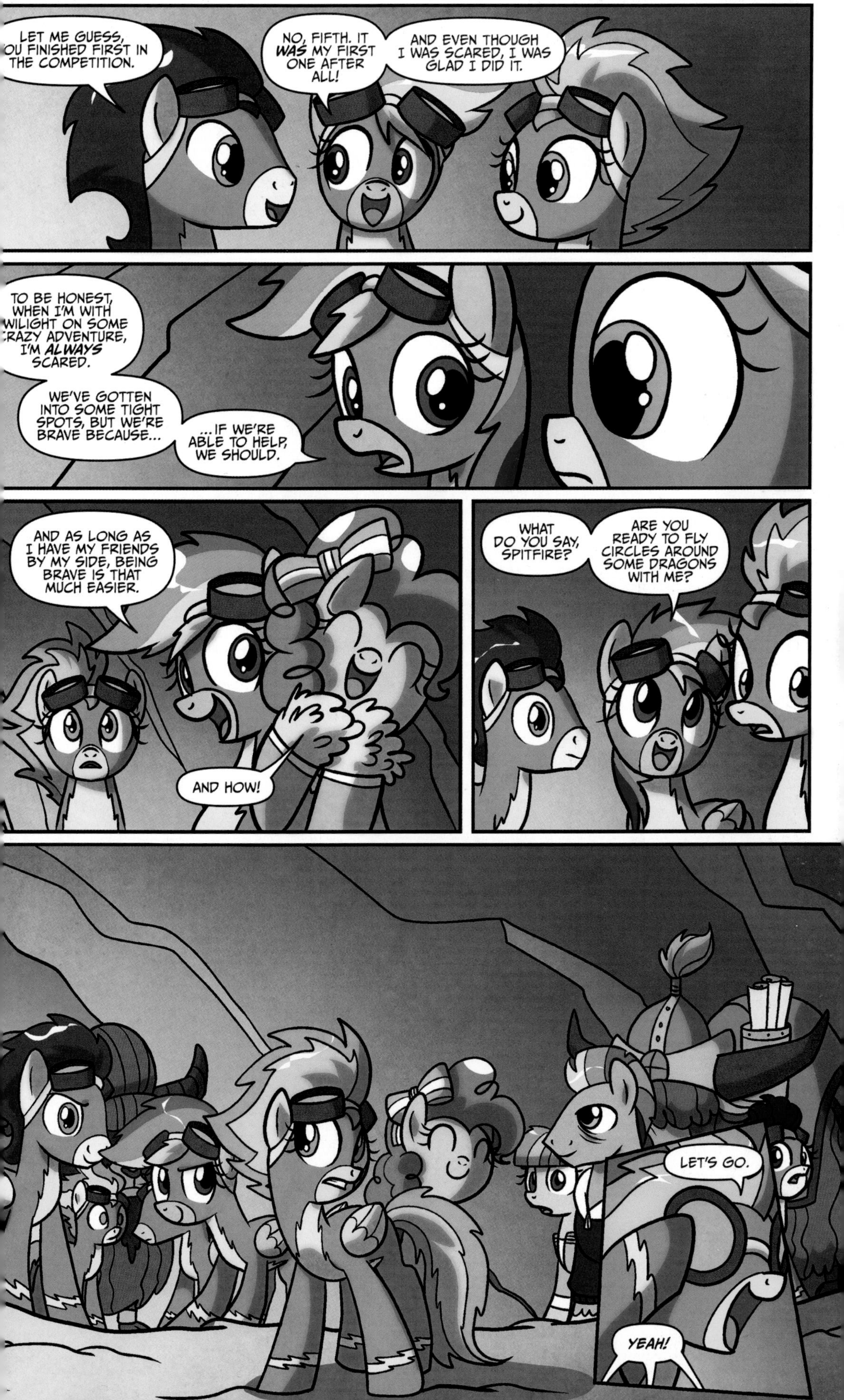

LET ME GUESS, OU FINISHED FIRST IN THE COMPETITION.
NO, FIFTH. IT *WAS* MY FIRST ONE AFTER ALL!
AND EVEN THOUGH I WAS SCARED, I WAS GLAD I DID IT.
TO BE HONEST, WHEN I'M WITH WILIGHT ON SOME RAZY ADVENTURE, I'M *ALWAYS* SCARED.
WE'VE GOTTEN INTO SOME TIGHT SPOTS, BUT WE'RE BRAVE BECAUSE...
...IF WE'RE ABLE TO HELP, WE SHOULD.
AND AS LONG AS I HAVE MY FRIENDS BY MY SIDE, BEING BRAVE IS THAT MUCH EASIER.
AND HOW!
WHAT DO YOU SAY, SPITFIRE?
ARE YOU READY TO FLY CIRCLES AROUND SOME DRAGONS WITH ME?
LET'S GO.
YEAH!

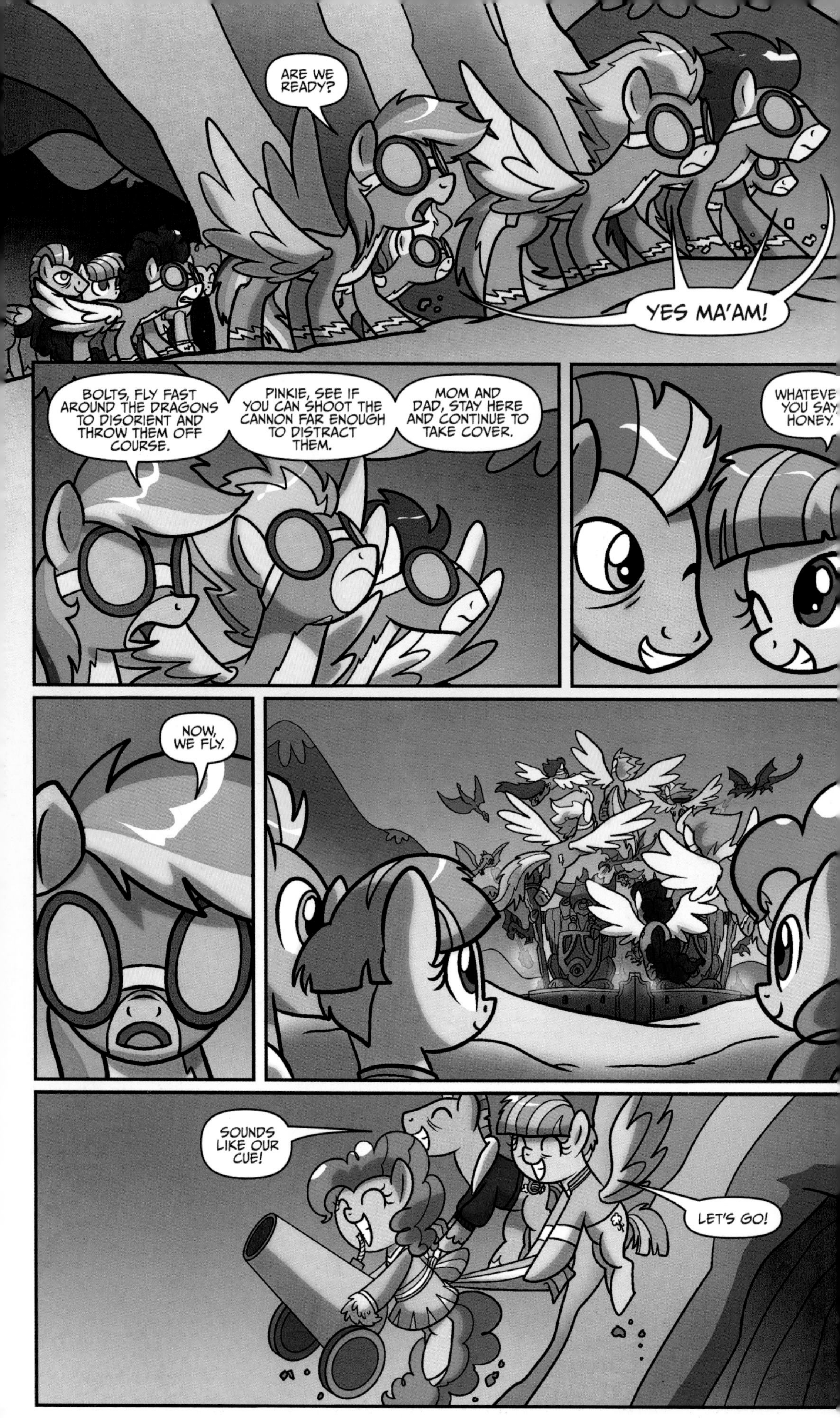
ARE WE READY?
YES MA'AM!
BOLTS, FLY FAST AROUND THE DRAGONS TO DISORIENT AND THROW THEM OFF COURSE.
PINKIE, SEE IF YOU CAN SHOOT THE CANNON FAR ENOUGH TO DISTRACT THEM.
MOM AND DAD, STAY HERE AND CONTINUE TO TAKE COVER.
WHATEVE YOU SAY HONEY.
NOW, WE FLY.
SOUNDS LIKE OUR CUE!
LET'S GO!

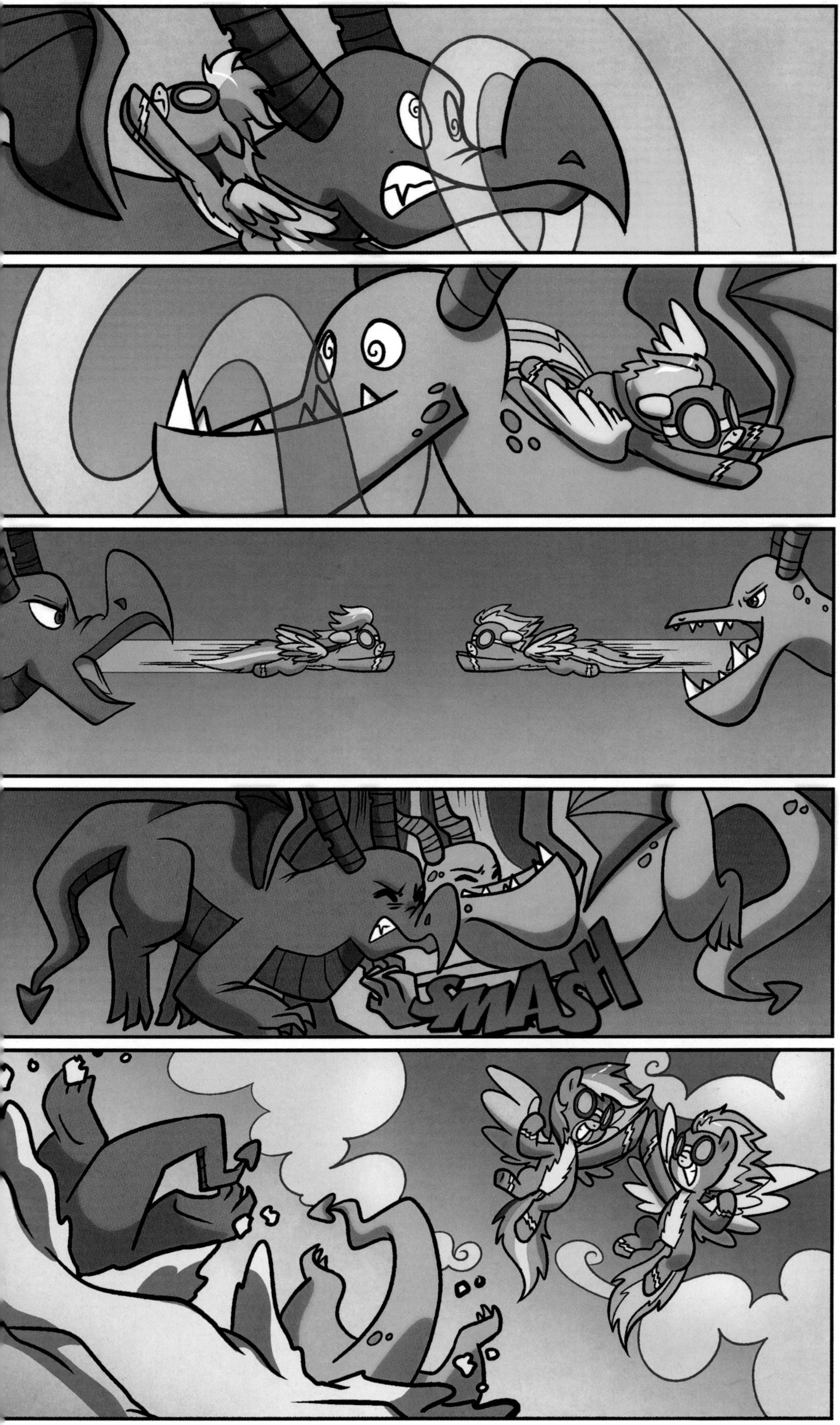
SMASH

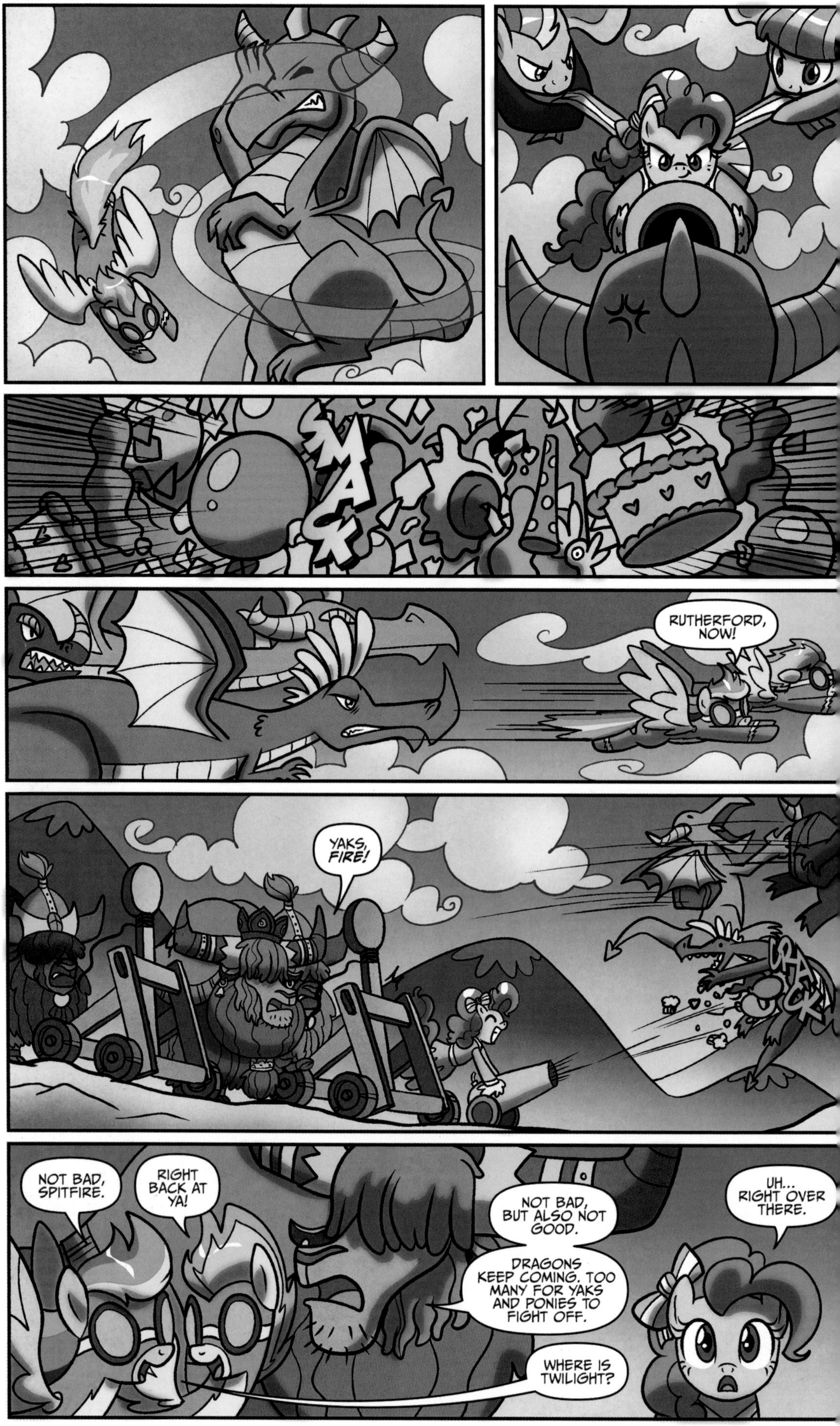
SMACK
RUTHERFORD, NOW!
YAKS, FIRE!
CRACK
NOT BAD, SPITFIRE.
RIGHT BACK AT YA!
NOT BAD, BUT ALSO NOT GOOD.
DRAGONS KEEP COMING. TOO MANY FOR YAKS AND PONIES TO FIGHT OFF.
WHERE IS TWILIGHT?
UH... RIGHT OVER THERE.

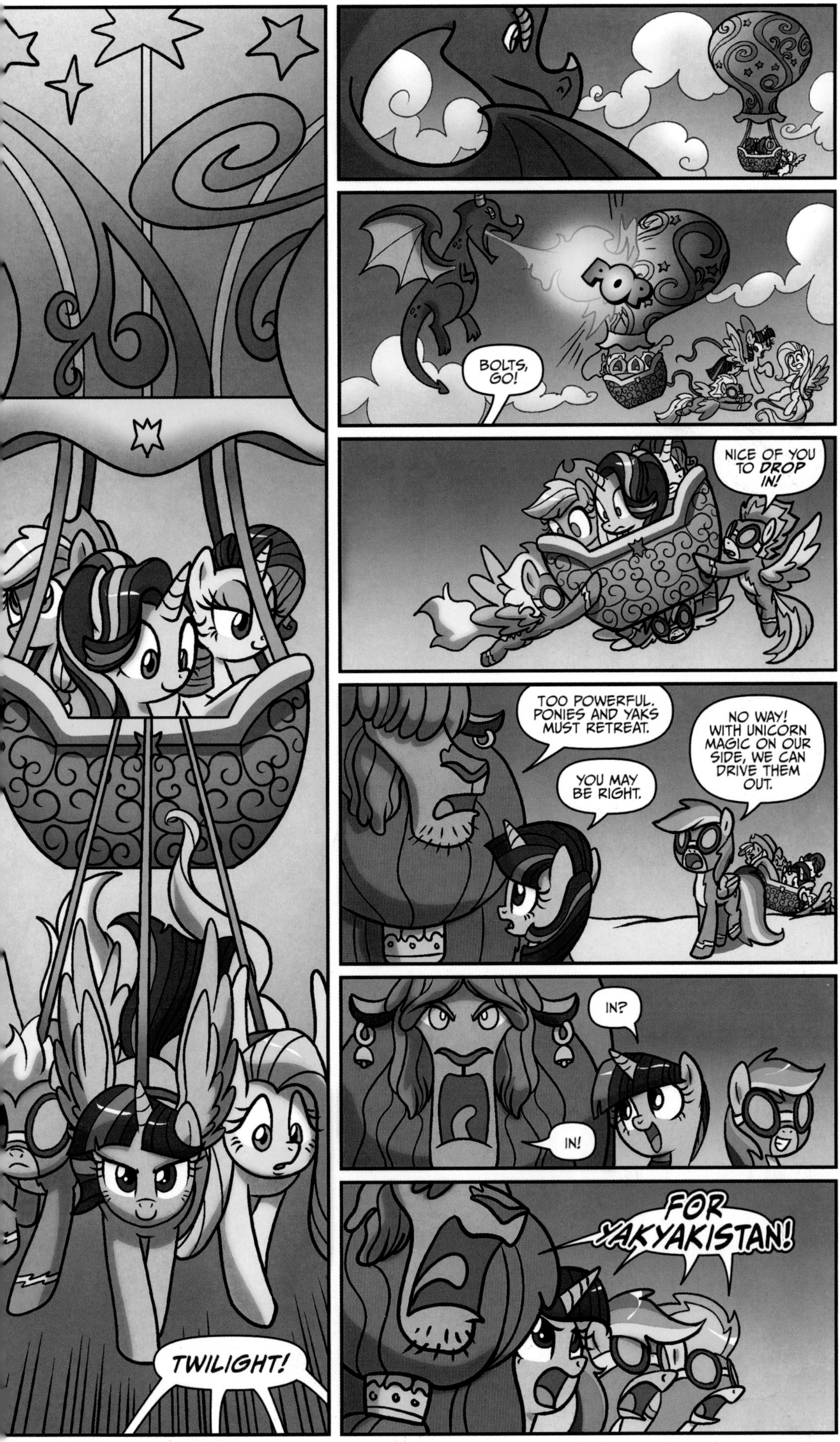
TWILIGHT!
POP
BOLTS, GO!
NICE OF YOU TO DROP IN!
TOO POWERFUL. PONIES AND YAKS MUST RETREAT.
YOU MAY BE RIGHT.
NO WAY! WITH UNICORN MAGIC ON OUR SIDE, WE CAN DRIVE THEM OUT.
IN?
IN!
FOR YAKYAKISTAN!

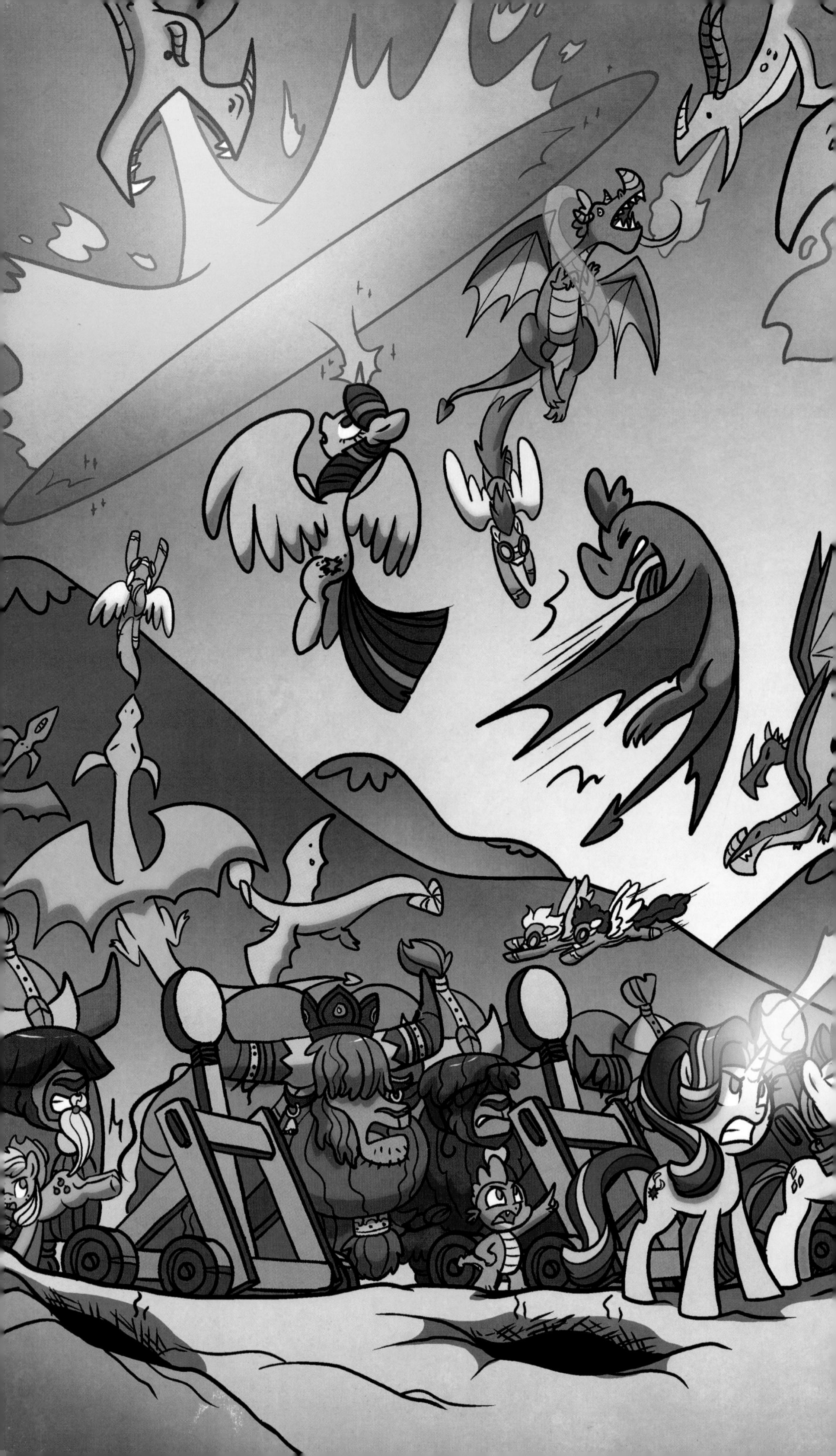

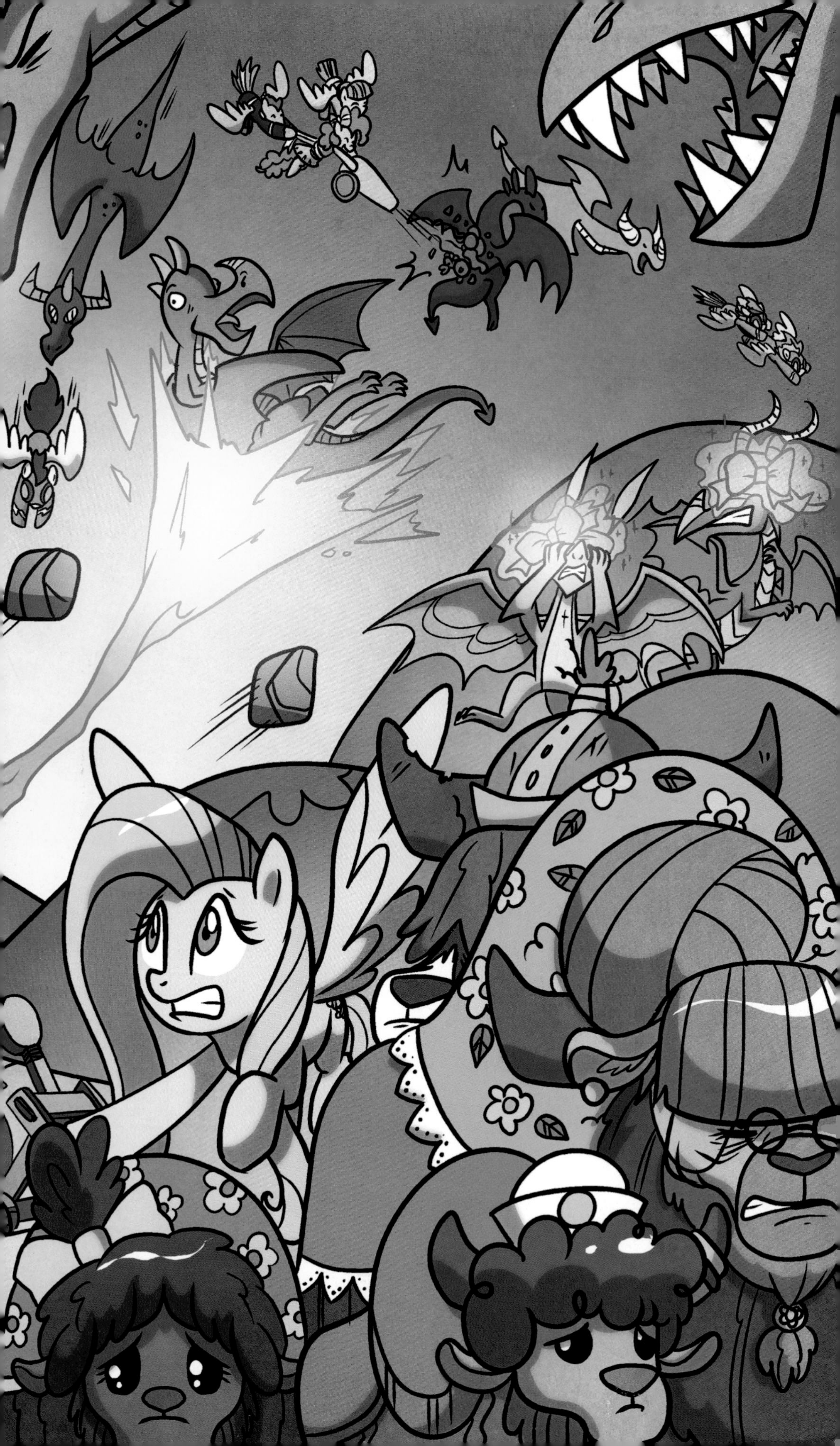

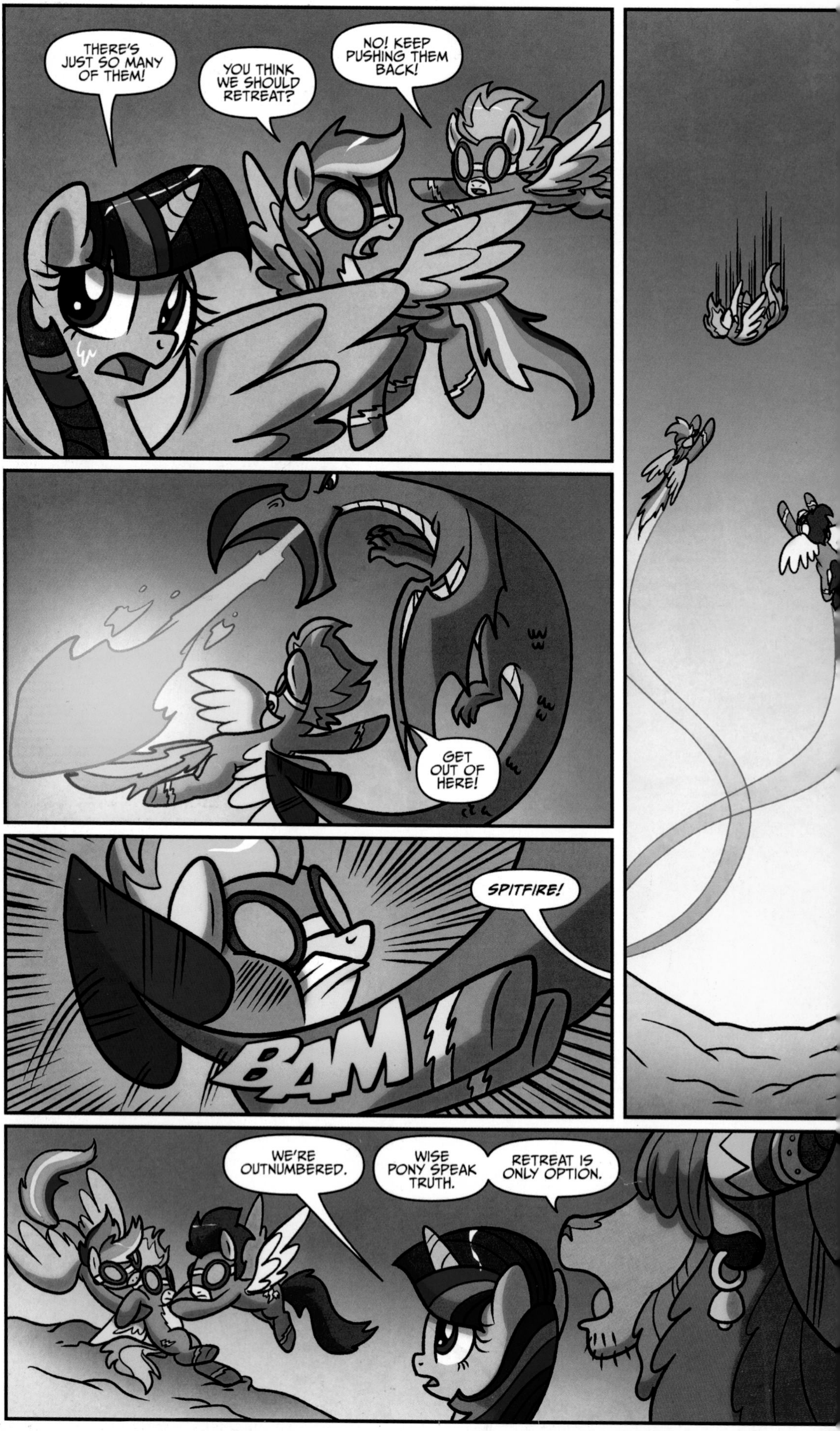
THERE'S JUST SO MANY OF THEM!
YOU THINK WE SHOULD RETREAT?
NO! KEEP PUSHING THEM BACK!
GET OUT OF HERE!
SPITFIRE!
BAM!
WE'RE OUTNUMBERED.
WISE PONY SPEAK TRUTH.
RETREAT IS ONLY OPTION.

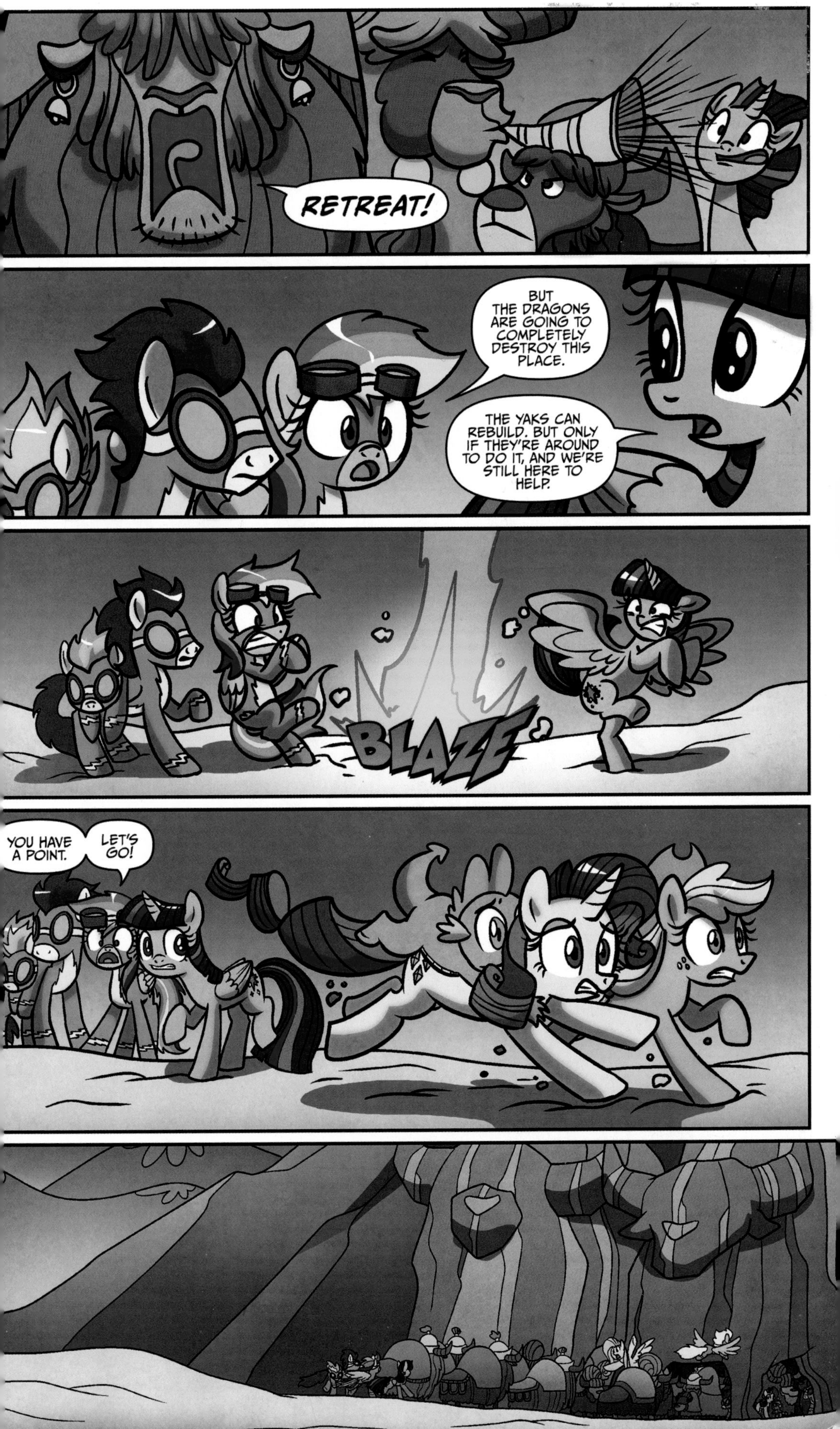
RETREAT!
BUT THE DRAGONS ARE GOING TO COMPLETELY DESTROY THIS PLACE.
THE YAKS CAN REBUILD. BUT ONLY IF THEY'RE AROUND TO DO IT, AND WE'RE STILL HERE TO HELP.
BLAZE
YOU HAVE A POINT.
LET'S GO!

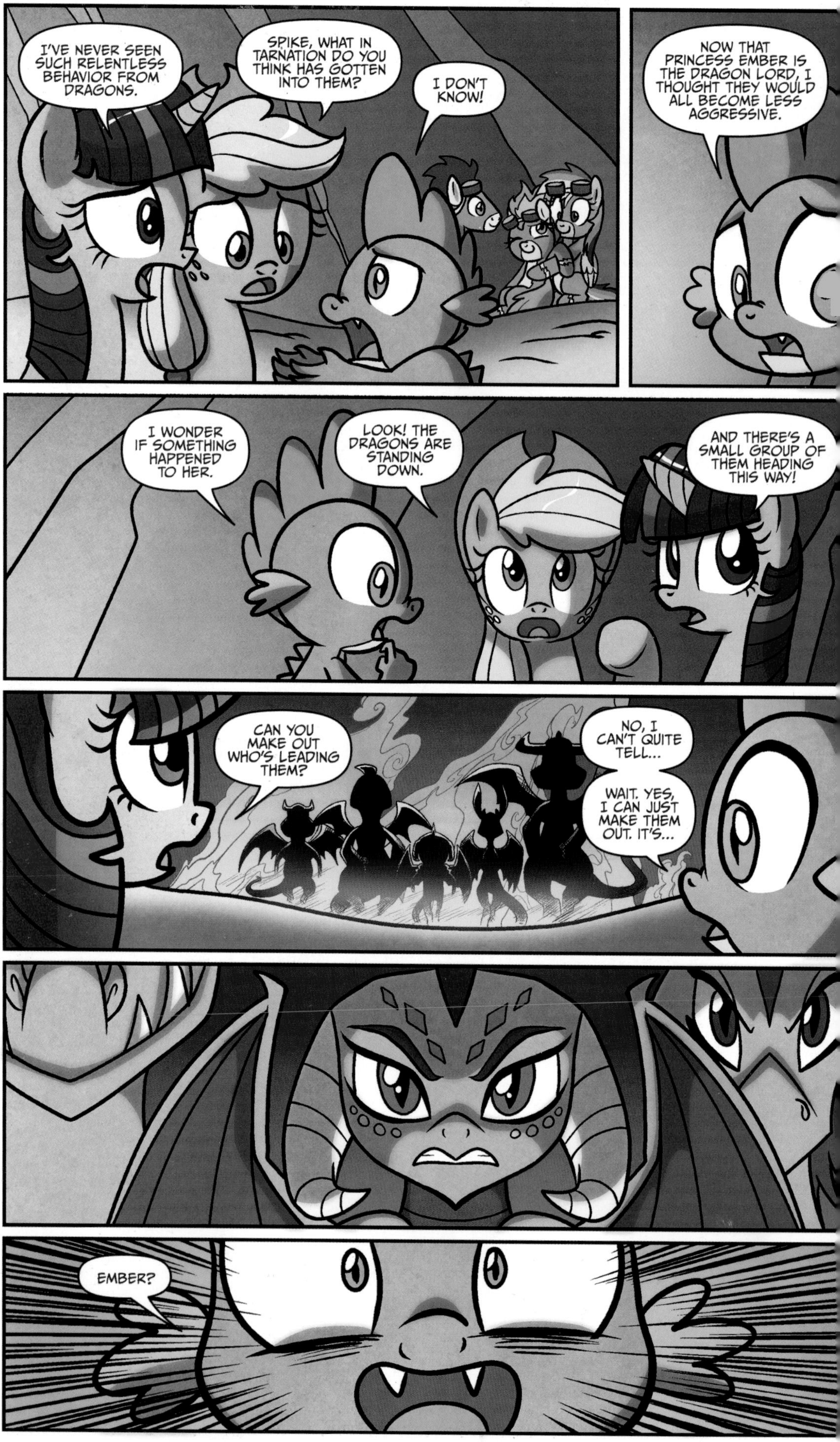

I'VE NEVER SEEN SUCH RELENTLESS BEHAVIOR FROM DRAGONS.
SPIKE, WHAT IN TARNATION DO YOU THINK HAS GOTTEN INTO THEM?
I DON'T KNOW!
NOW THAT PRINCESS EMBER IS THE DRAGON LORD, I THOUGHT THEY WOULD ALL BECOME LESS AGGRESSIVE.
I WONDER IF SOMETHING HAPPENED TO HER.
LOOK! THE DRAGONS ARE STANDING DOWN.
AND THERE'S A SMALL GROUP OF THEM HEADING THIS WAY!
CAN YOU MAKE OUT WHO'S LEADING THEM?
NO, I CAN'T QUITE TELL...
WAIT. YES, I CAN JUST MAKE THEM OUT. IT'S...
EMBER?

I GUESS THERE IS ONE GOOD THING ABOUT THIS DRAGON ATTACK ON YAKYAKISTAN.

PRINCE RUTHERFORD HAS GIVEN ME FULL ACCESS TO THE ANCIENT SCROLLS!

I DON'T THINK ANYPONY HAS HAD THIS MUCH INSIGHT INTO YAK CULTURE.

NOT EVEN PINKIE PIE.

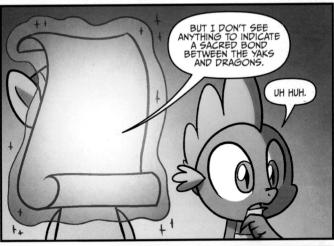

BUT I DON'T SEE ANYTHING TO INDICATE A SACRED BOND BETWEEN THE YAKS AND DRAGONS.

UH HUH.

SOMETHING TELLS ME YOU'RE NOT EXACTLY LISTENING TO ANYTHING I SAY.

I DON'T UNDERSTAND.

WHY WOULD EMBER DO THIS?

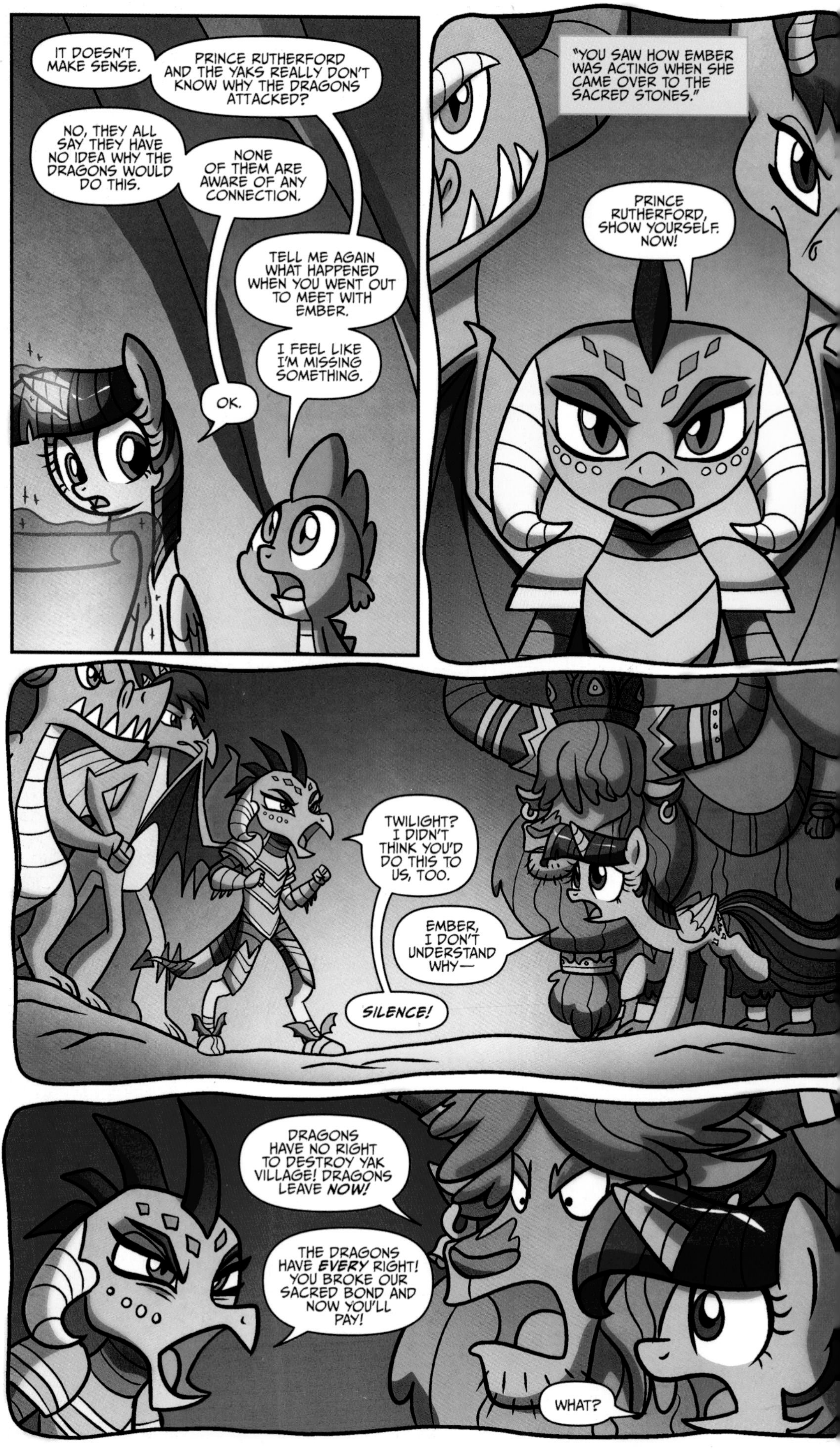
IT DOESN'T MAKE SENSE.
PRINCE RUTHERFORD AND THE YAKS REALLY DON'T KNOW WHY THE DRAGONS ATTACKED?
NO, THEY ALL SAY THEY HAVE NO IDEA WHY THE DRAGONS WOULD DO THIS.
NONE OF THEM ARE AWARE OF ANY CONNECTION.
TELL ME AGAIN WHAT HAPPENED WHEN YOU WENT OUT TO MEET WITH EMBER.
I FEEL LIKE I'M MISSING SOMETHING.
OK.
"YOU SAW HOW EMBER WAS ACTING WHEN SHE CAME OVER TO THE SACRED STONES."
PRINCE RUTHERFORD, SHOW YOURSELF. NOW!
TWILIGHT? I DIDN'T THINK YOU'D DO THIS TO US, TOO.
EMBER, I DON'T UNDERSTAND WHY—
SILENCE!
DRAGONS HAVE NO RIGHT TO DESTROY YAK VILLAGE! DRAGONS LEAVE NOW!
THE DRAGONS HAVE EVERY RIGHT! YOU BROKE OUR SACRED BOND AND NOW YOU'LL PAY!
WHAT?

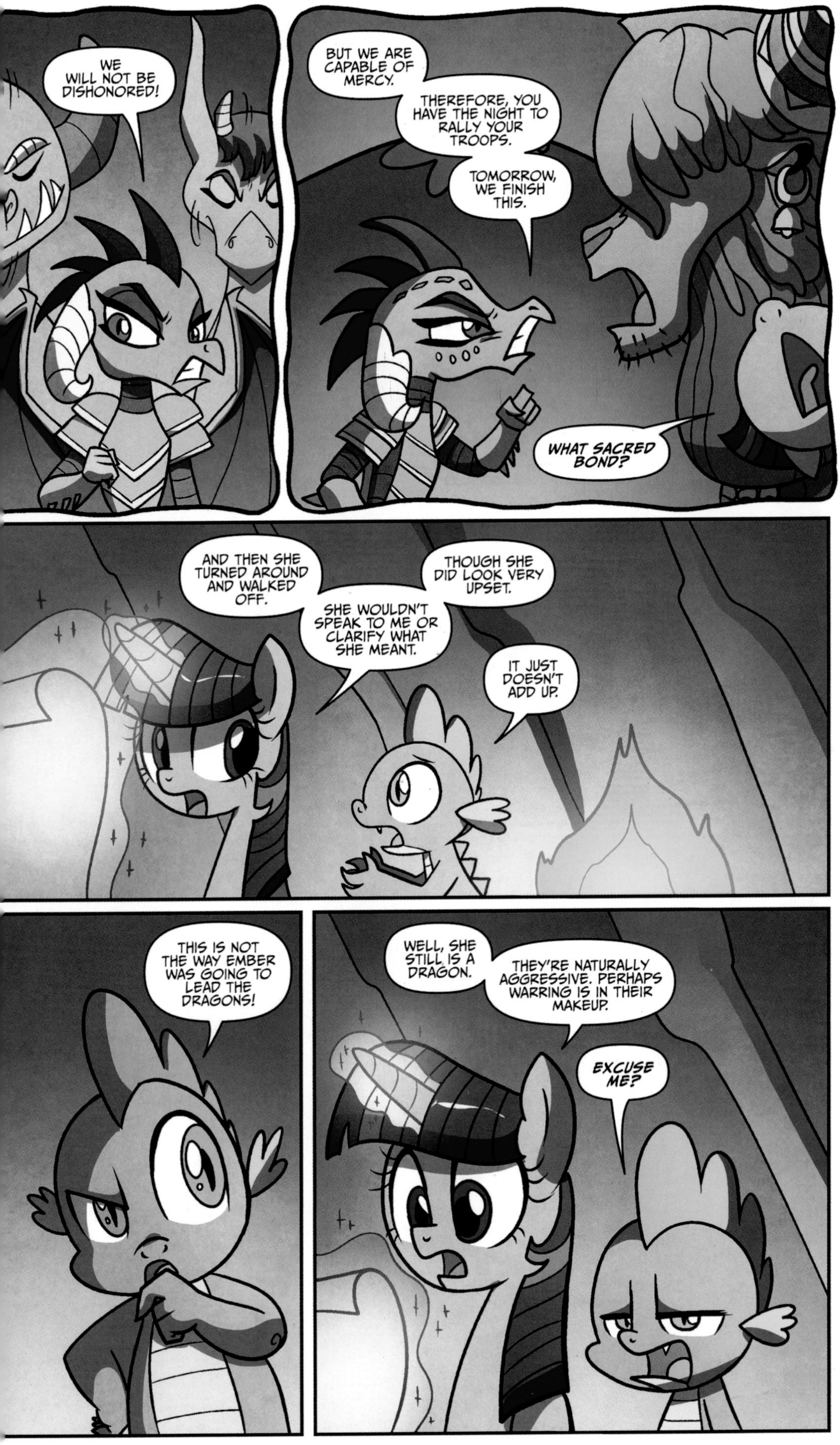
WE WILL NOT BE DISHONORED!
BUT WE ARE CAPABLE OF MERCY.
THEREFORE, YOU HAVE THE NIGHT TO RALLY YOUR TROOPS.
TOMORROW, WE FINISH THIS.
WHAT SACRED BOND?
AND THEN SHE TURNED AROUND AND WALKED OFF.
SHE WOULDN'T SPEAK TO ME OR CLARIFY WHAT SHE MEANT.
THOUGH SHE DID LOOK VERY UPSET.
IT JUST DOESN'T ADD UP.
THIS IS NOT THE WAY EMBER WAS GOING TO LEAD THE DRAGONS!
WELL, SHE STILL IS A DRAGON.
THEY'RE NATURALLY AGGRESSIVE. PERHAPS WARRING IS IN THEIR MAKEUP.
EXCUSE ME?

HAVE YOU FORGOTTEN THAT I AM A DRAGON?

OH! I GUESS I ACTUALLY DID FORGET.

YOU'RE MORE LIKE A PONY THAN A DRAGON, ANYWAY.

GEE, THANKS.

MAYBE EMBER'S NATURAL INSTINCT IS TOO POWERFUL FOR HER TO OVERCOME.

I JUST DON'T THINK IT'S THAT.

THEN WHAT IS IT?

I'M NOT SURE.

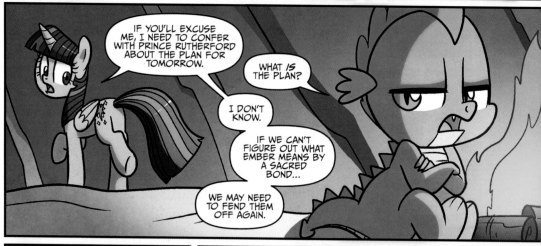

IF YOU'LL EXCUSE ME, I NEED TO CONFER WITH PRINCE RUTHERFORD ABOUT THE PLAN FOR TOMORROW.

WHAT *IS* THE PLAN?

I DON'T KNOW.

IF WE CAN'T FIGURE OUT WHAT EMBER MEANS BY A SACRED BOND...

WE MAY NEED TO FEND THEM OFF AGAIN.

WHY WOULD EMBER DO THIS?

AND WHAT DID SHE MEAN WHEN SHE SAID SHE DIDN'T THINK TWILIGHT WOULD DO THAT TO THEM TOO?

WELL, I'M GONNA GO AND FIND OUT!

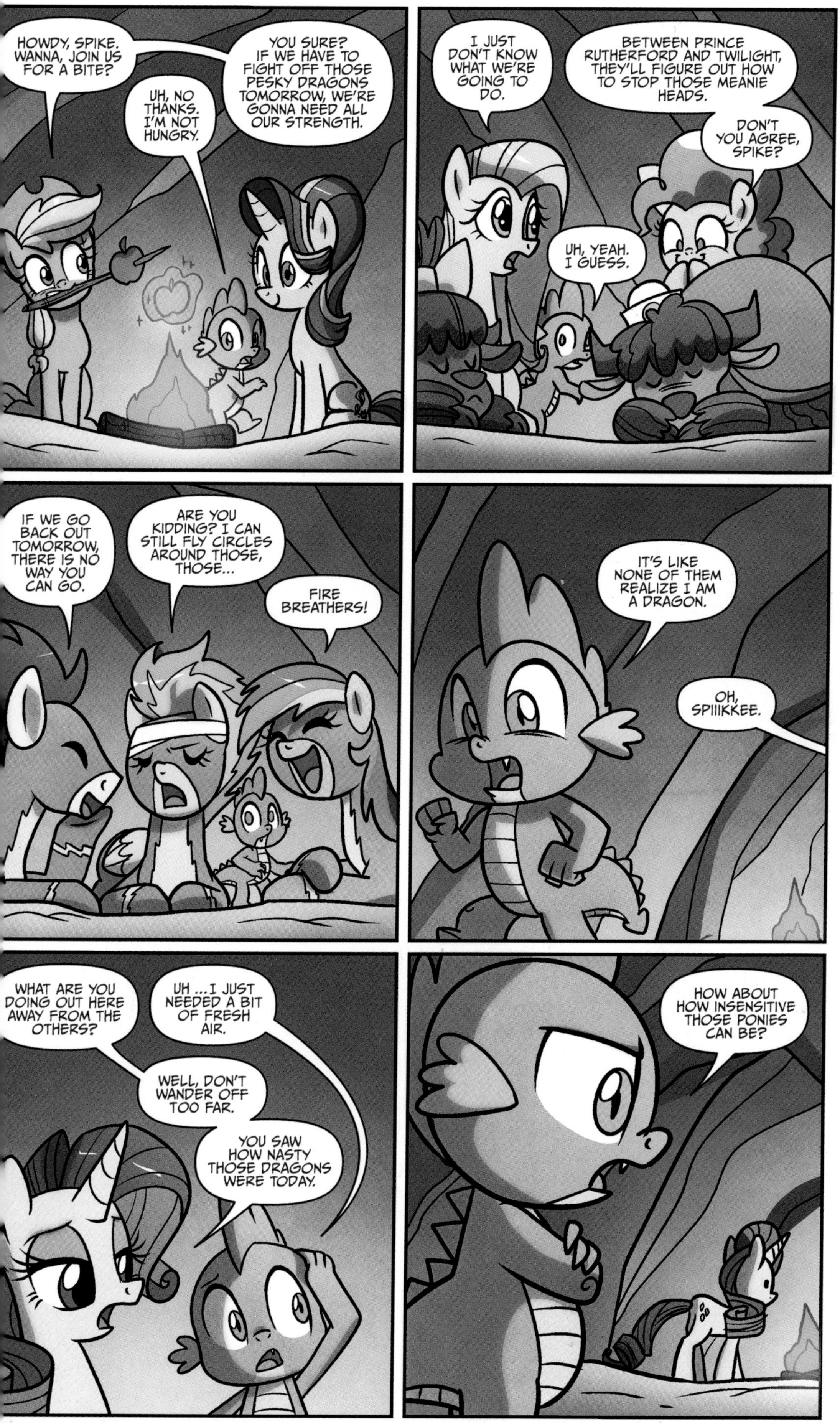
HOWDY, SPIKE. WANNA, JOIN US FOR A BITE?
UH, NO THANKS. I'M NOT HUNGRY.
YOU SURE? IF WE HAVE TO FIGHT OFF THOSE PESKY DRAGONS TOMORROW, WE'RE GONNA NEED ALL OUR STRENGTH.
I JUST DON'T KNOW WHAT WE'RE GOING TO DO.
BETWEEN PRINCE RUTHERFORD AND TWILIGHT, THEY'LL FIGURE OUT HOW TO STOP THOSE MEANIE HEADS.
DON'T YOU AGREE, SPIKE?
UH, YEAH. I GUESS.
IF WE GO BACK OUT TOMORROW, THERE IS NO WAY YOU CAN GO.
ARE YOU KIDDING? I CAN STILL FLY CIRCLES AROUND THOSE, THOSE...
FIRE BREATHERS!
IT'S LIKE NONE OF THEM REALIZE I AM A DRAGON.
OH, SPIIIKKEE.
WHAT ARE YOU DOING OUT HERE AWAY FROM THE OTHERS?
UH ...I JUST NEEDED A BIT OF FRESH AIR.
WELL, DON'T WANDER OFF TOO FAR.
YOU SAW HOW NASTY THOSE DRAGONS WERE TODAY.
HOW ABOUT HOW INSENSITIVE THOSE PONIES CAN BE?

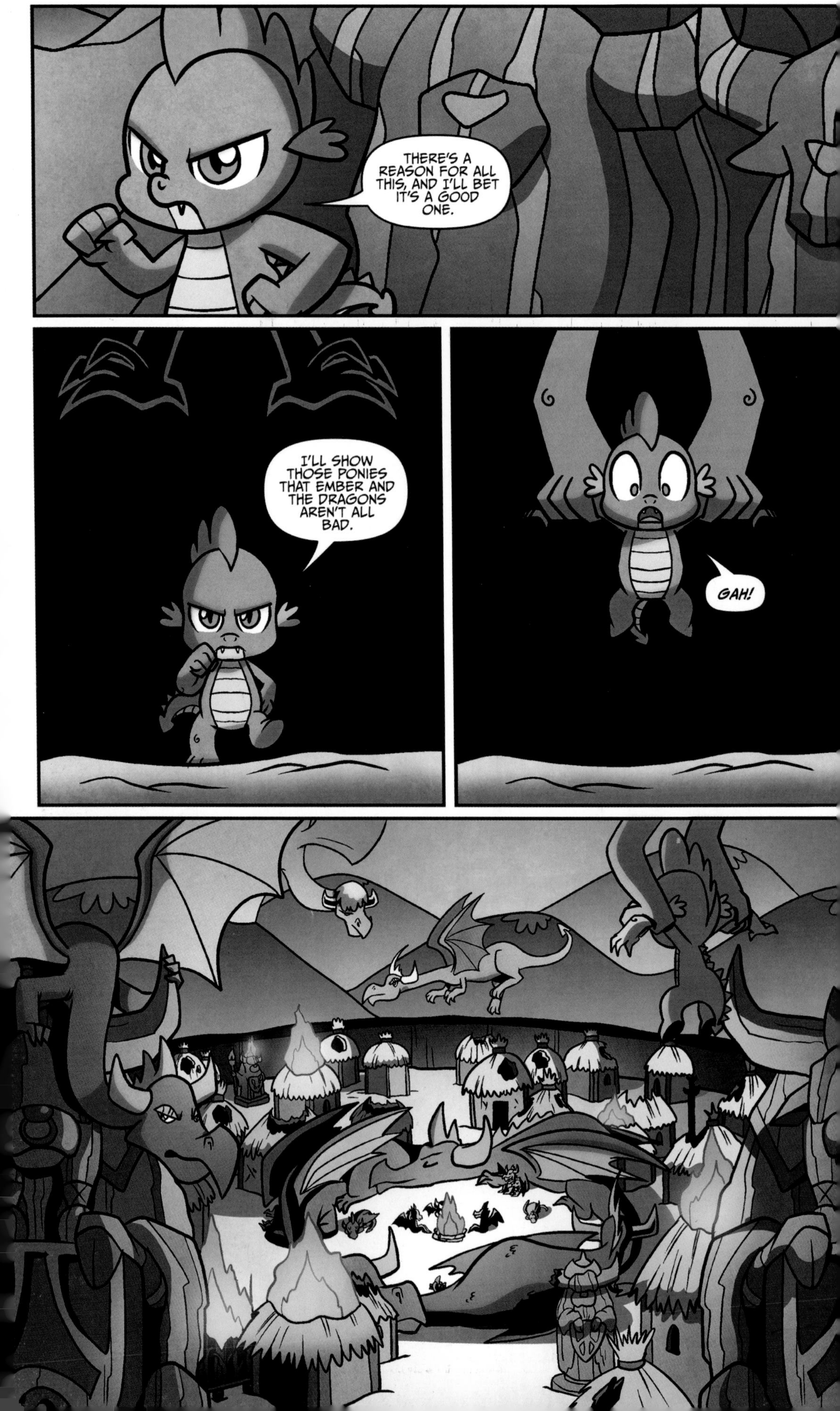
THERE'S A REASON FOR ALL THIS, AND I'LL BET IT'S A GOOD ONE.
I'LL SHOW THOSE PONIES THAT EMBER AND THE DRAGONS AREN'T ALL BAD.
GAH!

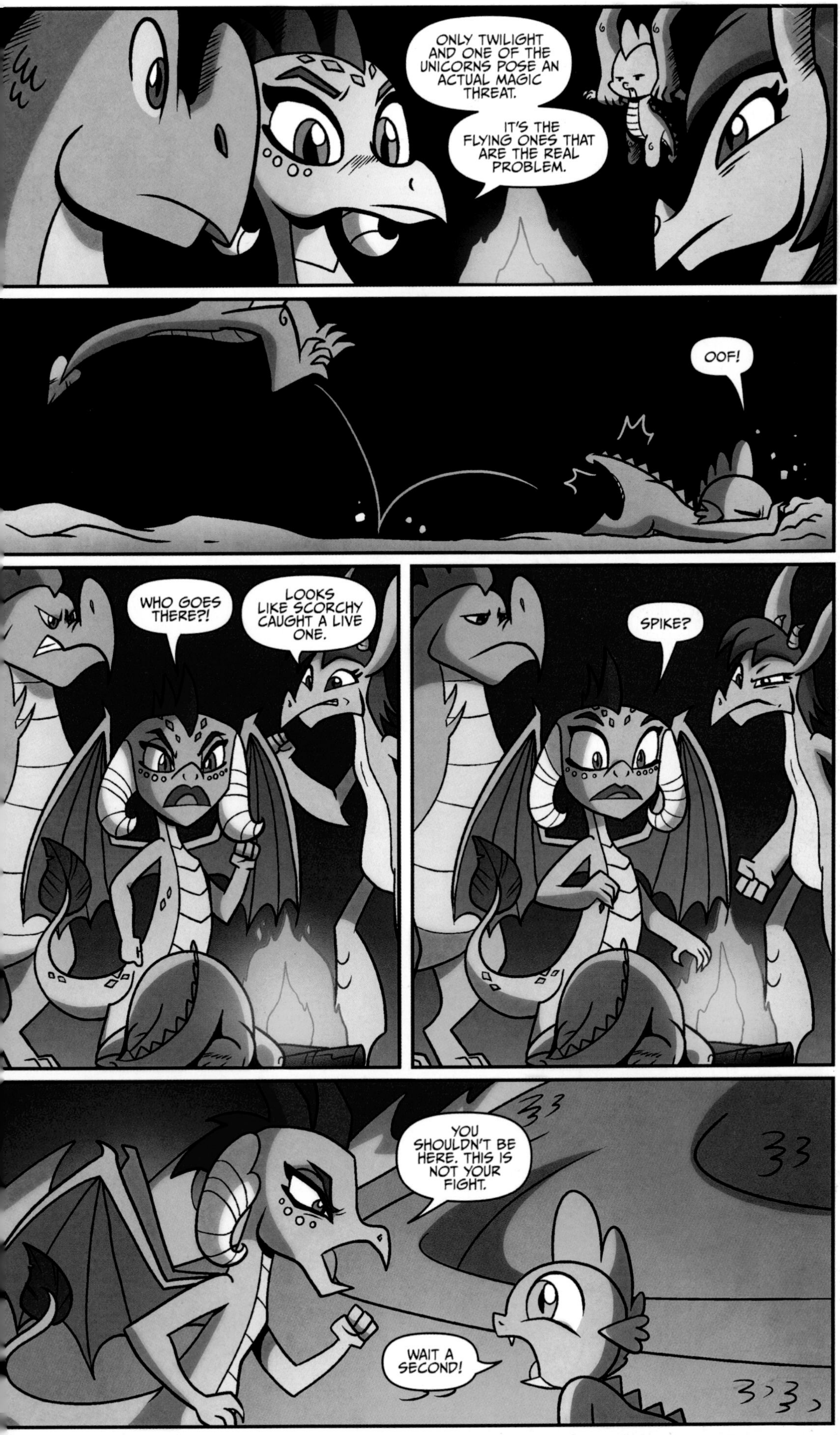
ONLY TWILIGHT AND ONE OF THE UNICORNS POSE AN ACTUAL MAGIC THREAT.
IT'S THE FLYING ONES THAT ARE THE REAL PROBLEM.
OOF!
WHO GOES THERE?!
LOOKS LIKE SCORCHY CAUGHT A LIVE ONE.
SPIKE?
YOU SHOULDN'T BE HERE. THIS IS NOT YOUR FIGHT.
WAIT A SECOND!

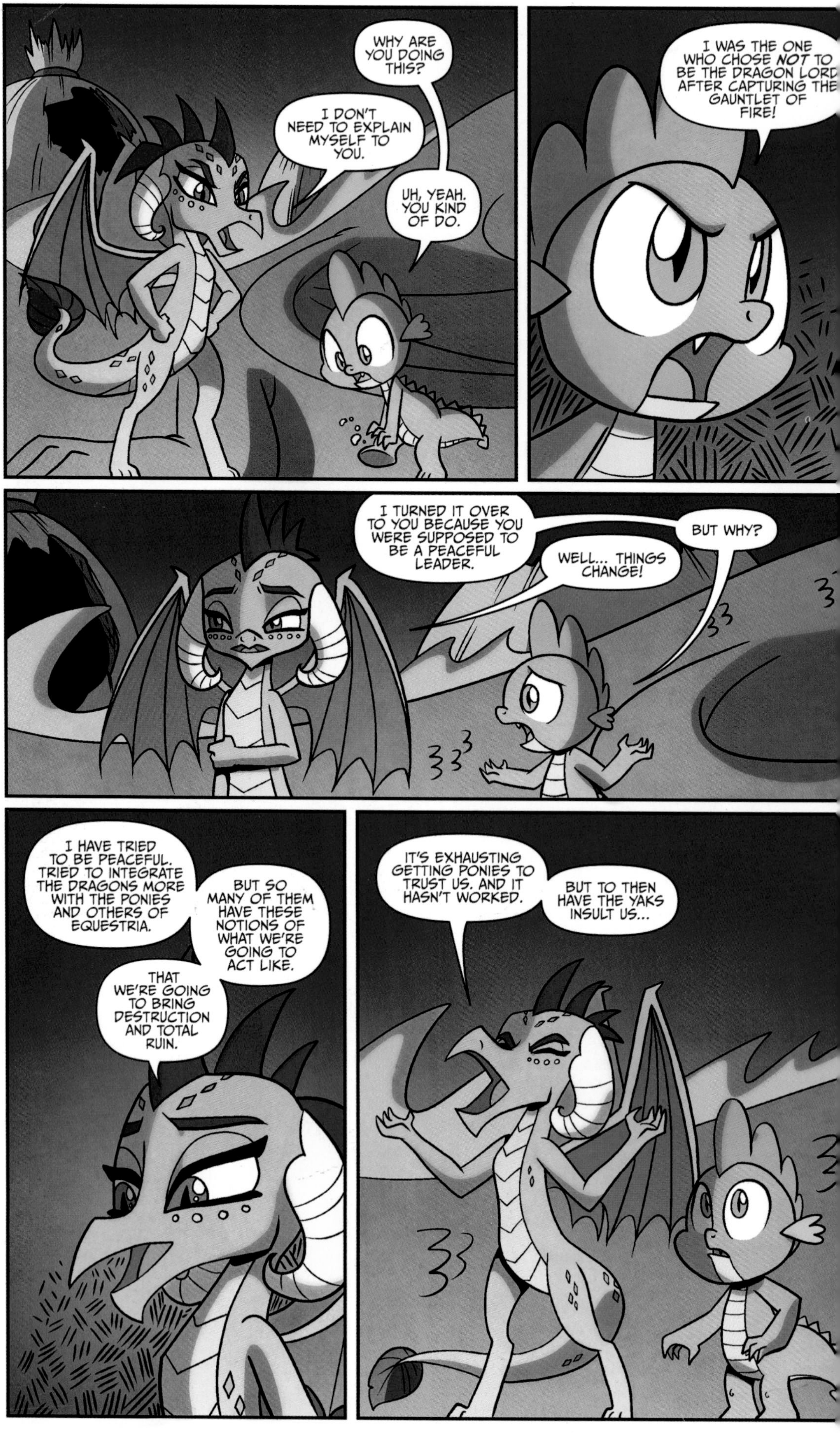
WHY ARE YOU DOING THIS?
I DON'T NEED TO EXPLAIN MYSELF TO YOU.
UH, YEAH. YOU KIND OF DO.
I WAS THE ONE WHO CHOSE *NOT* TO BE THE DRAGON LORD AFTER CAPTURING THE GAUNTLET OF FIRE!
I TURNED IT OVER TO YOU BECAUSE YOU WERE SUPPOSED TO BE A PEACEFUL LEADER.
BUT WHY?
WELL... THINGS CHANGE!
I HAVE TRIED TO BE PEACEFUL. TRIED TO INTEGRATE THE DRAGONS MORE WITH THE PONIES AND OTHERS OF EQUESTRIA.
BUT SO MANY OF THEM HAVE THESE NOTIONS OF WHAT WE'RE GOING TO ACT LIKE.
THAT WE'RE GOING TO BRING DESTRUCTION AND TOTAL RUIN.
IT'S EXHAUSTING GETTING PONIES TO TRUST US. AND IT HASN'T WORKED.
BUT TO THEN HAVE THE YAKS INSULT US...

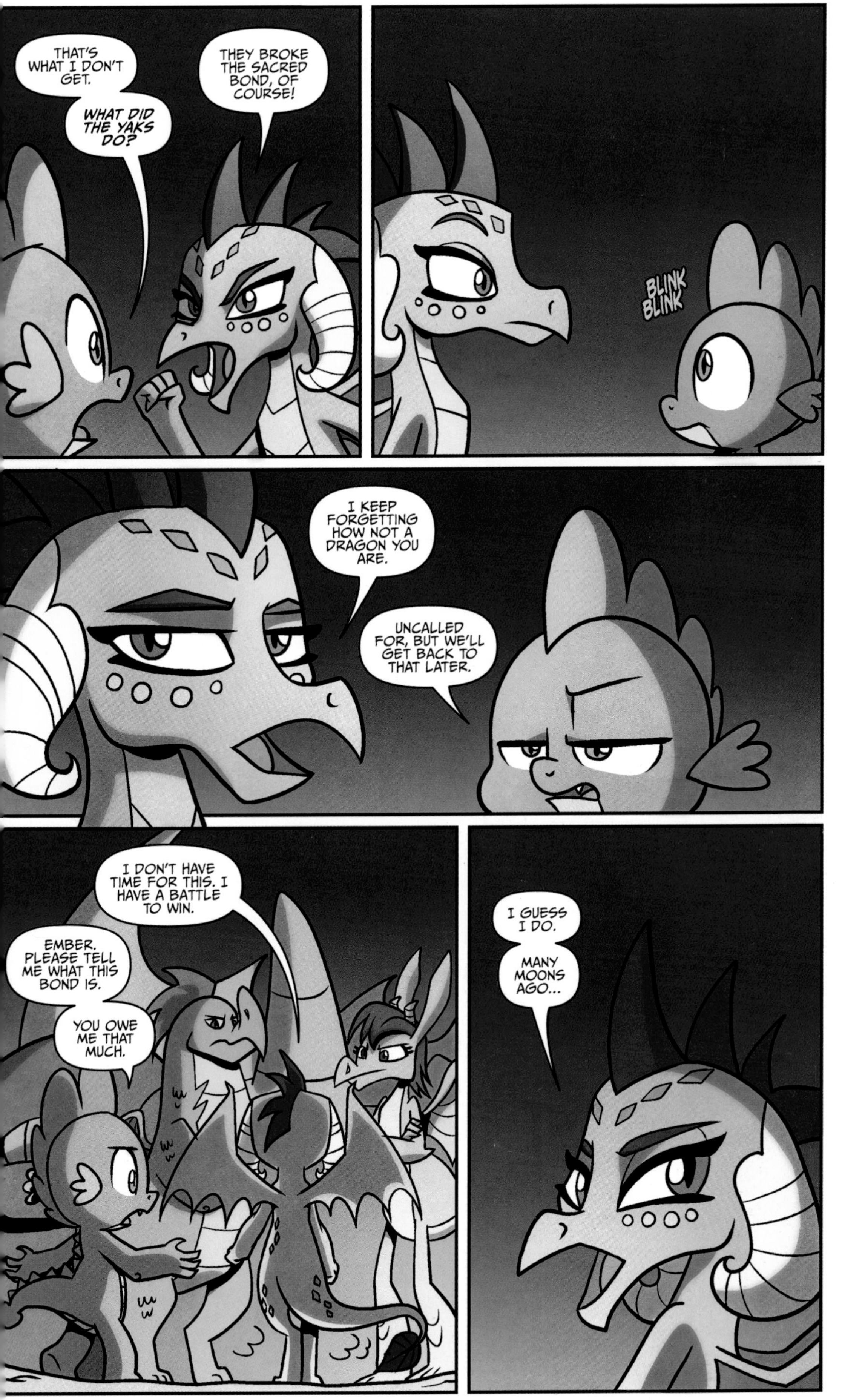

THAT'S WHAT I DON'T GET.
WHAT DID THE YAKS DO?
THEY BROKE THE SACRED BOND, OF COURSE!
BLINK BLINK
I KEEP FORGETTING HOW NOT A DRAGON YOU ARE.
UNCALLED FOR, BUT WE'LL GET BACK TO THAT LATER.
I DON'T HAVE TIME FOR THIS. I HAVE A BATTLE TO WIN.
EMBER. PLEASE TELL ME WHAT THIS BOND IS.
YOU OWE ME THAT MUCH.
I GUESS I DO.
MANY MOONS AGO...

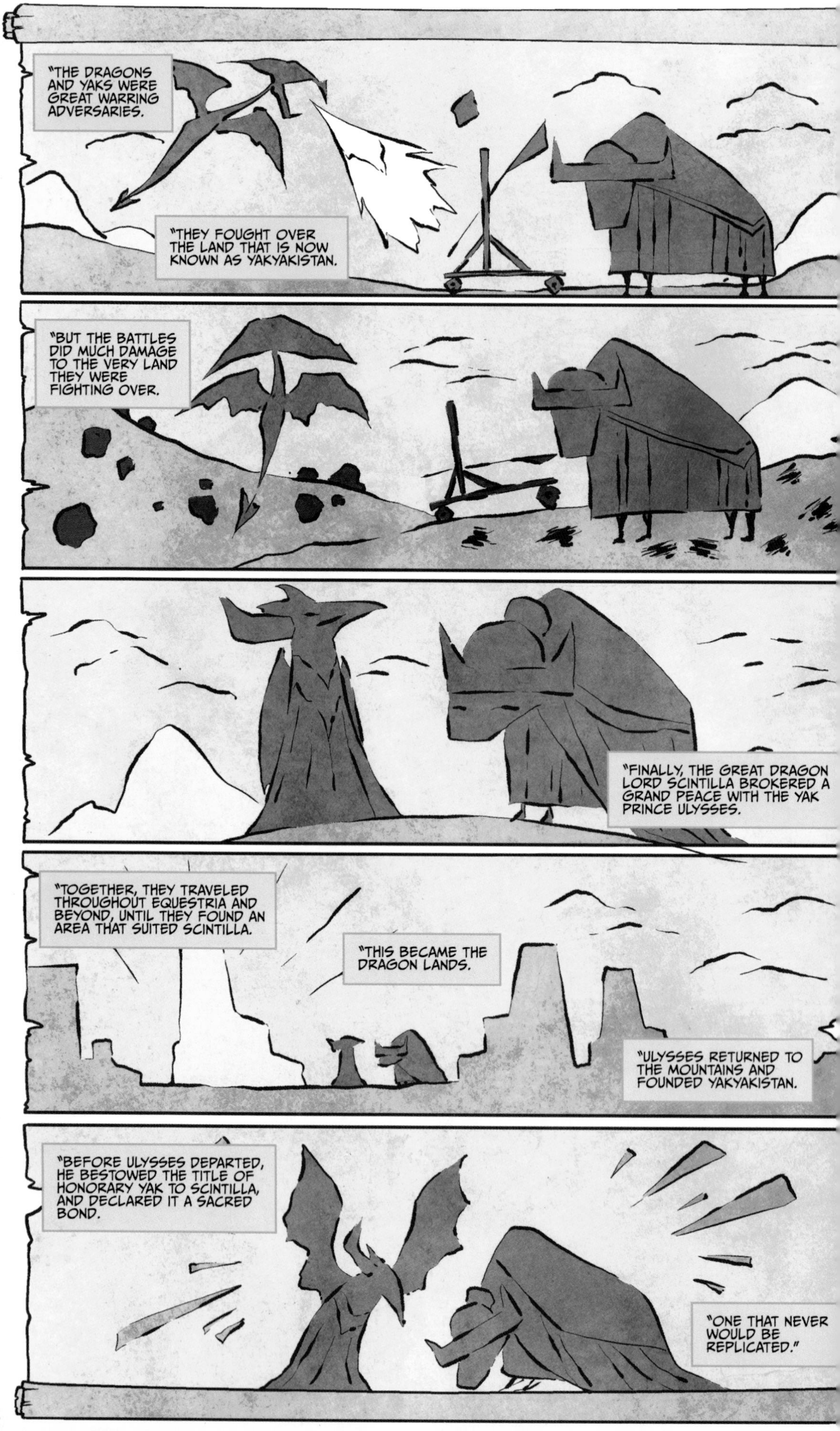
"THE DRAGONS AND YAKS WERE GREAT WARRING ADVERSARIES.
"THEY FOUGHT OVER THE LAND THAT IS NOW KNOWN AS YAKYAKISTAN.
"BUT THE BATTLES DID MUCH DAMAGE TO THE VERY LAND THEY WERE FIGHTING OVER.
"FINALLY, THE GREAT DRAGON LORD SCINTILLA BROKERED A GRAND PEACE WITH THE YAK PRINCE ULYSSES.
"TOGETHER, THEY TRAVELED THROUGHOUT EQUESTRIA AND BEYOND, UNTIL THEY FOUND AN AREA THAT SUITED SCINTILLA.
"THIS BECAME THE DRAGON LANDS.
"ULYSSES RETURNED TO THE MOUNTAINS AND FOUNDED YAKYAKISTAN.
"BEFORE ULYSSES DEPARTED, HE BESTOWED THE TITLE OF HONORARY YAK TO SCINTILLA, AND DECLARED IT A SACRED BOND.
"ONE THAT NEVER WOULD BE REPLICATED."

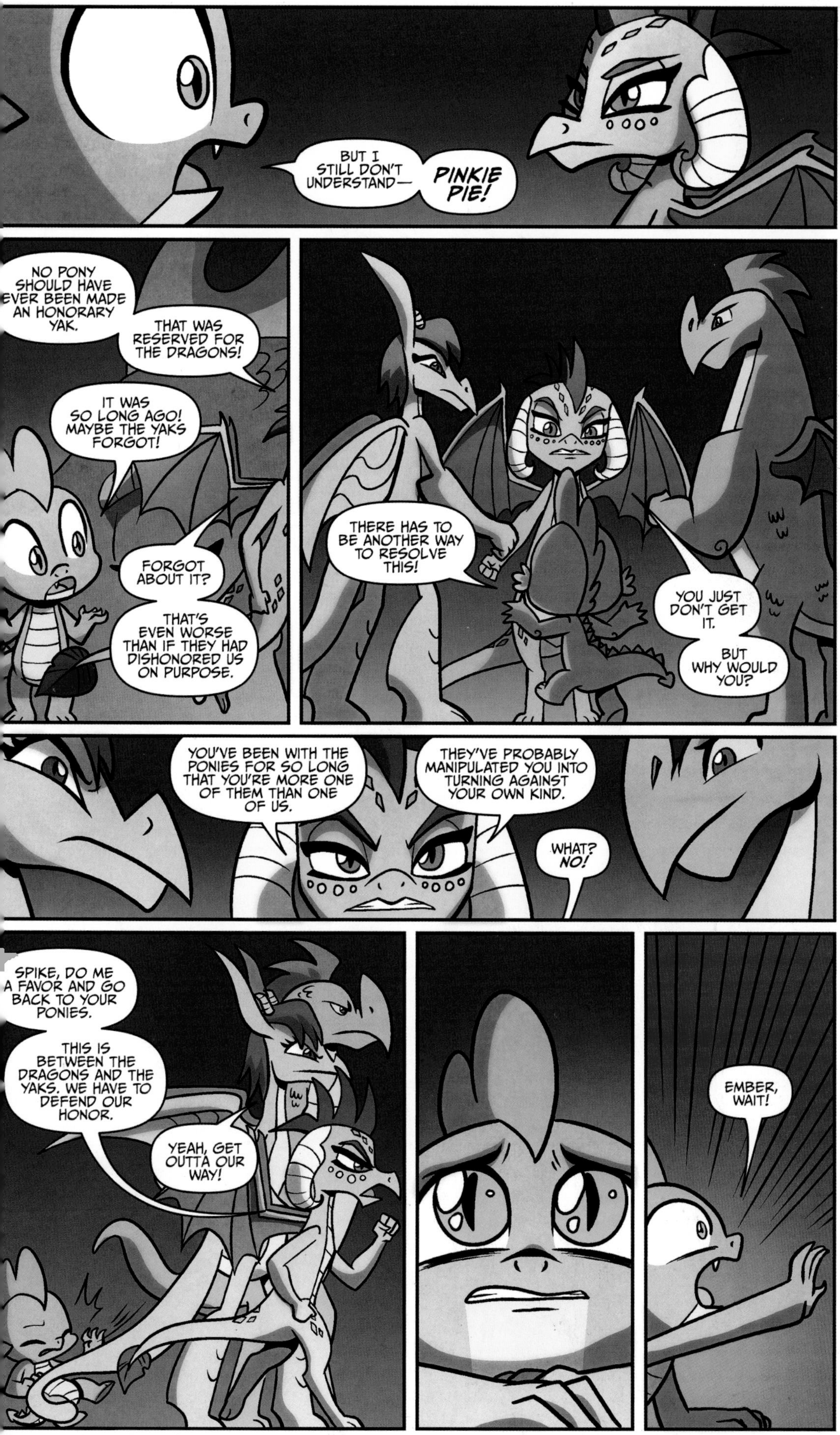
BUT I STILL DON'T UNDERSTAND—
PINKIE PIE!
NO PONY SHOULD HAVE EVER BEEN MADE AN HONORARY YAK.
THAT WAS RESERVED FOR THE DRAGONS!
IT WAS SO LONG AGO! MAYBE THE YAKS FORGOT!
FORGOT ABOUT IT?
THAT'S EVEN WORSE THAN IF THEY HAD DISHONORED US ON PURPOSE.
THERE HAS TO BE ANOTHER WAY TO RESOLVE THIS!
YOU JUST DON'T GET IT.
BUT WHY WOULD YOU?
YOU'VE BEEN WITH THE PONIES FOR SO LONG THAT YOU'RE MORE ONE OF THEM THAN ONE OF US.
THEY'VE PROBABLY MANIPULATED YOU INTO TURNING AGAINST YOUR OWN KIND.
WHAT? NO!
SPIKE, DO ME A FAVOR AND GO BACK TO YOUR PONIES.
THIS IS BETWEEN THE DRAGONS AND THE YAKS. WE HAVE TO DEFEND OUR HONOR.
YEAH, GET OUTTA OUR WAY!
EMBER, WAIT!

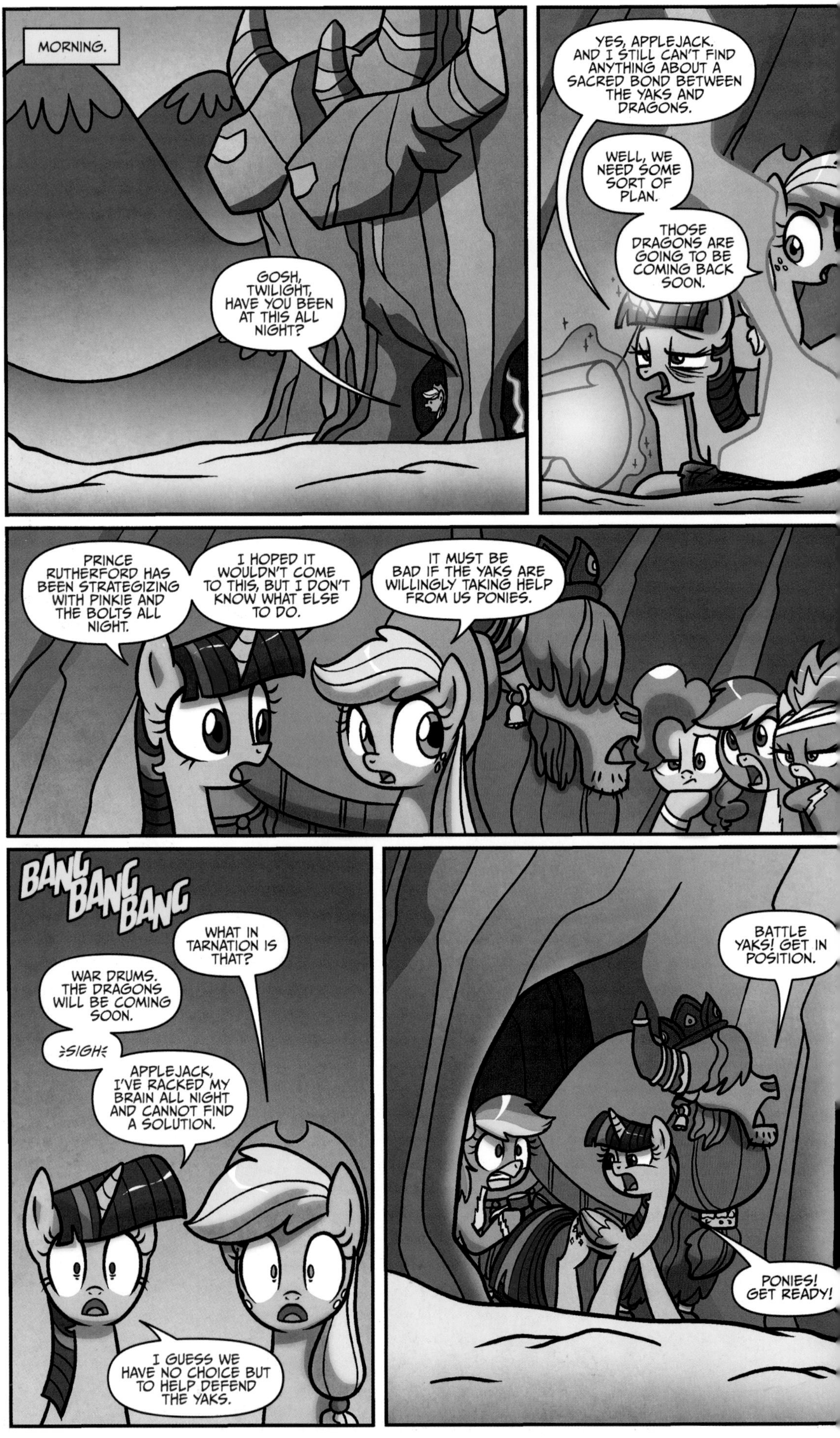
MORNING.
GOSH, TWILIGHT, HAVE YOU BEEN AT THIS ALL NIGHT?
YES, APPLEJACK. AND I STILL CAN'T FIND ANYTHING ABOUT A SACRED BOND BETWEEN THE YAKS AND DRAGONS.
WELL, WE NEED SOME SORT OF PLAN.
THOSE DRAGONS ARE GOING TO BE COMING BACK SOON.
PRINCE RUTHERFORD HAS BEEN STRATEGIZING WITH PINKIE AND THE BOLTS ALL NIGHT.
I HOPED IT WOULDN'T COME TO THIS, BUT I DON'T KNOW WHAT ELSE TO DO.
IT MUST BE BAD IF THE YAKS ARE WILLINGLY TAKING HELP FROM US PONIES.
BANG BANG BANG
WHAT IN TARNATION IS THAT?
WAR DRUMS. THE DRAGONS WILL BE COMING SOON.
SIGH
APPLEJACK, I'VE RACKED MY BRAIN ALL NIGHT AND CANNOT FIND A SOLUTION.
I GUESS WE HAVE NO CHOICE BUT TO HELP DEFEND THE YAKS.
BATTLE YAKS! GET IN POSITION.
PONIES! GET READY!

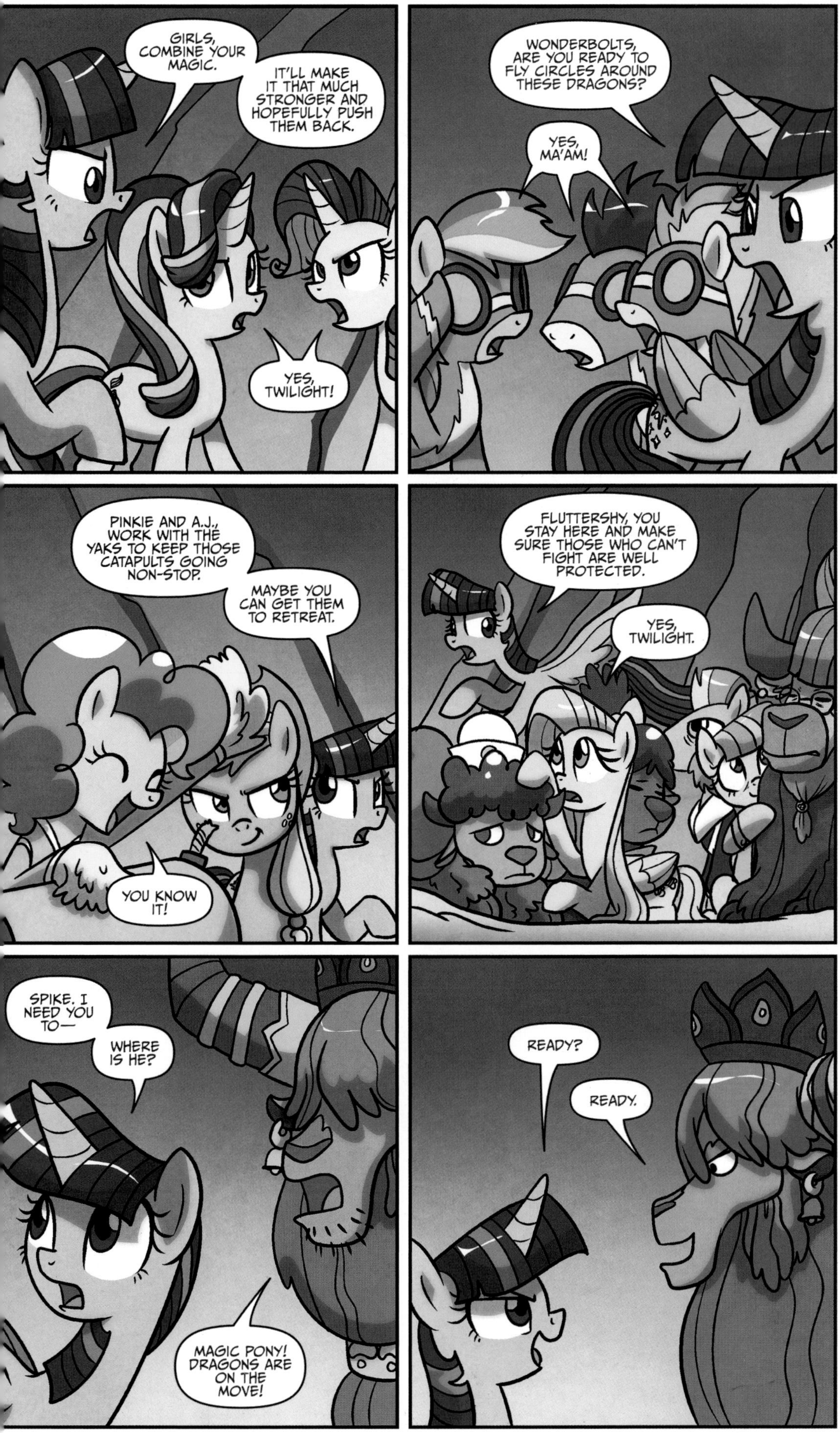
GIRLS, COMBINE YOUR MAGIC.
IT'LL MAKE IT THAT MUCH STRONGER AND HOPEFULLY PUSH THEM BACK.
YES, TWILIGHT!
WONDERBOLTS, ARE YOU READY TO FLY CIRCLES AROUND THESE DRAGONS?
YES, MA'AM!
PINKIE AND A.J., WORK WITH THE YAKS TO KEEP THOSE CATAPULTS GOING NON-STOP.
MAYBE YOU CAN GET THEM TO RETREAT.
YOU KNOW IT!
FLUTTERSHY, YOU STAY HERE AND MAKE SURE THOSE WHO CAN'T FIGHT ARE WELL PROTECTED.
YES, TWILIGHT.
SPIKE. I NEED YOU TO—
WHERE IS HE?
MAGIC PONY! DRAGONS ARE ON THE MOVE!
READY?
READY.

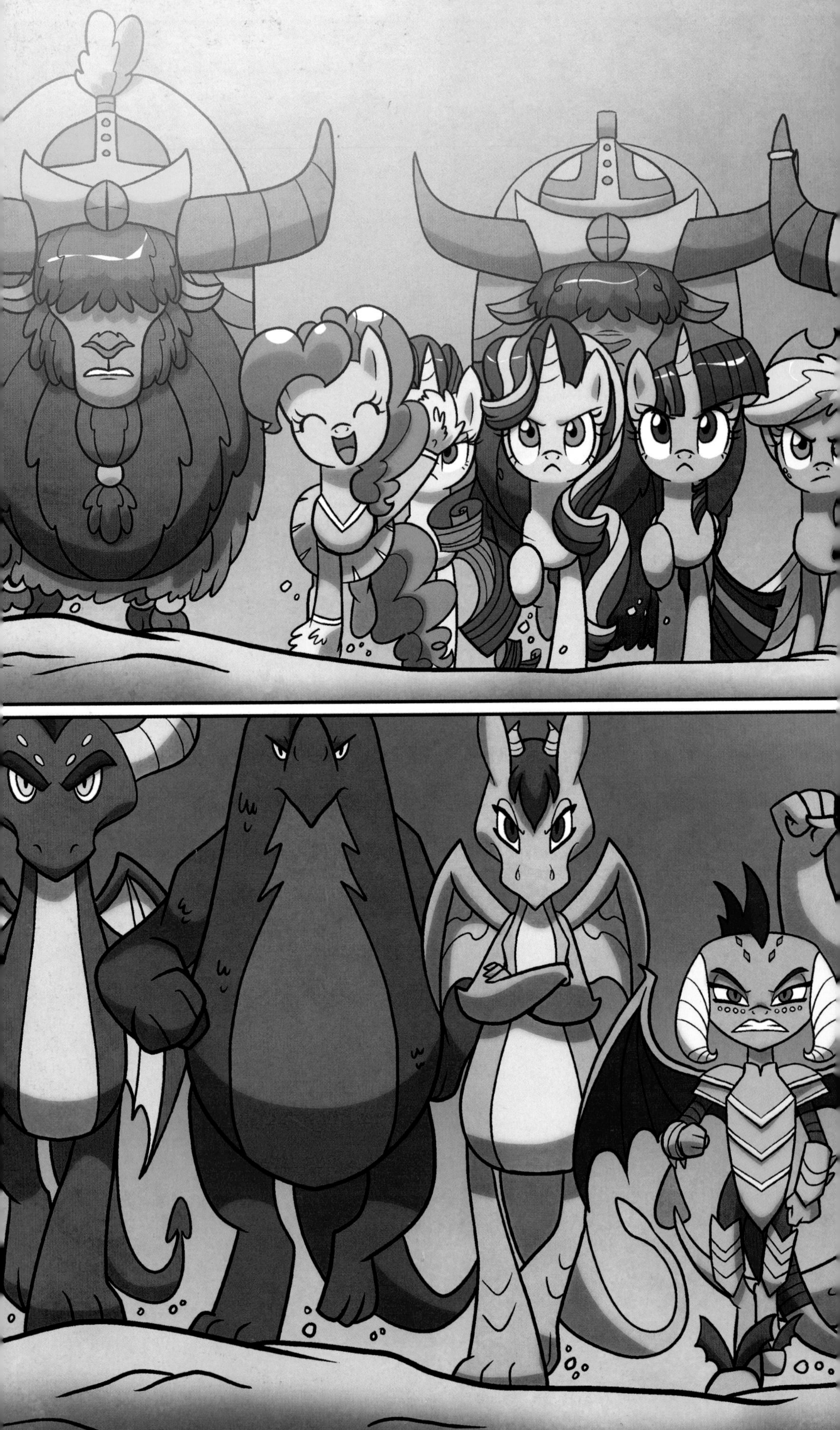

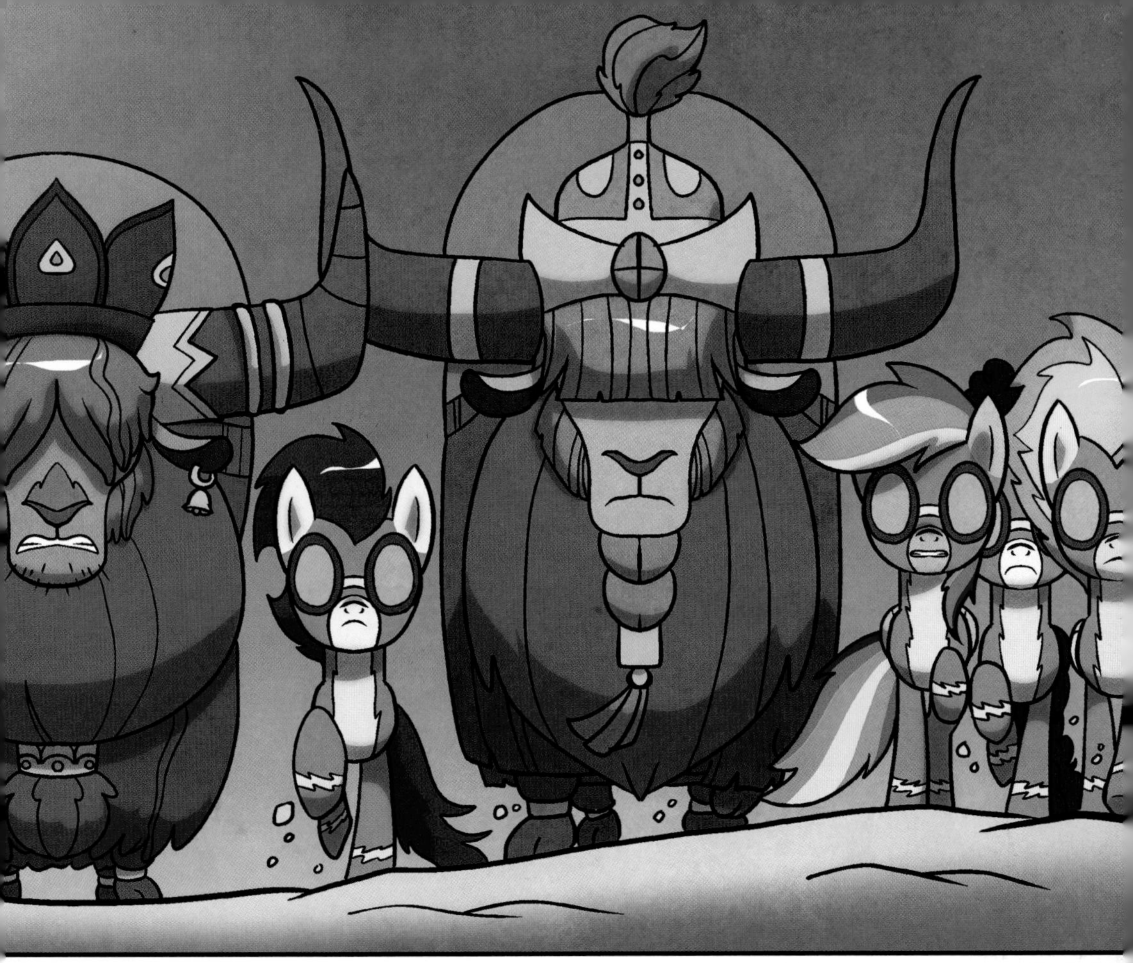

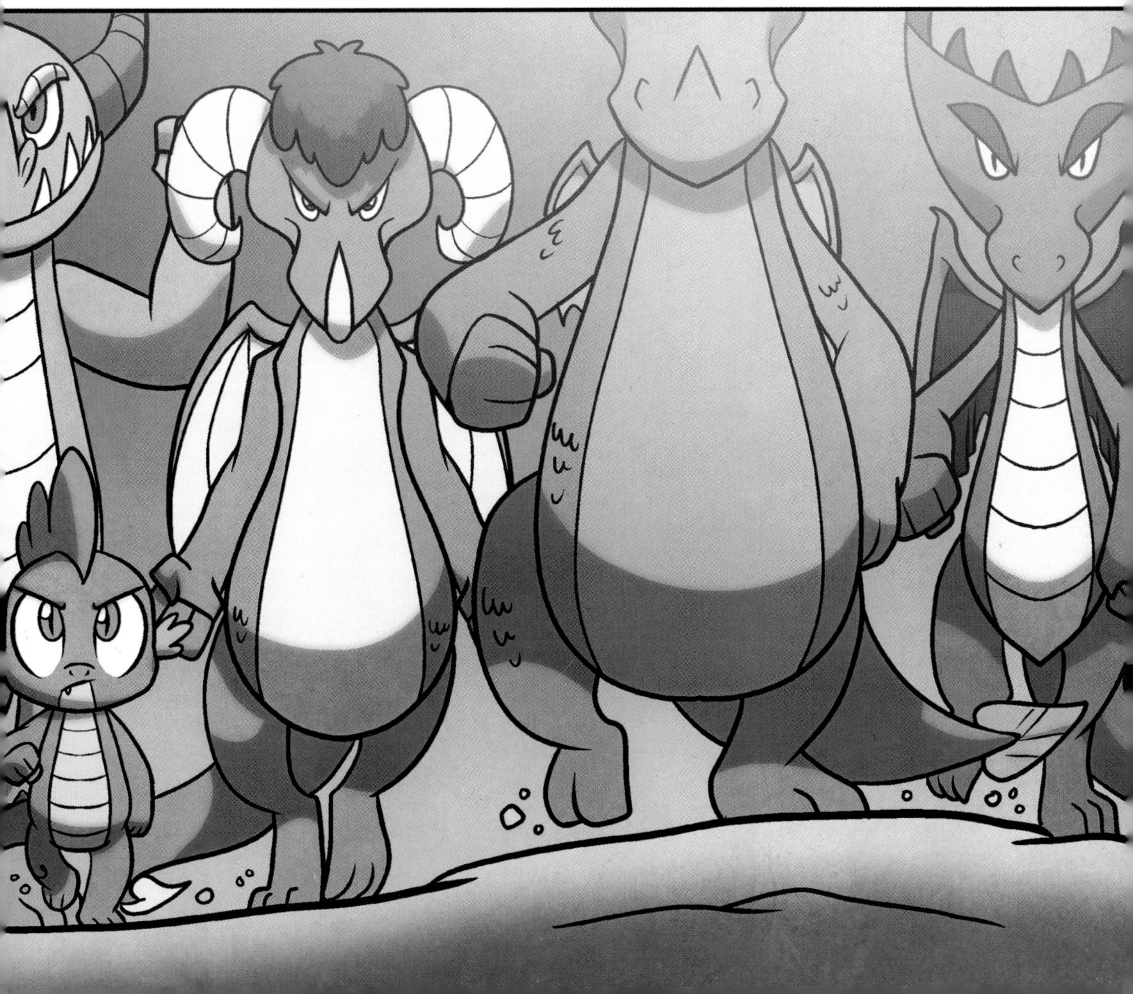

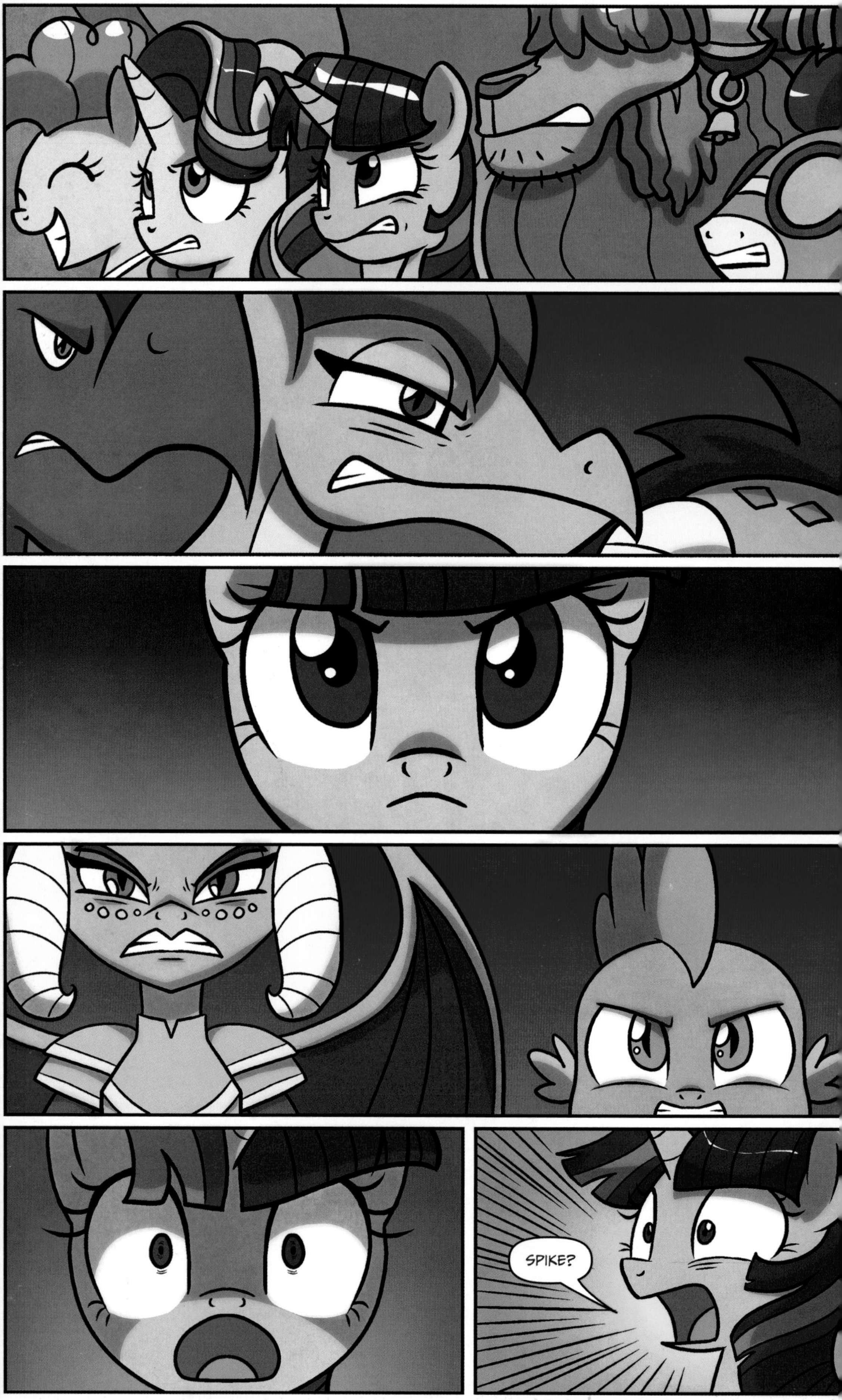
SPIKE?

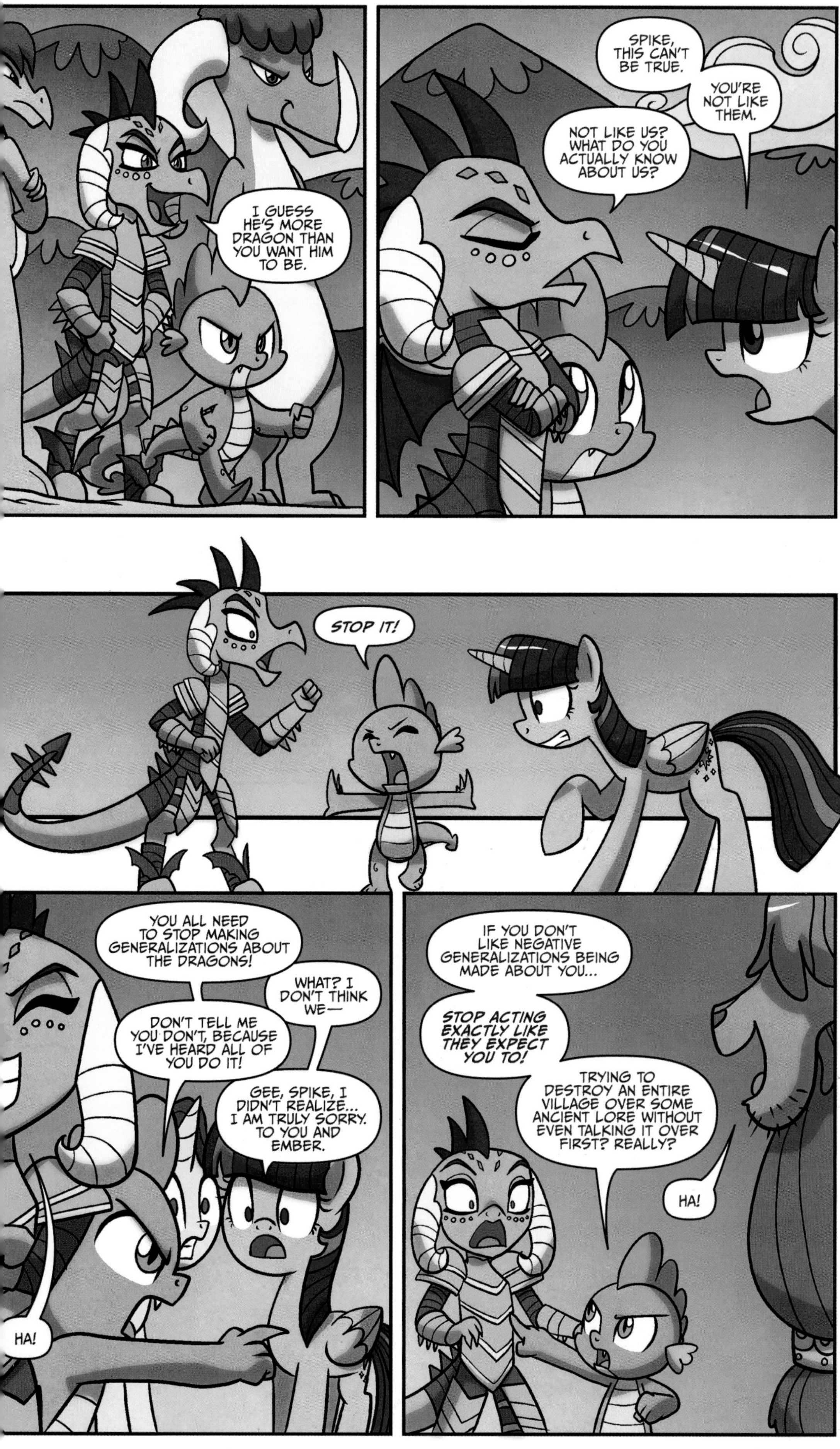
I GUESS HE'S MORE DRAGON THAN YOU WANT HIM TO BE.
SPIKE, THIS CAN'T BE TRUE.
YOU'RE NOT LIKE THEM.
NOT LIKE US? WHAT DO YOU ACTUALLY KNOW ABOUT US?
STOP IT!
YOU ALL NEED TO STOP MAKING GENERALIZATIONS ABOUT THE DRAGONS!
WHAT? I DON'T THINK WE—
DON'T TELL ME YOU DON'T, BECAUSE I'VE HEARD ALL OF YOU DO IT!
GEE, SPIKE, I DIDN'T REALIZE... I AM TRULY SORRY. TO YOU AND EMBER.
HA!
IF YOU DON'T LIKE NEGATIVE GENERALIZATIONS BEING MADE ABOUT YOU...
STOP ACTING EXACTLY LIKE THEY EXPECT YOU TO!
TRYING TO DESTROY AN ENTIRE VILLAGE OVER SOME ANCIENT LORE WITHOUT EVEN TALKING IT OVER FIRST? REALLY?
HA!

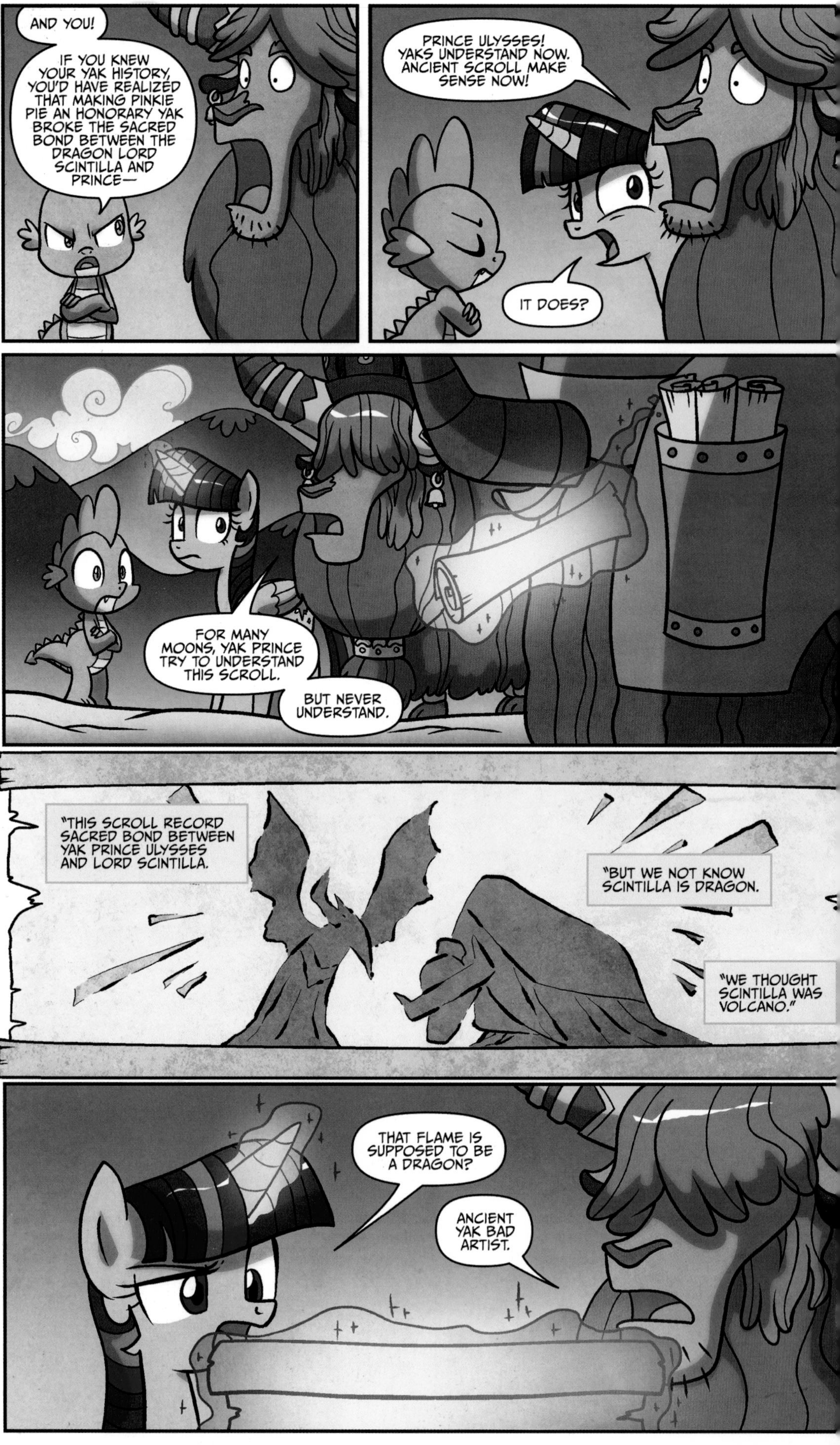
AND YOU!
IF YOU KNEW YOUR YAK HISTORY, YOU'D HAVE REALIZED THAT MAKING PINKIE PIE AN HONORARY YAK BROKE THE SACRED BOND BETWEEN THE DRAGON LORD SCINTILLA AND PRINCE—
PRINCE ULYSSES! YAKS UNDERSTAND NOW. ANCIENT SCROLL MAKE SENSE NOW!
IT DOES?
FOR MANY MOONS, YAK PRINCE TRY TO UNDERSTAND THIS SCROLL.
BUT NEVER UNDERSTAND.
"THIS SCROLL RECORD SACRED BOND BETWEEN YAK PRINCE ULYSSES AND LORD SCINTILLA.
"BUT WE NOT KNOW SCINTILLA IS DRAGON.
"WE THOUGHT SCINTILLA WAS VOLCANO."
THAT FLAME IS SUPPOSED TO BE A DRAGON?
ANCIENT YAK BAD ARTIST.

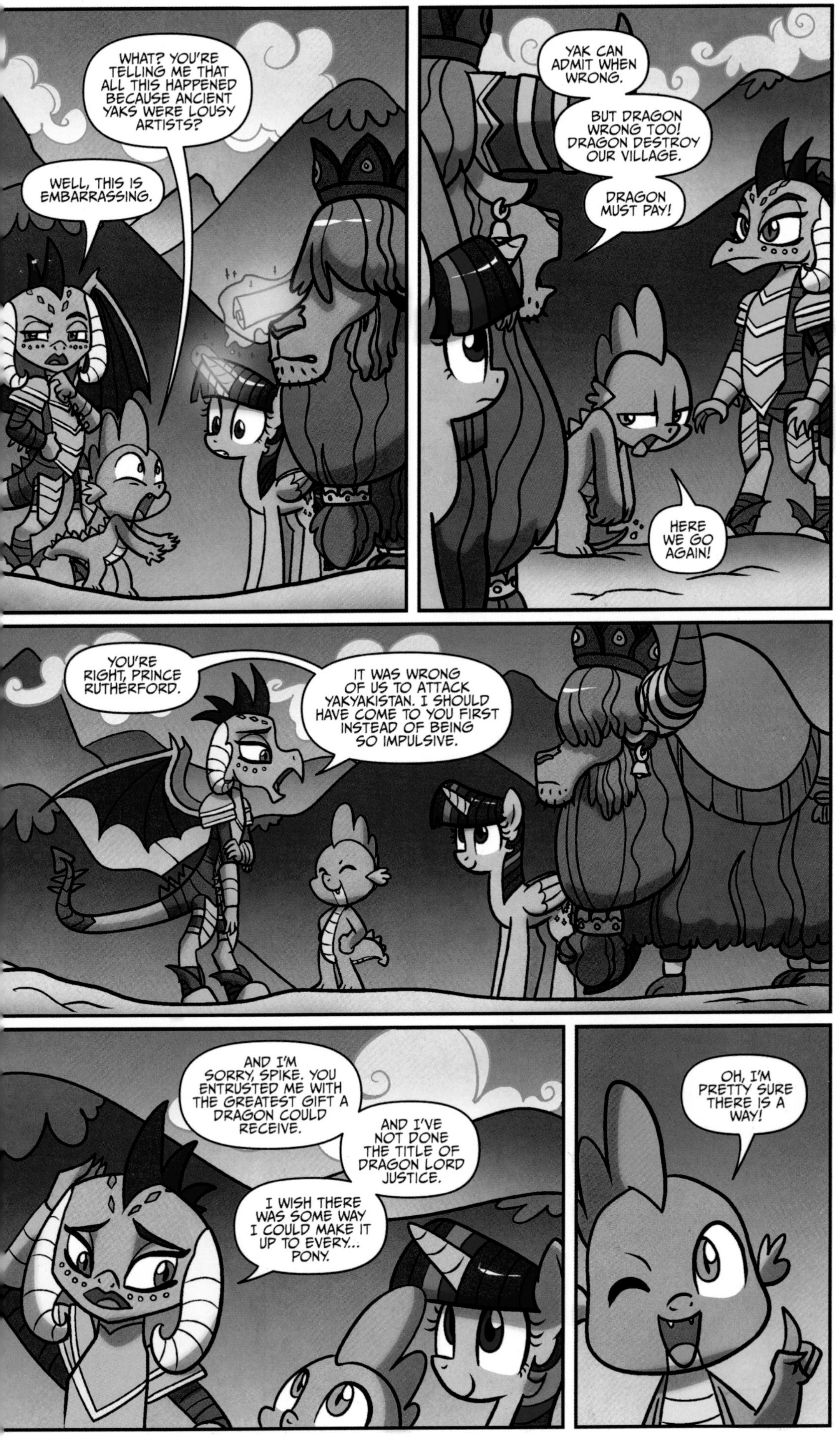

WHAT? YOU'RE TELLING ME THAT ALL THIS HAPPENED BECAUSE ANCIENT YAKS WERE LOUSY ARTISTS?
WELL, THIS IS EMBARRASSING.
YAK CAN ADMIT WHEN WRONG.
BUT DRAGON WRONG TOO! DRAGON DESTROY OUR VILLAGE.
DRAGON MUST PAY!
HERE WE GO AGAIN!
YOU'RE RIGHT, PRINCE RUTHERFORD.
IT WAS WRONG OF US TO ATTACK YAKYAKISTAN. I SHOULD HAVE COME TO YOU FIRST INSTEAD OF BEING SO IMPULSIVE.
AND I'M SORRY, SPIKE. YOU ENTRUSTED ME WITH THE GREATEST GIFT A DRAGON COULD RECEIVE.
AND I'VE NOT DONE THE TITLE OF DRAGON LORD JUSTICE.
I WISH THERE WAS SOME WAY I COULD MAKE IT UP TO EVERY... PONY.
OH, I'M PRETTY SURE THERE IS A WAY!

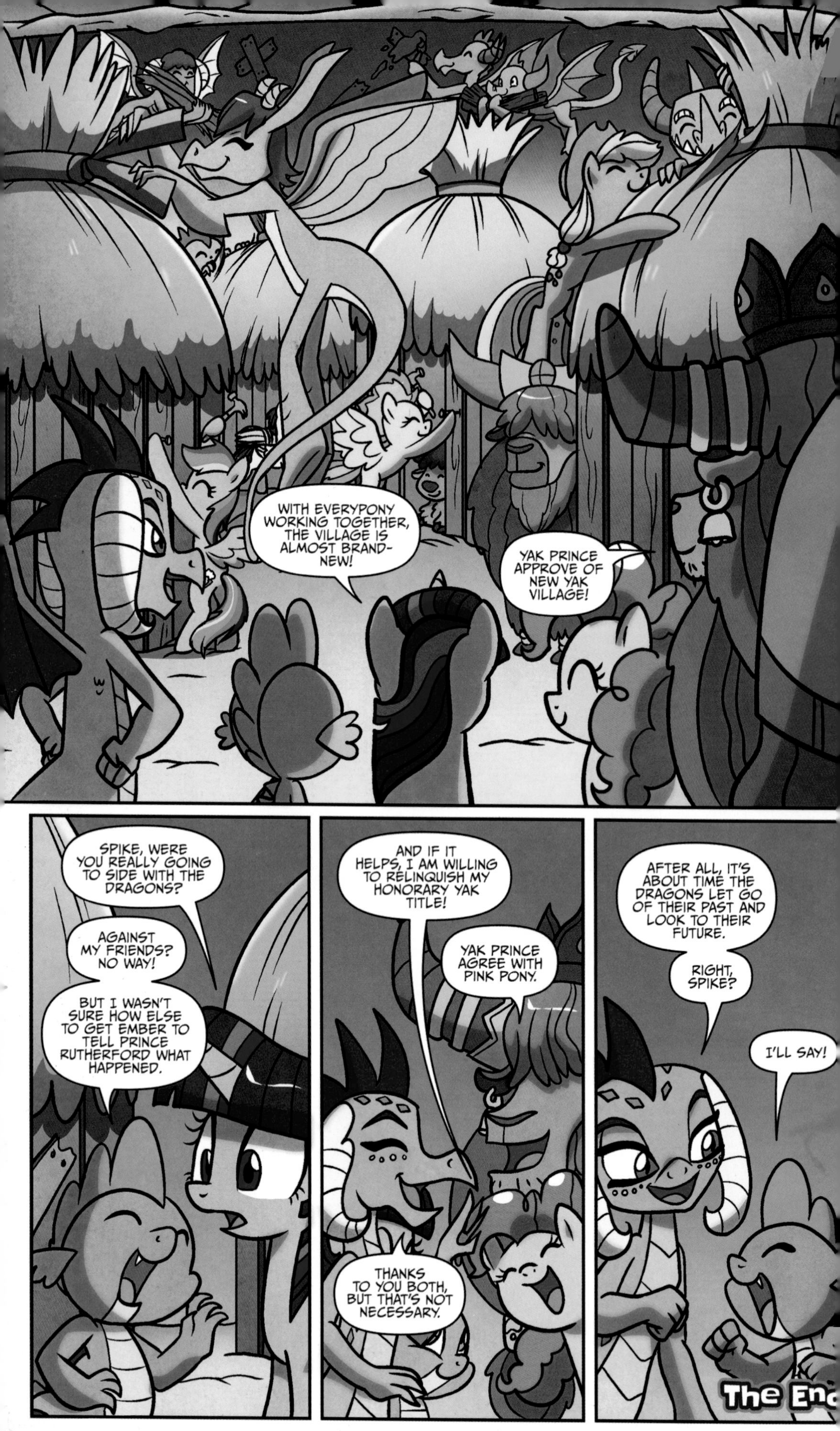

WITH EVERYPONY WORKING TOGETHER, THE VILLAGE IS ALMOST BRAND-NEW!
YAK PRINCE APPROVE OF NEW YAK VILLAGE!
SPIKE, WERE YOU REALLY GOING TO SIDE WITH THE DRAGONS?
AGAINST MY FRIENDS? NO WAY!
BUT I WASN'T SURE HOW ELSE TO GET EMBER TO TELL PRINCE RUTHERFORD WHAT HAPPENED.
AND IF IT HELPS, I AM WILLING TO RELINQUISH MY HONORARY YAK TITLE!
YAK PRINCE AGREE WITH PINK PONY.
THANKS TO YOU BOTH, BUT THAT'S NOT NECESSARY.
AFTER ALL, IT'S ABOUT TIME THE DRAGONS LET GO OF THEIR PAST AND LOOK TO THEIR FUTURE.
RIGHT, SPIKE?
I'LL SAY!
The En

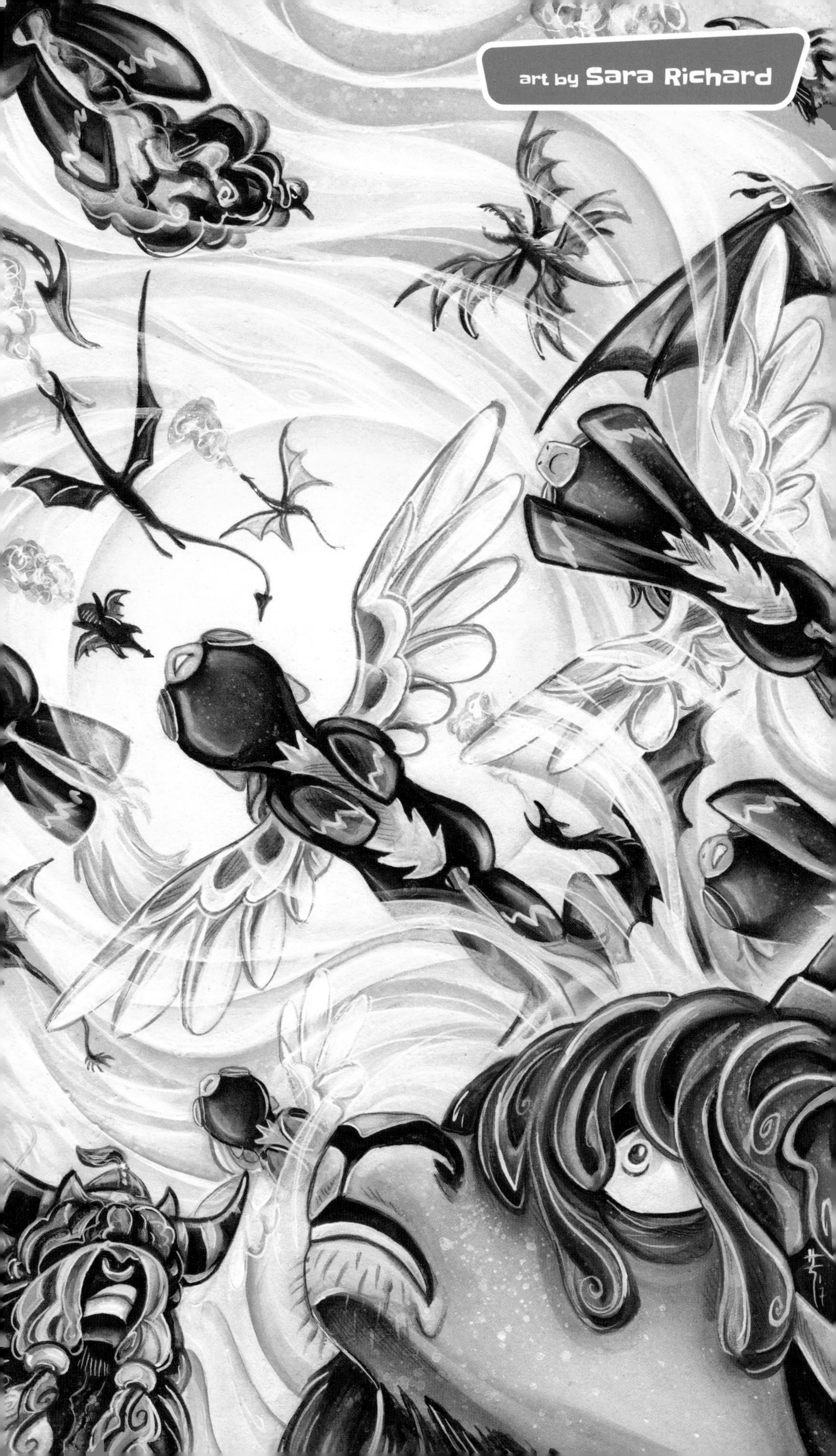

art by Sara Richard

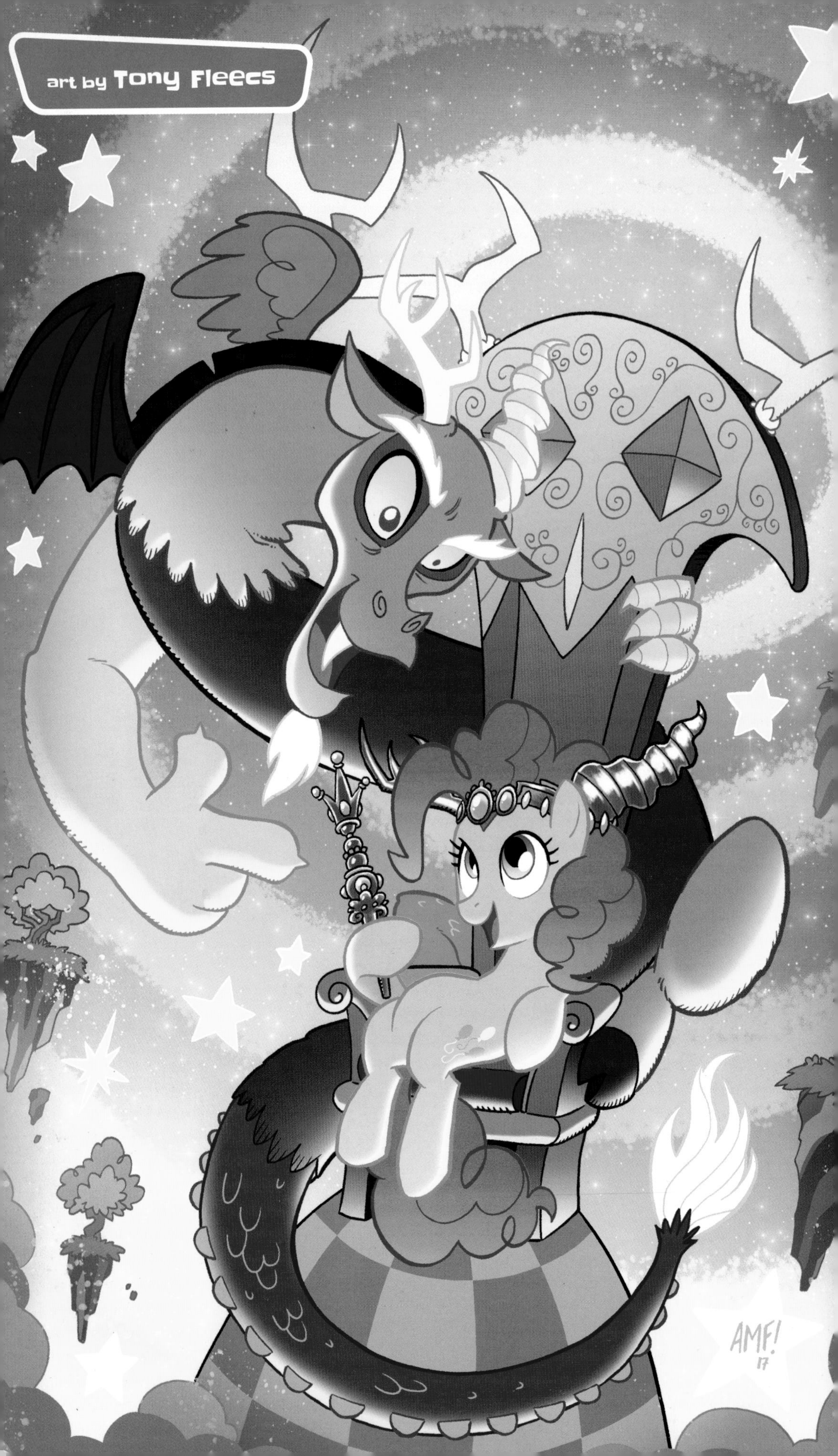
art by Tony Fleecs
AMF! 17

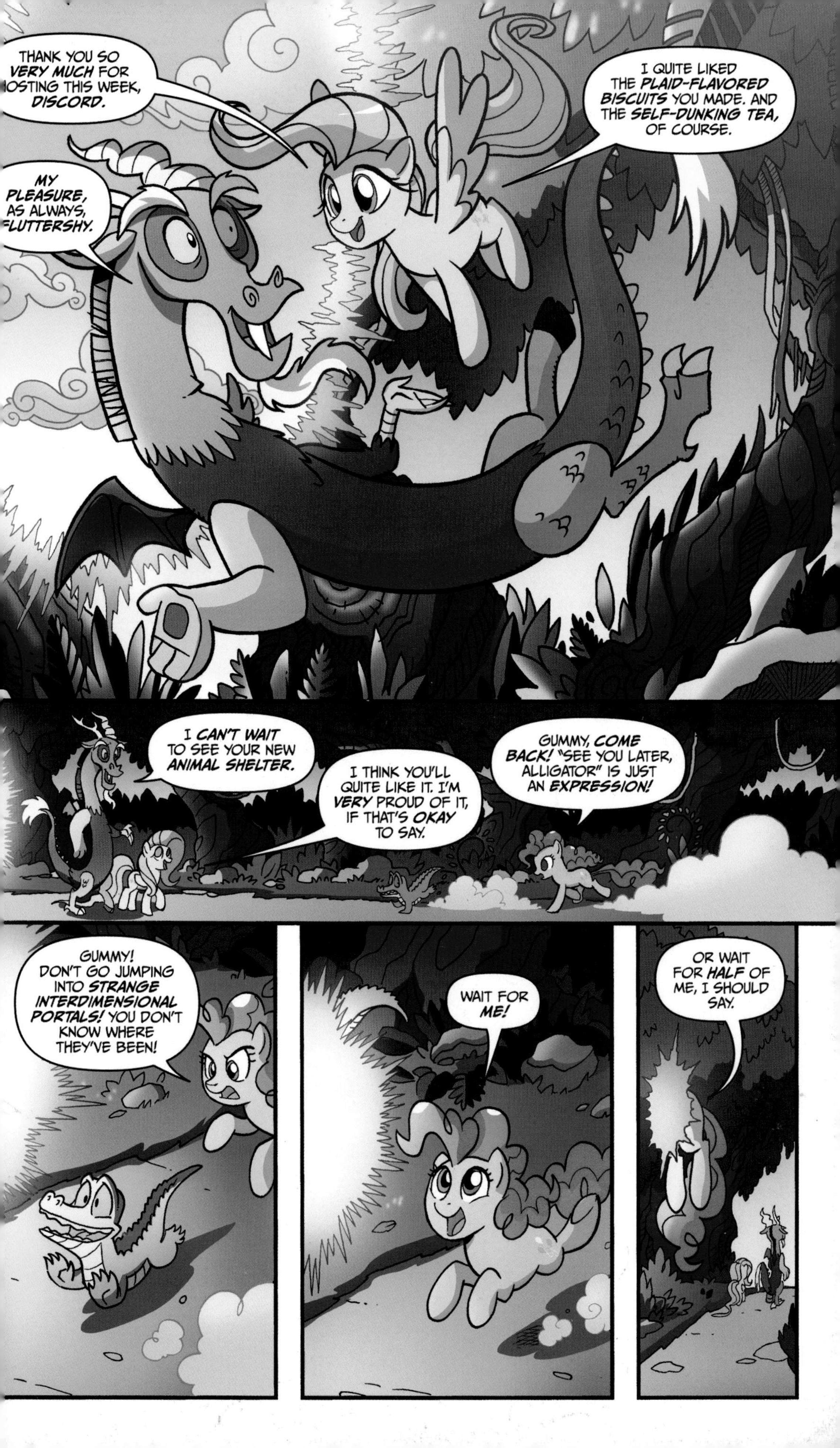
THANK YOU SO VERY MUCH FOR HOSTING THIS WEEK, DISCORD.
I QUITE LIKED THE PLAID-FLAVORED BISCUITS YOU MADE. AND THE SELF-DUNKING TEA, OF COURSE.
MY PLEASURE, AS ALWAYS, FLUTTERSHY.
I CAN'T WAIT TO SEE YOUR NEW ANIMAL SHELTER.
I THINK YOU'LL QUITE LIKE IT. I'M VERY PROUD OF IT, IF THAT'S OKAY TO SAY.
GUMMY, COME BACK! "SEE YOU LATER, ALLIGATOR" IS JUST AN EXPRESSION!
GUMMY! DON'T GO JUMPING INTO STRANGE INTERDIMENSIONAL PORTALS! YOU DON'T KNOW WHERE THEY'VE BEEN!
WAIT FOR ME!
OR WAIT FOR HALF OF ME, I SHOULD SAY.

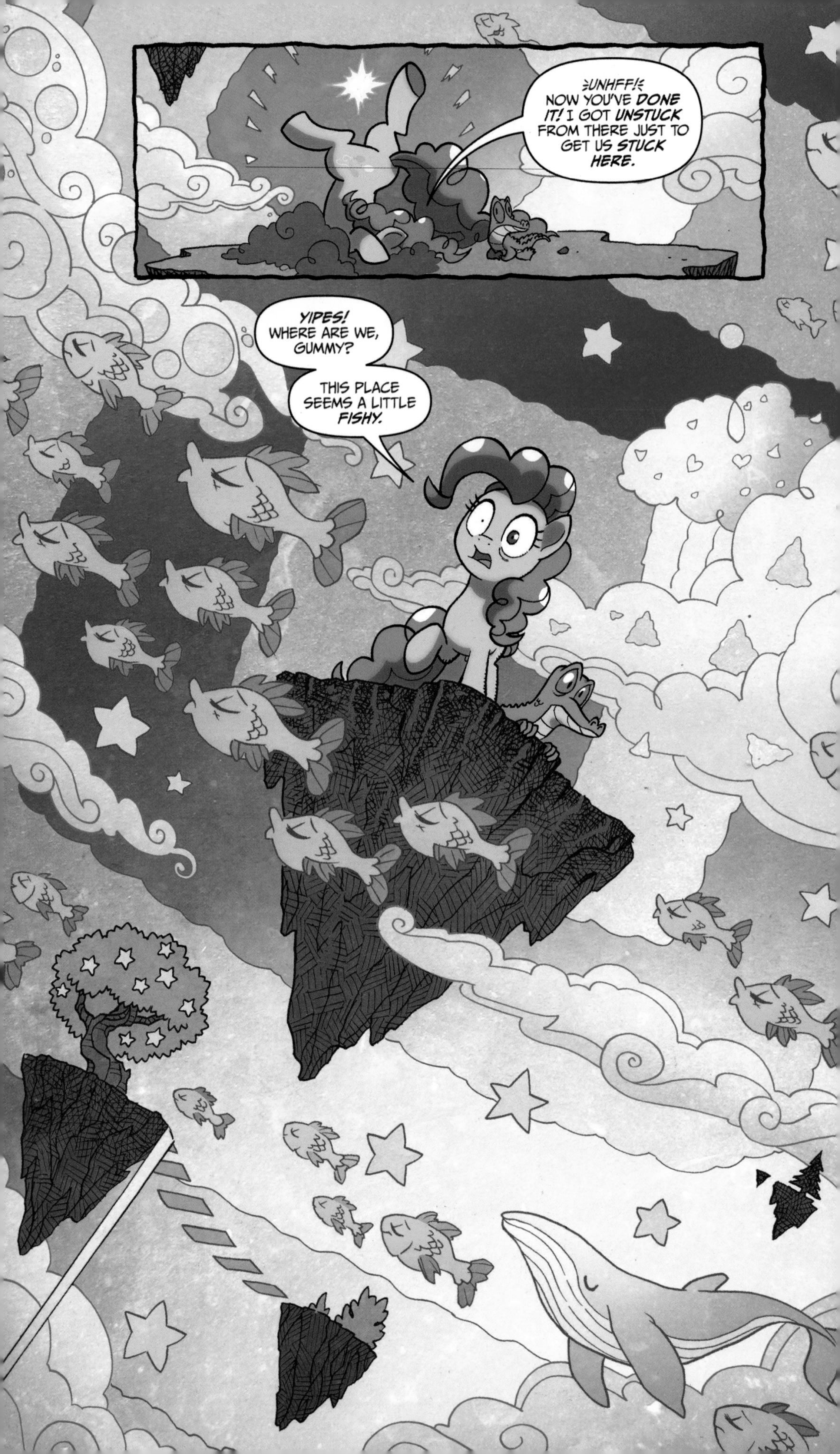

≋UNHFF!≋ NOW YOU'VE *DONE IT!* I GOT *UNSTUCK* FROM THERE JUST TO GET US *STUCK HERE.*
YIPES! WHERE ARE WE, GUMMY?
THIS PLACE SEEMS A LITTLE *FISHY.*

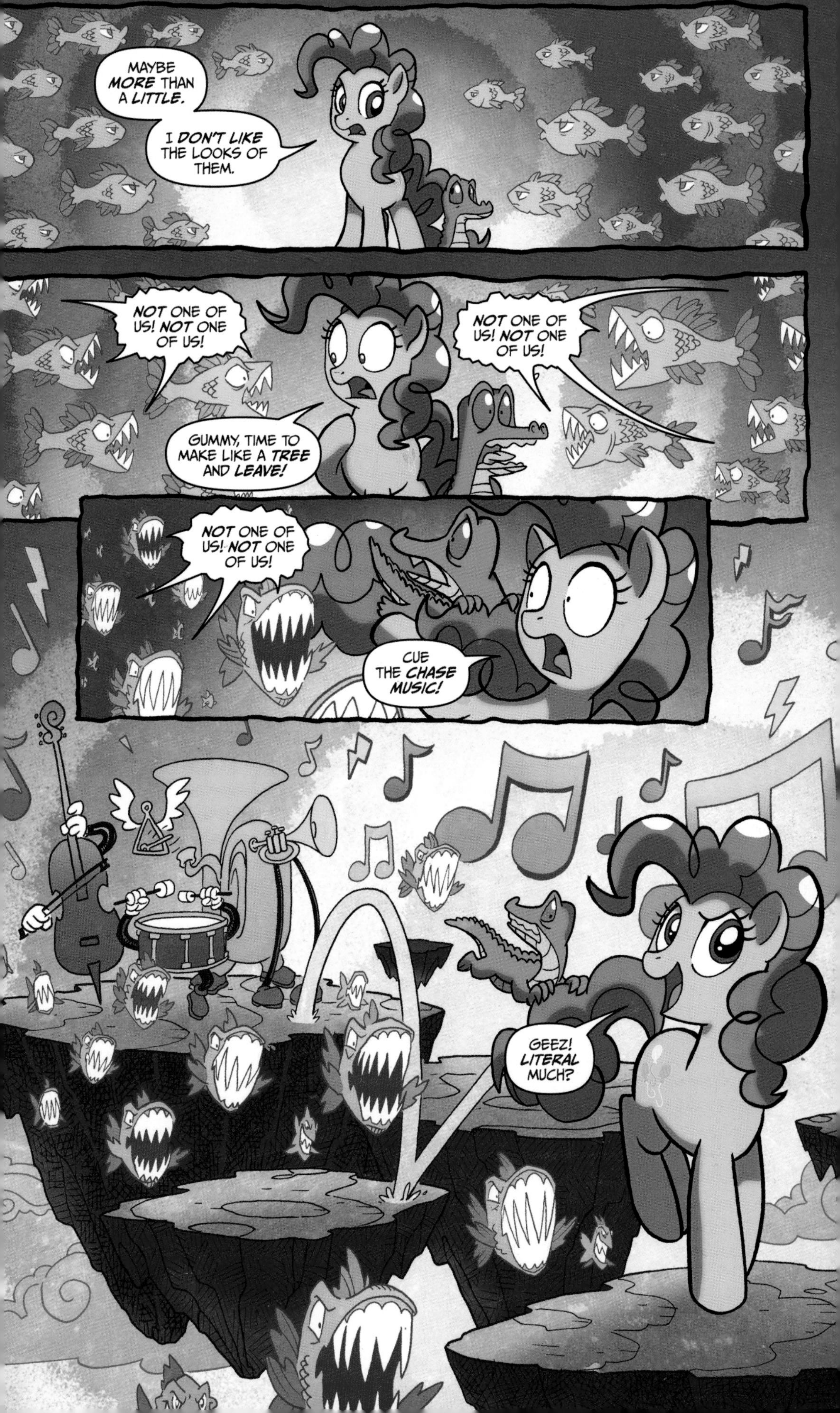
MAYBE MORE THAN A LITTLE.
I DON'T LIKE THE LOOKS OF THEM.
NOT ONE OF US! NOT ONE OF US!
NOT ONE OF US! NOT ONE OF US!
GUMMY, TIME TO MAKE LIKE A TREE AND LEAVE!
NOT ONE OF US! NOT ONE OF US!
CUE THE CHASE MUSIC!
GEEZ! LITERAL MUCH?

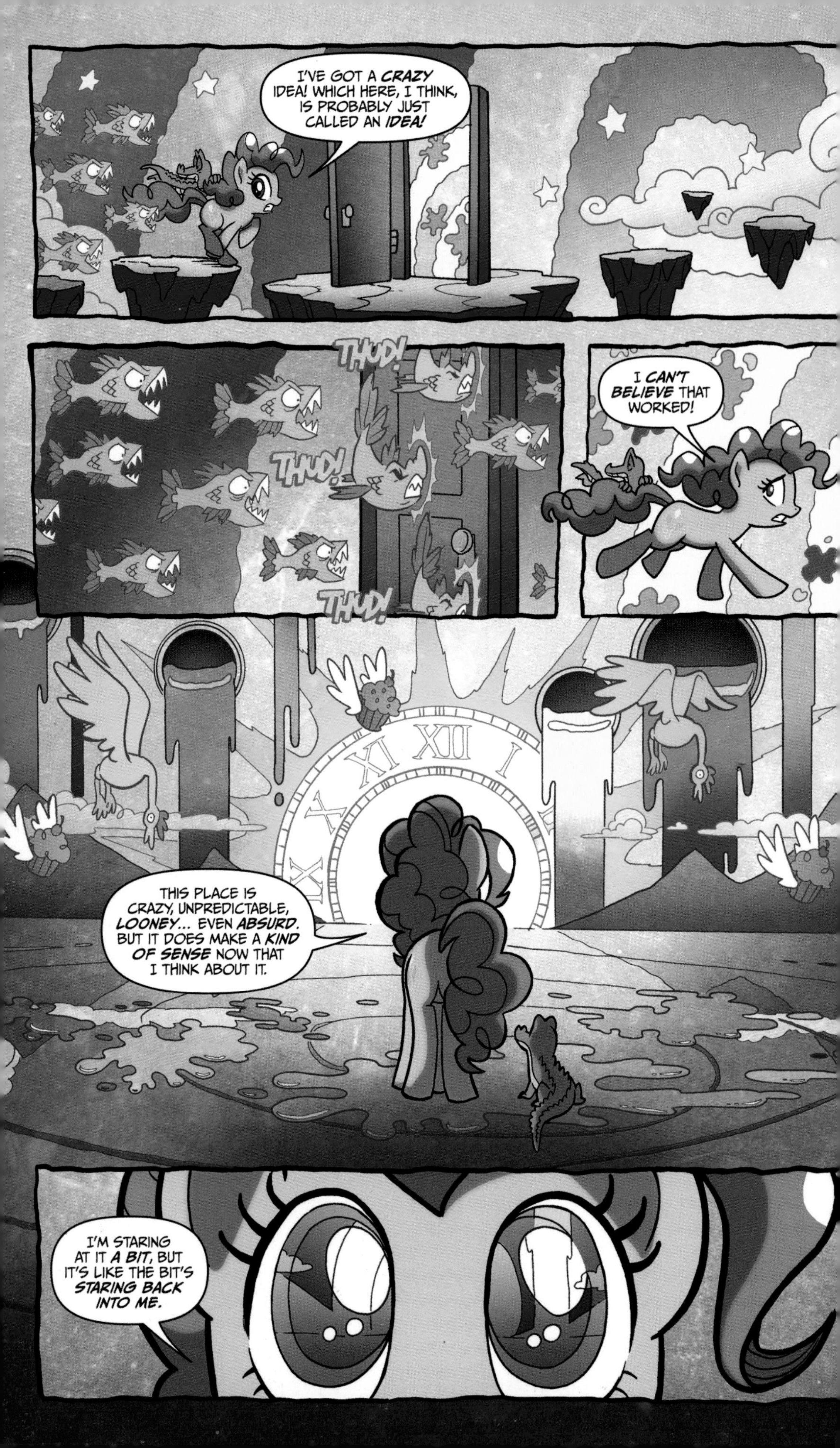
I'VE GOT A CRAZY IDEA! WHICH HERE, I THINK, IS PROBABLY JUST CALLED AN IDEA!
THUD!
THUD!
THUD!
I CAN'T BELIEVE THAT WORKED!
THIS PLACE IS CRAZY, UNPREDICTABLE, LOONEY... EVEN ABSURD. BUT IT DOES MAKE A KIND OF SENSE NOW THAT I THINK ABOUT IT.
I'M STARING AT IT A BIT, BUT IT'S LIKE THE BIT'S STARING BACK INTO ME.

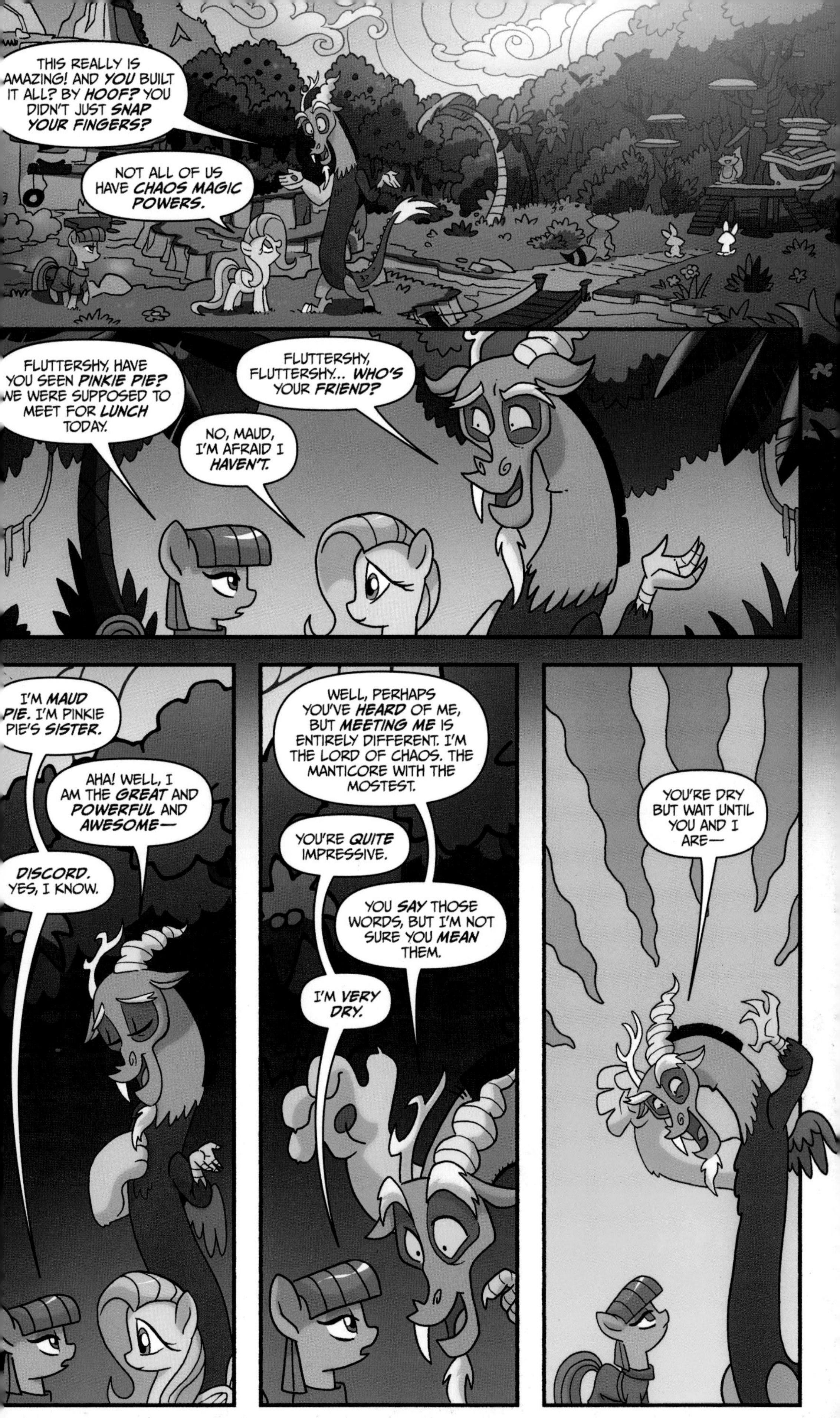
THIS REALLY IS AMAZING! AND YOU BUILT IT ALL? BY HOOF? YOU DIDN'T JUST SNAP YOUR FINGERS?
NOT ALL OF US HAVE CHAOS MAGIC POWERS.
FLUTTERSHY, HAVE YOU SEEN PINKIE PIE? WE WERE SUPPOSED TO MEET FOR LUNCH TODAY.
NO, MAUD, I'M AFRAID I HAVEN'T.
FLUTTERSHY, FLUTTERSHY... WHO'S YOUR FRIEND?
I'M MAUD PIE. I'M PINKIE PIE'S SISTER.
AHA! WELL, I AM THE GREAT AND POWERFUL AND AWESOME—
DISCORD. YES, I KNOW.
WELL, PERHAPS YOU'VE HEARD OF ME, BUT MEETING ME IS ENTIRELY DIFFERENT. I'M THE LORD OF CHAOS. THE MANTICORE WITH THE MOSTEST.
YOU'RE QUITE IMPRESSIVE.
YOU SAY THOSE WORDS, BUT I'M NOT SURE YOU MEAN THEM.
I'M VERY DRY.
YOU'RE DRY BUT WAIT UNTIL YOU AND I ARE—

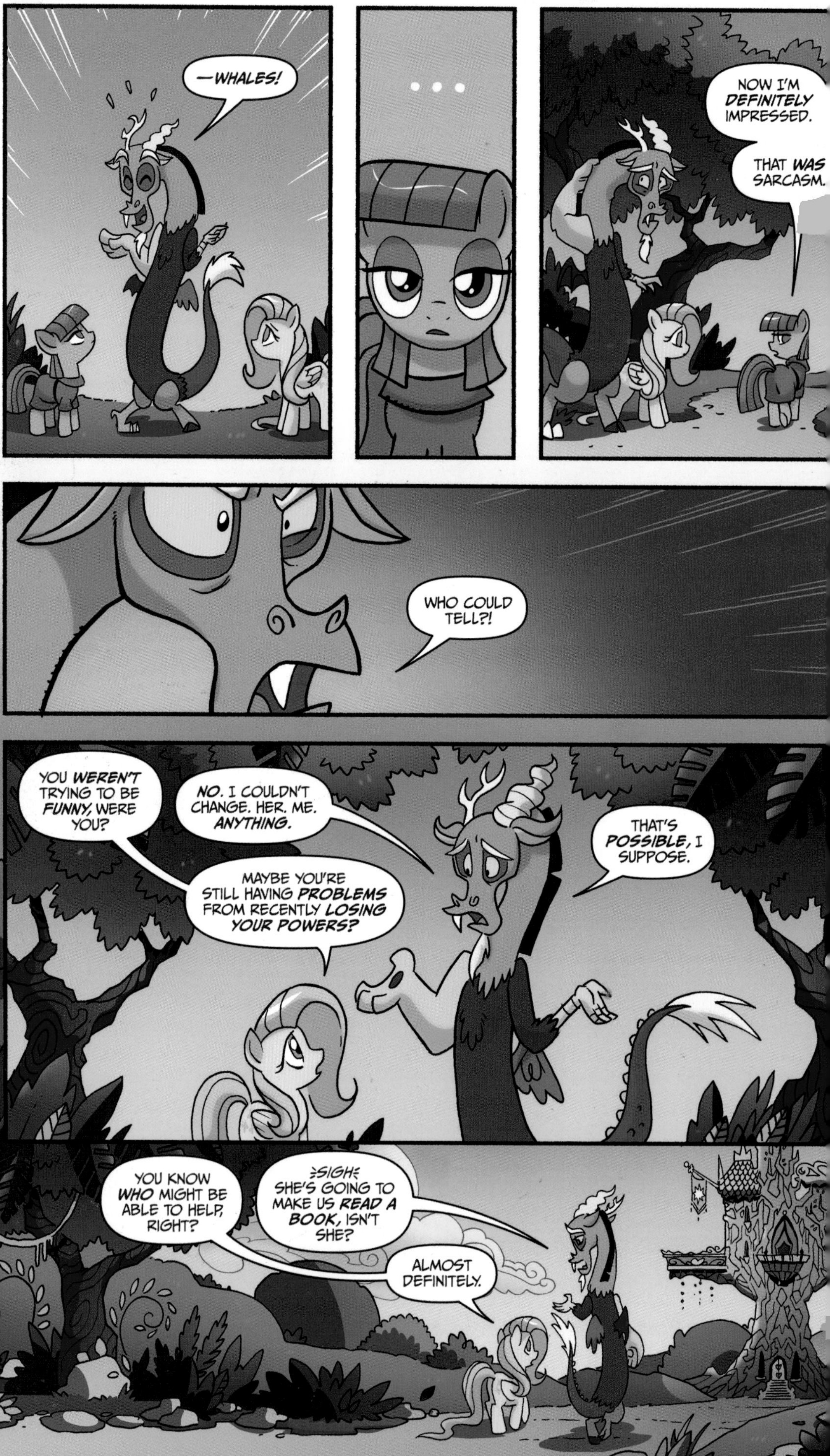
—WHALES!
. . .
NOW I'M DEFINITELY IMPRESSED.
THAT WAS SARCASM.
WHO COULD TELL?!
YOU WEREN'T TRYING TO BE FUNNY, WERE YOU?
NO. I COULDN'T CHANGE. HER. ME. ANYTHING.
MAYBE YOU'RE STILL HAVING PROBLEMS FROM RECENTLY LOSING YOUR POWERS?
THAT'S POSSIBLE, I SUPPOSE.
YOU KNOW WHO MIGHT BE ABLE TO HELP, RIGHT?
SIGH
SHE'S GOING TO MAKE US READ A BOOK, ISN'T SHE?
ALMOST DEFINITELY.

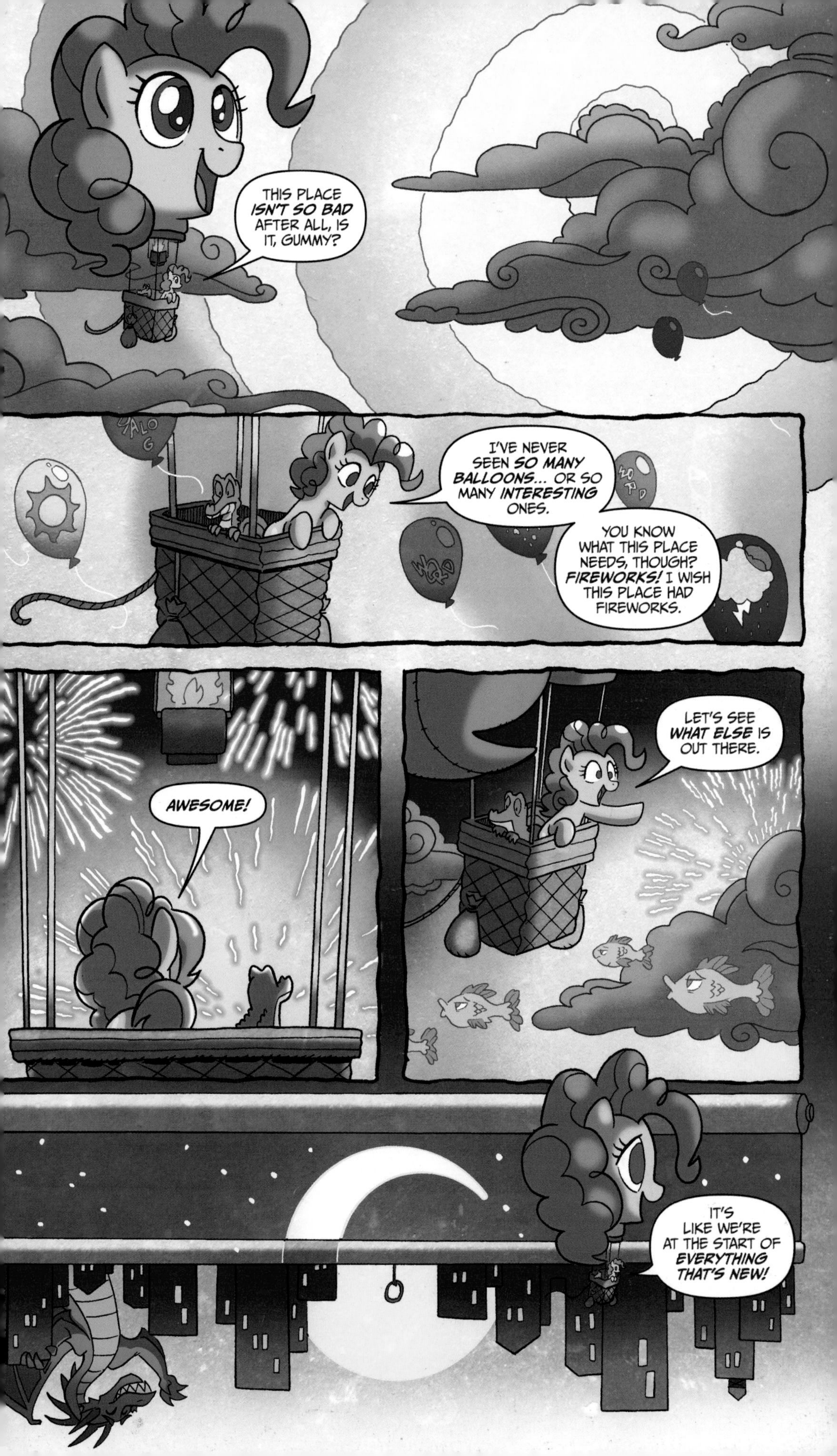
THIS PLACE ISN'T SO BAD AFTER ALL, IS IT, GUMMY?
I'VE NEVER SEEN SO MANY BALLOONS... OR SO MANY INTERESTING ONES.
YOU KNOW WHAT THIS PLACE NEEDS, THOUGH? FIREWORKS! I WISH THIS PLACE HAD FIREWORKS.
AWESOME!
LET'S SEE WHAT ELSE IS OUT THERE.
IT'S LIKE WE'RE AT THE START OF EVERYTHING THAT'S NEW!

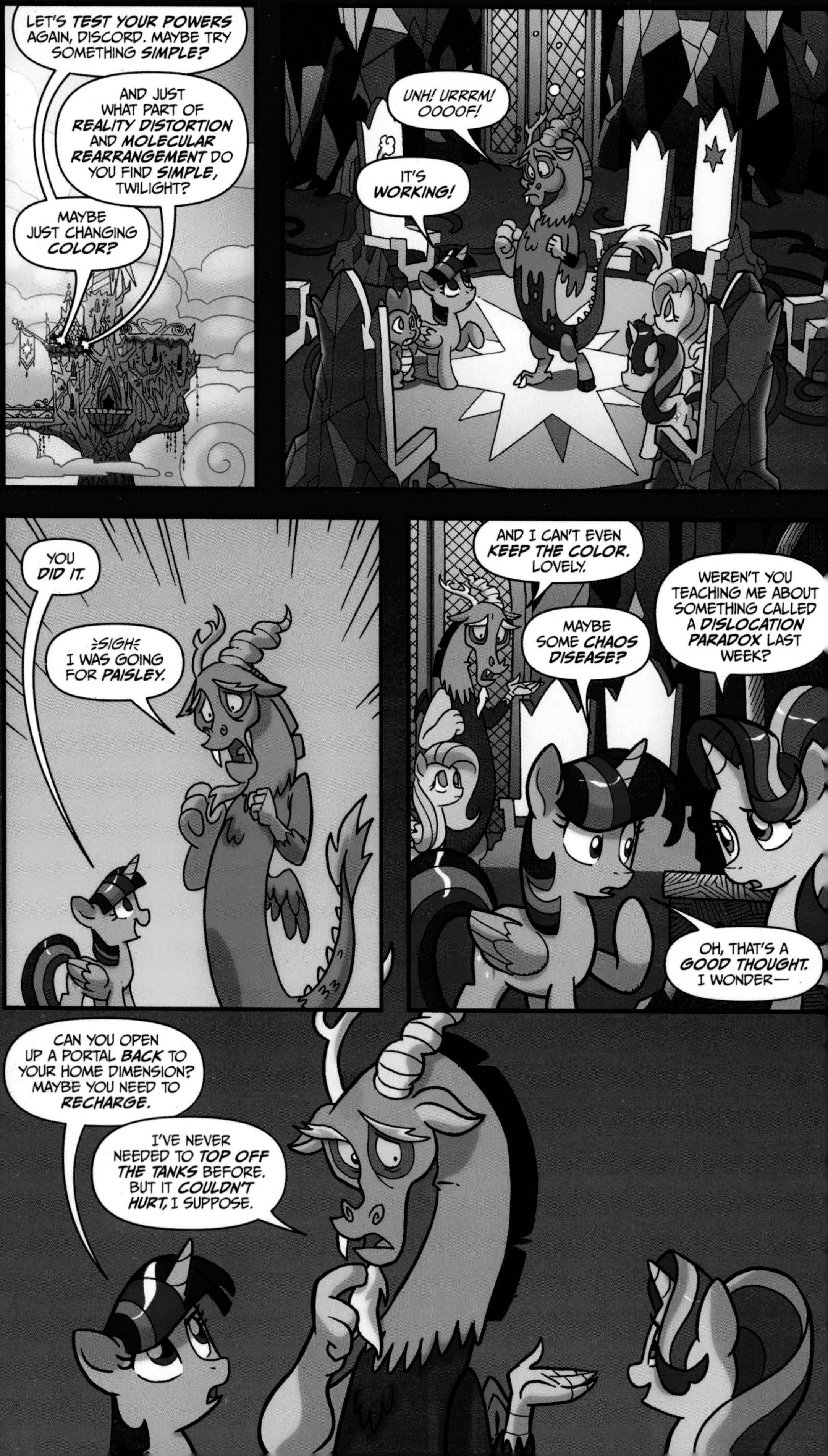

LET'S *TEST YOUR POWERS* AGAIN, DISCORD. MAYBE TRY SOMETHING *SIMPLE?*
AND JUST WHAT PART OF *REALITY DISTORTION* AND *MOLECULAR REARRANGEMENT* DO YOU FIND *SIMPLE,* TWILIGHT?
MAYBE JUST CHANGING *COLOR?*
UNH! URRRM! OOOOF!
IT'S *WORKING!*
YOU *DID IT.*
SIGH I WAS GOING FOR *PAISLEY.*
AND I CAN'T EVEN *KEEP THE COLOR.* LOVELY.
MAYBE SOME *CHAOS DISEASE?*
WEREN'T YOU TEACHING ME ABOUT SOMETHING CALLED A *DISLOCATION PARADOX* LAST WEEK?
OH, THAT'S A *GOOD THOUGHT.* I WONDER—
CAN YOU OPEN UP A PORTAL *BACK* TO YOUR HOME DIMENSION? MAYBE YOU NEED TO *RECHARGE.*
I'VE NEVER NEEDED TO *TOP OFF THE TANKS* BEFORE. BUT IT *COULDN'T HURT,* I SUPPOSE.

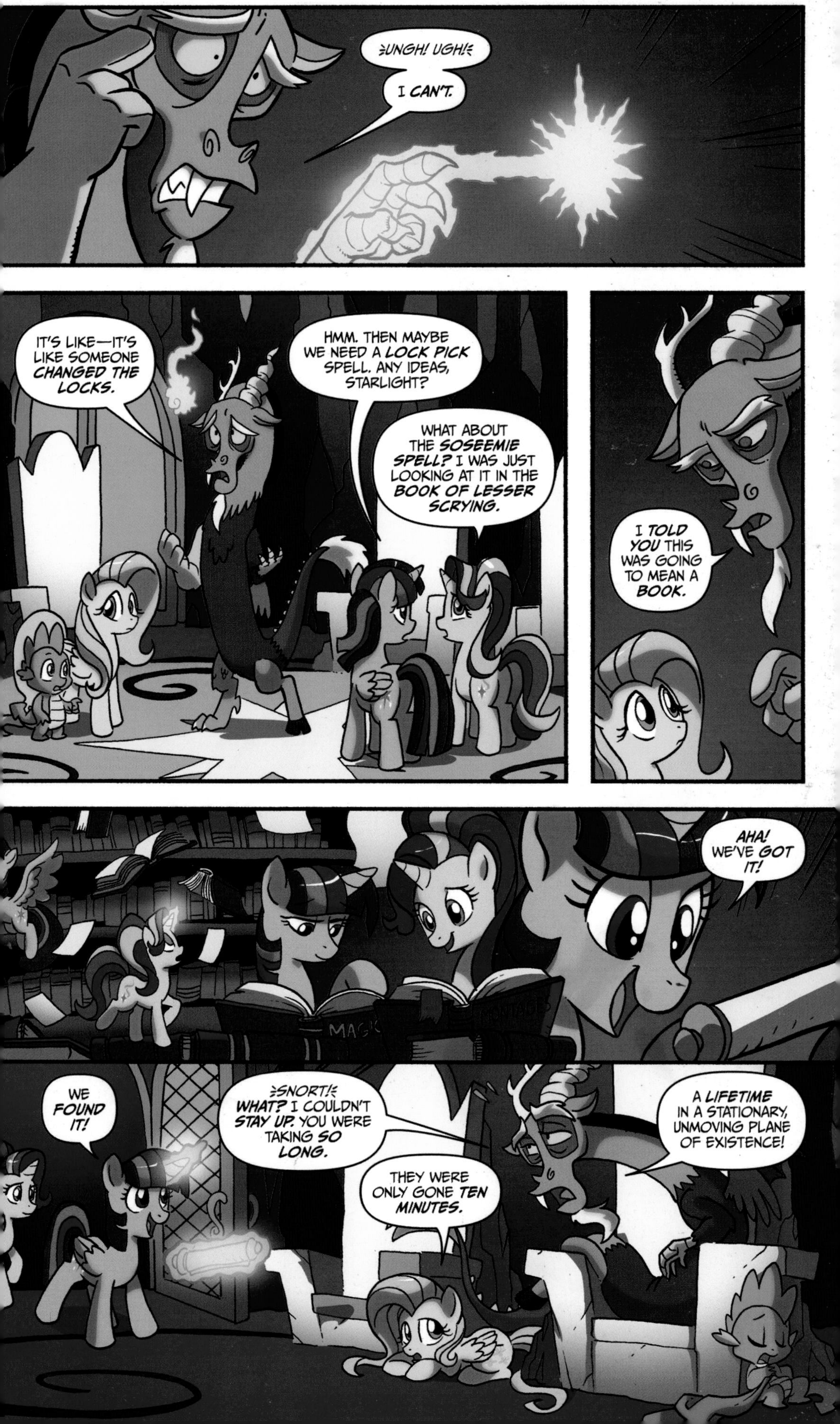

UNGH! UGH!
I CAN'T.
IT'S LIKE—IT'S LIKE SOMEONE CHANGED THE LOCKS.
HMM. THEN MAYBE WE NEED A LOCK PICK SPELL. ANY IDEAS, STARLIGHT?
WHAT ABOUT THE SOSEEMIE SPELL? I WAS JUST LOOKING AT IT IN THE BOOK OF LESSER SCRYING.
I TOLD YOU THIS WAS GOING TO MEAN A BOOK.
AHA! WE'VE GOT IT!
WE FOUND IT!
SNORT! WHAT? I COULDN'T STAY UP. YOU WERE TAKING SO LONG.
THEY WERE ONLY GONE TEN MINUTES.
A LIFETIME IN A STATIONARY, UNMOVING PLANE OF EXISTENCE!

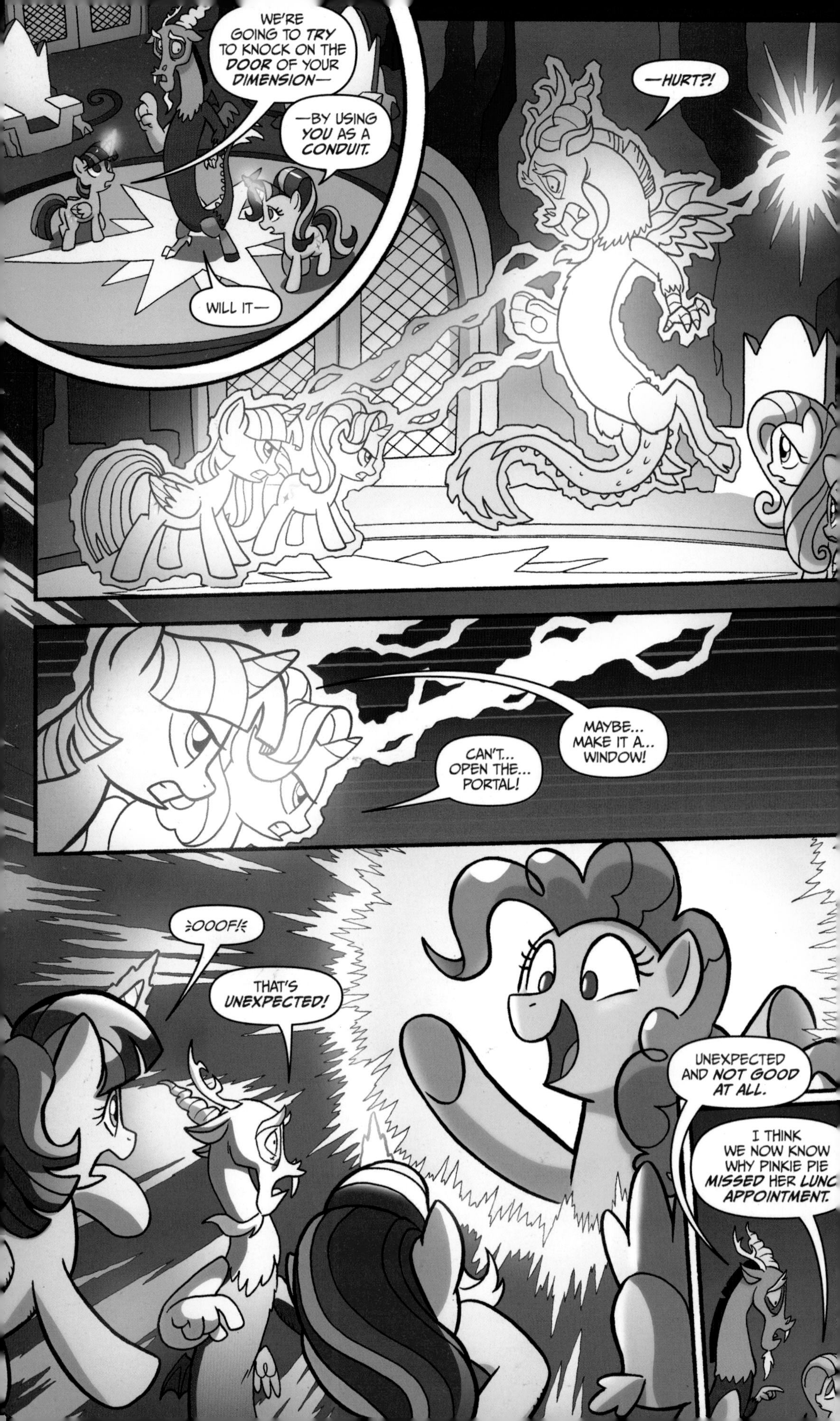
WE'RE GOING TO TRY TO KNOCK ON THE DOOR OF YOUR DIMENSION—
—BY USING YOU AS A CONDUIT.
WILL IT—
—HURT?!
CAN'T... OPEN THE... PORTAL!
MAYBE... MAKE IT A... WINDOW!
OOOF!
THAT'S UNEXPECTED!
UNEXPECTED AND NOT GOOD AT ALL.
I THINK WE NOW KNOW WHY PINKIE PIE MISSED HER LUNC APPOINTMENT.

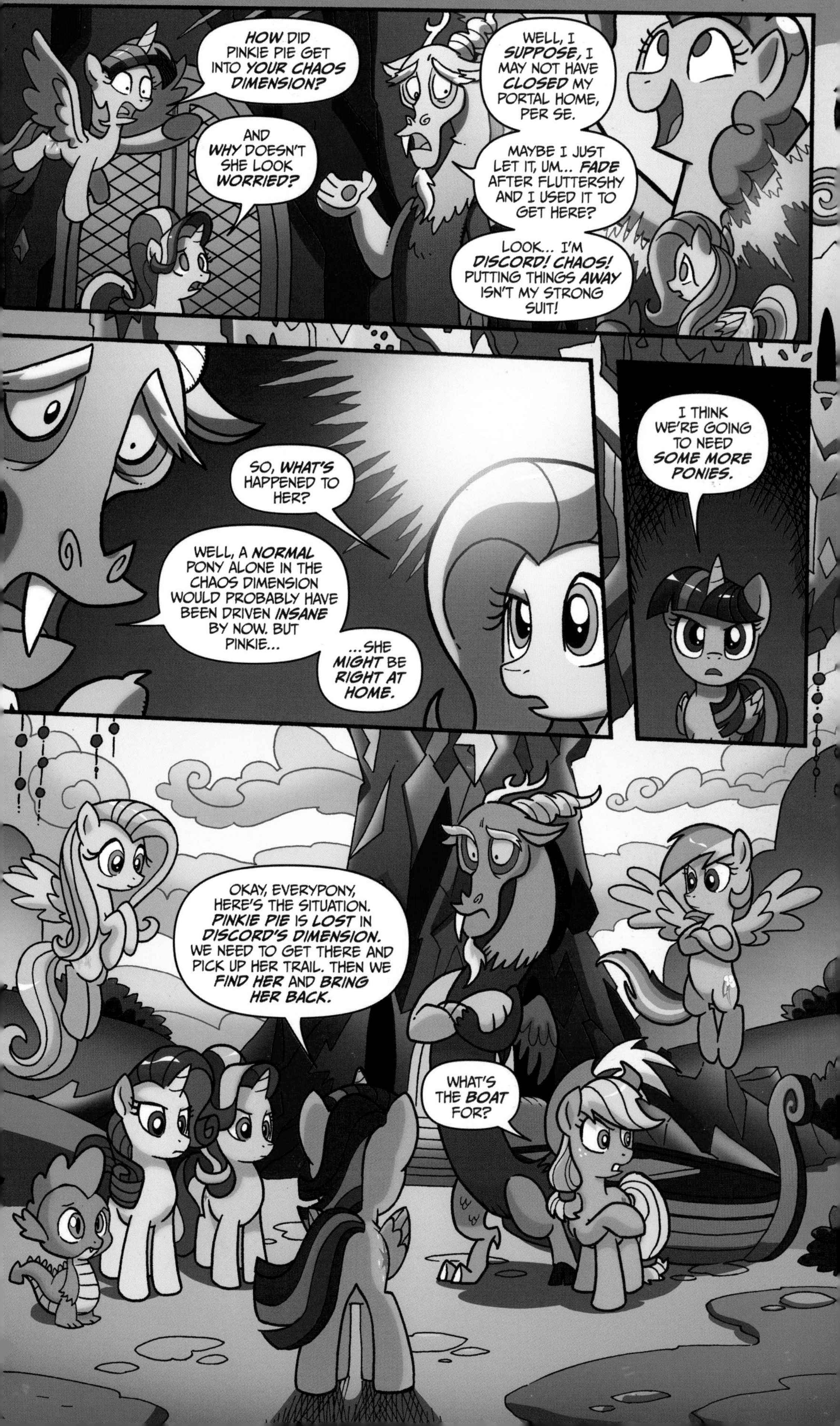
HOW DID PINKIE PIE GET INTO YOUR CHAOS DIMENSION?
AND WHY DOESN'T SHE LOOK WORRIED?
WELL, I SUPPOSE, I MAY NOT HAVE CLOSED MY PORTAL HOME, PER SE.
MAYBE I JUST LET IT, UM... FADE AFTER FLUTTERSHY AND I USED IT TO GET HERE?
LOOK... I'M DISCORD! CHAOS! PUTTING THINGS AWAY ISN'T MY STRONG SUIT!
SO, WHAT'S HAPPENED TO HER?
WELL, A NORMAL PONY ALONE IN THE CHAOS DIMENSION WOULD PROBABLY HAVE BEEN DRIVEN INSANE BY NOW. BUT PINKIE...
...SHE MIGHT BE RIGHT AT HOME.
I THINK WE'RE GOING TO NEED SOME MORE PONIES.
OKAY, EVERYPONY, HERE'S THE SITUATION. PINKIE PIE IS LOST IN DISCORD'S DIMENSION. WE NEED TO GET THERE AND PICK UP HER TRAIL. THEN WE FIND HER AND BRING HER BACK.
WHAT'S THE BOAT FOR?

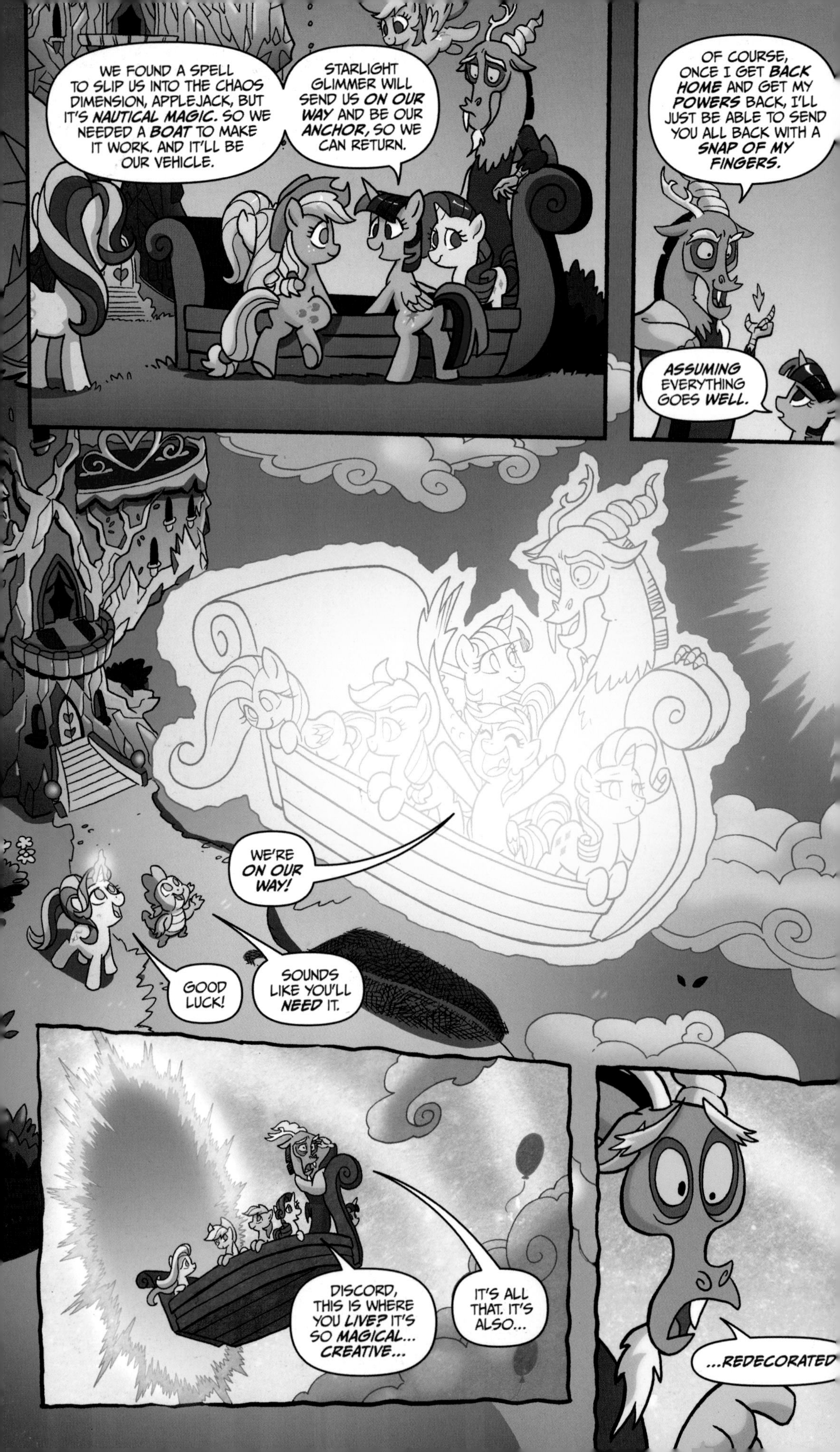

WE FOUND A SPELL TO SLIP US INTO THE CHAOS DIMENSION, APPLEJACK, BUT IT'S **NAUTICAL MAGIC.** SO WE NEEDED A **BOAT** TO MAKE IT WORK. AND IT'LL BE OUR VEHICLE.
STARLIGHT GLIMMER WILL SEND US **ON OUR WAY** AND BE OUR **ANCHOR,** SO WE CAN RETURN.
OF COURSE, ONCE I GET **BACK HOME** AND GET MY **POWERS** BACK, I'LL JUST BE ABLE TO SEND YOU ALL BACK WITH A **SNAP OF MY FINGERS.**
ASSUMING EVERYTHING GOES **WELL.**
WE'RE **ON OUR WAY!**
GOOD LUCK!
SOUNDS LIKE YOU'LL **NEED** IT.
DISCORD, THIS IS WHERE YOU **LIVE?** IT'S SO **MAGICAL... CREATIVE...**
IT'S ALL THAT. IT'S ALSO...
...REDECORATED

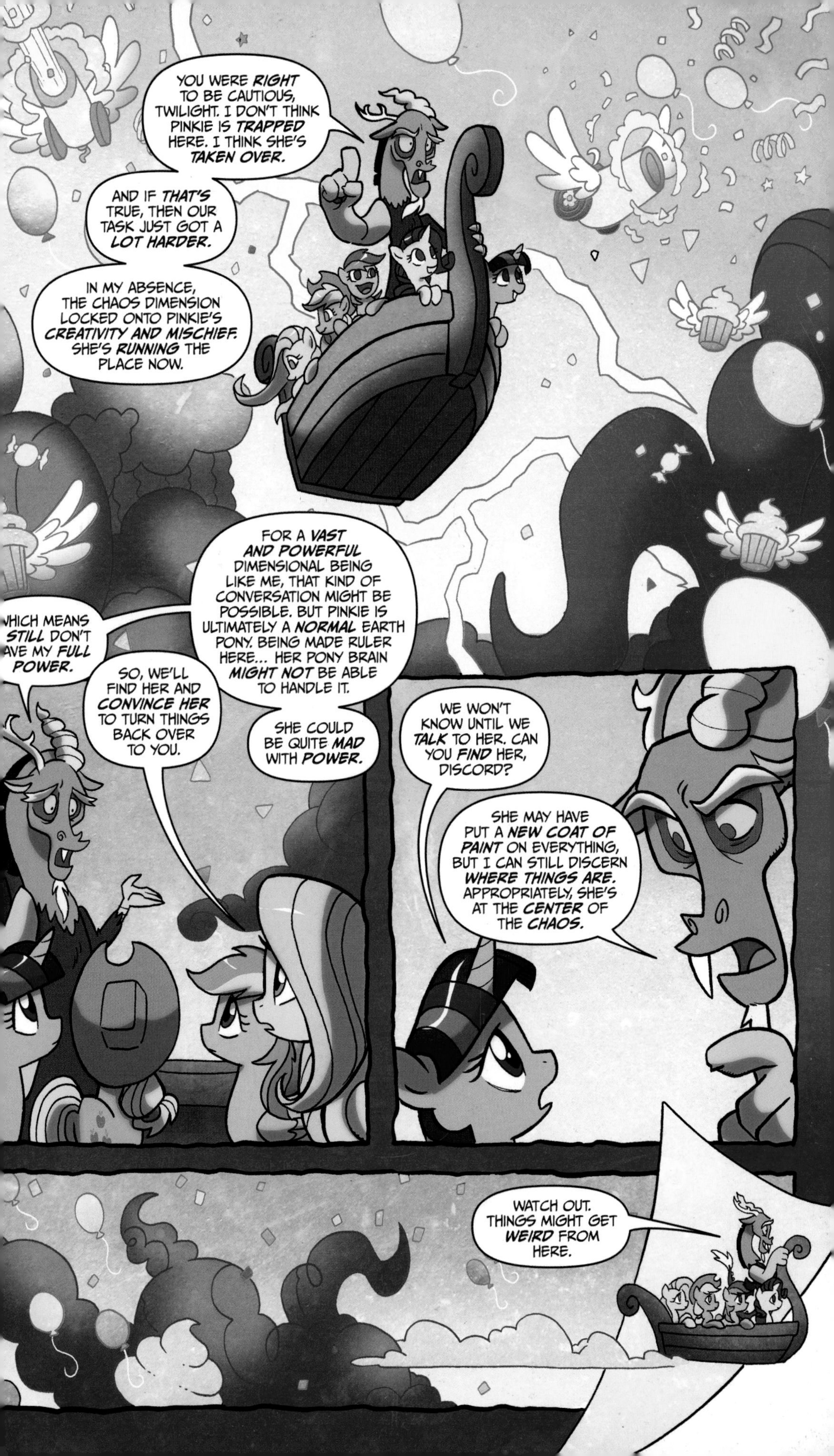
YOU WERE RIGHT TO BE CAUTIOUS, TWILIGHT. I DON'T THINK PINKIE IS TRAPPED HERE. I THINK SHE'S TAKEN OVER.
AND IF THAT'S TRUE, THEN OUR TASK JUST GOT A LOT HARDER.
IN MY ABSENCE, THE CHAOS DIMENSION LOCKED ONTO PINKIE'S CREATIVITY AND MISCHIEF. SHE'S RUNNING THE PLACE NOW.
WHICH MEANS STILL DON'T AVE MY FULL POWER.
SO, WE'LL FIND HER AND CONVINCE HER TO TURN THINGS BACK OVER TO YOU.
FOR A VAST AND POWERFUL DIMENSIONAL BEING LIKE ME, THAT KIND OF CONVERSATION MIGHT BE POSSIBLE. BUT PINKIE IS ULTIMATELY A NORMAL EARTH PONY. BEING MADE RULER HERE... HER PONY BRAIN MIGHT NOT BE ABLE TO HANDLE IT.
SHE COULD BE QUITE MAD WITH POWER.
WE WON'T KNOW UNTIL WE TALK TO HER. CAN YOU FIND HER, DISCORD?
SHE MAY HAVE PUT A NEW COAT OF PAINT ON EVERYTHING, BUT I CAN STILL DISCERN WHERE THINGS ARE. APPROPRIATELY, SHE'S AT THE CENTER OF THE CHAOS.
WATCH OUT. THINGS MIGHT GET WEIRD FROM HERE.

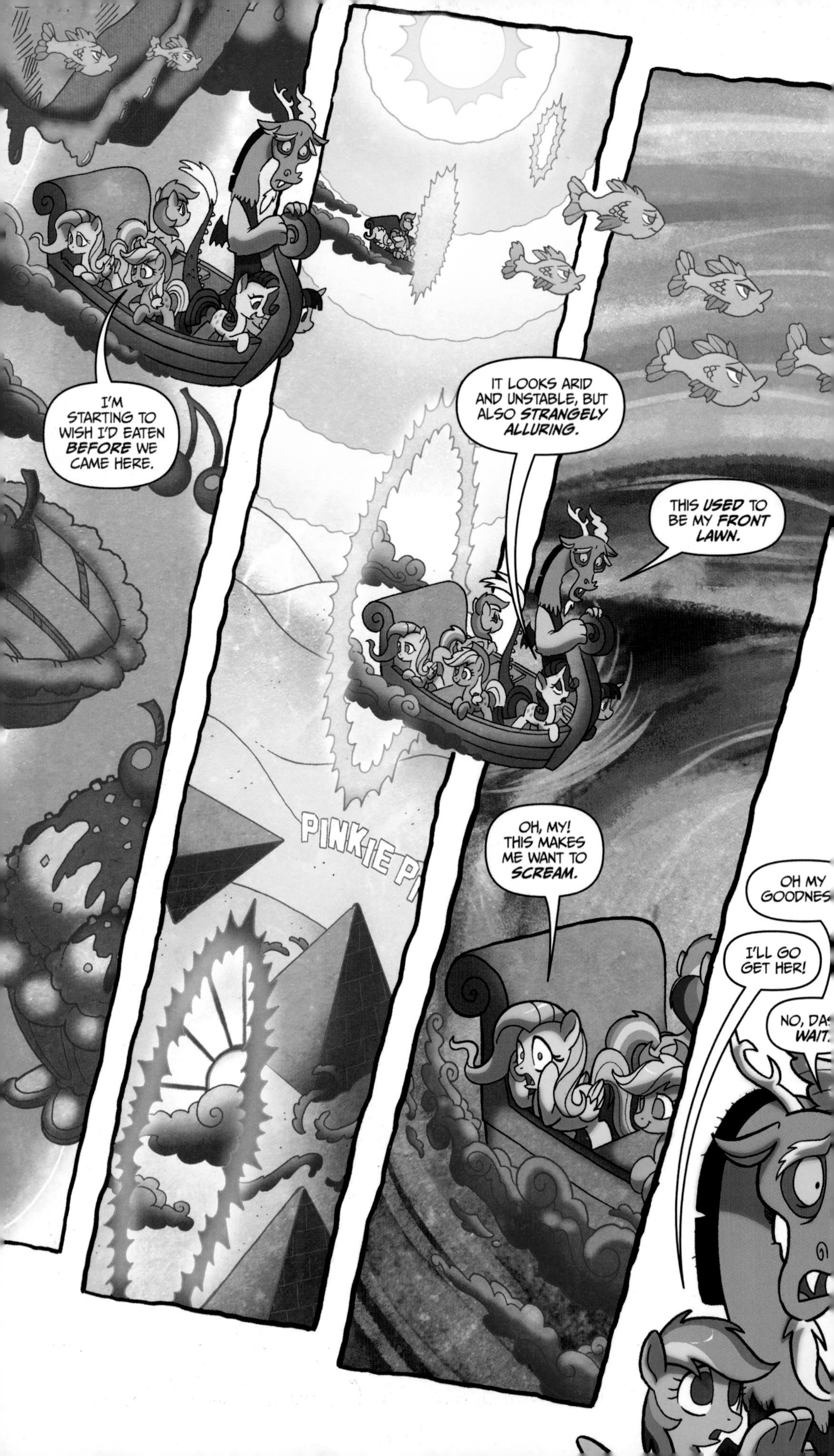
I'M STARTING TO WISH I'D EATEN BEFORE WE CAME HERE.
IT LOOKS ARID AND UNSTABLE, BUT ALSO STRANGELY ALLURING.
PINKIE PI
THIS USED TO BE MY FRONT LAWN.
OH, MY! THIS MAKES ME WANT TO SCREAM.
OH MY GOODNES
I'LL GO GET HER!
NO, DA WAIT.

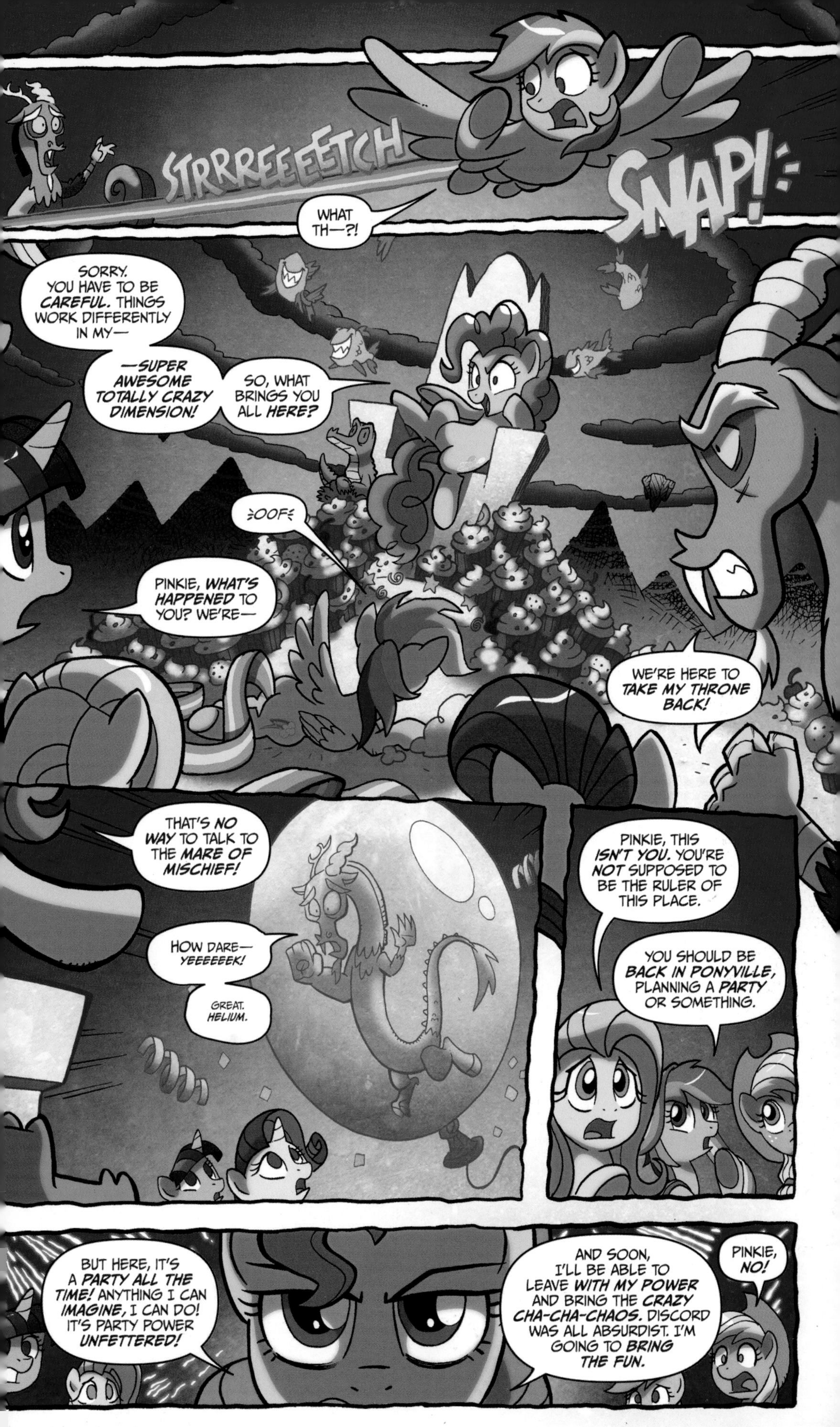
STRRREEEETCH
SNAP!
WHAT TH—?!
SORRY. YOU HAVE TO BE CAREFUL. THINGS WORK DIFFERENTLY IN MY—
—SUPER AWESOME TOTALLY CRAZY DIMENSION!
SO, WHAT BRINGS YOU ALL HERE?
OOF
PINKIE, WHAT'S HAPPENED TO YOU? WE'RE—
WE'RE HERE TO TAKE MY THRONE BACK!
THAT'S NO WAY TO TALK TO THE MARE OF MISCHIEF!
HOW DARE— YEEEEEEK!
GREAT. HELIUM.
PINKIE, THIS ISN'T YOU. YOU'RE NOT SUPPOSED TO BE THE RULER OF THIS PLACE.
YOU SHOULD BE BACK IN PONYVILLE, PLANNING A PARTY OR SOMETHING.
BUT HERE, IT'S A PARTY ALL THE TIME! ANYTHING I CAN IMAGINE, I CAN DO! IT'S PARTY POWER UNFETTERED!
AND SOON, I'LL BE ABLE TO LEAVE WITH MY POWER AND BRING THE CRAZY CHA-CHA-CHAOS. DISCORD WAS ALL ABSURDIST. I'M GOING TO BRING THE FUN.
PINKIE, NO!

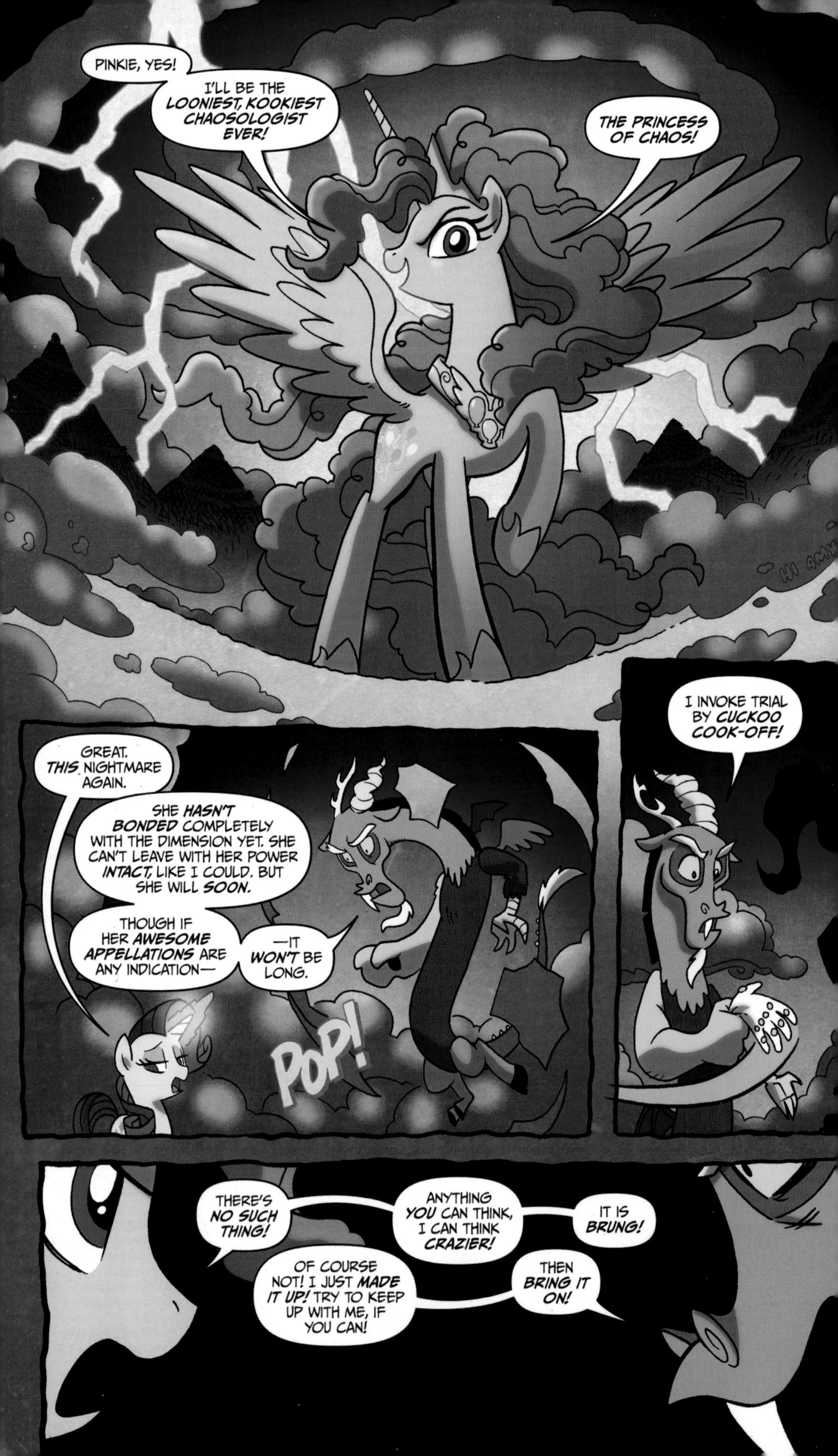
PINKIE, YES!
I'LL BE THE LOONIEST, KOOKIEST CHAOSOLOGIST EVER!
THE PRINCESS OF CHAOS!
GREAT. THIS NIGHTMARE AGAIN.
SHE HASN'T BONDED COMPLETELY WITH THE DIMENSION YET. SHE CAN'T LEAVE WITH HER POWER INTACT, LIKE I COULD. BUT SHE WILL SOON.
THOUGH IF HER AWESOME APPELLATIONS ARE ANY INDICATION—
—IT WON'T BE LONG.
POP!
I INVOKE TRIAL BY CUCKOO COOK-OFF!
THERE'S NO SUCH THING!
ANYTHING YOU CAN THINK, I CAN THINK CRAZIER!
IT IS BRUNG!
OF COURSE NOT! I JUST MADE IT UP! TRY TO KEEP UP WITH ME, IF YOU CAN!
THEN BRING IT ON!

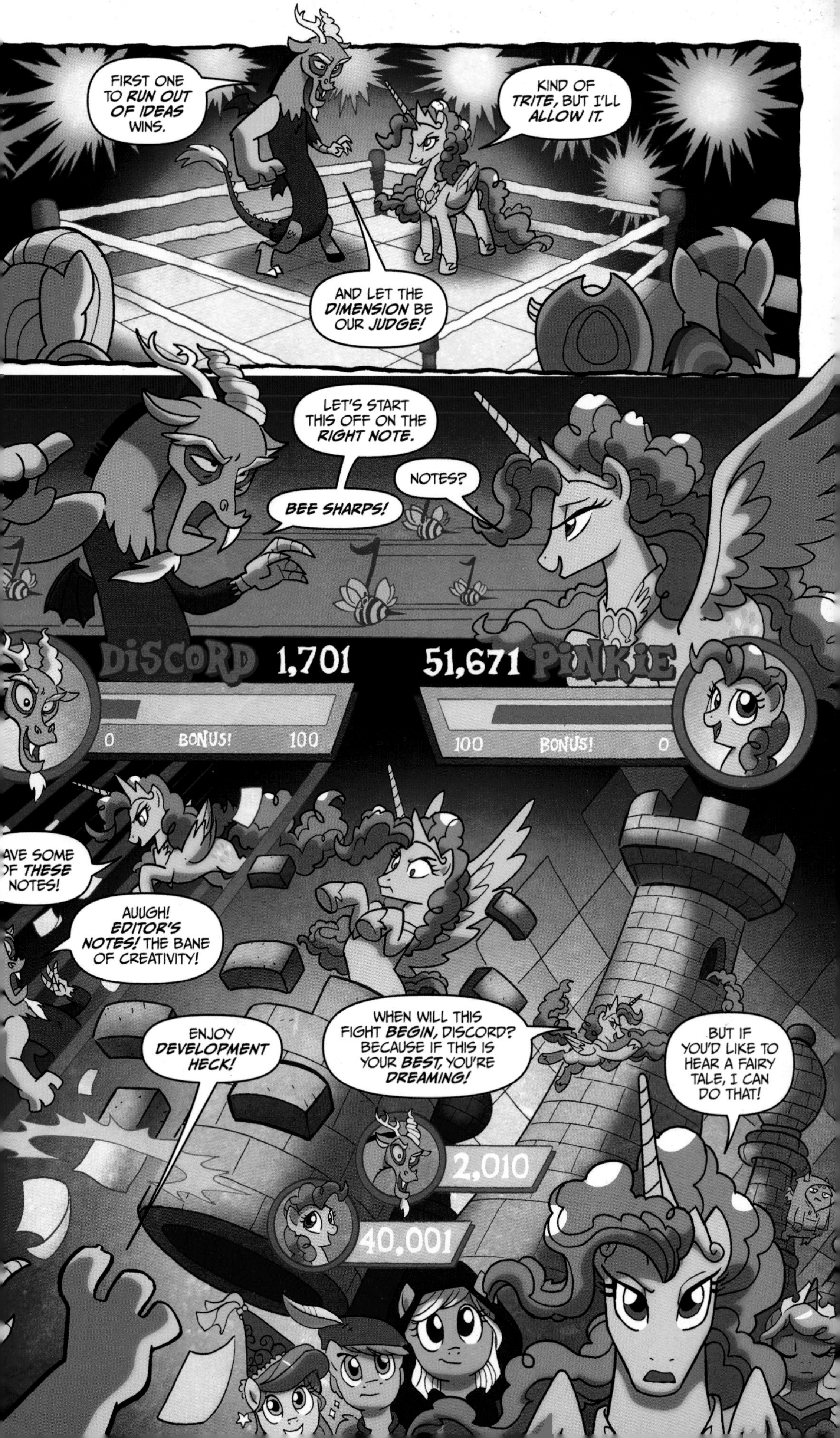

FIRST ONE TO RUN OUT OF IDEAS WINS.
KIND OF TRITE, BUT I'LL ALLOW IT.
AND LET THE DIMENSION BE OUR JUDGE!
LET'S START THIS OFF ON THE RIGHT NOTE.
NOTES?
BEE SHARPS!
DISCORD 1,701
51,671 PINKIE
0 BONUS! 100
100 BONUS! 0
AVE SOME OF THESE NOTES!
AUUGH! EDITOR'S NOTES! THE BANE OF CREATIVITY!
ENJOY DEVELOPMENT HECK!
WHEN WILL THIS FIGHT BEGIN, DISCORD? BECAUSE IF THIS IS YOUR BEST, YOU'RE DREAMING!
BUT IF YOU'D LIKE TO HEAR A FAIRY TALE, I CAN DO THAT!
2,010
40,001

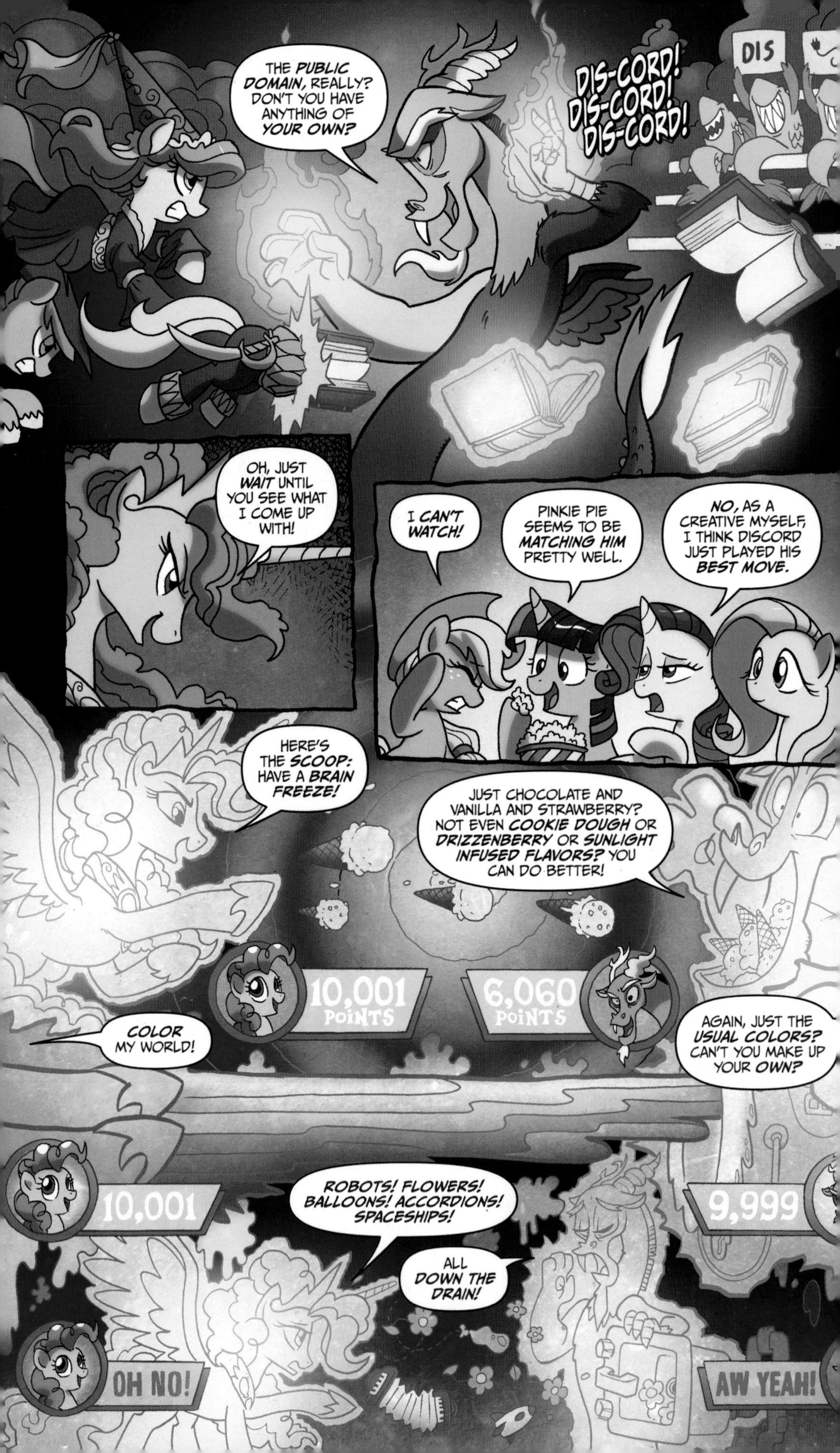
THE PUBLIC DOMAIN, REALLY? DON'T YOU HAVE ANYTHING OF YOUR OWN?
DIS-CORD! DIS-CORD! DIS-CORD!
DIS
OH, JUST WAIT UNTIL YOU SEE WHAT I COME UP WITH!
I CAN'T WATCH!
PINKIE PIE SEEMS TO BE MATCHING HIM PRETTY WELL.
NO, AS A CREATIVE MYSELF, I THINK DISCORD JUST PLAYED HIS BEST MOVE.
HERE'S THE SCOOP: HAVE A BRAIN FREEZE!
JUST CHOCOLATE AND VANILLA AND STRAWBERRY? NOT EVEN COOKIE DOUGH OR DRIZZENBERRY OR SUNLIGHT INFUSED FLAVORS? YOU CAN DO BETTER!
10,001 POINTS
6,060 POINTS
COLOR MY WORLD!
AGAIN, JUST THE USUAL COLORS? CAN'T YOU MAKE UP YOUR OWN?
10,001
ROBOTS! FLOWERS! BALLOONS! ACCORDIONS! SPACESHIPS!
9,999
ALL DOWN THE DRAIN!
OH NO!
AW YEAH!

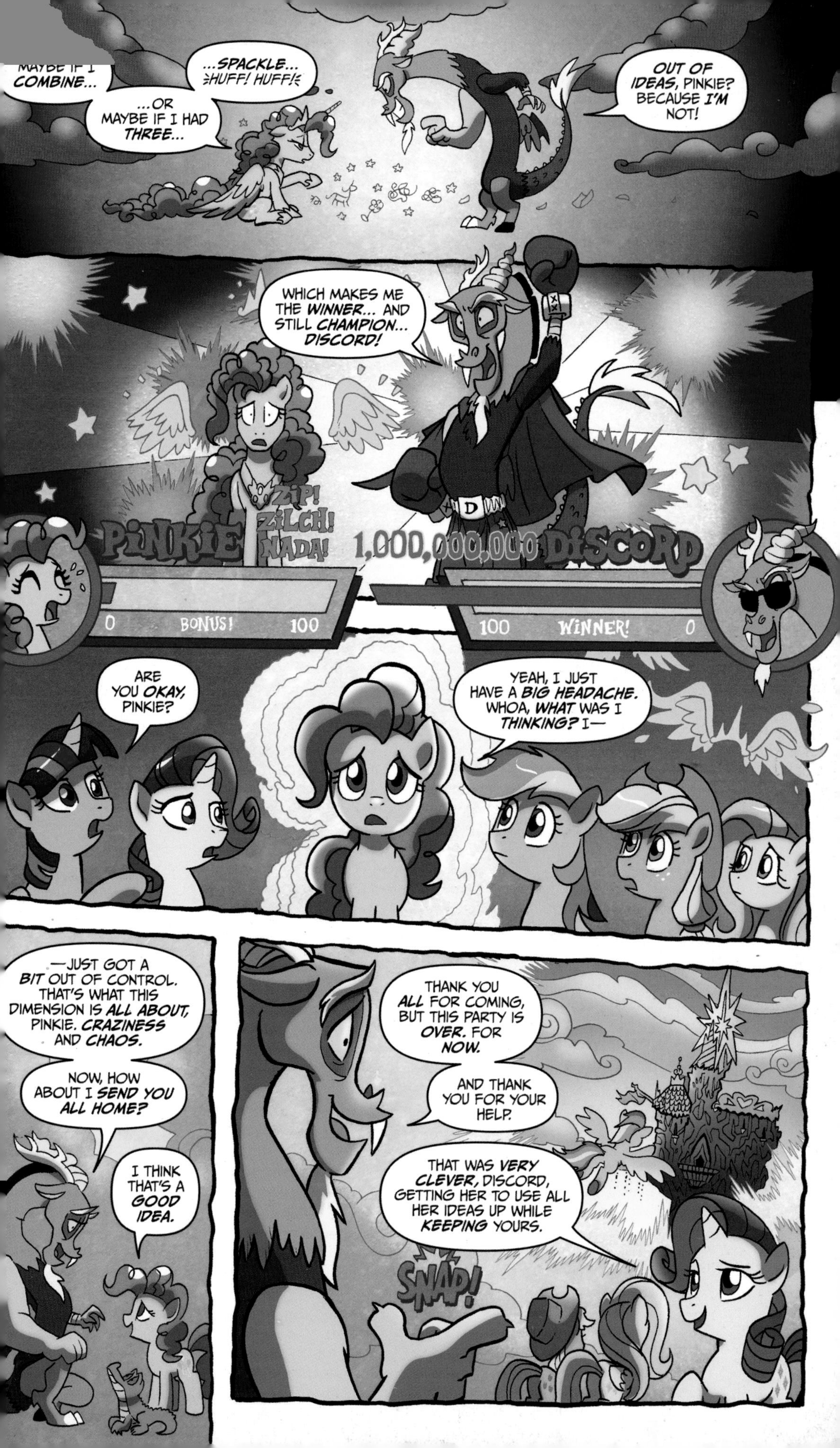

MAYBE IF I COMBINE...
...SPACKLE... HUFF! HUFF!
...OR MAYBE IF I HAD THREE...
OUT OF IDEAS, PINKIE? BECAUSE I'M NOT!
WHICH MAKES ME THE WINNER... AND STILL CHAMPION... DISCORD!
ZIP! ZILCH! NADA!
1,000,000,000
PINKIE
DISCORD
0 BONUS! 100
100 WINNER! 0
ARE YOU OKAY, PINKIE?
YEAH, I JUST HAVE A BIG HEADACHE. WHOA, WHAT WAS I THINKING? I—
—JUST GOT A BIT OUT OF CONTROL. THAT'S WHAT THIS DIMENSION IS ALL ABOUT, PINKIE. CRAZINESS AND CHAOS.
NOW, HOW ABOUT I SEND YOU ALL HOME?
I THINK THAT'S A GOOD IDEA.
THANK YOU ALL FOR COMING, BUT THIS PARTY IS OVER. FOR NOW.
AND THANK YOU FOR YOUR HELP.
THAT WAS VERY CLEVER, DISCORD, GETTING HER TO USE ALL HER IDEAS UP WHILE KEEPING YOURS.
SNAP!

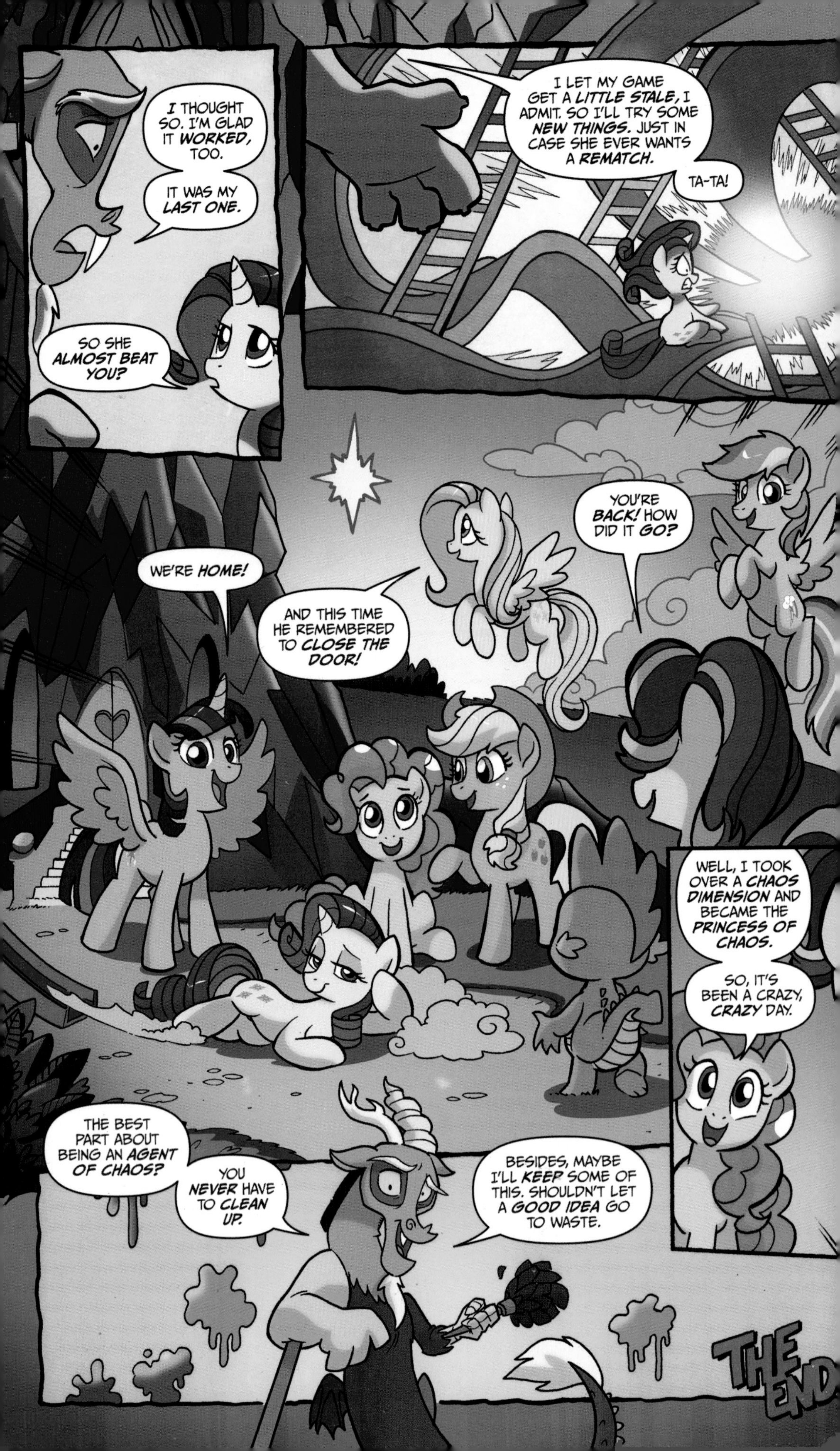
I THOUGHT SO. I'M GLAD IT WORKED, TOO.
IT WAS MY LAST ONE.
SO SHE ALMOST BEAT YOU?
I LET MY GAME GET A LITTLE STALE, I ADMIT. SO I'LL TRY SOME NEW THINGS. JUST IN CASE SHE EVER WANTS A REMATCH.
TA-TA!
WE'RE HOME!
AND THIS TIME HE REMEMBERED TO CLOSE THE DOOR!
YOU'RE BACK! HOW DID IT GO?
WELL, I TOOK OVER A CHAOS DIMENSION AND BECAME THE PRINCESS OF CHAOS.
SO, IT'S BEEN A CRAZY, CRAZY DAY.
THE BEST PART ABOUT BEING AN AGENT OF CHAOS?
YOU NEVER HAVE TO CLEAN UP.
BESIDES, MAYBE I'LL KEEP SOME OF THIS. SHOULDN'T LET A GOOD IDEA GO TO WASTE.
THE END

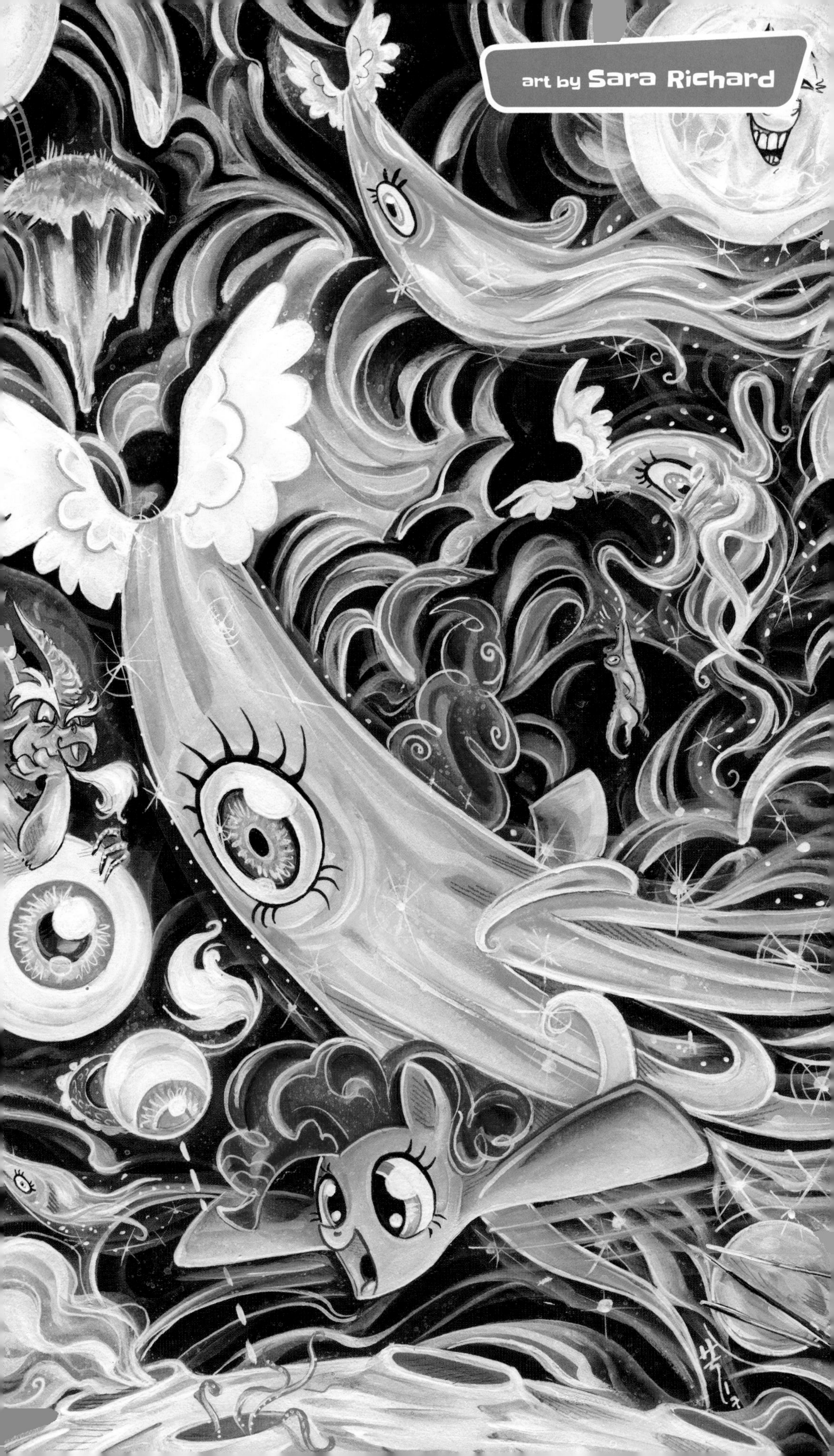

art by Sara Richard

art by Agnes Garbowska

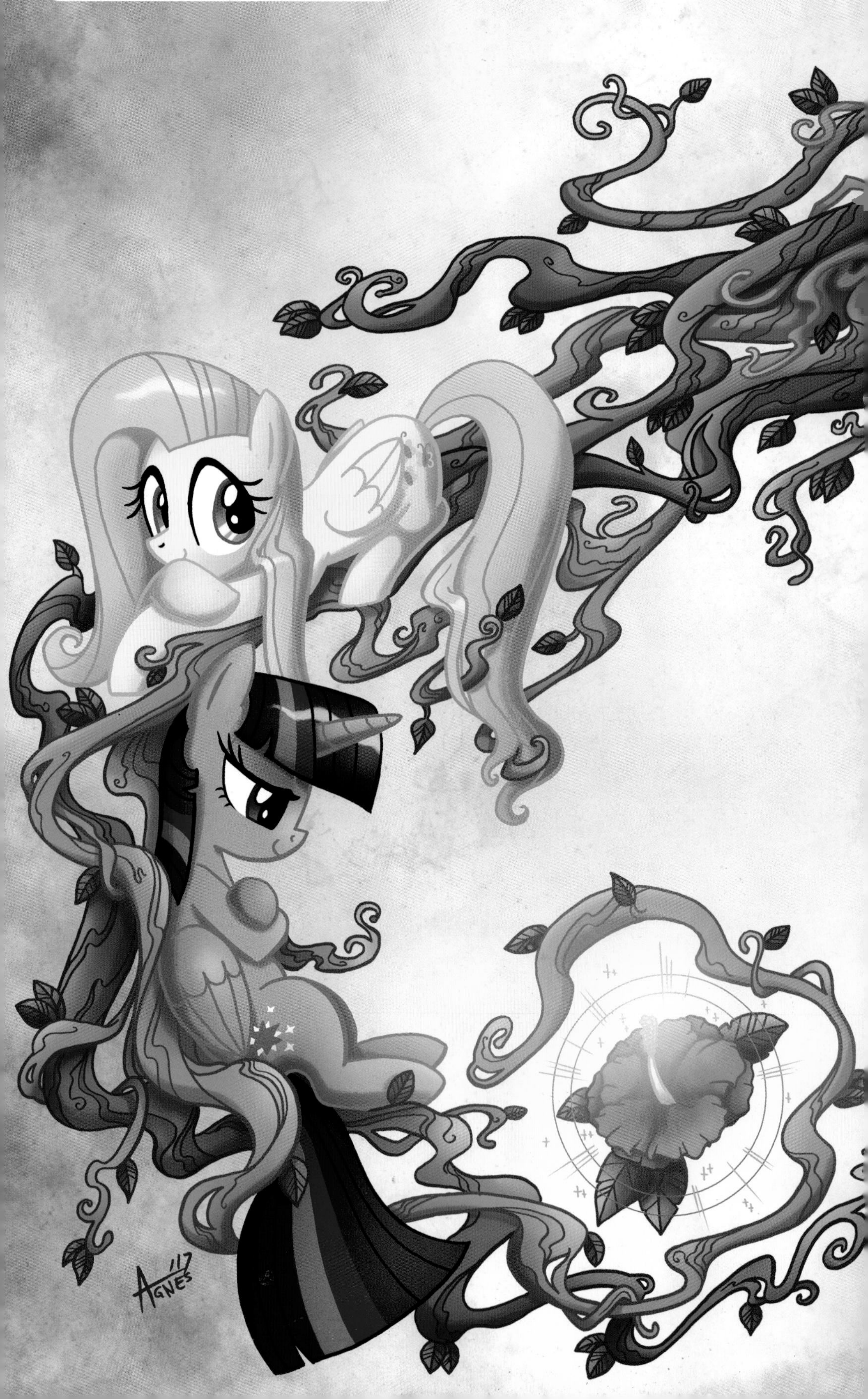

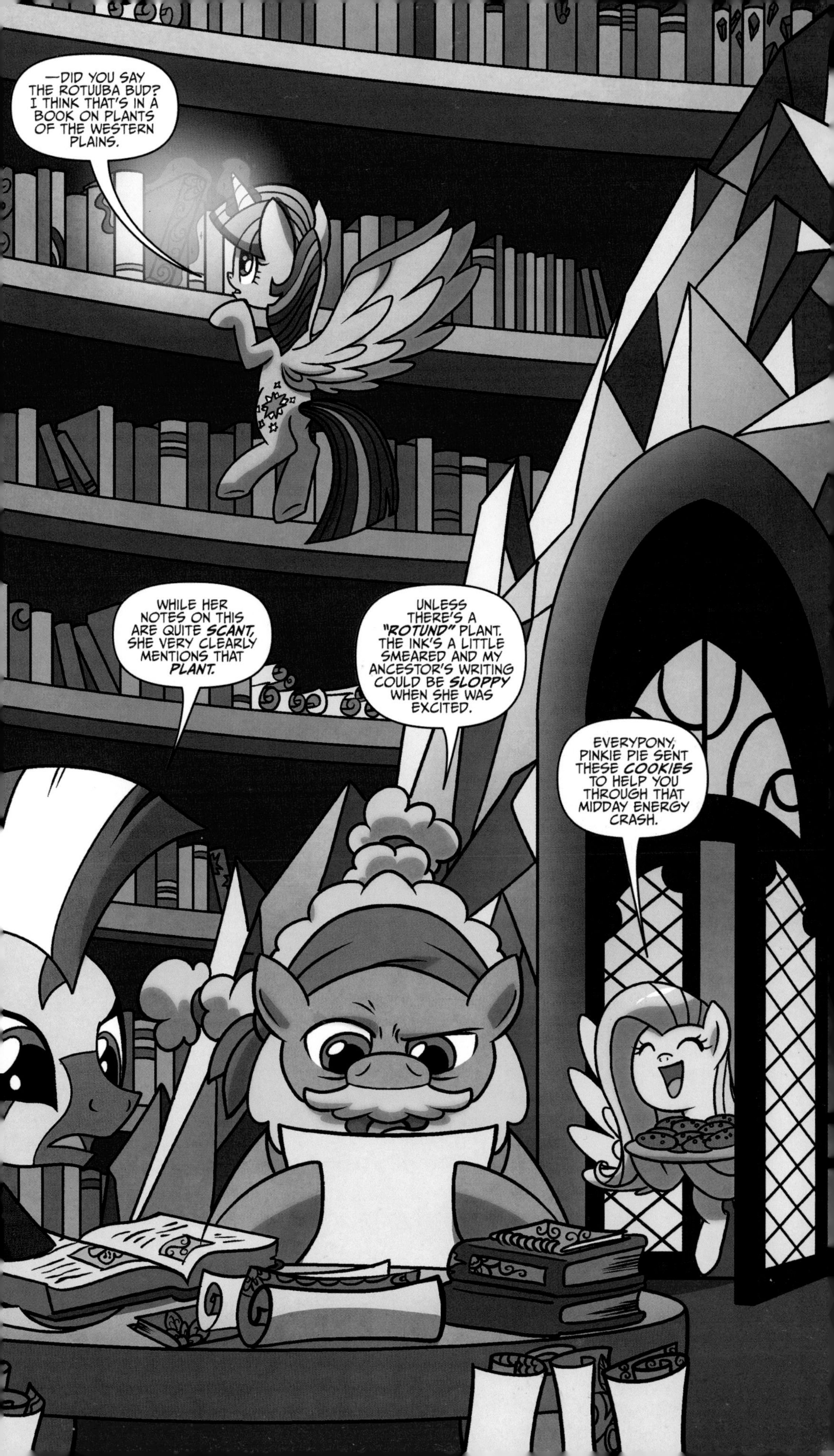
—DID YOU SAY THE ROTUUBA BUD? I THINK THAT'S IN A BOOK ON PLANTS OF THE WESTERN PLAINS.
WHILE HER NOTES ON THIS ARE QUITE SCANT, SHE VERY CLEARLY MENTIONS THAT PLANT.
UNLESS THERE'S A "ROTUND" PLANT. THE INK'S A LITTLE SMEARED AND MY ANCESTOR'S WRITING COULD BE SLOPPY WHEN SHE WAS EXCITED.
EVERYPONY, PINKIE PIE SENT THESE COOKIES TO HELP YOU THROUGH THAT MIDDAY ENERGY CRASH.

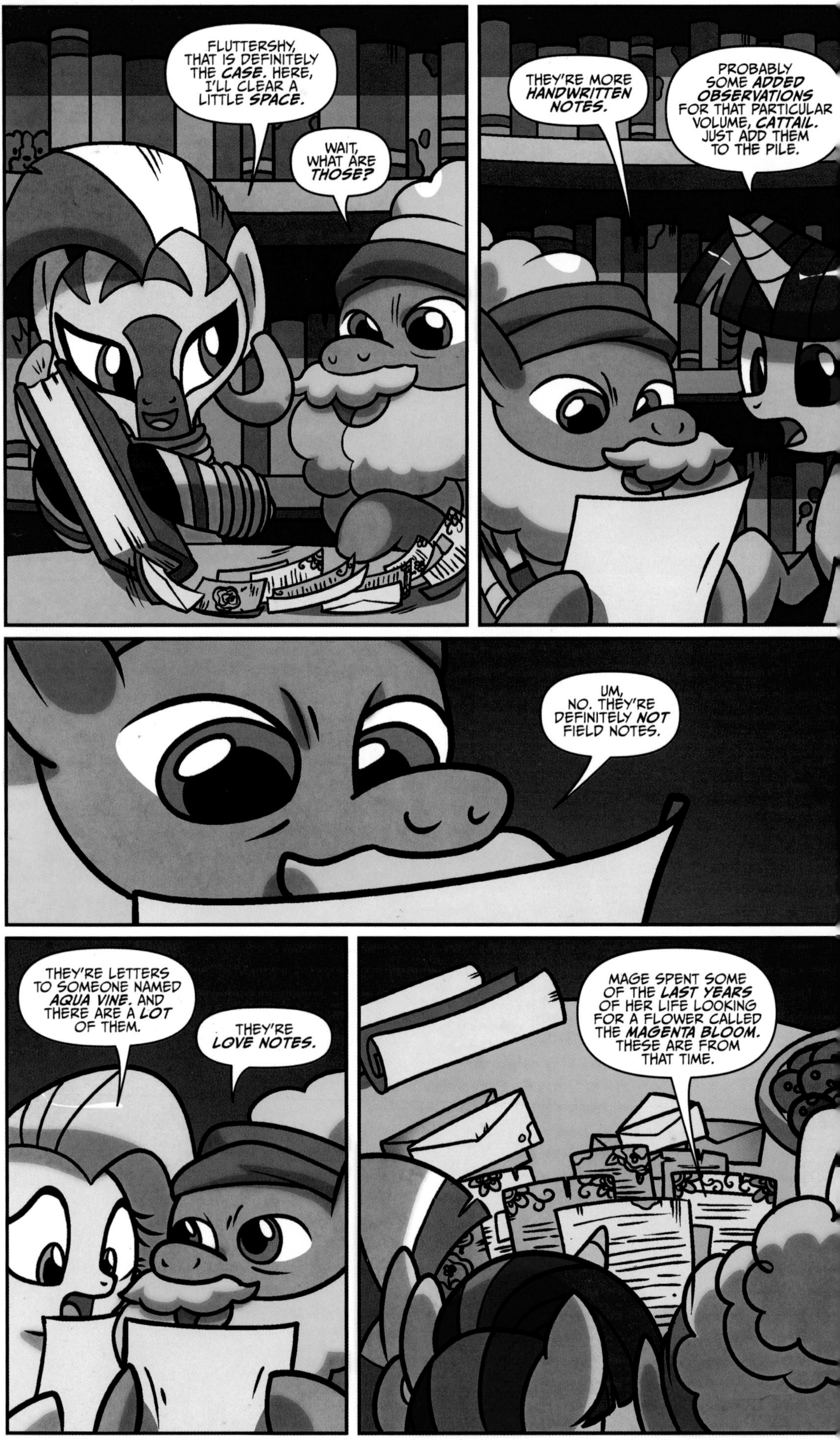
FLUTTERSHY, THAT IS DEFINITELY THE CASE. HERE, I'LL CLEAR A LITTLE SPACE.
WAIT, WHAT ARE THOSE?
THEY'RE MORE HANDWRITTEN NOTES.
PROBABLY SOME ADDED OBSERVATIONS FOR THAT PARTICULAR VOLUME, CATTAIL. JUST ADD THEM TO THE PILE.
UM, NO. THEY'RE DEFINITELY NOT FIELD NOTES.
THEY'RE LETTERS TO SOMEONE NAMED AQUA VINE. AND THERE ARE A LOT OF THEM.
THEY'RE LOVE NOTES.
MAGE SPENT SOME OF THE LAST YEARS OF HER LIFE LOOKING FOR A FLOWER CALLED THE MAGENTA BLOOM. THESE ARE FROM THAT TIME.

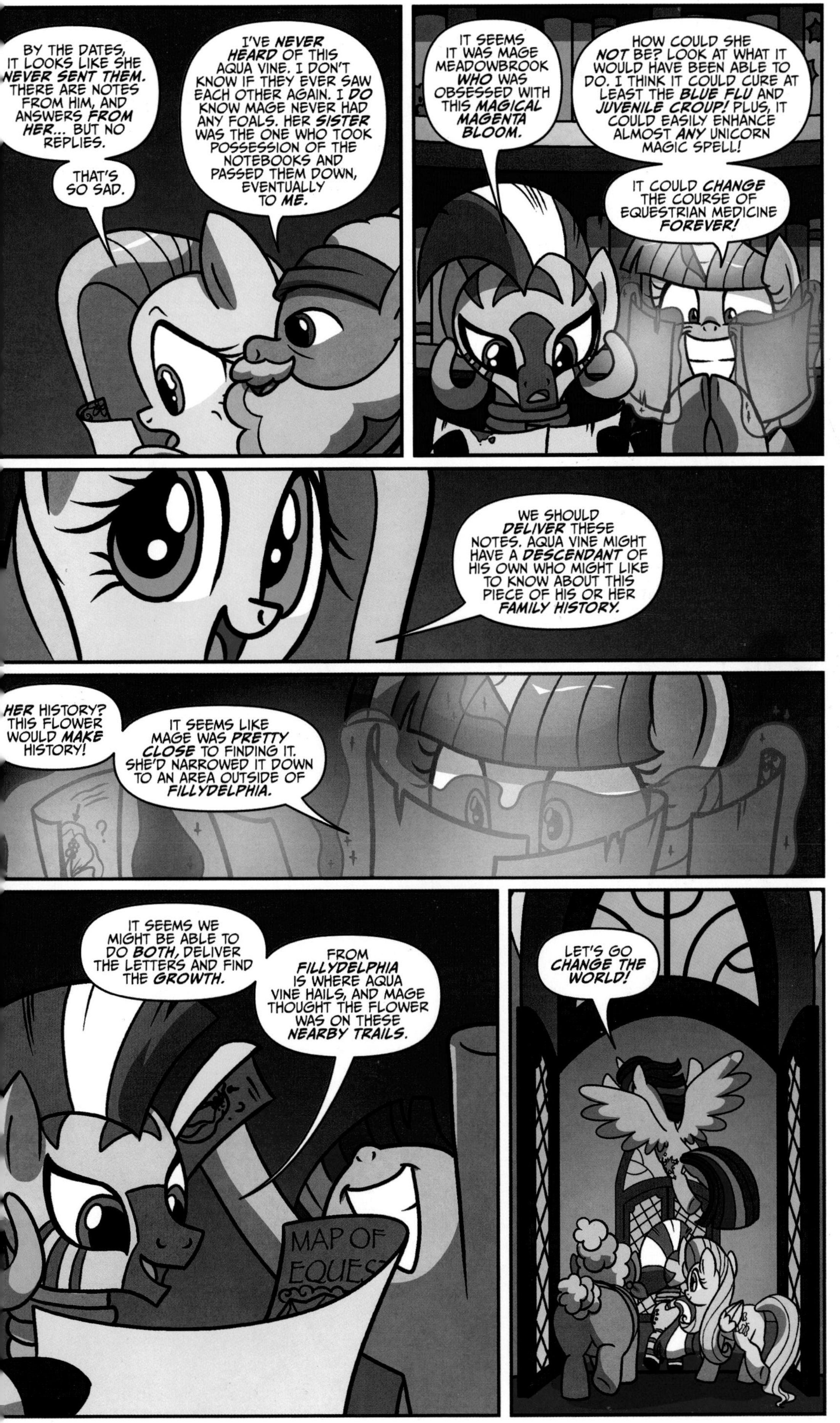

BY THE DATES, IT LOOKS LIKE SHE NEVER SENT THEM. THERE ARE NOTES FROM HIM, AND ANSWERS FROM HER... BUT NO REPLIES.
I'VE NEVER HEARD OF THIS AQUA VINE. I DON'T KNOW IF THEY EVER SAW EACH OTHER AGAIN. I DO KNOW MAGE NEVER HAD ANY FOALS. HER SISTER WAS THE ONE WHO TOOK POSSESSION OF THE NOTEBOOKS AND PASSED THEM DOWN, EVENTUALLY TO ME.
THAT'S SO SAD.
IT SEEMS IT WAS MAGE MEADOWBROOK WHO WAS OBSESSED WITH THIS MAGICAL MAGENTA BLOOM.
HOW COULD SHE NOT BE? LOOK AT WHAT IT WOULD HAVE BEEN ABLE TO DO. I THINK IT COULD CURE AT LEAST THE BLUE FLU AND JUVENILE CROUP! PLUS, IT COULD EASILY ENHANCE ALMOST ANY UNICORN MAGIC SPELL!
IT COULD CHANGE THE COURSE OF EQUESTRIAN MEDICINE FOREVER!
WE SHOULD DELIVER THESE NOTES. AQUA VINE MIGHT HAVE A DESCENDANT OF HIS OWN WHO MIGHT LIKE TO KNOW ABOUT THIS PIECE OF HIS OR HER FAMILY HISTORY.
HER HISTORY? THIS FLOWER WOULD MAKE HISTORY!
IT SEEMS LIKE MAGE WAS PRETTY CLOSE TO FINDING IT. SHE'D NARROWED IT DOWN TO AN AREA OUTSIDE OF FILLYDELPHIA.
IT SEEMS WE MIGHT BE ABLE TO DO BOTH, DELIVER THE LETTERS AND FIND THE GROWTH.
FROM FILLYDELPHIA IS WHERE AQUA VINE HAILS, AND MAGE THOUGHT THE FLOWER WAS ON THESE NEARBY TRAILS.
MAP OF EQUES
LET'S GO CHANGE THE WORLD!

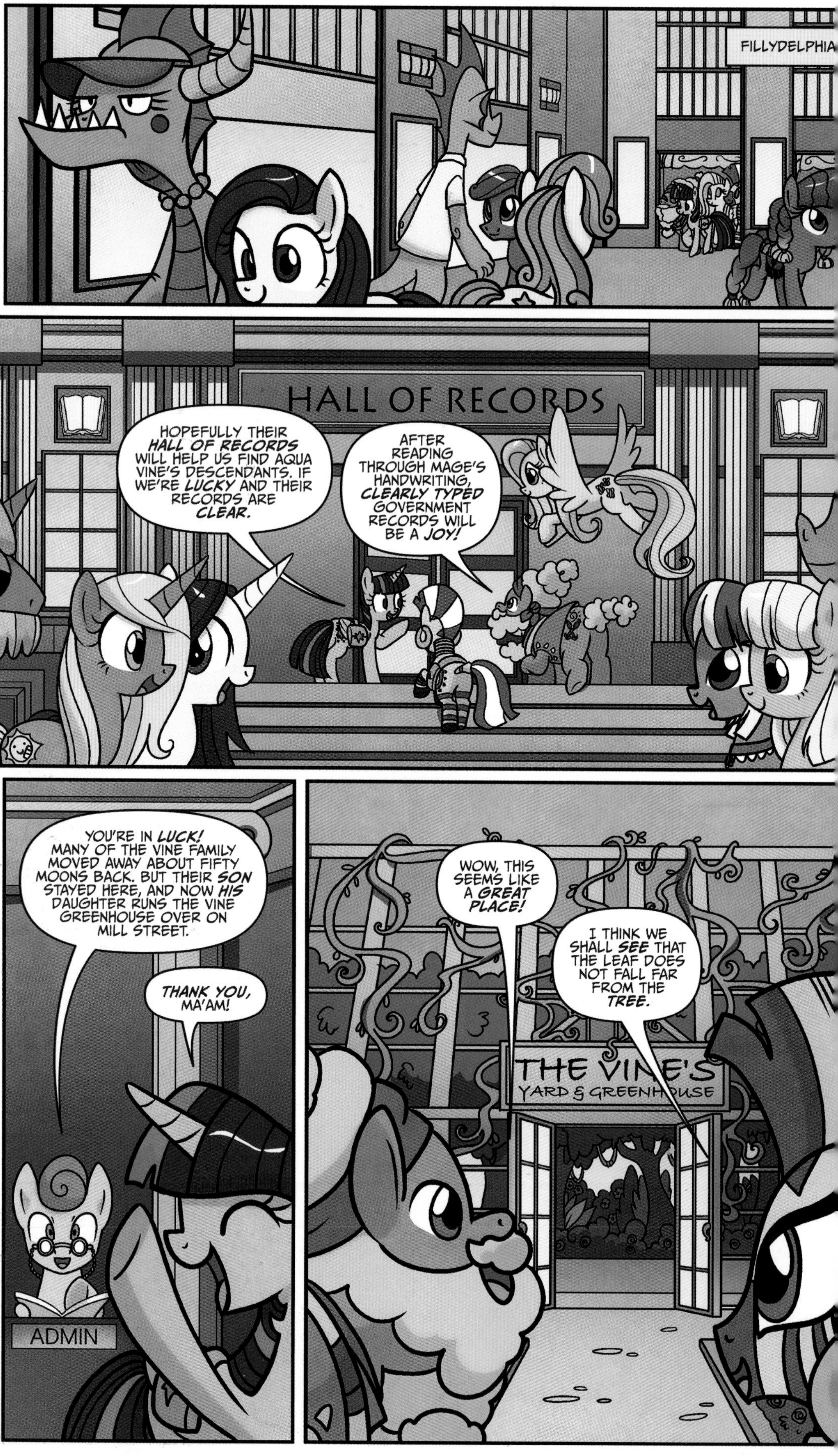
FILLYDELPHIA
HALL OF RECORDS
HOPEFULLY THEIR ***HALL OF RECORDS*** WILL HELP US FIND AQUA VINE'S DESCENDANTS. IF WE'RE ***LUCKY*** AND THEIR RECORDS ARE ***CLEAR.***
AFTER READING THROUGH MAGE'S HANDWRITING, ***CLEARLY TYPED*** GOVERNMENT RECORDS WILL BE A ***JOY!***
YOU'RE IN ***LUCK!*** MANY OF THE VINE FAMILY MOVED AWAY ABOUT FIFTY MOONS BACK. BUT THEIR ***SON*** STAYED HERE, AND NOW ***HIS*** DAUGHTER RUNS THE VINE GREENHOUSE OVER ON MILL STREET.
THANK YOU, MA'AM!
ADMIN
WOW, THIS SEEMS LIKE A ***GREAT PLACE!***
I THINK WE SHALL ***SEE*** THAT THE LEAF DOES NOT FALL FAR FROM THE ***TREE.***
THE VINE'S
YARD & GREENHOUSE

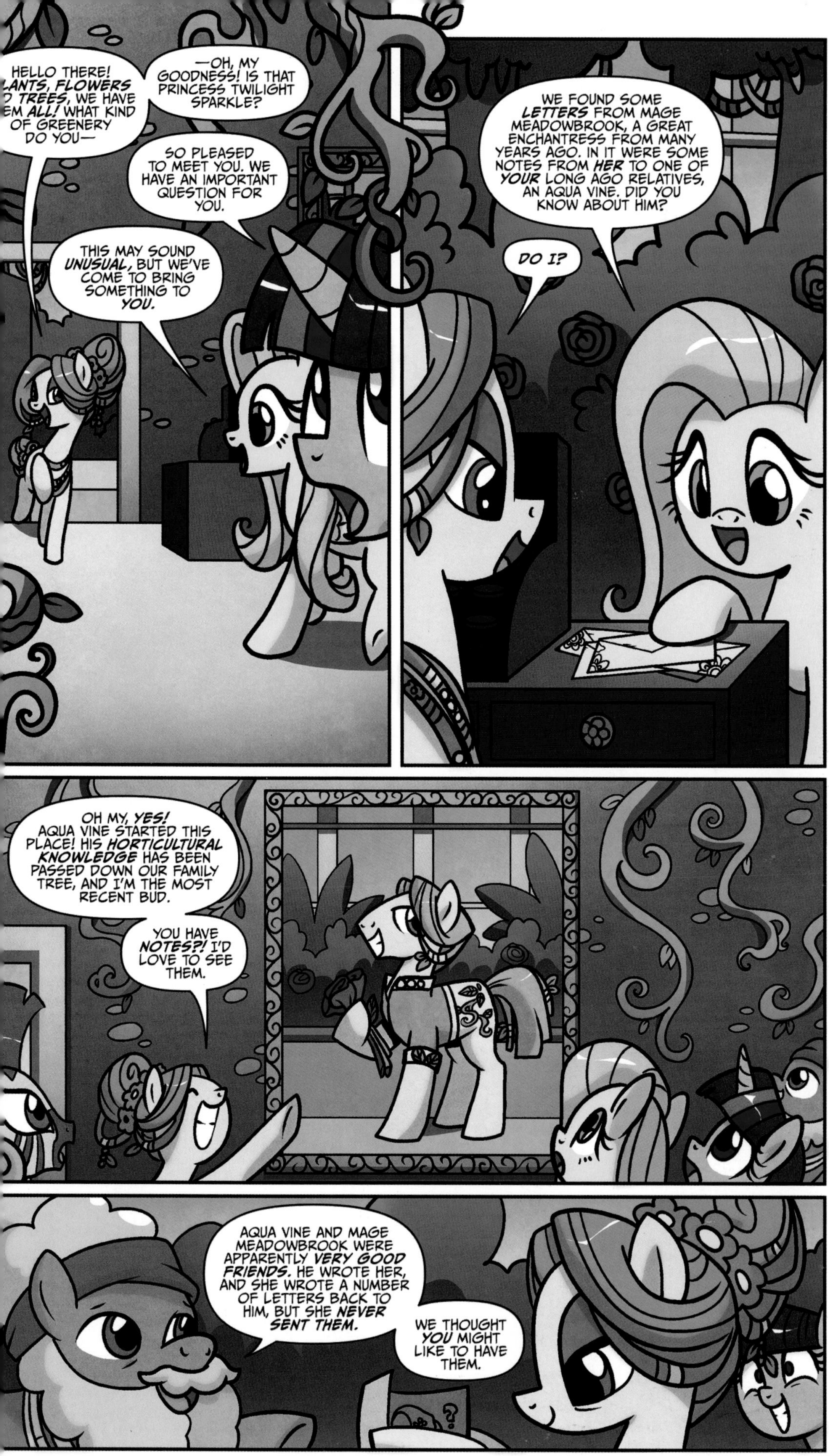

HELLO THERE! PLANTS, FLOWERS AND TREES, WE HAVE THEM ALL! WHAT KIND OF GREENERY DO YOU—
—OH, MY GOODNESS! IS THAT PRINCESS TWILIGHT SPARKLE?
SO PLEASED TO MEET YOU. WE HAVE AN IMPORTANT QUESTION FOR YOU.
THIS MAY SOUND UNUSUAL, BUT WE'VE COME TO BRING SOMETHING TO YOU.
WE FOUND SOME LETTERS FROM MAGE MEADOWBROOK, A GREAT ENCHANTRESS FROM MANY YEARS AGO. IN IT WERE SOME NOTES FROM HER TO ONE OF YOUR LONG AGO RELATIVES, AN AQUA VINE. DID YOU KNOW ABOUT HIM?
DO I?
OH MY, YES! AQUA VINE STARTED THIS PLACE! HIS HORTICULTURAL KNOWLEDGE HAS BEEN PASSED DOWN OUR FAMILY TREE, AND I'M THE MOST RECENT BUD.
YOU HAVE NOTES?! I'D LOVE TO SEE THEM.
AQUA VINE AND MAGE MEADOWBROOK WERE APPARENTLY VERY GOOD FRIENDS. HE WROTE HER, AND SHE WROTE A NUMBER OF LETTERS BACK TO HIM, BUT SHE NEVER SENT THEM.
WE THOUGHT YOU MIGHT LIKE TO HAVE THEM.

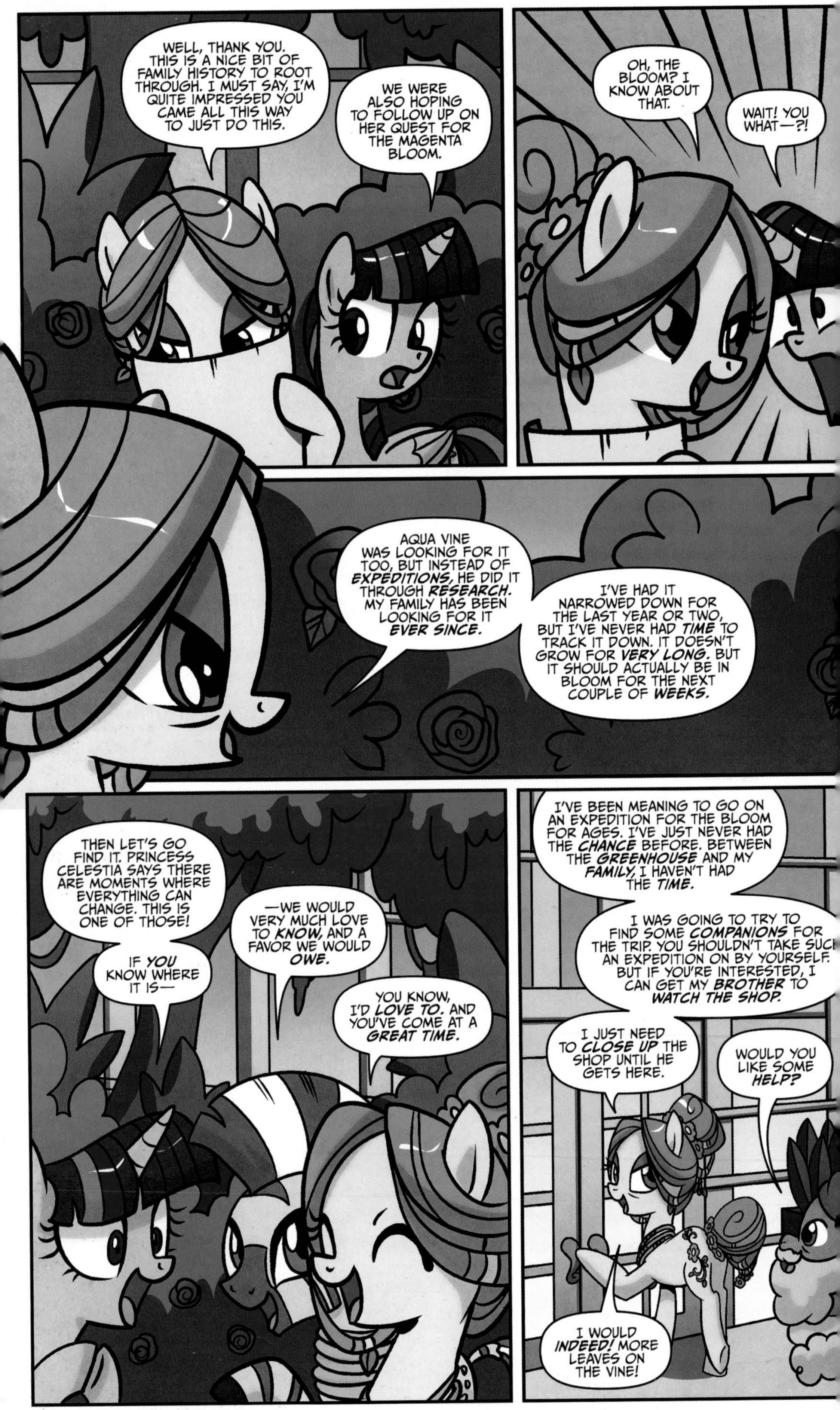
WELL, THANK YOU. THIS IS A NICE BIT OF FAMILY HISTORY TO ROOT THROUGH. I MUST SAY, I'M QUITE IMPRESSED YOU CAME ALL THIS WAY TO JUST DO THIS.
WE WERE ALSO HOPING TO FOLLOW UP ON HER QUEST FOR THE MAGENTA BLOOM.
OH, THE BLOOM? I KNOW ABOUT THAT.
WAIT! YOU WHAT—?!
AQUA VINE WAS LOOKING FOR IT TOO, BUT INSTEAD OF EXPEDITIONS, HE DID IT THROUGH RESEARCH. MY FAMILY HAS BEEN LOOKING FOR IT EVER SINCE.
I'VE HAD IT NARROWED DOWN FOR THE LAST YEAR OR TWO, BUT I'VE NEVER HAD TIME TO TRACK IT DOWN. IT DOESN'T GROW FOR VERY LONG. BUT IT SHOULD ACTUALLY BE IN BLOOM FOR THE NEXT COUPLE OF WEEKS.
THEN LET'S GO FIND IT. PRINCESS CELESTIA SAYS THERE ARE MOMENTS WHERE EVERYTHING CAN CHANGE. THIS IS ONE OF THOSE!
IF YOU KNOW WHERE IT IS—
—WE WOULD VERY MUCH LOVE TO KNOW, AND A FAVOR WE WOULD OWE.
YOU KNOW, I'D LOVE TO. AND YOU'VE COME AT A GREAT TIME.
I'VE BEEN MEANING TO GO ON AN EXPEDITION FOR THE BLOOM FOR AGES. I'VE JUST NEVER HAD THE CHANCE BEFORE. BETWEEN THE GREENHOUSE AND MY FAMILY, I HAVEN'T HAD THE TIME.
I WAS GOING TO TRY TO FIND SOME COMPANIONS FOR THE TRIP. YOU SHOULDN'T TAKE SUCH AN EXPEDITION ON BY YOURSELF. BUT IF YOU'RE INTERESTED, I CAN GET MY BROTHER TO WATCH THE SHOP.
I JUST NEED TO CLOSE UP THE SHOP UNTIL HE GETS HERE.
WOULD YOU LIKE SOME HELP?
I WOULD INDEED! MORE LEAVES ON THE VINE!

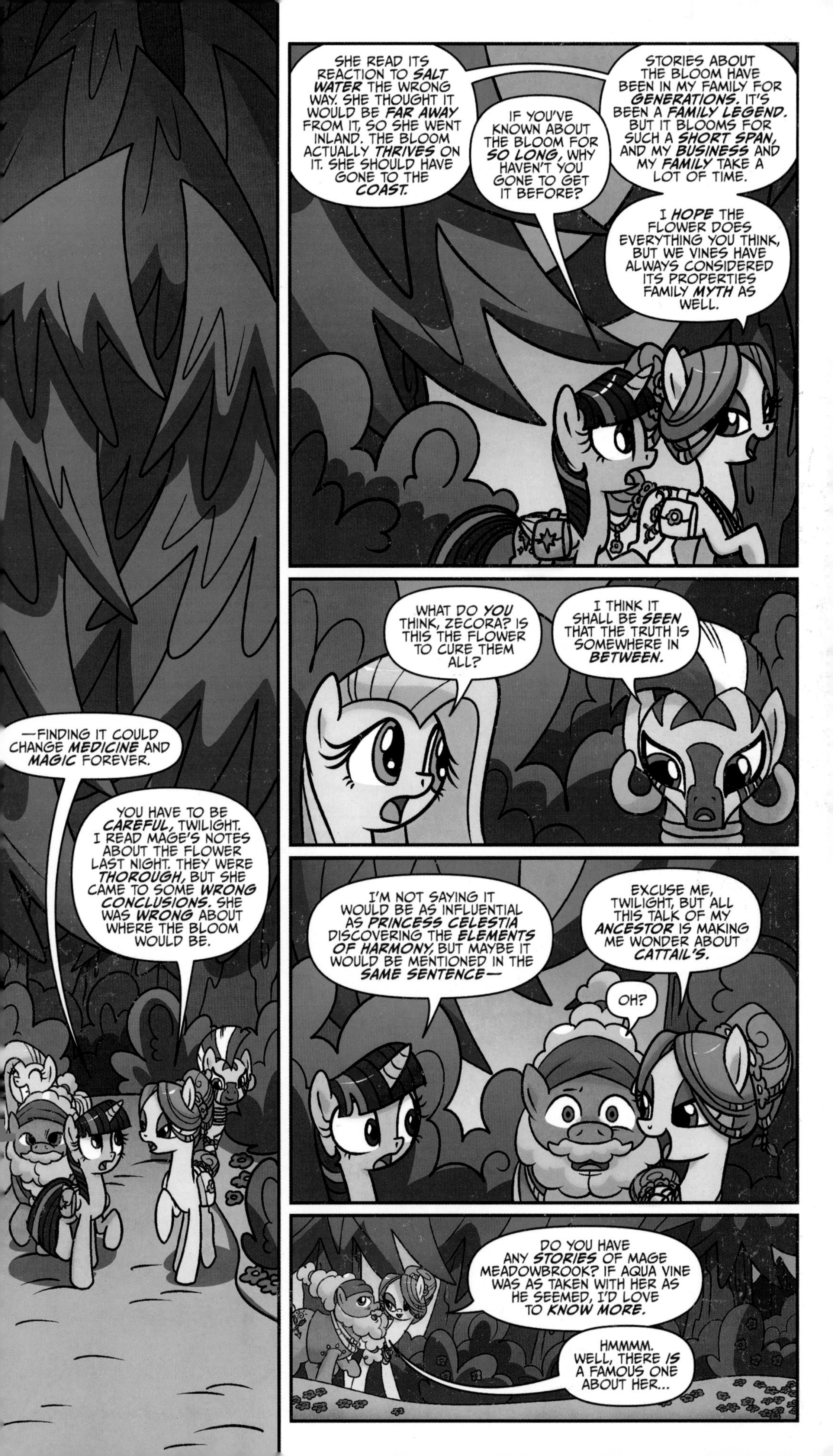

—FINDING IT COULD CHANGE MEDICINE AND MAGIC FOREVER.
YOU HAVE TO BE CAREFUL, TWILIGHT. I READ MAGE'S NOTES ABOUT THE FLOWER LAST NIGHT. THEY WERE THOROUGH, BUT SHE CAME TO SOME WRONG CONCLUSIONS. SHE WAS WRONG ABOUT WHERE THE BLOOM WOULD BE.
SHE READ ITS REACTION TO SALT WATER THE WRONG WAY. SHE THOUGHT IT WOULD BE FAR AWAY FROM IT, SO SHE WENT INLAND. THE BLOOM ACTUALLY THRIVES ON IT. SHE SHOULD HAVE GONE TO THE COAST.
IF YOU'VE KNOWN ABOUT THE BLOOM FOR SO LONG, WHY HAVEN'T YOU GONE TO GET IT BEFORE?
STORIES ABOUT THE BLOOM HAVE BEEN IN MY FAMILY FOR GENERATIONS. IT'S BEEN A FAMILY LEGEND. BUT IT BLOOMS FOR SUCH A SHORT SPAN, AND MY BUSINESS AND MY FAMILY TAKE A LOT OF TIME.
I HOPE THE FLOWER DOES EVERYTHING YOU THINK, BUT WE VINES HAVE ALWAYS CONSIDERED ITS PROPERTIES FAMILY MYTH AS WELL.
WHAT DO YOU THINK, ZECORA? IS THIS THE FLOWER TO CURE THEM ALL?
I THINK IT SHALL BE SEEN THAT THE TRUTH IS SOMEWHERE IN BETWEEN.
I'M NOT SAYING IT WOULD BE AS INFLUENTIAL AS PRINCESS CELESTIA DISCOVERING THE ELEMENTS OF HARMONY, BUT MAYBE IT WOULD BE MENTIONED IN THE SAME SENTENCE—
EXCUSE ME, TWILIGHT, BUT ALL THIS TALK OF MY ANCESTOR IS MAKING ME WONDER ABOUT CATTAIL'S.
OH?
DO YOU HAVE ANY STORIES OF MAGE MEADOWBROOK? IF AQUA VINE WAS AS TAKEN WITH HER AS HE SEEMED, I'D LOVE TO KNOW MORE.
HMMMM. WELL, THERE IS A FAMOUS ONE ABOUT HER...

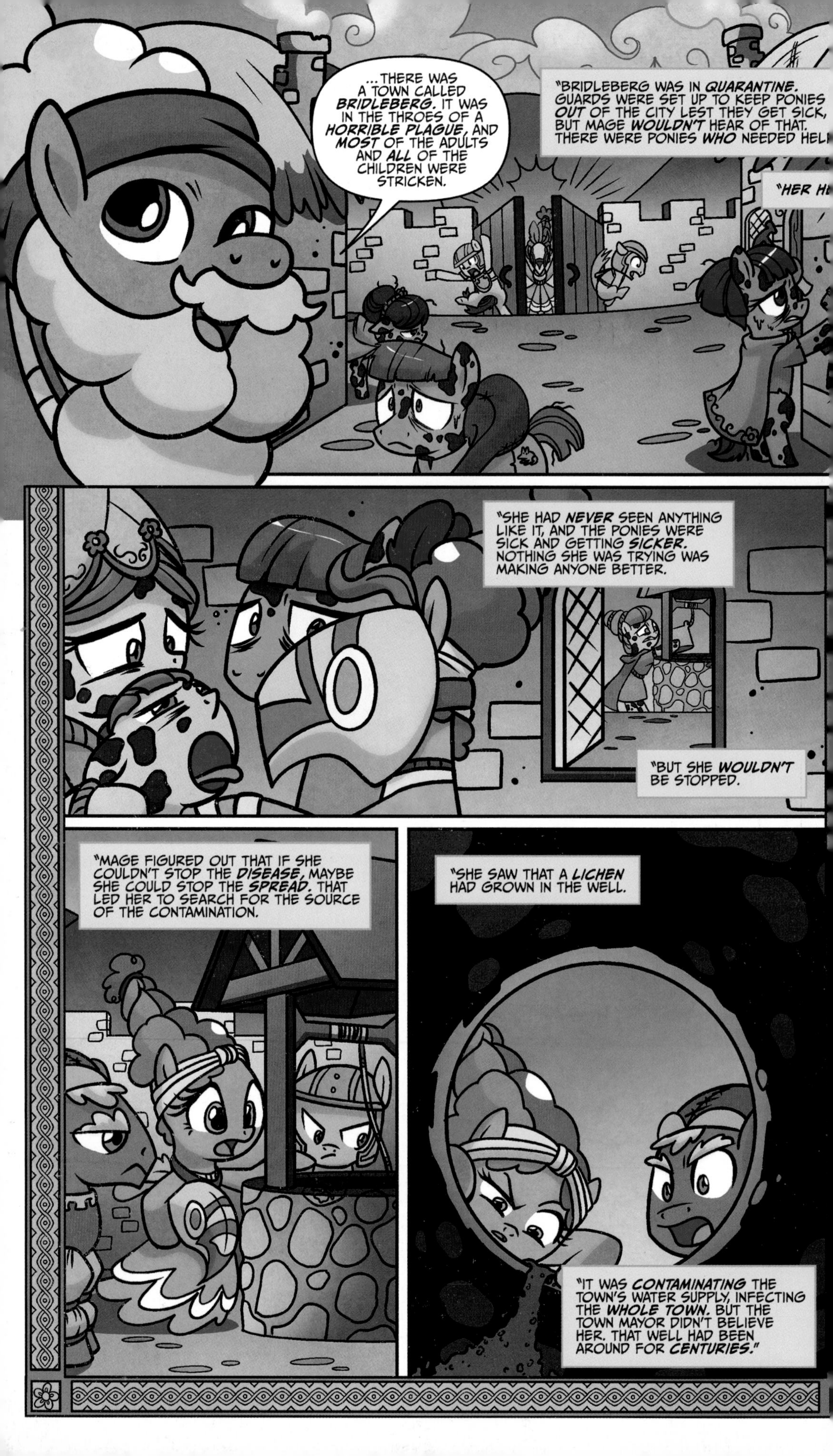
...THERE WAS A TOWN CALLED BRIDLEBERG. IT WAS IN THE THROES OF A HORRIBLE PLAGUE, AND MOST OF THE ADULTS AND ALL OF THE CHILDREN WERE STRICKEN.
"BRIDLEBERG WAS IN QUARANTINE. GUARDS WERE SET UP TO KEEP PONIES OUT OF THE CITY LEST THEY GET SICK, BUT MAGE WOULDN'T HEAR OF THAT. THERE WERE PONIES WHO NEEDED HEL
"HER H
"SHE HAD NEVER SEEN ANYTHING LIKE IT, AND THE PONIES WERE SICK AND GETTING SICKER. NOTHING SHE WAS TRYING WAS MAKING ANYONE BETTER.
"BUT SHE WOULDN'T BE STOPPED.
"MAGE FIGURED OUT THAT IF SHE COULDN'T STOP THE DISEASE, MAYBE SHE COULD STOP THE SPREAD. THAT LED HER TO SEARCH FOR THE SOURCE OF THE CONTAMINATION.
"SHE SAW THAT A LICHEN HAD GROWN IN THE WELL.
"IT WAS CONTAMINATING THE TOWN'S WATER SUPPLY, INFECTING THE WHOLE TOWN. BUT THE TOWN MAYOR DIDN'T BELIEVE HER. THAT WELL HAD BEEN AROUND FOR CENTURIES."

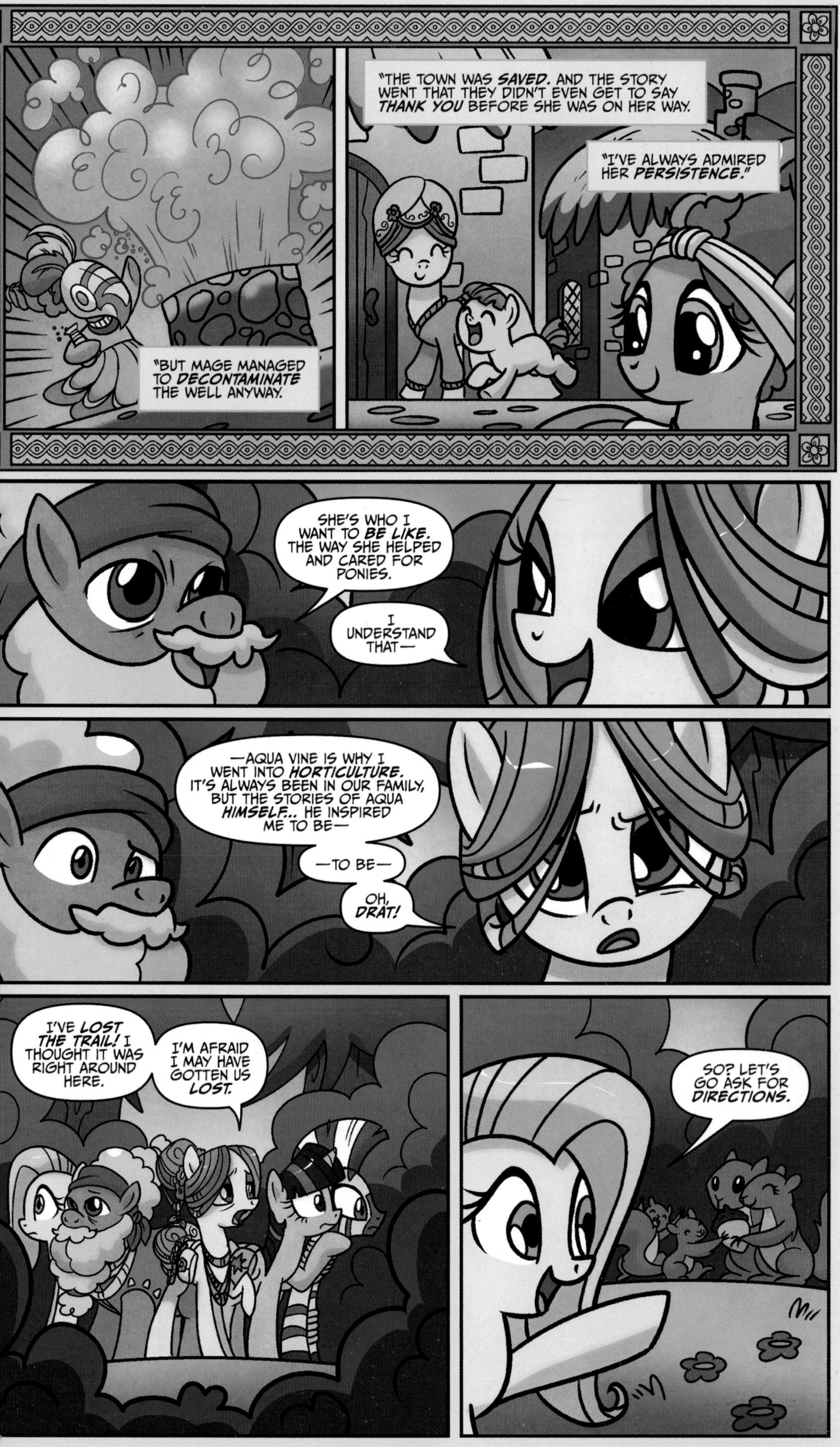
"BUT MAGE MANAGED TO *DECONTAMINATE* THE WELL ANYWAY.
"THE TOWN WAS *SAVED*. AND THE STORY WENT THAT THEY DIDN'T EVEN GET TO SAY *THANK YOU* BEFORE SHE WAS ON HER WAY.
"I'VE ALWAYS ADMIRED HER *PERSISTENCE*."
SHE'S WHO I WANT TO *BE LIKE*. THE WAY SHE HELPED AND CARED FOR PONIES.
I UNDERSTAND THAT—
—AQUA VINE IS WHY I WENT INTO *HORTICULTURE*. IT'S ALWAYS BEEN IN OUR FAMILY, BUT THE STORIES OF AQUA *HIMSELF*.. HE INSPIRED ME TO BE—
—TO BE—
OH, *DRAT!*
I'VE *LOST THE TRAIL!* I THOUGHT IT WAS RIGHT AROUND HERE.
I'M AFRAID I MAY HAVE GOTTEN US *LOST*.
SO? LET'S GO ASK FOR *DIRECTIONS*.

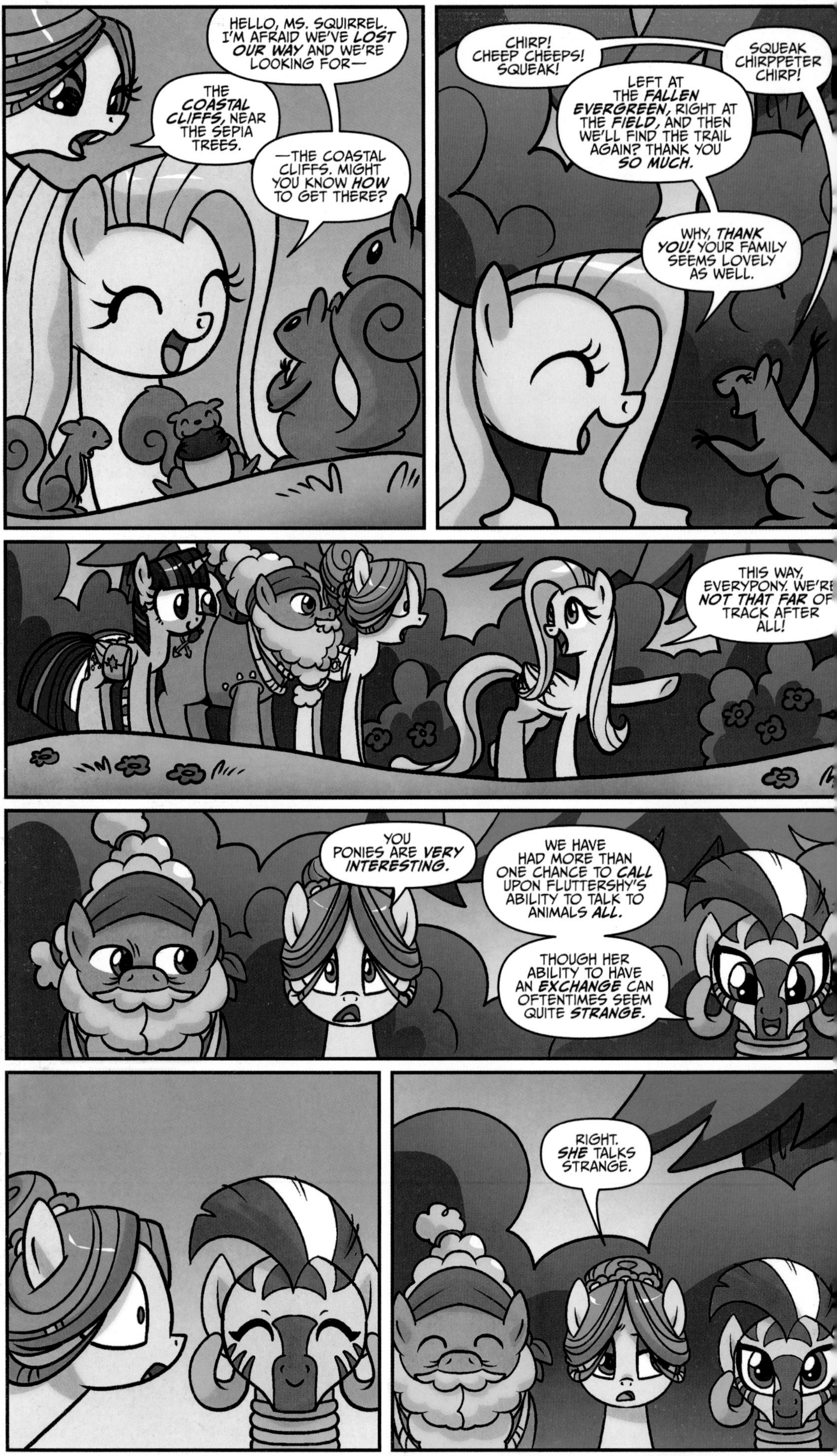

HELLO, MS. SQUIRREL. I'M AFRAID WE'VE LOST OUR WAY AND WE'RE LOOKING FOR—
THE COASTAL CLIFFS, NEAR THE SEPIA TREES.
—THE COASTAL CLIFFS. MIGHT YOU KNOW HOW TO GET THERE?
CHIRP! CHEEP CHEEPS! SQUEAK!
SQUEAK CHIRPPETER CHIRP!
LEFT AT THE FALLEN EVERGREEN, RIGHT AT THE FIELD, AND THEN WE'LL FIND THE TRAIL AGAIN? THANK YOU SO MUCH.
WHY, THANK YOU! YOUR FAMILY SEEMS LOVELY AS WELL.
THIS WAY, EVERYPONY. WE'RE NOT THAT FAR OFF TRACK AFTER ALL!
YOU PONIES ARE VERY INTERESTING.
WE HAVE HAD MORE THAN ONE CHANCE TO CALL UPON FLUTTERSHY'S ABILITY TO TALK TO ANIMALS ALL.
THOUGH HER ABILITY TO HAVE AN EXCHANGE CAN OFTENTIMES SEEM QUITE STRANGE.
RIGHT. SHE TALKS STRANGE.

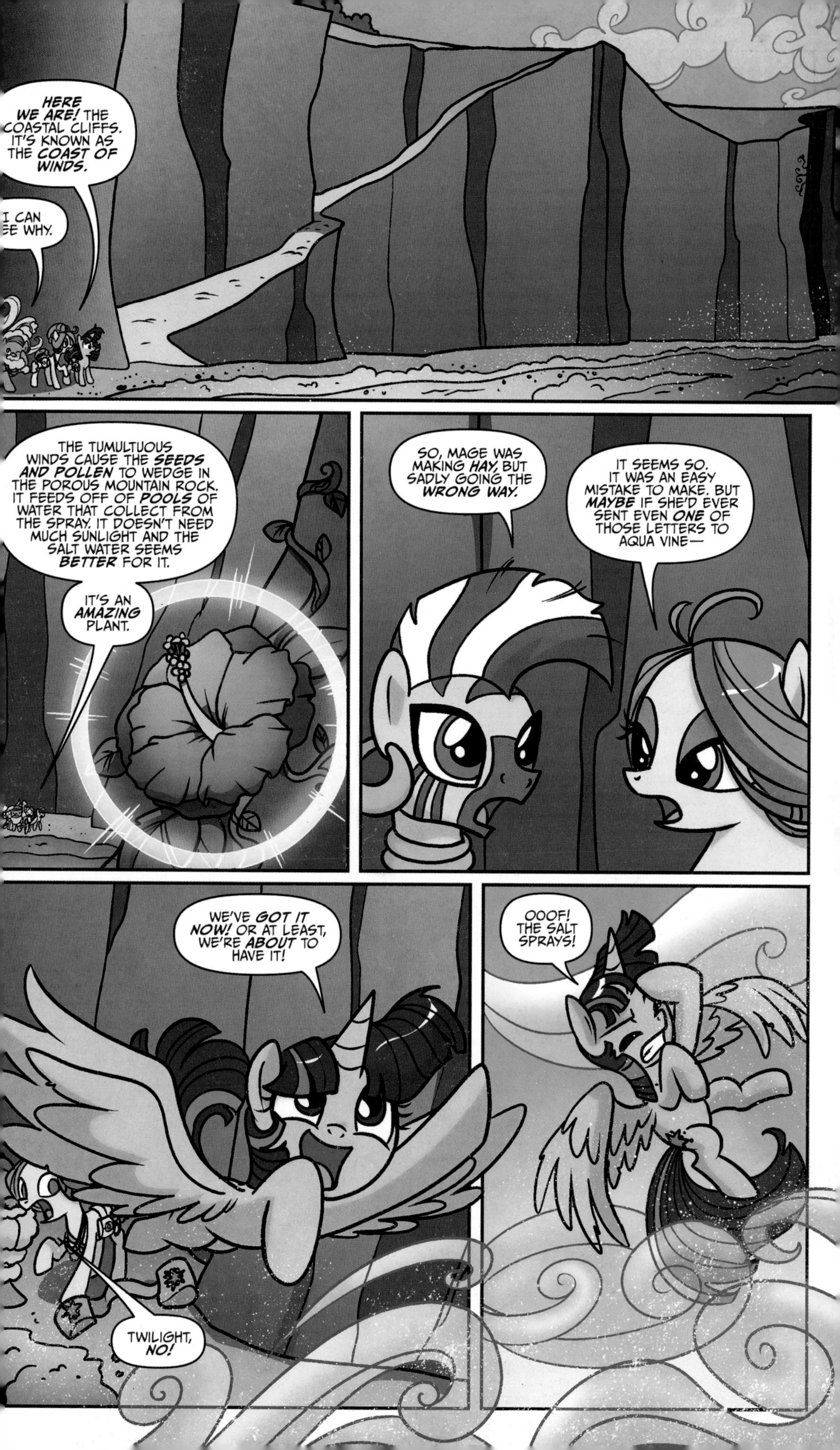
HERE WE ARE! THE COASTAL CLIFFS. IT'S KNOWN AS THE COAST OF WINDS.
I CAN SEE WHY.
THE TUMULTUOUS WINDS CAUSE THE SEEDS AND POLLEN TO WEDGE IN THE POROUS MOUNTAIN ROCK. IT FEEDS OFF OF POOLS OF WATER THAT COLLECT FROM THE SPRAY. IT DOESN'T NEED MUCH SUNLIGHT AND THE SALT WATER SEEMS BETTER FOR IT.
IT'S AN AMAZING PLANT.
SO, MAGE WAS MAKING HAY, BUT SADLY GOING THE WRONG WAY.
IT SEEMS SO. IT WAS AN EASY MISTAKE TO MAKE. BUT MAYBE IF SHE'D EVER SENT EVEN ONE OF THOSE LETTERS TO AQUA VINE—
WE'VE GOT IT NOW! OR AT LEAST, WE'RE ABOUT TO HAVE IT!
TWILIGHT, NO!
OOOF! THE SALT SPRAYS!

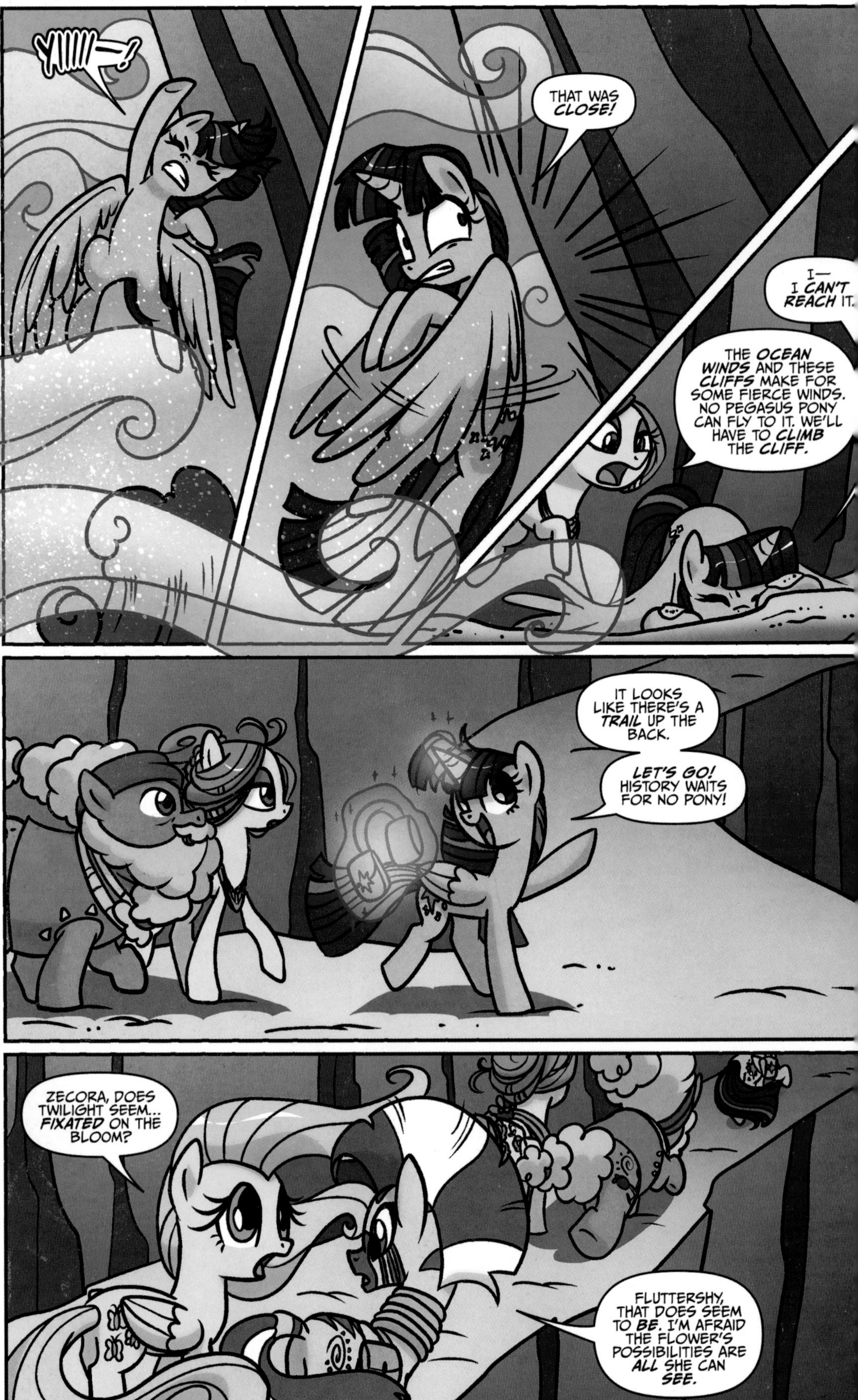
YIIIII—!
THAT WAS CLOSE!
I— I CAN'T REACH IT.
THE OCEAN WINDS AND THESE CLIFFS MAKE FOR SOME FIERCE WINDS. NO PEGASUS PONY CAN FLY TO IT. WE'LL HAVE TO CLIMB THE CLIFF.
IT LOOKS LIKE THERE'S A TRAIL UP THE BACK.
LET'S GO! HISTORY WAITS FOR NO PONY!
ZECORA, DOES TWILIGHT SEEM... FIXATED ON THE BLOOM?
FLUTTERSHY, THAT DOES SEEM TO BE. I'M AFRAID THE FLOWER'S POSSIBILITIES ARE ALL SHE CAN SEE.

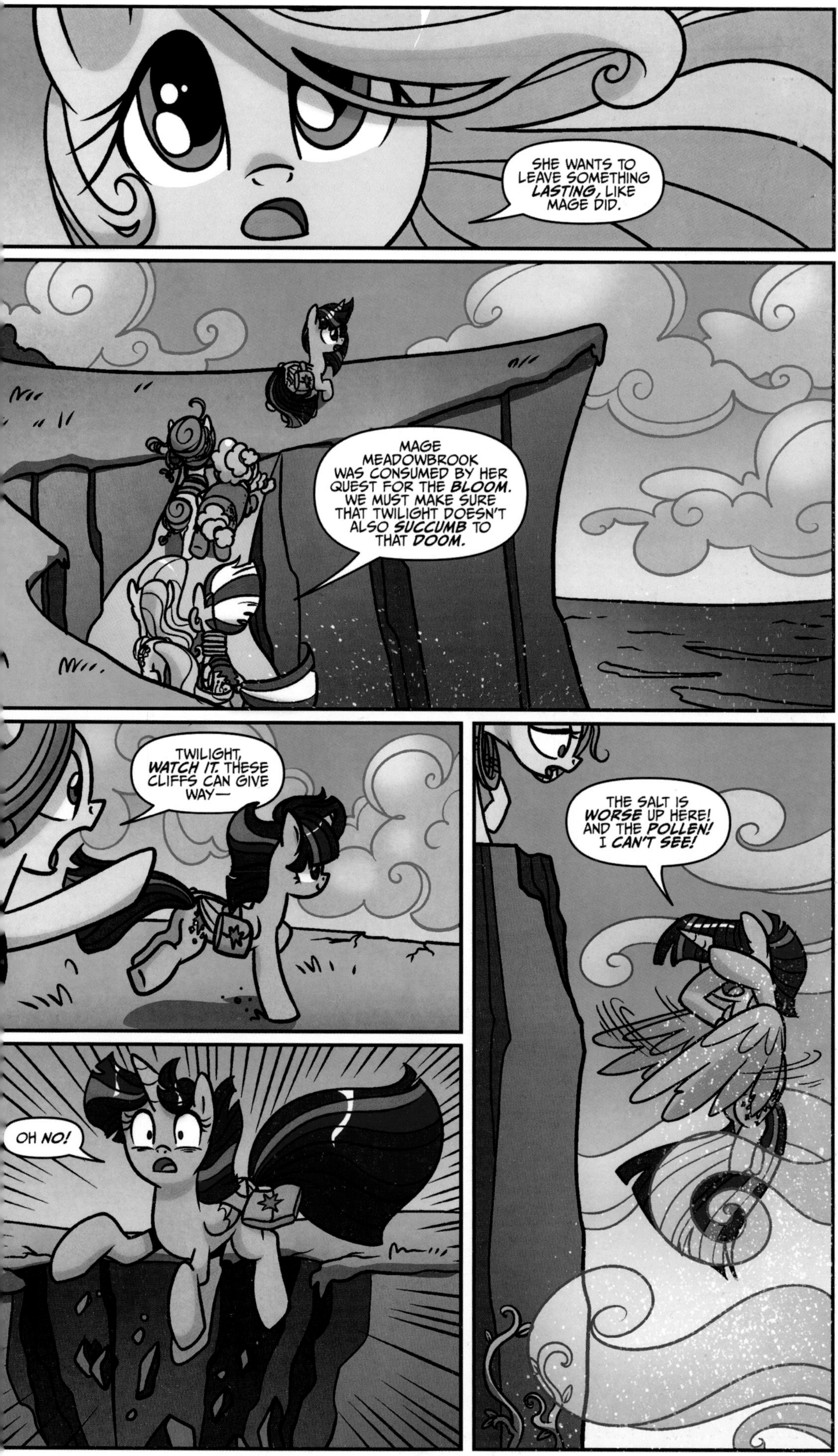
SHE WANTS TO LEAVE SOMETHING LASTING, LIKE MAGE DID.
MAGE MEADOWBROOK WAS CONSUMED BY HER QUEST FOR THE BLOOM. WE MUST MAKE SURE THAT TWILIGHT DOESN'T ALSO SUCCUMB TO THAT DOOM.
TWILIGHT, WATCH IT. THESE CLIFFS CAN GIVE WAY—
THE SALT IS WORSE UP HERE! AND THE POLLEN! I CAN'T SEE!
OH NO!

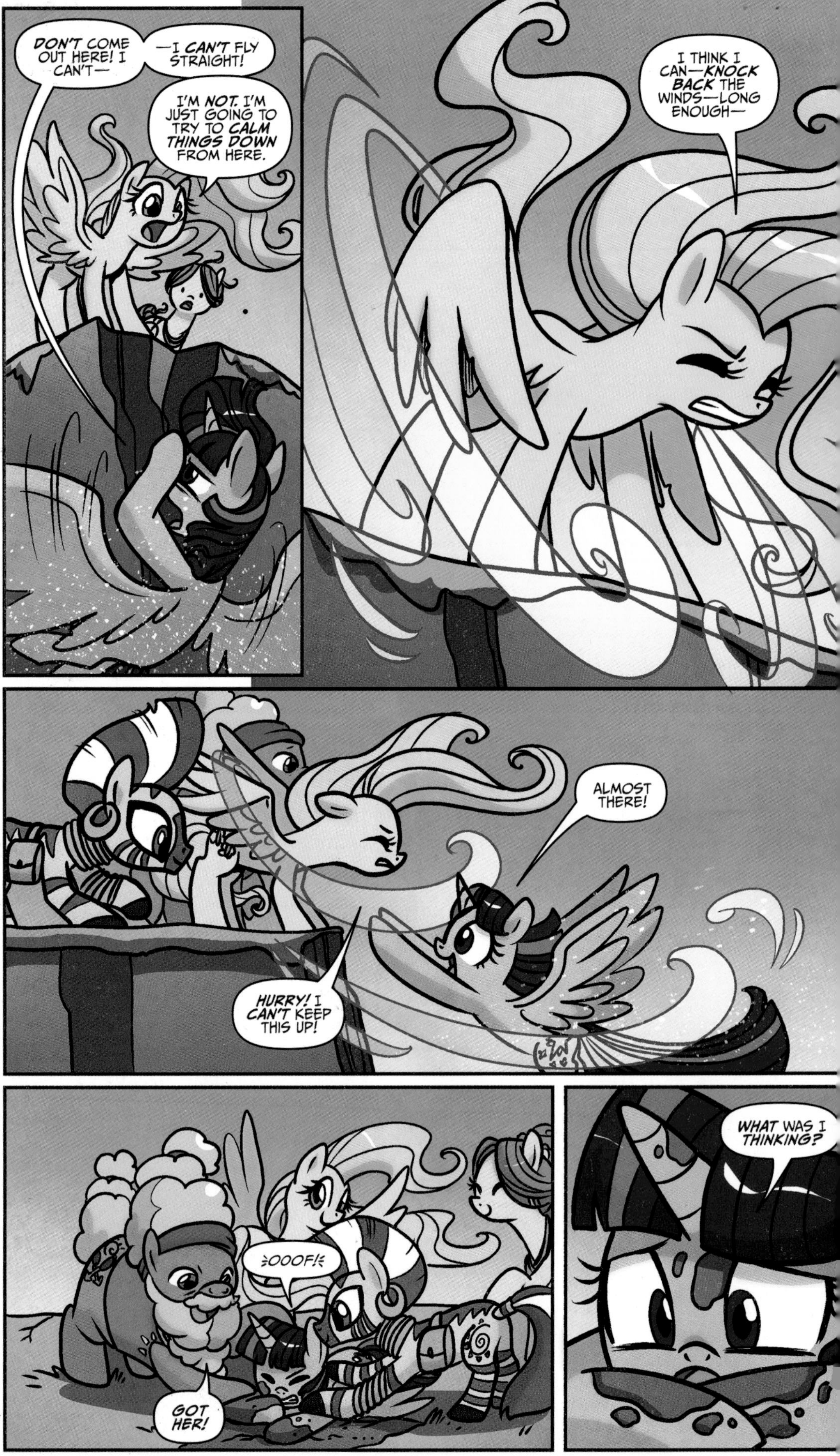
DON'T COME OUT HERE! I CAN'T—
—I CAN'T FLY STRAIGHT!
I'M NOT. I'M JUST GOING TO TRY TO CALM THINGS DOWN FROM HERE.
I THINK I CAN—KNOCK BACK THE WINDS—LONG ENOUGH—
ALMOST THERE!
HURRY! I CAN'T KEEP THIS UP!
OOOF!
GOT HER!
WHAT WAS I THINKING?

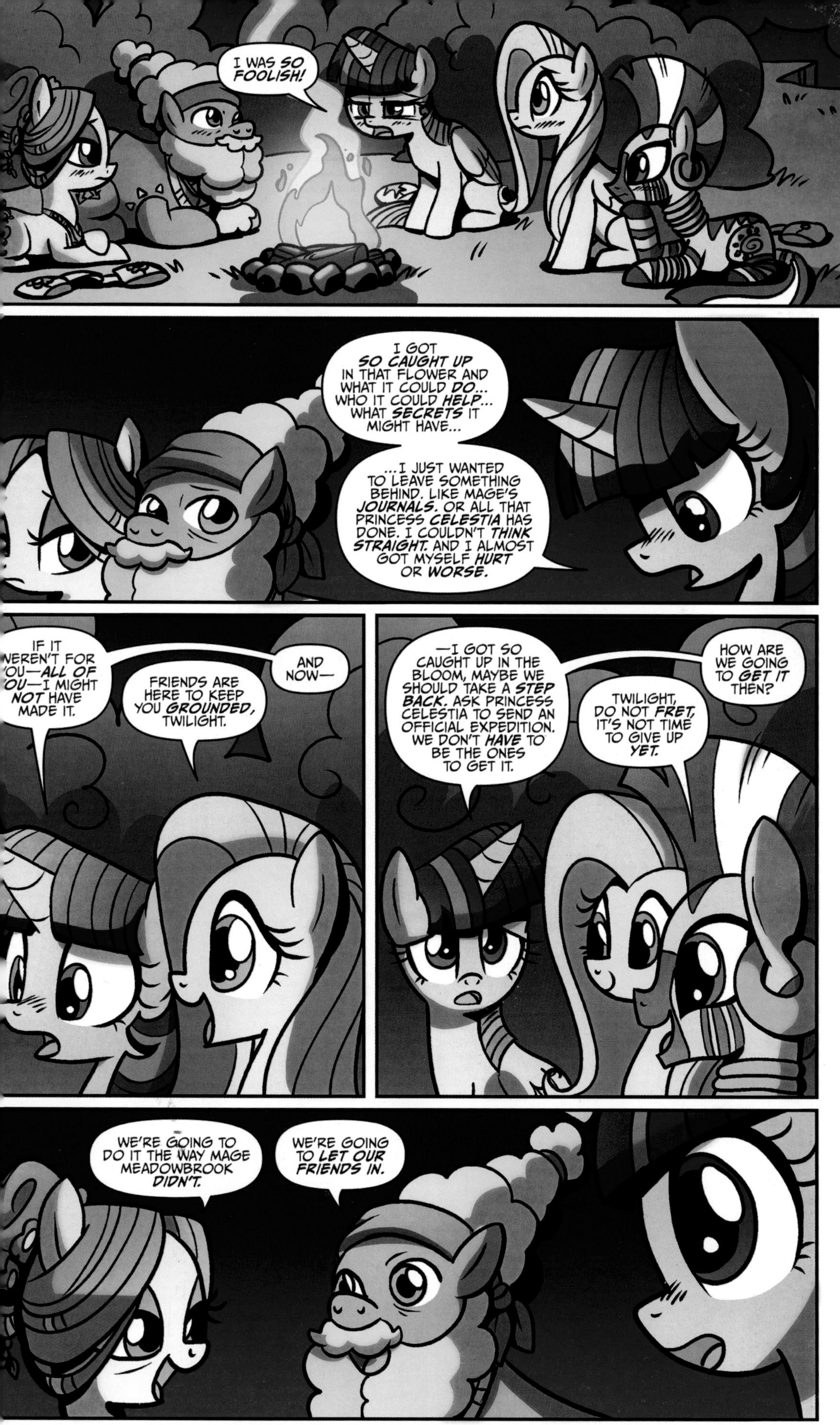
I WAS SO FOOLISH!
I GOT SO CAUGHT UP IN THAT FLOWER AND WHAT IT COULD DO... WHO IT COULD HELP... WHAT SECRETS IT MIGHT HAVE...
...I JUST WANTED TO LEAVE SOMETHING BEHIND. LIKE MAGE'S JOURNALS. OR ALL THAT PRINCESS CELESTIA HAS DONE. I COULDN'T THINK STRAIGHT. AND I ALMOST GOT MYSELF HURT OR WORSE.
IF IT WEREN'T FOR YOU—ALL OF YOU—I MIGHT NOT HAVE MADE IT.
FRIENDS ARE HERE TO KEEP YOU GROUNDED, TWILIGHT.
AND NOW—
—I GOT SO CAUGHT UP IN THE BLOOM, MAYBE WE SHOULD TAKE A STEP BACK. ASK PRINCESS CELESTIA TO SEND AN OFFICIAL EXPEDITION. WE DON'T HAVE TO BE THE ONES TO GET IT.
TWILIGHT, DO NOT FRET, IT'S NOT TIME TO GIVE UP YET.
HOW ARE WE GOING TO GET IT THEN?
WE'RE GOING TO DO IT THE WAY MAGE MEADOWBROOK DIDN'T.
WE'RE GOING TO LET OUR FRIENDS IN.

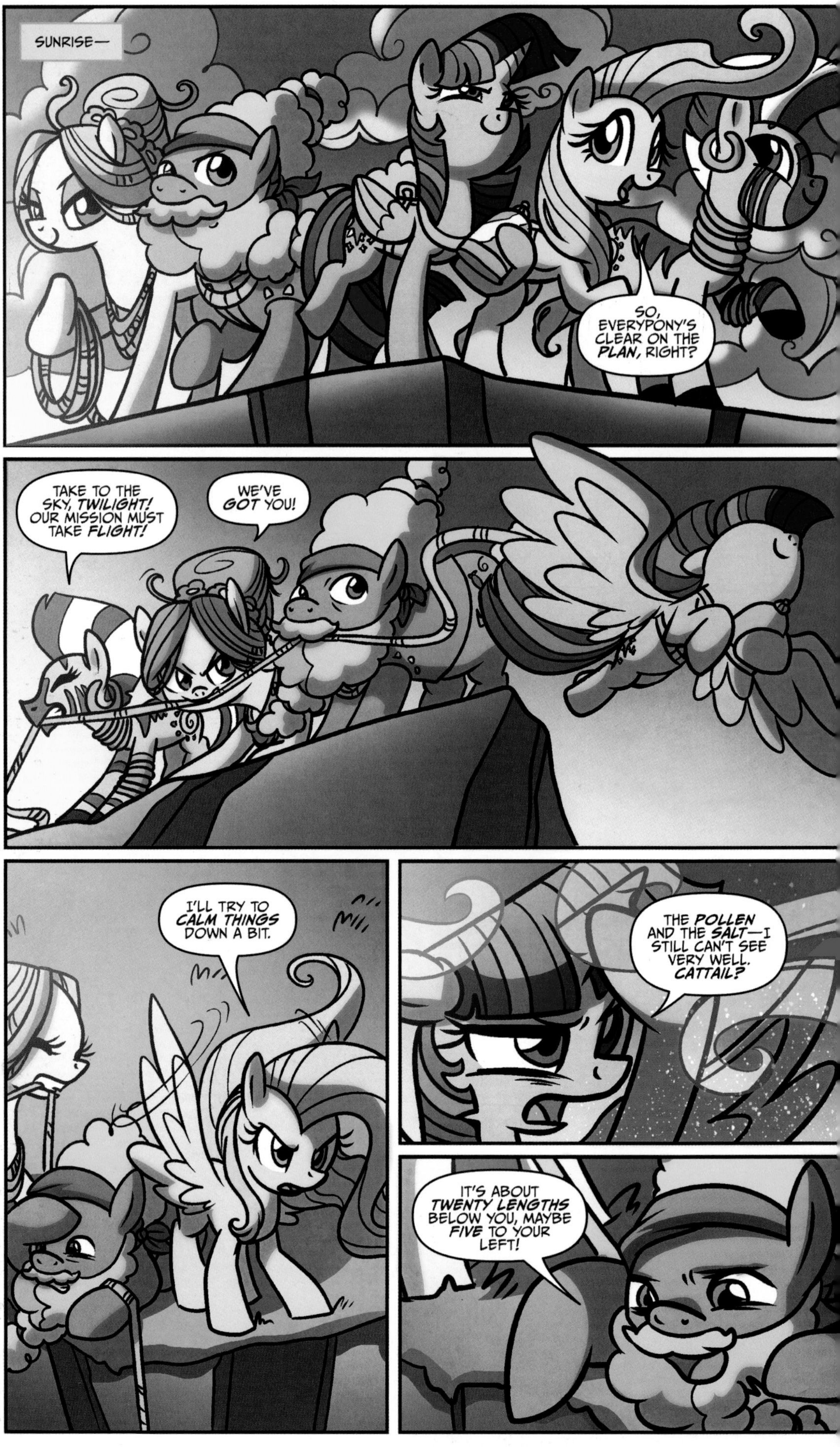
SUNRISE—
SO, EVERYPONY'S CLEAR ON THE PLAN, RIGHT?
TAKE TO THE SKY, TWILIGHT! OUR MISSION MUST TAKE FLIGHT!
WE'VE GOT YOU!
I'LL TRY TO CALM THINGS DOWN A BIT.
THE POLLEN AND THE SALT—I STILL CAN'T SEE VERY WELL. CATTAIL?
IT'S ABOUT TWENTY LENGTHS BELOW YOU, MAYBE FIVE TO YOUR LEFT!

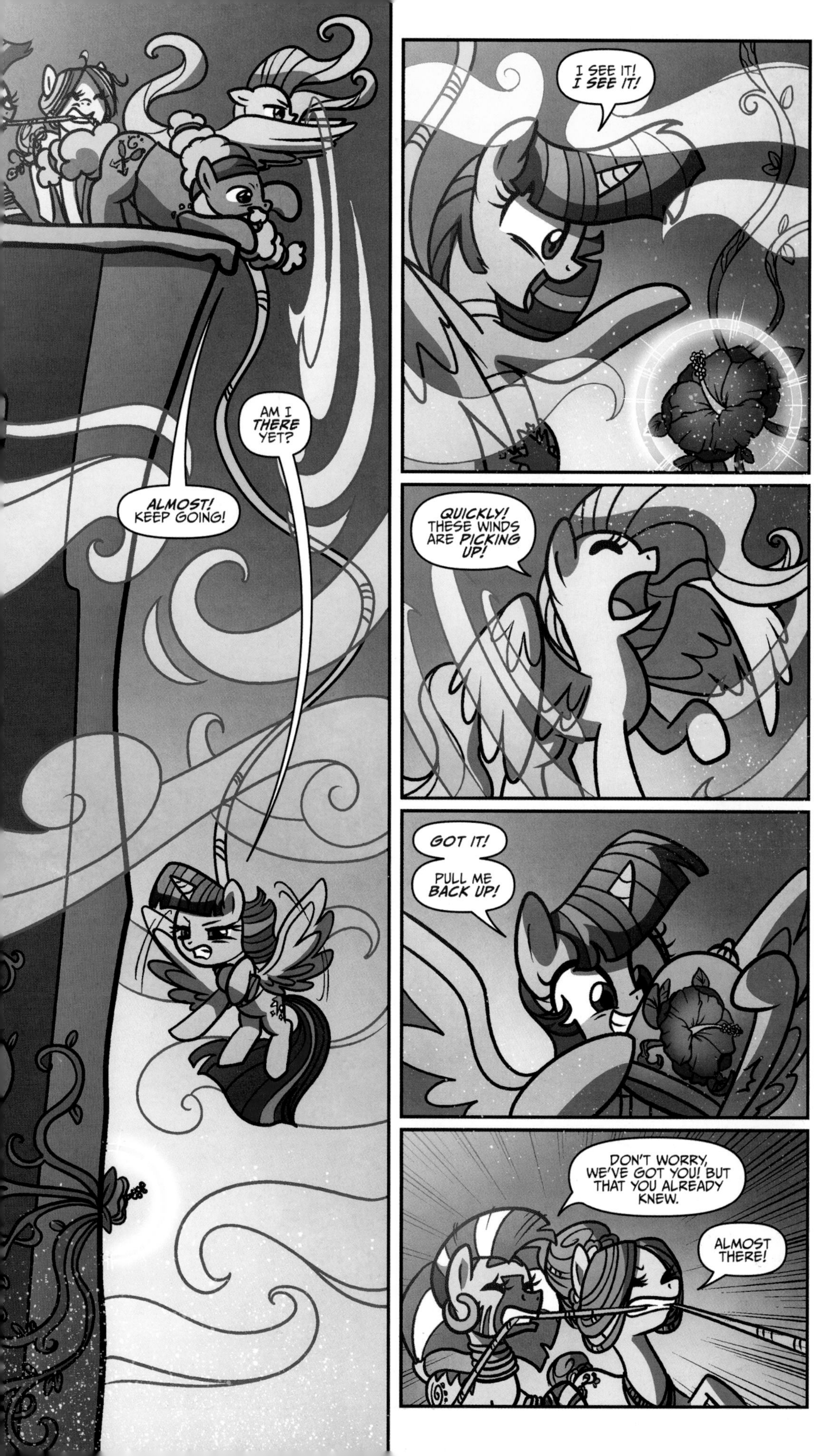
AM I THERE YET?
ALMOST! KEEP GOING!
I SEE IT! I SEE IT!
QUICKLY! THESE WINDS ARE PICKING UP!
GOT IT!
PULL ME BACK UP!
DON'T WORRY, WE'VE GOT YOU! BUT THAT YOU ALREADY KNEW.
ALMOST THERE!

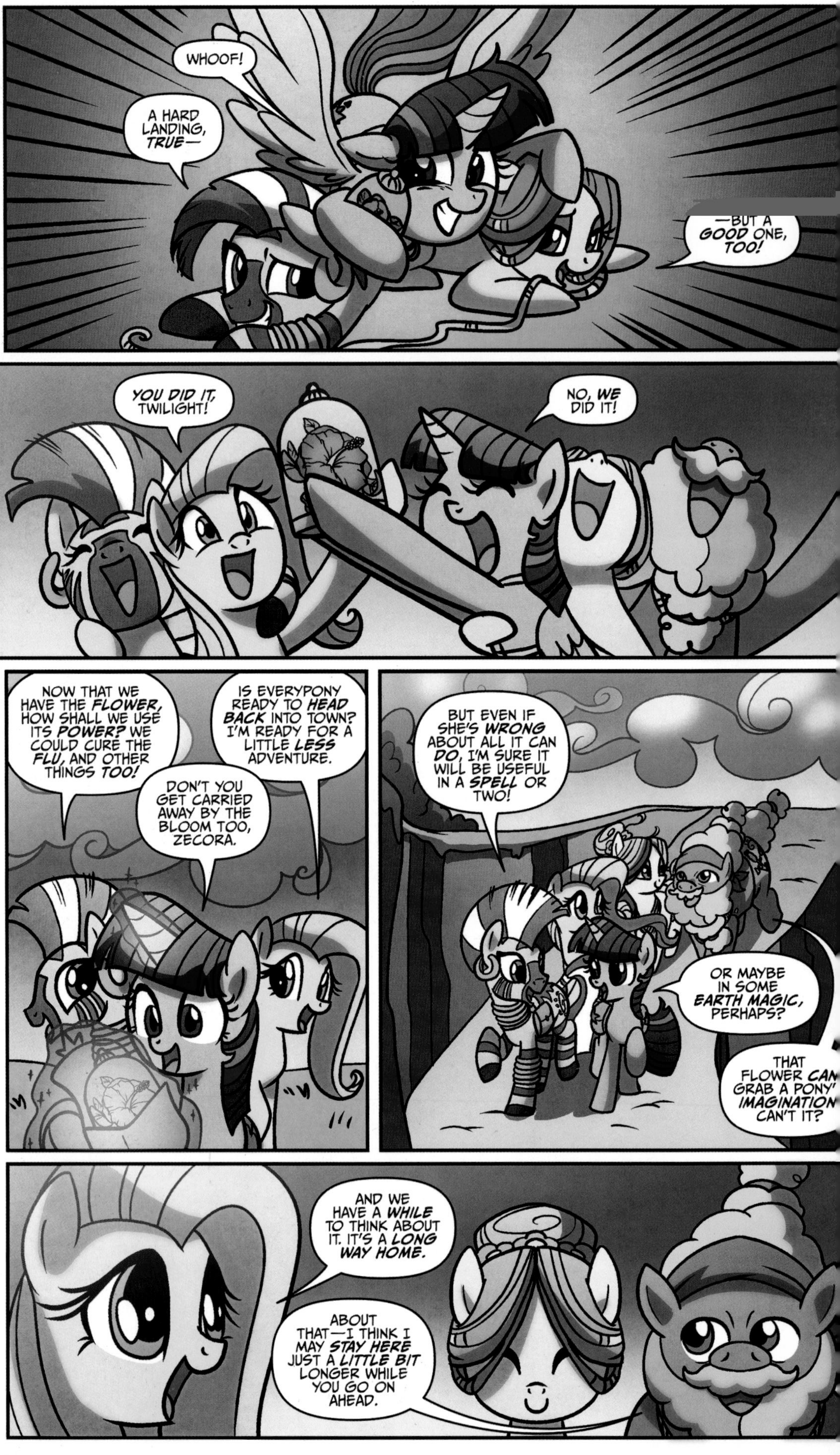

WHOOF!
A HARD LANDING, TRUE—
—BUT A GOOD ONE, TOO!
YOU DID IT, TWILIGHT!
NO, WE DID IT!
NOW THAT WE HAVE THE FLOWER, HOW SHALL WE USE ITS POWER? WE COULD CURE THE FLU, AND OTHER THINGS TOO!
IS EVERYPONY READY TO HEAD BACK INTO TOWN? I'M READY FOR A LITTLE LESS ADVENTURE.
DON'T YOU GET CARRIED AWAY BY THE BLOOM TOO, ZECORA.
BUT EVEN IF SHE'S WRONG ABOUT ALL IT CAN DO, I'M SURE IT WILL BE USEFUL IN A SPELL OR TWO!
OR MAYBE IN SOME EARTH MAGIC, PERHAPS?
THAT FLOWER CAN GRAB A PONY' IMAGINATION CAN'T IT?
AND WE HAVE A WHILE TO THINK ABOUT IT. IT'S A LONG WAY HOME.
ABOUT THAT—I THINK I MAY STAY HERE JUST A LITTLE BIT LONGER WHILE YOU GO ON AHEAD.

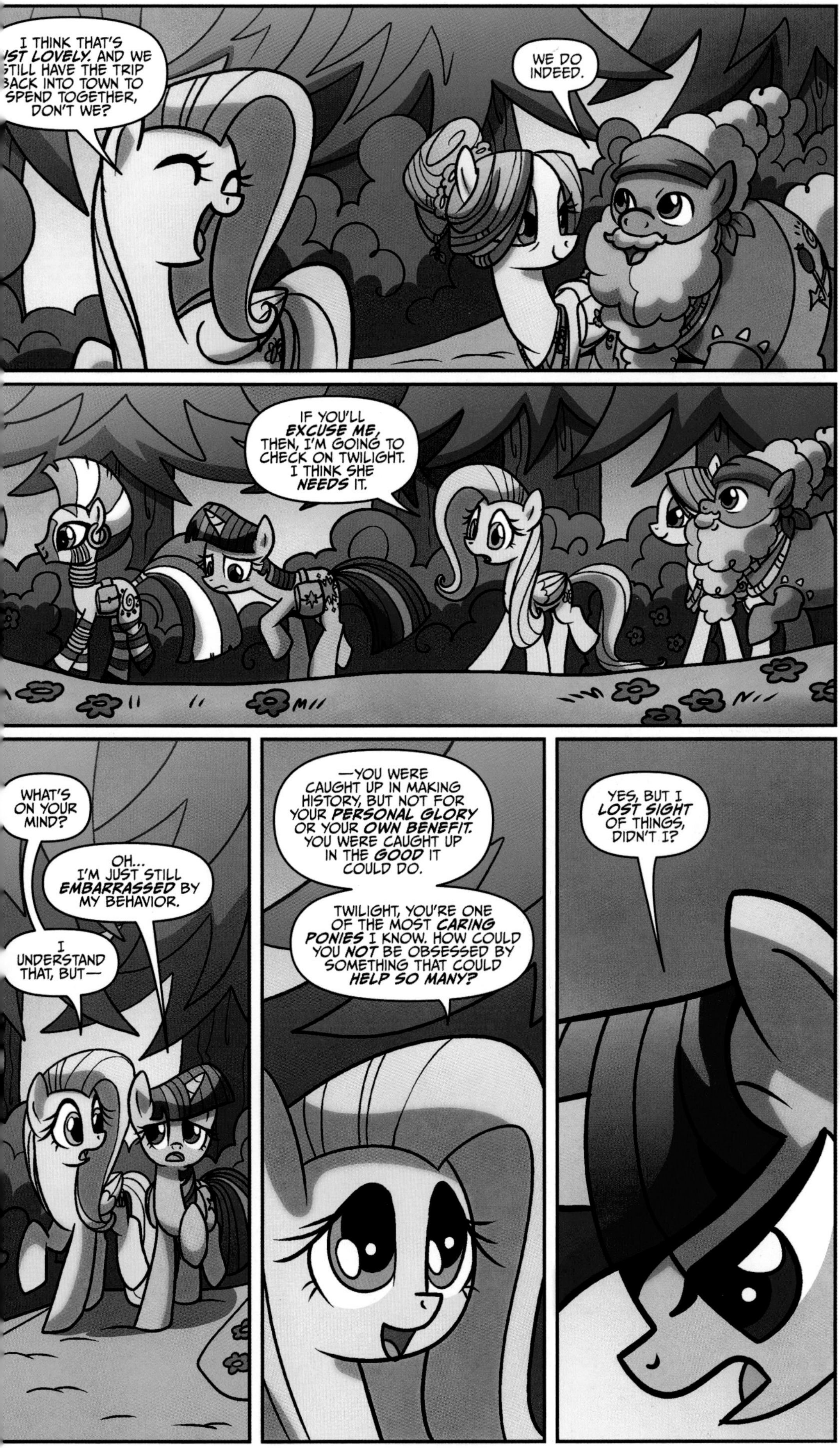
I THINK THAT'S JUST LOVELY. AND WE STILL HAVE THE TRIP BACK INTO TOWN TO SPEND TOGETHER, DON'T WE?
WE DO INDEED.
IF YOU'LL EXCUSE ME, THEN, I'M GOING TO CHECK ON TWILIGHT. I THINK SHE NEEDS IT.
WHAT'S ON YOUR MIND?
OH... I'M JUST STILL EMBARRASSED BY MY BEHAVIOR.
I UNDERSTAND THAT, BUT—
—YOU WERE CAUGHT UP IN MAKING HISTORY, BUT NOT FOR YOUR PERSONAL GLORY OR YOUR OWN BENEFIT. YOU WERE CAUGHT UP IN THE GOOD IT COULD DO.
TWILIGHT, YOU'RE ONE OF THE MOST CARING PONIES I KNOW. HOW COULD YOU NOT BE OBSESSED BY SOMETHING THAT COULD HELP SO MANY?
YES, BUT I LOST SIGHT OF THINGS, DIDN'T I?

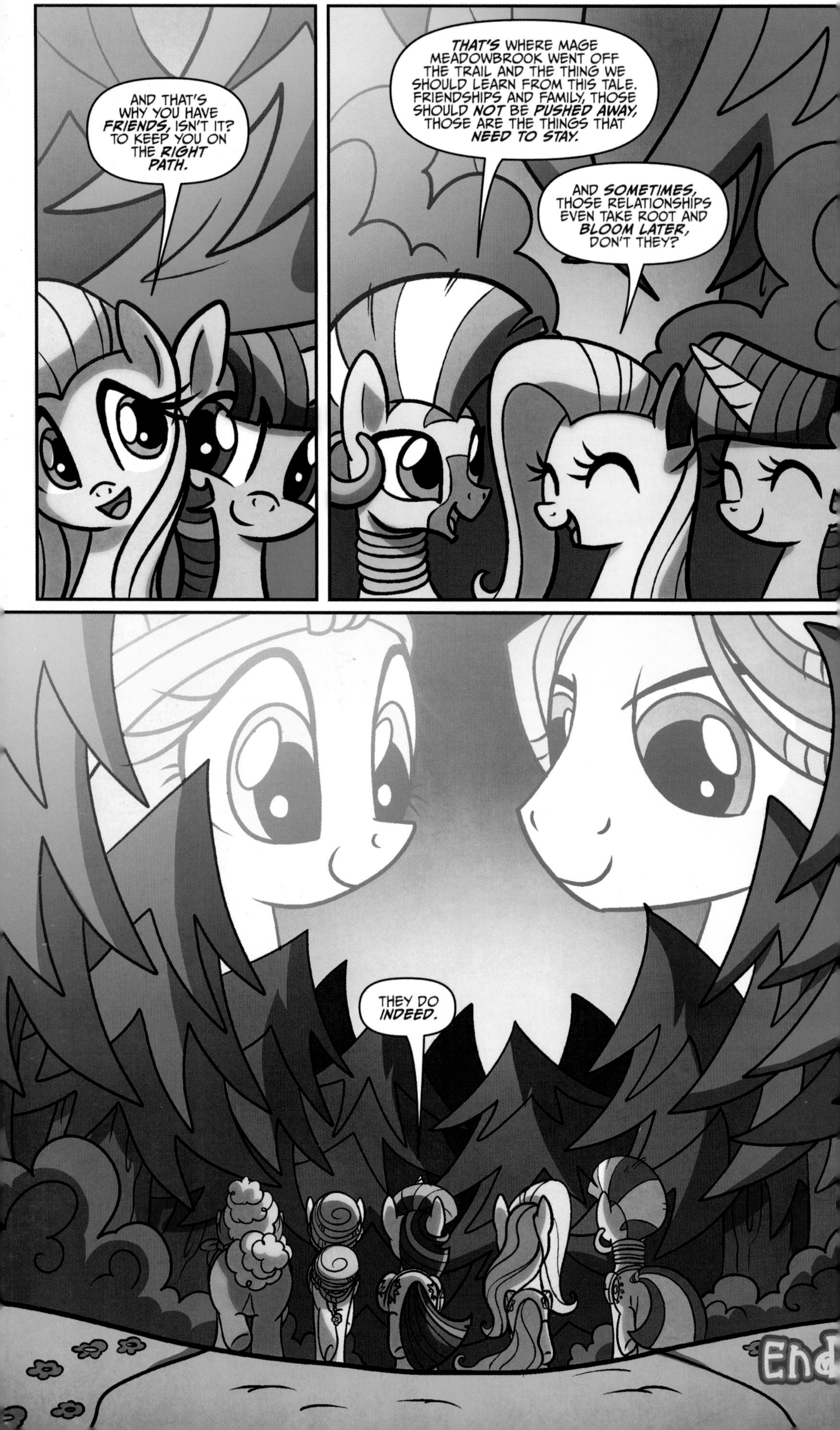
AND THAT'S WHY YOU HAVE FRIENDS, ISN'T IT? TO KEEP YOU ON THE RIGHT PATH.
THAT'S WHERE MAGE MEADOWBROOK WENT OFF THE TRAIL AND THE THING WE SHOULD LEARN FROM THIS TALE. FRIENDSHIPS AND FAMILY, THOSE SHOULD NOT BE PUSHED AWAY, THOSE ARE THE THINGS THAT NEED TO STAY.
AND SOMETIMES, THOSE RELATIONSHIPS EVEN TAKE ROOT AND BLOOM LATER, DON'T THEY?
THEY DO INDEED.
End

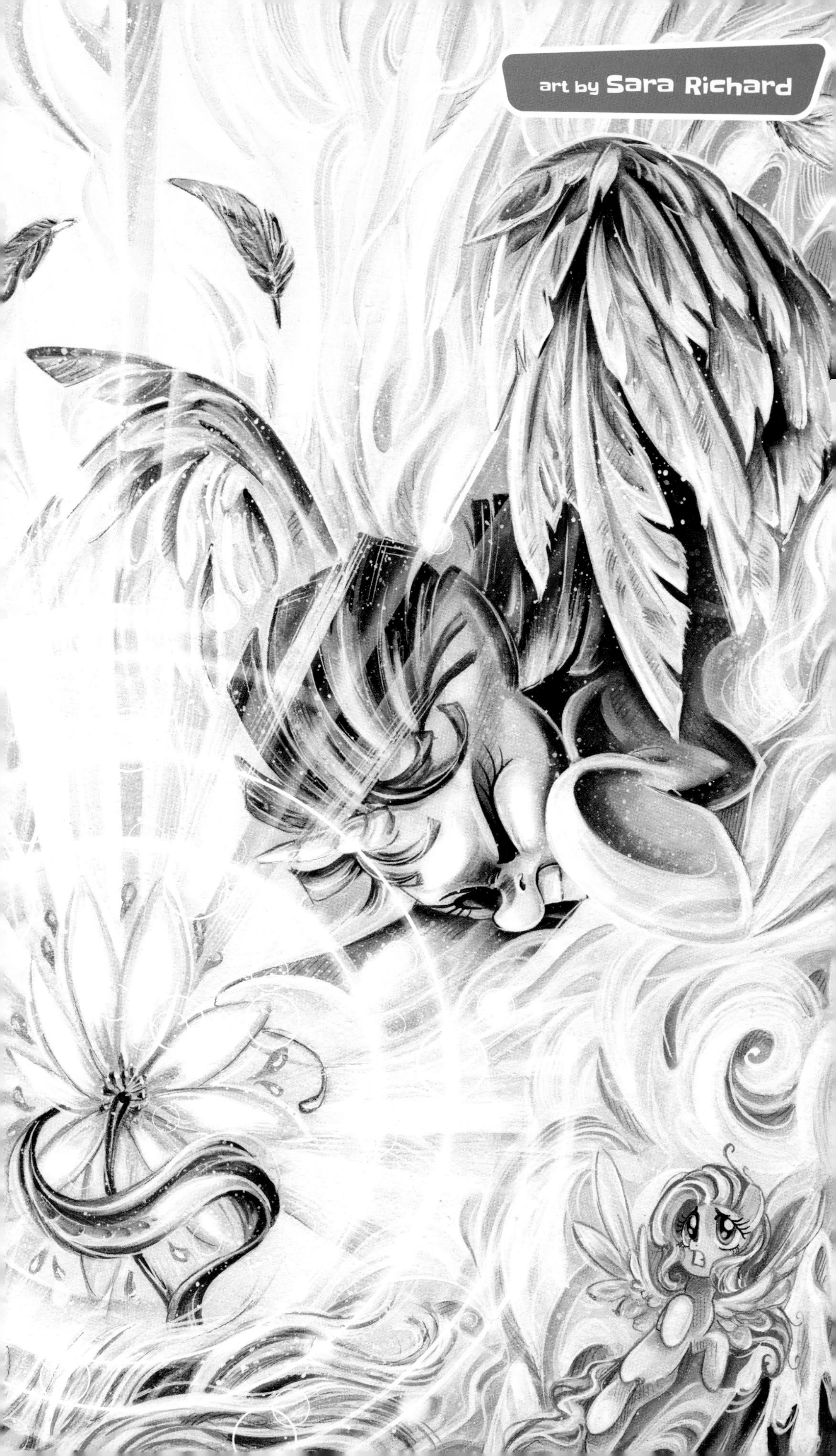
art by Sara Richard

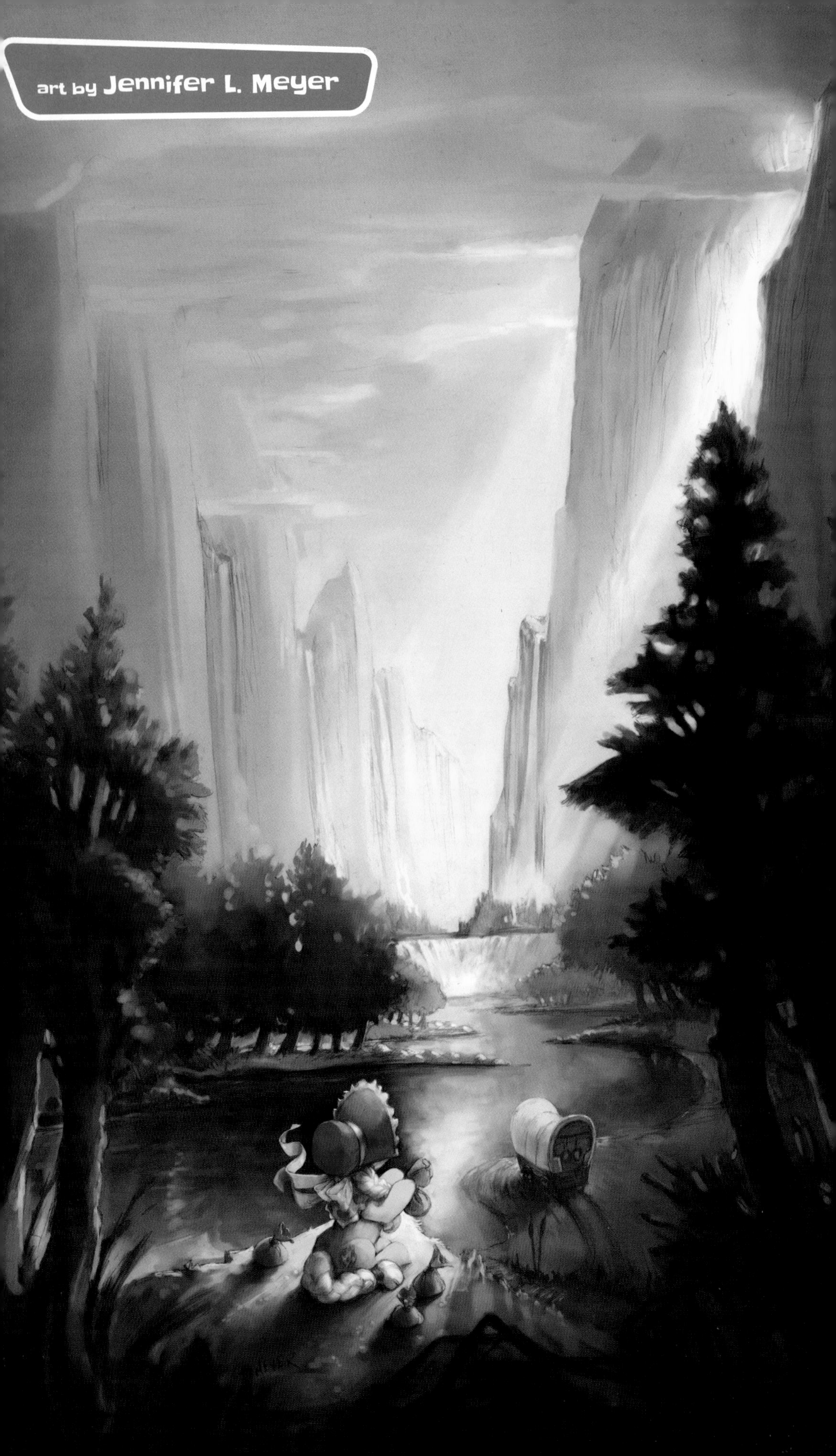
art by Jennifer L. Meyer

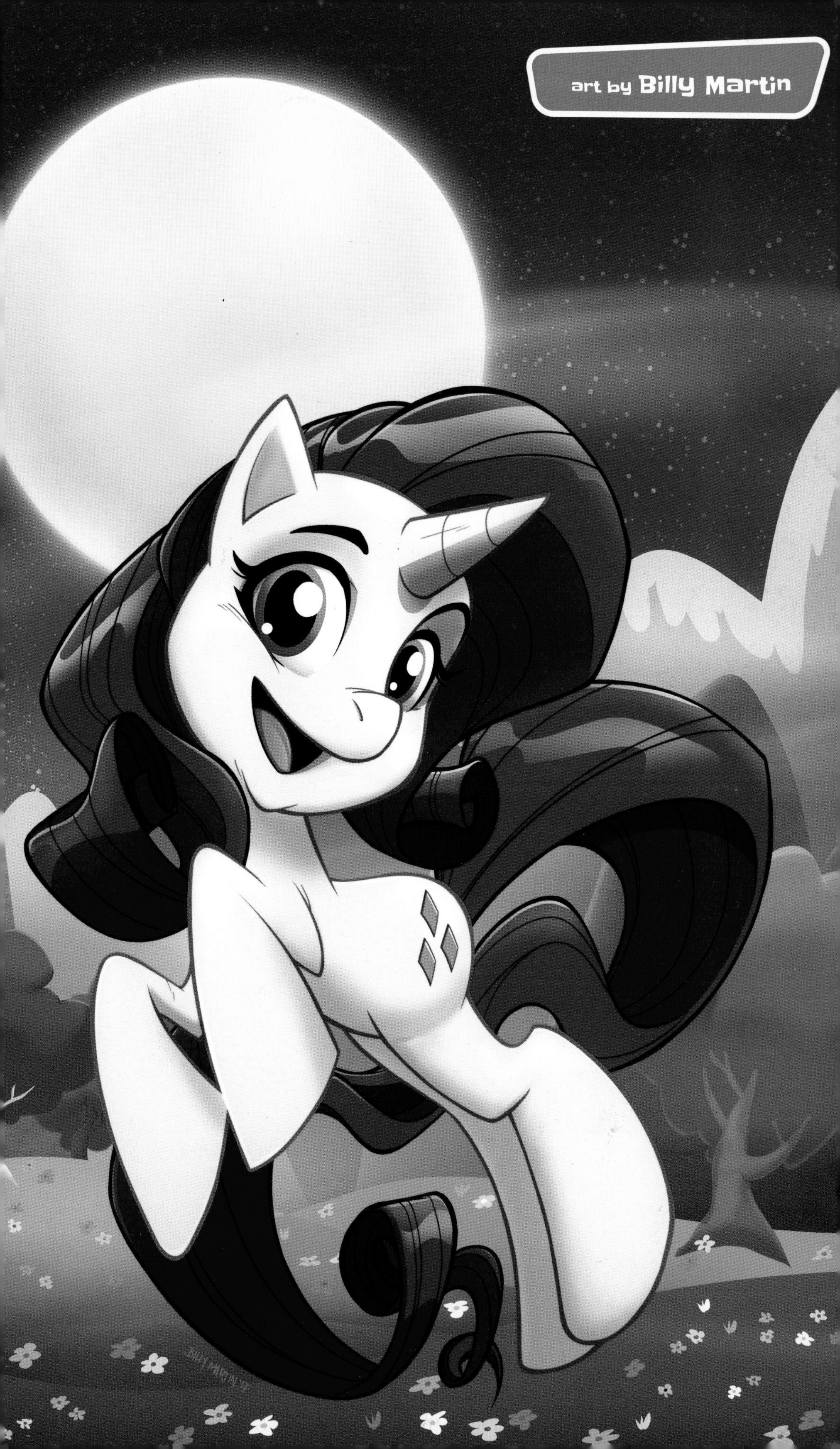
art by Billy Martin
BILLY MARTIN '17

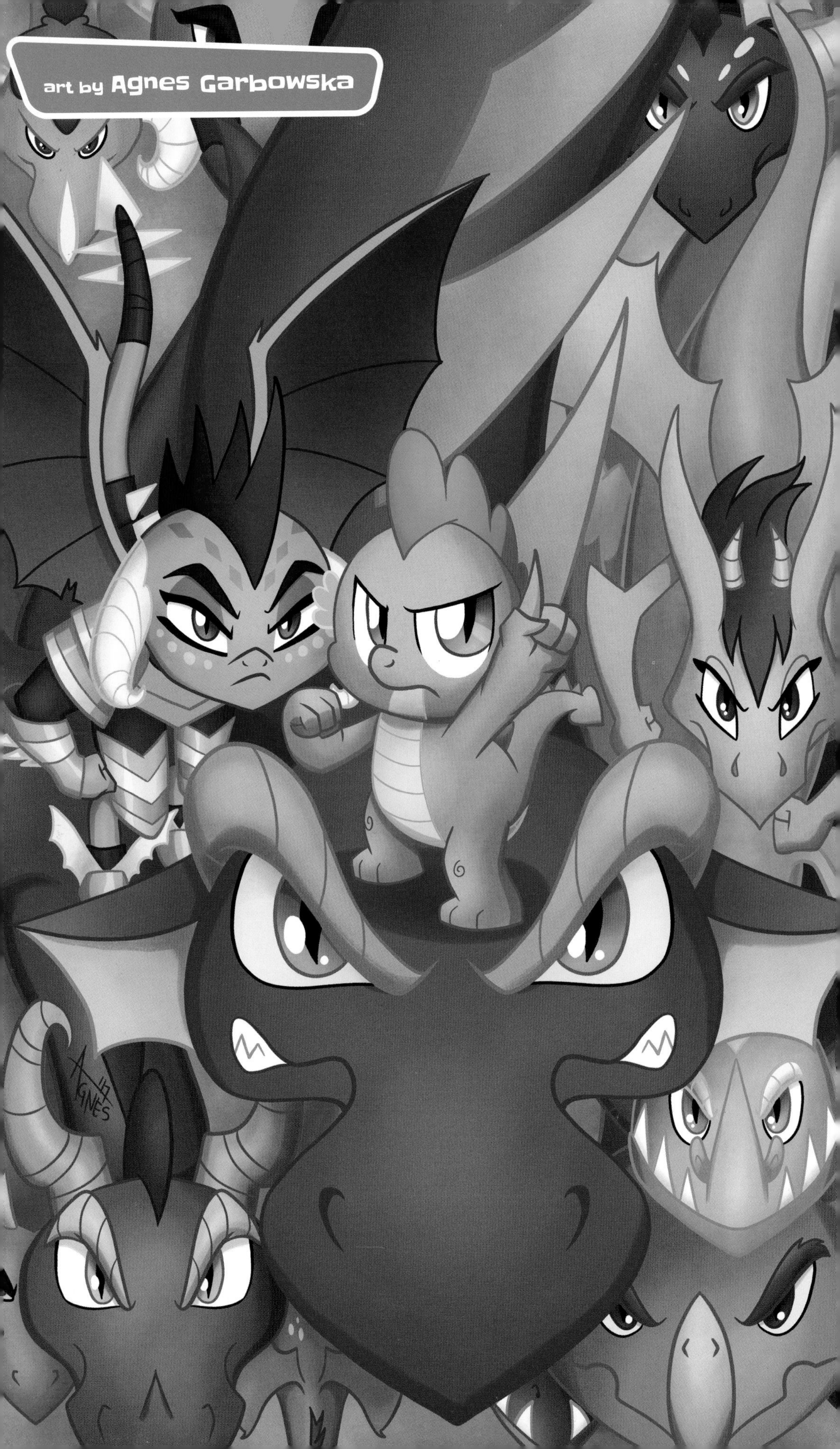

art by Agnes Garbowska

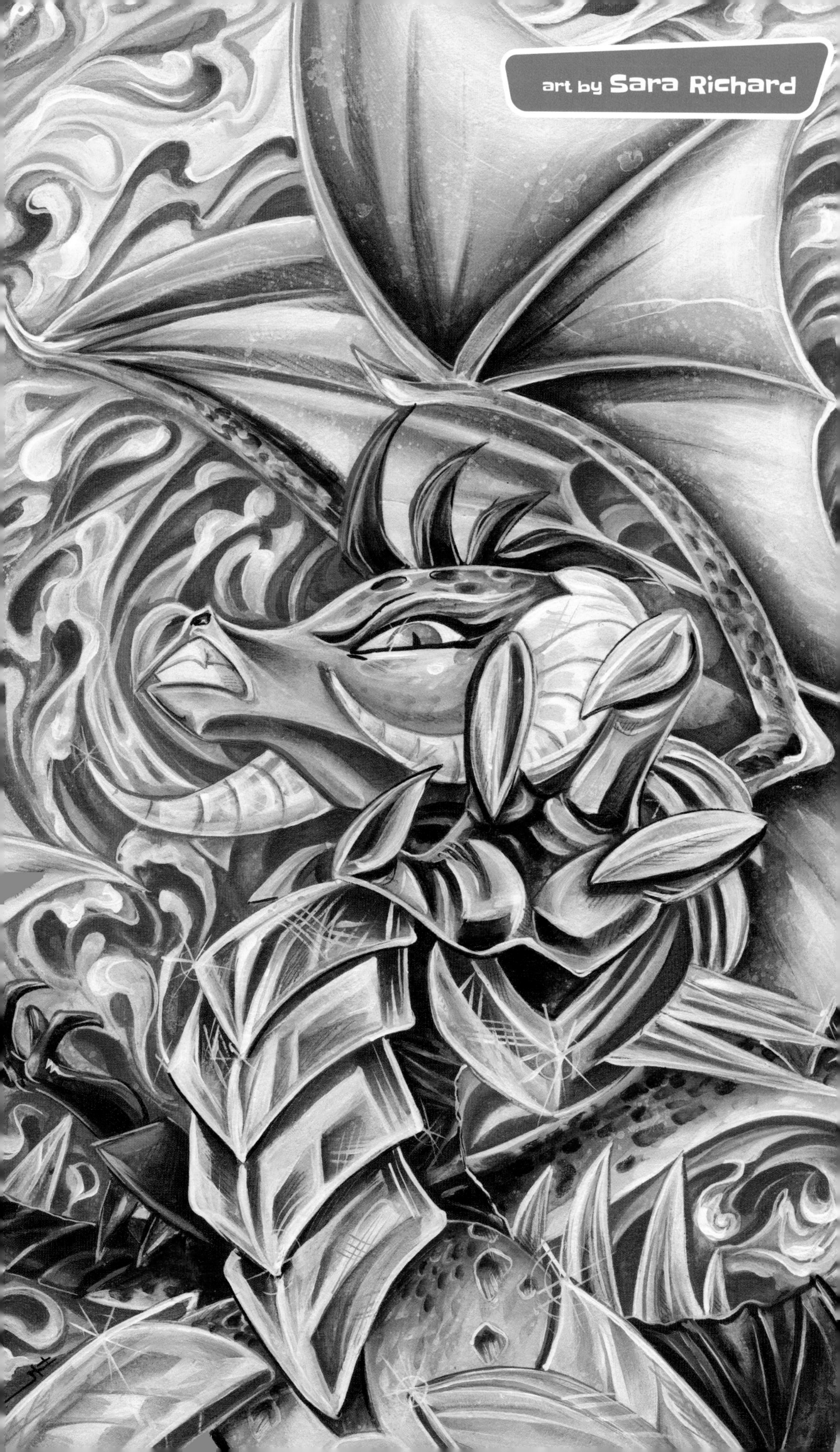
art by Sara Richard

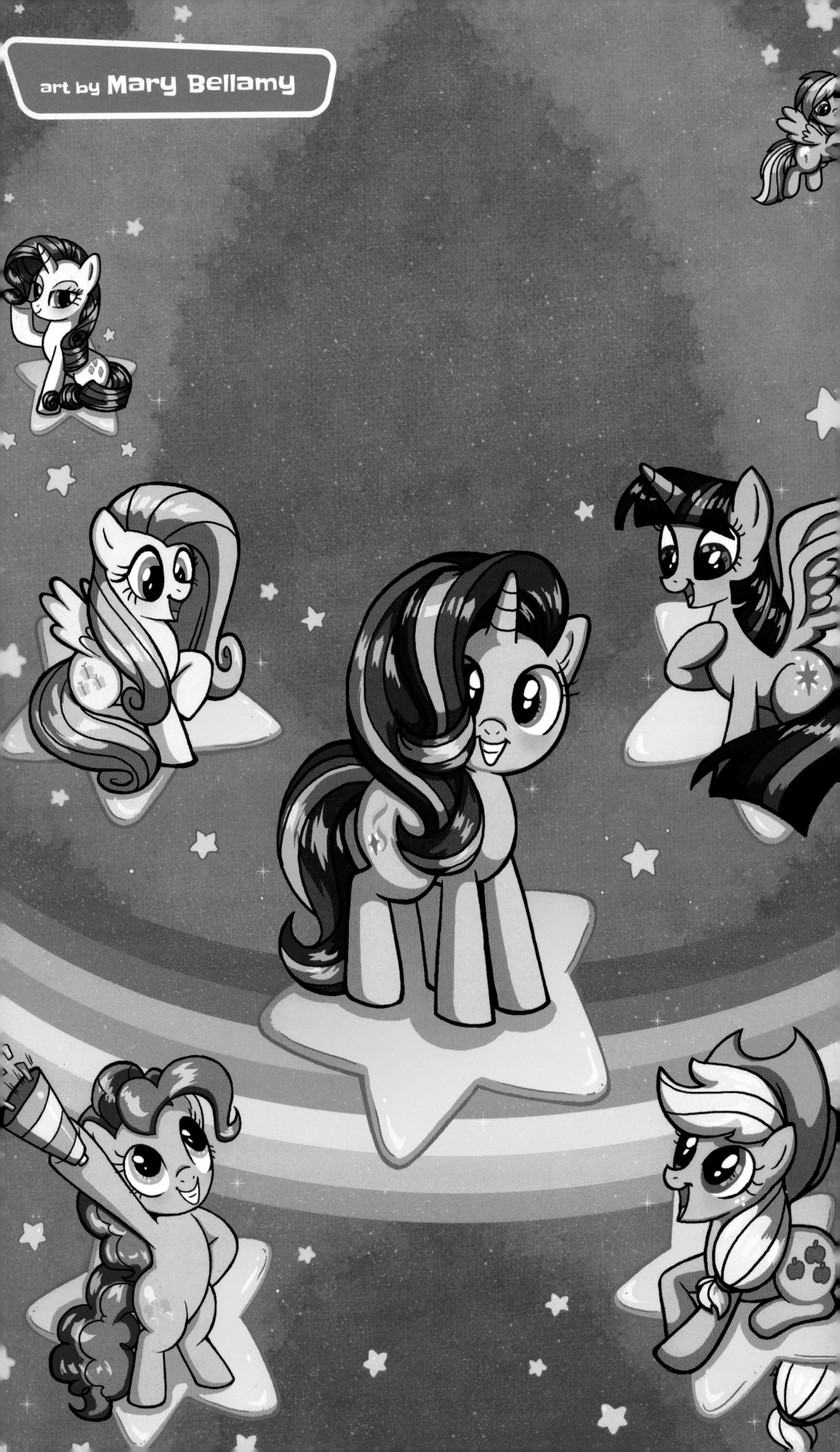
art by Mary Bellamy

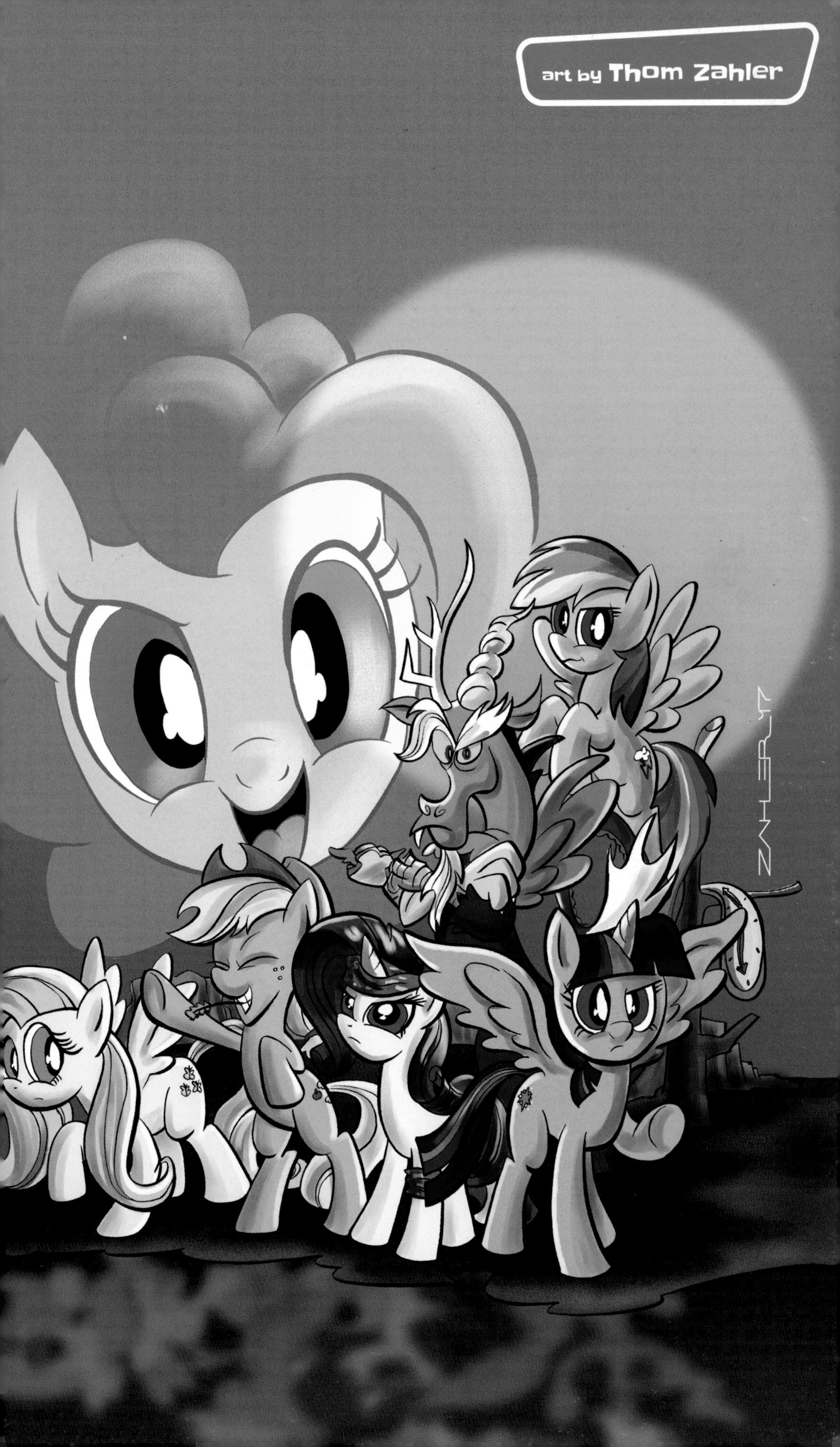

art by Thom Zahler

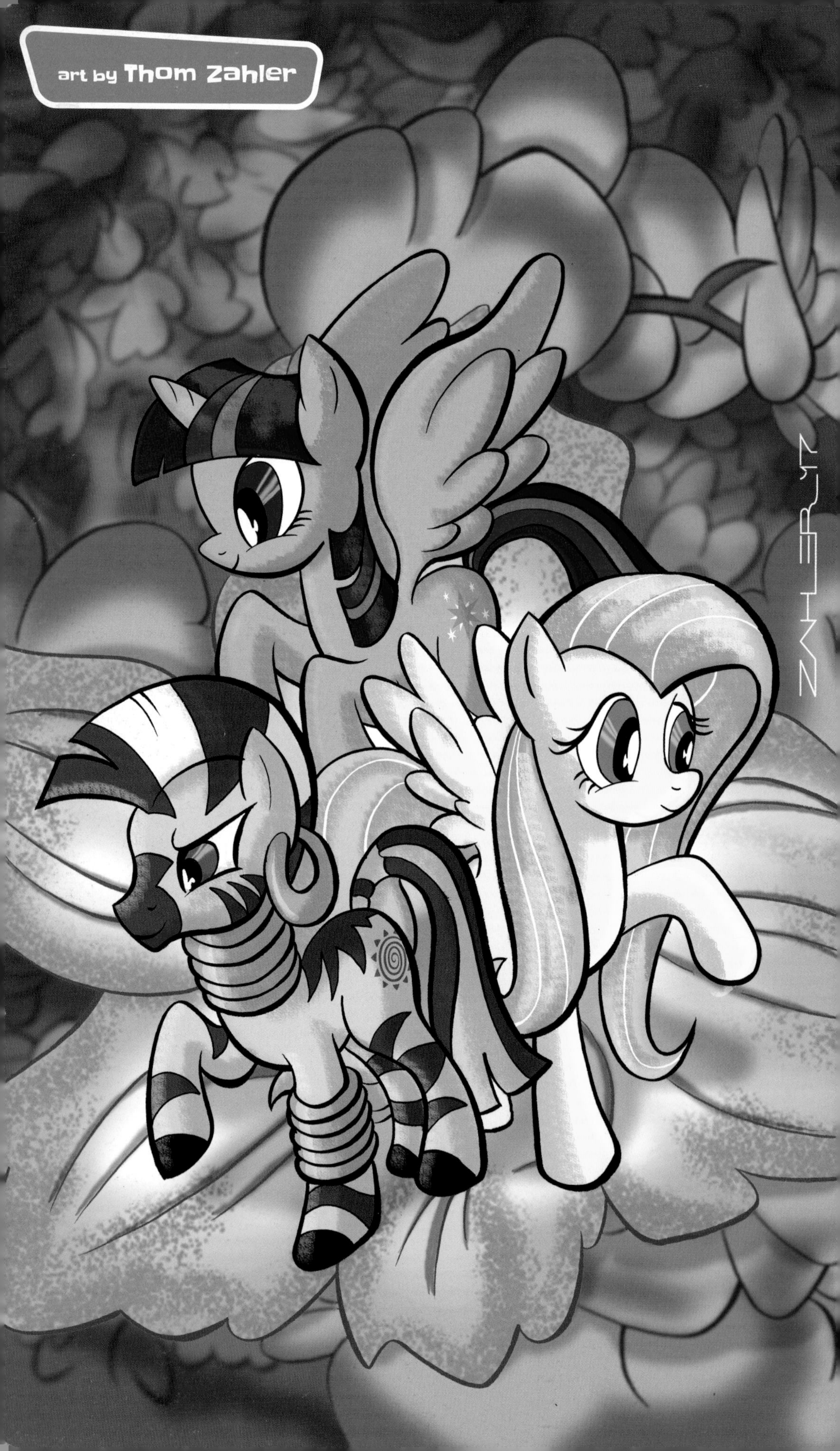

art by Thom Zahler

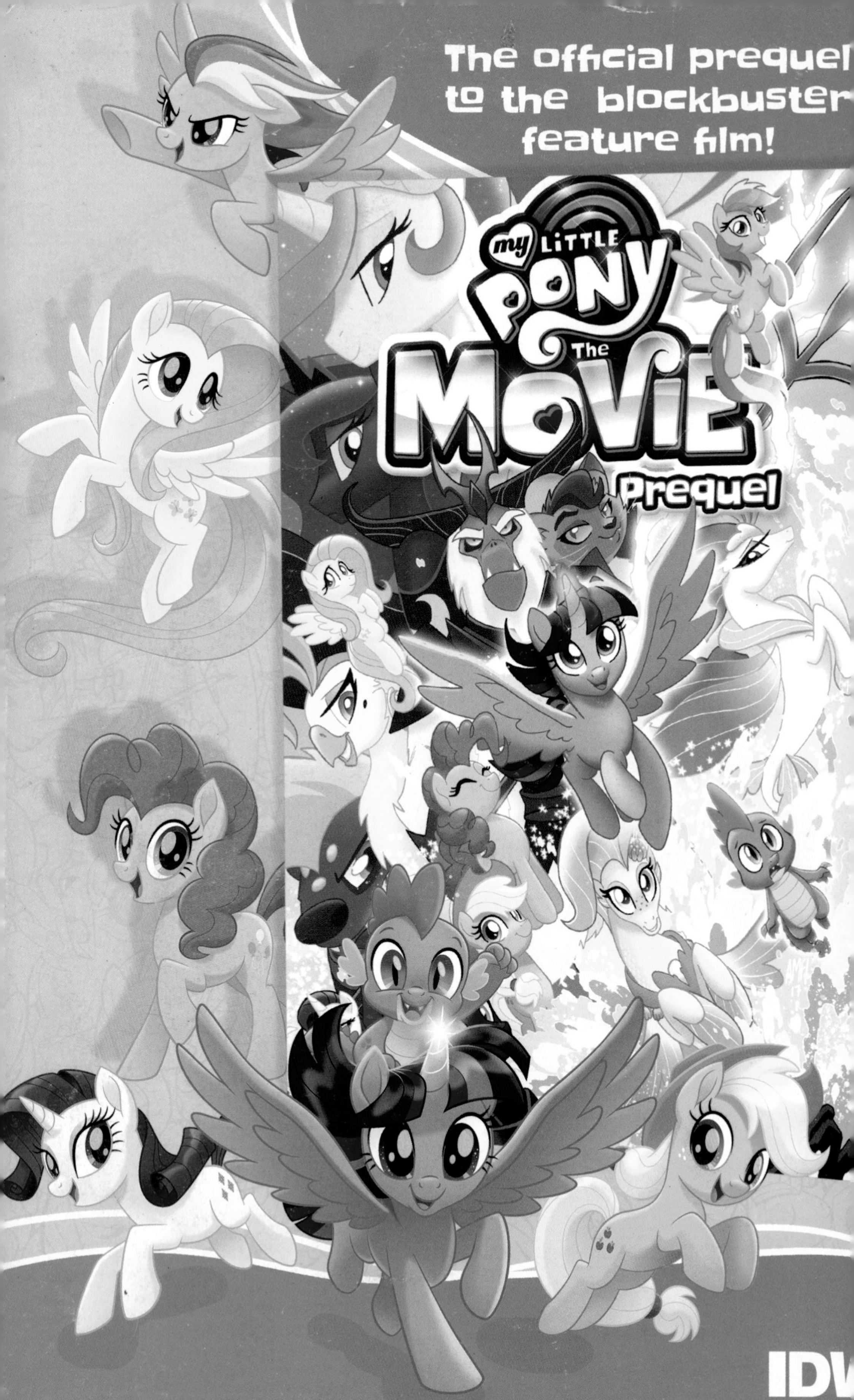

The official prequel
to the blockbuster
feature film!
My Little Pony
The Movie
Prequel